THE ROWAN'S DESTINY

KILLIAN BLADE SERIES BOOK 3

STELLA BRIE

Cover Design: Mayflower Studio

Editing: Bookish Dreams Editing

Proofreading: Kaye Kemp Book Polishing

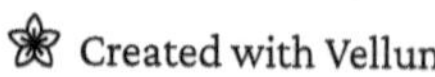 Created with Vellum

AUTHOR'S NOTE

This book is a Reverse Harem romance. The heroine does not have to choose between male interests. This book has a FMMMMM relationship. Recommended for 18+ due to mature content.

Playlist for all my books can be found on my YouTube channel - @authorstellabrie.

FYI: A glossary can be found at the end of this book. **IT CONTAINS SPOILERS!**

Playlist

"UNSTOPPABLE" - THE SCORE

"ROYALS'" - VITAMIN STRING QUARTET

"SWAY WITH ME_"- GALXARA

"GLORIOUS" - MACKLEMORE FEAT. SKYLAR GREY

"FOOLPROOF" - HAYDEN JAMES, GORGON CITY, NAT DUNN

"LEAVE BEFORE YOU LOVE ME" - MARSHMALLOW & JONAS BROTHERS

"SPACE GHOST COAST TO COAST" - GLASS ANIMALS

"CONFIDENT" - DEMI LOVATO

"GOOD TO BE ALIVE" - THE SCORE

"FALLIN'" - ADRENALINE

"UNDER YOUR SCARS" - GODSMACK

"THAT'S MY GIRL" - FIFTH HARMONY

"BORN FOR THIS" - THE SCORE

"POWER" - LITTLE MIX FEAT. STORMY

"WOLF TOTEM" - THE HU FEAT. JACOBY SHADDIX OF PAPA ROACH

"WE ARE GODS" - AUDIOMACHINE

DEDICATION

To my sweet girl, Bailey. You've brought us tremendous joy and unconditional love for over thirteen years. I treasure each day you are here, snoozing by my desk, while I type the next words. I love you.

CHAPTER
ONE

ARDEN

My heartbeat echoes loudly in my ears, and my fingers tremble as they trace the indented grooves of the letters over and over. *Catriona MacAllister.* The journal is smooth and worn from time and use, and the slight scent of beeswax, along with the suppleness of the leather, tells me its value. Taking in a deep breath, I let it out slowly in an attempt to calm my nerves. Agnes' journal and the MacAllister grimoire revealed my heritage, but these words come from my father's family.

An image of the beautiful red-haired lady who delivered the box fills my mind. Catriona herself? My grandmother? Another relative? Who was the man with her? Could he have been my father? Given our propensity for longevity, all are possibilities. The mahogany box wouldn't have been in the care of a stranger—not with the royal symbol emblazoned on it—which only leaves family. But if so, why wouldn't she say anything?

A maelstrom of emotions and questions swirl round and round like a whirlpool in my head, disappointment front and center. Instead of finding my father, I'm still traversing this path without him. My heart yearns to find my family, not more secrets.

Shuffling sounds fill the room, and I look up and smile. The yearning eases.

"Do you mind if we join you?" Theron asks quietly, considerate as usual.

Standing tall with his arms relaxed at his side, I almost believe the picture in front of me, until I see the tightness around his eyes.

"I might require a toll," I tease.

Interest sparks in his eyes. "I see. Before I pay, can I get a hint?" He strides forward and leans down close, waiting to hear my answer.

The smell of dark chocolate and peppermint drifts between us, and I shiver.

Hmm, he smells so delicious.

Knowing he expects me to ask for a kiss, I decide to have some fun. Staring into his violet eyes, I slowly walk my fingers down his suit and answer, "Would jeans for a week be too much to pay?" I almost laugh at the pained consternation on his face. Rolling my eyes, I decide to let him off the hook. "Fine, I won't torture you. How about a kiss?"

His cool, firm lips capture mine, and I slide right into his icy depths, instantly wanting more from this enigmatic male. When he pulls back, his violet eyes retain their watchful vigilance, but my reassurance helps ease his tension.

A hand grips Theron's shoulder and shoves him aside. Astor slides into view with a devious smirk on his sensual lips.

"My turn to pay the toll." Astor's hand captures the back of my head and pulls me forward.

I press my lips together. "I don't want a kiss from you," I say breathlessly, the lie slipping easily from my tongue.

Astor shudders. "Your delicious lies are going to tip me over the edge," he warns.

His lips skim mine, nibbling on each one until my resistance falls and I can't help but kiss him back. Shadows flick up and down my spine, making me arch up into him, and the kiss changes from teasing to serious between one heartbeat and the next. We leave the others behind while we lose ourselves in each other. When his full lips pull back, I sigh and reluctantly return to the world.

Air displaces behind me, then a strong hand grips my hair and pulls my head back. I'm already on edge, so when I see the flames in Daire's icy blue eyes, I can't help but arch my neck, offering him the very thing he craves, quite possibly more than my kiss.

He wavers but shakes his head and douses the flames.

"Soon," he promises.

He dips down to trail firm lips up my neck, inhaling deeply along the way, before moving over to my mouth and crushing my lips in a demanding kiss far more revealing than he probably intended. Tingles invade my body, but again, it's over a brief second later.

"So delicious. Read the journal. We'll be here with you."

I might normally demand a different ending to those kisses, but the solid weight of the book helps sharpen my focus. Smiling and settled now, I scoot over to the corner of the couch and begin to read.

PAGES AND PAGES are filled with Catriona's life. I'm tempted to flip to the back of the journal to quickly get the answers I seek, but I refrain. Barely. I want to *know* her, and that can only be accomplished by experiencing her life through her own words and in the order she wrote them.

The simple and blockish handwriting on the first page reflects the young age at which she started capturing her thoughts. Her days are filled with cute boys, fights with her mom, and excitement for the magic she learned in school that day. Her tone is light and carefree, as if darkness is absent from her life.

About a quarter of the way through the journal, her tone changes dramatically, starting with this entry.

My world is foggy. I'm numb. Sleep is elusive. Nightmare visions of their death stalk me in the dark. I prayed to the goddess over and over last night, but I woke this morning to find nothing changed. My parents are gone. Murdered. In the wrong place at the wrong time, they told me. A robbery on their way back home.

My parents were powerful witches, but only human, so I almost believed them. Until I shut out their words and listened to their silence. They were hiding something. The shock on their faces and fear in their voices while they quietly murmured in the corner told me more than any words could convey. My parents' death was neither simple nor a coincidence of location.

Details are scarce. Adults withholding information from "the child" for protection, but I'm no longer a child. I grew up the instant they told me my parents were murdered. My mind circles around that word, desperate to know how they died and yet afraid to find out. One day, I will.

Something about the words bothers me. I stare at them for a few minutes and realize both of Catriona's parents were human; therefore, Catriona was human, which means the lady who delivered the box wasn't Catriona. A pang of sadness hits me. Another MacAllister dead. I'm more determined than ever to get to know her.

Her next few entries are robotic, with their stark statements of facts and events. Her mother's parents passed shortly after Catriona was born, and her father had been abandoned as a baby. She had no one. An orphan.

An elderly witch in the village offers Catriona a home for the next year until she becomes an adult. The coven allows her to keep a few sentimental items, but they sell the rest of the household to provide for her future. A single wooden chest and this journal is all that remains of her previous life.

Catriona begins to write every day, as if pen and paper are her only confidants. While her daily routine seems to be the same, the entries describe the many changes happening around her. Invitations to friends' houses for sleepovers or parties disappear overnight. Few speak to her in school. Wherever she goes, side glances and silence become the norm instead of the usual greetings. Her isolation within the coven grows.

Catriona notices and writes about these things in a listless manner. Her entries are neat and concise statements filled only with fact. The only emotion she displays is when she writes about her future. Where will she live? How will she survive? Should she stay in the land of dragons or go somewhere else? Worry consumes her. Until Agnes MacAllister, the clan's matriarch, comes to visit.

Agnes introduces Catriona, along with four other orphans, to a powerful seer named Gemma Perrone. Gemma explains they have been blessed by destiny to save the MacAllister clan, and ultimately, the lineage of witches everywhere. In a year, they will be sent off with specific instructions to set them on their path, but first, they have a lot to learn.

For the next twenty pages or so, Catriona's journal entries become sporadic, the handwriting sloppy as if rushed or tired when she writes. The orphans' days are filled with lessons on everything from advanced magic to work skills to survivalist knowledge, but it's all accomplished in secret. The rest of the coven believes Agnes is simply dedicated to helping these young orphans become better witches. Few know the true reason, and while this makes most of the girls nervous, Catriona doesn't care about the secrecy.

For the first time since her parents died, Catriona feels hope and a sense of purpose again. Excitement and emotion bleed into her words. She's looking forward to starting a new life somewhere beyond the Kingdom of Dragons.

CHAPTER
TWO

<u>ARDEN</u>

I wake a couple of hours later and find myself surrounded by strong arms and low voices. Opening my eyes, I realize Valerian's holding me in his arms. The journal is lying on the coffee table in front of me, and the cadre is sprawled out around us. I debate the idea of moving, but I'm too cozy and comfortable, so I lie there, drifting in and out of sleep. Their voices barely penetrate the cocoon around me.

"I'll get it done over the next couple of days," Astor states firmly. "I've got some ideas on how to work the spells to send out notifications and possibly open a portal for each person."

"Once the spells are done, I can merge it with various technology, including our phones." Theron's quiet voice slides into the conversation.

Valerian's arms tighten around me. "What about Fallon?"

he questions, voice rumbling through his chest where my head lies.

"He will want to be included," Theron insists. "He's getting closer."

"In the meantime, the ball gives us the perfect sanctuary for a few days," Daire interjects.

"We're invited to a ball?" I ask sleepily before falling under Morpheus' spell again.

THE NEXT TIME I WAKE, I'm in Valerian's bed. I lie there for a few minutes, staring at the smoothed lines of his face and listening to his deep breaths. I vaguely recall him holding me in the lounge, but the details are fuzzy. His hand reaches out to grab mine, and I smile. He's so fierce to the outside world, but he has the biggest heart. Having lost so much, he loves deeply. I debate waking him up for some early morning fun, but the journal calls to me. I need to find out what happened to Catriona. Sliding out of bed, I grab some clothes and head toward the bathroom.

I'm delighted to see Daire on the couch reading a book called—I tilt my head—*Ancient Battle Strategies* when I enter the lounge. There's something incredibly sexy about a man engrossed in a book, and when it's Daire, it makes me want to crawl in his lap and read with him.

Leaning down, I capture his lips with mine, taking time to savor the rare moment alone with him. He immediately drops his book to cup the back of my neck and return my kiss. *Mmm...* I'm tempted to slide into his lap, but I don't want to get distracted from the reason I came in here. With a sigh, I release him from the kiss slowly, sucking lightly on his lower lip, until finally pulling away.

He groans. "It's been a long time since I've received one of your good morning kisses, but I seem to recall a different ending." His eyes are heavy-lidded as they capture mine. "Something much more satisfying."

He reaches out to take my hand, but I dance over to sit in the corner of the sofa and grab the journal. "I need to finish Catriona's journal."

I flip through the pages until I find the last words I remember reading last night. Glancing up, I catch him staring at the rapidly beating pulse at the base of my neck.

"Before you get engrossed in her story, I need to tell you about the ball," he drawls huskily. Dragging his eyes up to mine, he continues, "Lucifer is holding a ball to officially introduce Vargas as his second-in-command and to generate some goodwill after he cleaned house so thoroughly. He'd like you to attend the ball as a thank you." His eyes flicker with some undefined emotion. "I'd like you to attend as our date."

I want to squeal like a little girl. My previous isolation meant few parties or formal events.

"I haven't been to a ball," I tell him, my voice breathless with excitement. "When is it? I need to find something to wear." I mentally sift through a list of stores where I think I can find a ballgown. Should I order one to be delivered? Sleek or full? I need shoes too. Maybe I should call Solandis. My mind stutters to a stop. "Our date?"

Daire tilts his head and answers, "It's in two days. Both Astor and I are attending the ball, and we'd like for you to be our date." While his tone is light, his eyes are watching me intently.

This seems to be important. Is it because I'll be there with them both? Was this his idea or Astor's? He never had to share

Solange, so I can't help but wonder if it bothers him to share me.

"I'd love to attend with both of you," I assure him. His hands flex when I answer, but the tension seems to dissipate.

"I hope you don't mind, but we ordered you a dress and shoes," he murmurs. "They'll be waiting for us when we arrive."

I'm a bit disappointed I won't be able to shop for myself, but I'm also relieved. I'm not sure I could have found something in two days, and I know Daire will pick something suitable and beautiful. Astor, on the other hand, would probably have chosen something shocking and risqué.

"Thank you," I reply. "I know it will be gorgeous. And I can't wait to dance with you both."

A slow smile steals over his face. "You're always gorgeous." He stands and stretches. "I'm going to take care of a few things and leave you to your book." Bending down, he places a soft kiss on my temple, and not even a second later, he's gone.

CHAPTER
THREE

<u>ARDEN</u>

It sounds like we'll be staying in the Underworld for at least a day or two, which suits me fine. I always love visiting there. *Hmmm...* If the ball is to introduce Vargas, I'm sure Solandis and Callyx will be there. I shoot off a text to confirm, but she doesn't reply.

Sighing, I open the journal and force myself to focus. Based on the number of pages remaining, I'm halfway through it. The first sentence immediately captures my attention.

After a year of training, this is it. The day we leave the MacAl-lister clan forever. Last night, Agnes pulled each one of us aside and gave us the coordinates to our destination and instructions for what to do when we get there.

She called in Lara first, who came out smiling about ten minutes later. With a wave, she left to pack. Then Aileen went in and returned shortly after, and she was also smiling. She gave us a quick hug and hurried out the door.

She called for Sima, but their conversation lasted much longer than ten minutes. When Sima came out, she was clutching a piece of paper, a medallion, and a dreamy smile on her face. I glanced at Fiona, and I could tell she was also dying to know what Agnes had told Sima to put such a lovestruck smile on her face. After giving Fiona and me a sweet hug, she left, practically floating out the door.

Next, Agnes requested Fiona. After their discussion, Fiona exited with a piece of paper in her hand and a medallion, but instead of a smile, tears were flowing like a river down her cheeks. Deep sadness was etched into her face, and when her eyes met mine, more tears fell. We stood staring at each other for a minute. Her with the knowledge Agnes had given her, and me, clueless but worried. She nodded to herself and straightened her shoulders, physically pushing the sadness away. Then her eyes filled with excitement and hope, but she never said a word. After a long hug, she left.

Agnes beckoned me into the room and shut the door. She stared at me for several minutes, and I started to worry whether I'd leave smiling or in tears. When she started speaking, she didn't stop until it was all laid bare. She told me about Gemma Perrone and her visions. The fall of the MacAllister witches and the subsequent eradication of us from everyone's memory. The reason she had been training the five of us, witches and orphans, for the last year. The purpose of the medallions.

Shock rendered me speechless, and I remember staring at her in horror. Only the five of us will survive the first wave of the massacre, and of us five, only one will ultimately survive to carry the MacAllister lineage forward. She continued to explain about the Rowan, born from the survivor's line, who will save witches and our magic. The Rowan who will shine a light on the MacAl-

listers again, telling of our downfall and heritage. But until that time, everything must remain secret. The world will forget the MacAllisters ever existed, and we can never tell anyone different.

She handed me a medallion and a piece of paper with coordinates. I'm to enter the light Elven territory first, but she cautioned me to keep moving until my heart and magic felt the urge to settle. She refused to tell me which of us will survive. Before I left, I gave her a fierce hug. I'm in awe of her, our matriarch, standing tall against the incoming tide, knowing what comes on the other side. I feel a fierce, unending gratitude for the chance I've been given to survive. I don't smile or cry when I leave. I take my cue from Agnes. I stand tall and face the world with determination and resolve. Regardless of my destiny, I will not let her down.

Catriona's next entry was brief. She arrived in the light Elven territory, but after only one night, felt the urgency to continue traveling. Over the next few months, she would wander in and out of territories, never staying more than a couple of weeks at most, until she reached the dark Elven territory. After making her way from village to village, she found herself in the king's village. When she'd been there a couple of months with no desire to leave, she knew it was time to create a home for herself.

If I'm staying here, I need to work, but few places need help. Liana, my neighbor, told me to go to the castle. I did, and thankfully, they had an open position in the kitchen.

The next few entries are filled with basic information about her daily life. I skim them quickly and land on one more interesting.

I met the most insufferable male today who thinks he's a gift from the goddess to all of us poor females. Given the number of women flocking around him, I can see why he might think we'd all be willing to wait on him hand and foot. I've better things to do.

The following entries are a hilarious account of her antagonizing the king's son, Conall Balinor. Over time, her tone changes from exasperation to love, and they find their mates in each other. She decides to tell him and his father, the king, about the MacAllister witches.

The king swore to keep her past a secret but felt he needed to confirm the facts. He sent a carefully worded letter to the dark Fae king to see if he had any news. The reply was startling but expected. His fellow king had no knowledge of the MacAllister witches or a massacre. Satisfied, he let the matter drop.

I skim the next few pages, but they mainly consist of quick posts about her married life. The posts get fewer and fewer. A specific entry catches my eye, and I almost cry with happiness and surprise.

Our daughter was born today. With her birth, I know I'm not the only MacAllister witch alive anymore. Does this mean I'm the sole MacAllister survivor? Is it wrong to hope I am? It would mean Fiona, Sima, and the others are all gone. My heart breaks at the thought, but I can't bear such sadness on this glorious day, so I push them away and concentrate on my beautiful baby. She's pale like me, but with her father's green eyes and her grandfather's red hair. She's beautiful. My darling girl. We shall call her Elora. Elora Agnes Balinor.

Was the red-haired lady who delivered the box my grandmother? My gut clenches with the thought. Could I have more Elven relatives out there? A picture of the rowan tapestry flashes in my mind. I don't recall very many leaves on the MacAllister branches. It takes everything I have not to take a portal to Witchwood, but I get a grip on myself. This isn't knowledge I want to share with anyone in the coven. I'll check it out during the next council meeting. Sighing, I return to reading the journal.

After her daughter is born, Catriona's posts get fewer and fewer, as if daily life takes up all her time, but toward the end, I find two hastily written entries.

I messed up. Agnes warned me not to tell anyone what happened, but I felt I had to tell my husband and his father the truth to protect themselves. When nothing happened right away, I let my guard down. Now, ten years later, the repercussions reverberate through the village and kingdom. The dark Elven king is dead, and a new one has taken the throne. My husband, our daughter, and I fled in the middle of the night to the dark Fae, where we've been offered sanctuary in a remote village. Yesterday, word reached us of the villagers' punishment for staying loyal to us. I pray to the goddess Liana is okay.

And the last entry...

For fifteen years, we've stayed here raising our daughter, hiding behind this simple life. My husband became the local blacksmith, and while our home is nothing like the castle we left, we couldn't be happier. And we've gone largely unnoticed until today.

When I answered the door this morning, a beautiful puck stood there with his hand propped casually against the doorframe as if he were a friendly neighbor dropping by for a chat.

Thick caramel hair waved carelessly in the wind and brown eyes twinkled with mischief, but it was his devilish smile that promised delightful fun. Clothes made of the finest materials draped his tall, muscular physique, lending him an air of stylish wealth. The puck's entire package was designed to entice others and compel them to commit mischief with him, but not me.

I frowned, but he chuckled, introduced himself as Bran, and asked for my husband. About to close the door to this trickster, I realized he asked for my husband by his true name, Conall Balinor, not the blacksmith name, Keir Balanthir, he'd adopted years ago.

When he entered our home, his countenance changed, becoming serious and intense, which made me uneasy. My husband took him behind the house, where they spoke for a long time. When they shook hands, I assumed a deal was struck, but instead of coming back into the house, they entered the blacksmith shop, and for the next three days, worked together in the forge.

The puck's fine linen sleeves were casually rolled up and sweat dripped down his face in rivers, but his expression was fierce and focused as he swung the hammer and pounded the metal. He created and forged each initial piece, and when finished, he would pass it to my husband, who would start bending and layering intricate details into the metal until the puck was satisfied. While they worked, I could see their magic coalescing in the air, green from my husband and a sparkly golden aura I assume came from the puck. When they finished, they presented the three beautiful daggers they had crafted and named the Killian blades. I don't know their purpose, and apparently, I'm not supposed to know. My husband says my knowledge of the information will influence the future, so I remain in the dark.

With his task accomplished, the puck turned to leave, but he stopped suddenly in the doorway. Without looking at me, he said, "The Rowan will be your legacy."

Stunned, I stood frozen in place while I contemplated his words. Did I believe him? The fact he knew about the Rowan indi-

cated some knowledge. How? Did he know Gemma? While I sifted through the possibilities, a flicker of fire caught the corner of my eye, and puzzled, I glanced over at the table. The Killian blades, reflecting the flames from the nearby hearth, lay vibrating on the table as if they were alive. Suddenly, I knew his words to be true.

Somehow, he knows the future, and for some reason, he's decided to lend his magic and knowledge to helping us. The blades are proof of his intent. Unending sorrow and joy filled me as I thanked the goddess over and over. Now, I know. I am the MacAllister survivor. My daughter will live, and through her, so will the MacAllister line.

I take a deep breath and read the last entry several times. It's stunning how a few hundred words can impact you. Six words were all Catriona needed to hear to find peace. For me, the words on this page confirm the Killian blades and my destiny are intrinsically tied together. We have a purpose.

A puck. I have very little knowledge of pucks. Honestly, I thought they were a myth, a creature supernatural parents referenced when their children were misbehaving. Both utterly divine and deceiving, they were mischief makers.

In all the legends of the blades, nothing mentioned a puck. Every story questions how an Elven blacksmith managed to make the Killian blades permanently sentient with the ability to kill the Fae. While Elven magic can animate objects, it requires a tremendous amount of magic to sustain the anima- tion. The permanency of this animation and the sentient life in the blades makes sense now. The puck's magic must have helped in some way, but I've no idea what type of magic they possess.

Hearing a chime, I pick up my phone and see a text from Solandis confirming she will be at the ball, and she's excited I'm going to be there too. She asks if I have a dress, and I tell her Daire picked out something for me. She sends me several heart emojis, and I laugh.

I pull up another chat to ask Theron for a book on pucks. Dots start and stop several times before he explains he doesn't have one here but can borrow a couple from the dark Fae king's library. I tell him we're going to need them. Knowledge is power, after all.

Picking up the journal, I flip through to the next page and the next, but all the rest are blank. It's worrisome. Catriona kept this journal her entire life. I'd have expected to see at least one or two entries in the twilight of her life. Biting my lip, I try to think about other possibilities beyond the most obvious, but nothing comes to mind. About to close the book, I see a small note slipped in between the last couple of pages.

Dearest Arden,

The dark Elven king's spies are everywhere, so I'm allowed to deliver the box, but I cannot introduce myself in person. Nobody said I couldn't leave you a note.

As you've might have noticed, the journal entries end abruptly. My mother, Catriona, died not long after the puck came to our house. We're not sure if he was followed or if he told our location to another, but my father and I came home to find her body in the doorway and our house ransacked. Given nothing of value was taken, we know her death was deliberate, and she was murdered. The journal and blades were hidden in the forge, so we took them, left everything else, and started over in a new location.

We never felt safe again. Over the years, we maintained absolute secrecy until my son, your father, met and fell in love with a witch named Gia.

I break the line of secrecy again because I refuse to wait another second to introduce myself. I'm your grandmother, Elora, and I promise we'll be reunited soon.

Love,

EAB

Tears slip down my face at the thought of another senseless MacAllister death. Faced with a monumental task, Catriona not only survived, but thrived. She knew love, laughter, and the joy of being a mother. Through it all, she faced her destiny with the same grace and determination she exuded the day she walked out of the Kingdom of Dragons. I'm proud to be her legacy.

CHAPTER
FOUR

<u>ARDEN</u>

Daire, Astor, and I arrive in the Underworld two days later. Daire immediately orders me to go find Solandis and Vargas. When I point to the luggage, he shrugs one elegant shoulder and reminds me of the many servants employed by the palace to take care of mundane matters. I raise an eyebrow and give him a look. He sighs and promises to take the luggage to my room himself. I reward him with a smile. I glance over at Astor, but he's immersed in some app on his phone, so I ask the nearby staff for directions to Vargas' room.

It takes forever to get there. Lucifer's palace is enormous, and it's a maze inside. Every hallway looks the same, with white marble on the walls and black marble on the floors. Even the sconces are identical, black wrought iron spikes with flames placed every six feet.

Exactly. My excellent sense of direction is challenged with every turn.

Finally, I spot a door with two guards in front of it which must be his. I walk up and request to see Vargas.

"Run along, witch," the burly demon demands with a sneer. "Vargas has no use for your kind." He glances at the soldier standing guard on the other side of the door, and they both chuckle. "Although, if you want to come back in about three hours, I'd be happy to take care of you." His hand drifts down to his crotch to convey his meaning.

Why would Vargas assign these morons to guard his door? And why does he need guards in Lucifer's house anyway? I guess it's a palace, not a house, but it would be hard for someone to breach its security.

Cocking my hip, I relax my stance and fold my arms across my chest to keep from throttling the idiot in front of me. *Patience. Channel Solandis,* I tell myself and take a controlled breath in and an equally slow exhale. Lucifer might be a tad angry if I maim or kill a couple of his guards.

"Open the door and tell Vargas his daughter is here to see him. You're not going to get in trouble for disturbing him, I promise. He's waiting for me."

"Good try," he says, taking a step forward to tower over me. "Everybody knows Vargas has a son, a demon son, not a puny witch daughter. Now get out of here before you really piss me off. I'm sure there are plenty of demons around here who will be happy to be your daddy."

I uncross my arms, step forward, and jab him in the chest with my finger. "Look here, asshole, your job is to guard the door, not insult Vargas' visitors. If we weren't in Lucifer's home, there wouldn't be a discussion, but I'm trying to be polite and respect the fact you're just doing your job. However, if you don't reach your hand behind you and knock on the damn door, I'm going to do it myself." I flash him my best smile.

The other guard laughs loudly. "Feisty, I like it." He reaches over and slaps a hand on the shoulder of the guard in front of me. "Hey, man, maybe we should knock on the door. Let Vargas deal with sparky here."

The meathead in front of me shoves him back. Turning his beet-red face toward me, he withdraws the dagger at his waist and waves it in front of my face.

"Nah, I think it's time I showed this witch how to show me proper respect," he bellows. "Maybe I should carve my mark on your pretty face for everyone to see?"

With a flick, the Killian blade is in my hand and pressed against his balls. "Take one step forward, and I'll cut them off." I press harder until I see him wince. "Now get the fuck out of my way." I shift my feet to get ready for his attack. He's too stupid to back off.

The smell of rotten eggs and dead animals fills the air, and the rune on my throat flares in warning. I immediately start breathing from my mouth to minimize the putrid stench. It's not until green slime starts oozing from his skin that I realize he's a swamp demon. While they're not known for being at the top of the demon food chain, they have one serious advantage —they can make their skin toxic.

Jumping back, I slide my blade into its holster and pull my sword to give myself room to maneuver while allowing me to avoid the poison. I'm barely in position when he charges toward me with his arms outstretched, trying to catch me. Using my witch power, I flip over him and down the hall a couple of feet. The other guard is still standing by the door laughing, but I refuse to take any chances.

My nemesis gives a loud bellow and whips around to locate me. Glaring at the other guard until he stops laughing, he snarls at him, "If you don't help me, I'll make sure you're given prison duty for a month."

When the other demon frowns and straightens from the door, I realize the idiot in front of me ranks higher than him. "Fine, but if this ends badly, don't think I won't find a way to make you pay," he warns him. He turns to me and shrugs. "Sorry, witch. He's a mean bastard on his best day."

I blink, and he's gone. Vanished. Sensing a disturbance behind me, I throw up a shield and start moving, but it's too late. He clamps down on my shoulders, pinning me in place, and my spells aren't having much impact against his armor.

The swamp demon in front of me starts laughing. "Let's play, shall we?" he says, clapping and rubbing his hands together to get them coated with poison. "This lovely toxin is a special blend I designed to attack the nerves. The instant I touch you, your nerves will feel raw, like they're on fire, and the agony will be intense. Soon, you'll be begging me to give you the antidote. Oh, and the best part—it will paralyze you, giving me extra playtime with my sweet little prey." His teeth gleam as he smiles at me.

"I didn't realize you wanted to play," I reply casually.

My brain quickly sifts through my defense options until I land on one giving me the ability to neutralize the primary threat, which is the toxin. Tuning out his babble, I send myself inward, pull the thread from my soul, and wrap it around the image in my head. Light, filled with intense heat, bursts inside me, and a second later, I'm ducking down, barely able to fit in the grand hallway. I might have underestimated my height.

With a swing of my spiked tail, I slam the demon behind me against the wall and pin him there while I use its strength to crush every one of his bones. His screams fill the air until he blinks out.

My head swivels to the demon with his hands pressed

against my scaled chest. He laughs with glee until I smile, showing him row after row of sharp teeth. My dragon scales are impenetrable to the toxin. His eyes widen, and he scrambles back quickly. His fear makes me snort, which makes fire shoot out of my nose, and I accidentally light him up like a match to tinder.

Oops.

A boisterous laugh echoes in the hall, and I swing my head to find Vargas, sword in hand, wiping tears from his eyes. Apparently, this is incredibly amusing. I narrow my eyes, but it has little effect on him.

The demon in front of me douses the fire and immediately starts spouting an elaborate story of how I attacked him and his buddy to get to Vargas. Apparently, I started with seduction but quickly changed my tactics when he resisted my charms.

Since I can't defend myself in this form, I picture my normal self and transform back. Swaying slightly, I wipe the sweat from my forehead. Transformation requires a tremendous amount of power, and I haven't been practicing enough to build up my stamina.

When the demon sees my form, he lunges forward, his toxic hand outstretched to grab me, but it quickly falls to the ground. Confused, he looks from me to the hand on the floor, and when he realizes it's his, screams erupt from his mouth.

Vargas steps in front of him and places the tip of his sword under the demon's chin to close his mouth. "Stop screaming," he orders him. "Nobody gave you permission to touch my daughter." He chuckles when the demon blanches. "That's right—she's my daughter. Let's take a walk so you can explain what happened." He snaps his fingers, and the other demon also appears. "I'd hate to leave your fellow soldier behind." In a blink, they all disappear together.

"Arden." Solandis' cool voice comes from the doorway.

"This is not how you act as a guest in someone else's home. I taught you better." Her eyes are twinkling, though.

She steps forward to give me a hug but stops and wrinkles her nose. "Darling, you smell terrible, and there seems to be green slime on your shirt. Let's go back to your suite so you can shower and change."

I glance down and see splatters of green on my shirt, which thankfully didn't soak all the way through. I'm going to have to cut it off to avoid touching the poison. *Damnit.* I don't have many clothes.

"I haven't been to my suite yet. Let me text Daire." I reply, pulling my phone from my back pocket. A minute later, a blur joins us in the hall.

Daire strides toward Solandis with a smile on his devastatingly handsome face, and she eats it up. After giving him a kiss on the cheek, she loops an arm through his and points to me. "Don't get close. A nasty swamp demon tried to teach Arden a lesson, and now she's covered in his poison and stench."

Daire's brows draw together while he assesses my appearance. When he finds the goo on my shirt, his eyes fill with concern. "Did you get any on you? Do we need to find an antidote?" When I shake my head no, he gives me a hard nod. His eyes dart around the hallway, taking in the rest of the scene, and his worry turns to rage. "A demon dared attack you in my father's house?"

"Two, actually," Solandis says in response. "They were guarding our door and took offense when Arden asked to see Vargas."

I glare at her and narrow my eyes, silently telling her to cut it out.

She smirks, then gives a delicate shudder. "If Arden hadn't transformed into a dragon, she would've been in excruciating pain." She smiles sweetly at me. "Quick thinking, my dear. I'm so proud of you."

His voice is soft, but his hands are clenched when he asks her, "Do you know where they are now?"

She waves an elegant hand. "Vargas took them away for a chat," she replies airily. "I'm sure he's taking care of the situation. In the meantime, would you mind escorting us to Arden's suite? I'd like to see this dress you picked out for her, and I'd like to avoid any more confrontations." She throws me a wink.

I roll my eyes at her antics.

A few minutes later, she nods in satisfaction when she enters my suite. "Oh, this is darling, much better than her room at The Abbey," she exclaims, her eyes swing to Daire. "Where's this dress you picked out?"

I frown at her. She didn't need to add the dig about my room at The Abbey, but she's right—the suite is beautiful, with its light and airy furnishings. My eyes drift from the fluffy comforter on the bed to the plush couch, and a sense of peace settles over me. Even the air smells divine, with a subtle scent of strawberries, honey, and mint, and I look around the room for the source.

Spotting a huge bouquet of freesias on the table, I walk over and bury my face in them. *Hmmm...* I should think about adding a few things to my room at The Abbey. It would be nice to have a fluffy bed and some flowers. Maybe a couch too.

"Do you like it?" Daire murmurs in my ear, causing me to shiver.

"If I weren't covered in putrid slime, I'd kick Solandis out and show you how much I like it," I answer softly.

He utters a low groan, and I turn to face him.

A muscle still ticks in his jaw, but desire has burned away some of the anger.

I stretch up, making sure to keep my distance from his impeccable suit, and give him a quick thank you kiss.

He smiles, steps through the door on the right, and returns a brief second later, carrying a long garment bag. He hangs it on the door and motions to the closet behind him. "All the accessories are in there. If you'll excuse me, I have something I need to do." He strides over to the door. "Astor will meet you here in two hours." With those brief words, he's gone. To kill a couple of demons, I'm guessing.

"Well, well. Things have certainly changed with him since I saw you last," Solandis remarks softly. "Now, go shower so we can try on your dress."

About thirty minutes later, I'm standing in front of the tall mirror in the corner and swiveling side to side to view the dress from every angle. Surprisingly, it's not a gown, but two separate pieces. The top half is a black corseted semi-sheer bodysuit with boning which molds to my curves. It's paired with a very full semi-sheer skirt that ties around the waist and drapes lightly to the floor. Tonal black flower appliques, along with a few sparkly beads, are placed strategically on the top and skirt, giving peek-a-boo glimpses of my body. I twirl, and the voluminous skirt slides open to reveal a slit from ankle to waist, exposing my entire leg for a microsecond before falling closed again.

It's stunning and bold. I would never have picked it out, but I can't tear my eyes or hands from it. Smoothing the gauzy fabric over my hips, I marvel at this masterpiece. I feel like I'm wearing nothing but air, and yet the material drapes and floats around my tall body and my curves, changing me from athletic to sensual.

I glance at Solandis in the mirror. "Daire certainly has impeccable taste," I murmur. I can tell by the stunned look on her face she agrees.

"You're beautiful, my darling," she confirms, pulling me into her arms and staring at the two of us in the mirror. "The dress only emphasizes your best features, but you are the star." Turning away, she claps her hands in happiness. "I'm so happy I can be here to share this experience with you."

With a snap of her fingers, her casual clothes disappear, and she's suddenly attired in a form-fitting silver beaded mermaid dress highlighting every single curve she possesses. I can't help but whistle. She's going to put Vargas on his knees if she wears that dress.

She steps to the side of me and bumps me with her hip. "Now, tell me about the journal, who you've been kissing, and well...everything, while I decide which dress to wear tonight."

Groaning, I back up, change clothes, and get comfortable. Knowing Solandis, she will want to try on all her dresses before choosing one.

<u>ASTOR</u>

Dashing around the corner, I find another empty hallway and yank my hand through my hair. *Fuck.* I spent too long working in the lab, and now I'm late meeting Arden. When I checked her suite, she'd already left, and she could be anywhere by now.

This is pointless. I stop and take a deep breath. The easiest way to find her would be to replicate my efforts. A flick of my wrist pulls the shadows to me, and I command them to search for her. Dark streaks take off down the various hallways, quietly whispering their findings back to me.

There. She's standing in the hallway by Lucifer's office. Calling my shadows back, I head toward her location. When I get there, she's standing outside the door with her fist raised to knock, but after a slight pause, she quickly lowers it. Tilting her head, she places her ear next to the door. I'm intrigued and slide in behind her so I can listen too.

"You're sure this is what you want to do? It's serious between you and Arden? What about Astor?" Lucifer questions someone in the room.

"Absolutely. Astor too," Daire confirms. "I don't want any more incidents like this morning, but it's more than a protective action. I want to claim her in front of everyone, and an announcement would make it official. I'm sure Astor will agree."

"I see. Will you give her the Mate's Kiss?" Lucifer probes quietly.

"No," Daire replies, his voice raw with emotion. "I can't."

"I'll talk to Astor," Lucifer informs him. "I want to hear it directly from him, but I also think it's a good solution. Now, let's discuss the territory I went to see last week."

I place my mouth next to Arden's ear and whisper, "Naughty, naughty. Eavesdropping on someone else's conversation." Although I'm glad we did, because now I'm curious about Daire's request to Lucifer and how it includes me. There was one high note in the conversation. Guilt washes over me, but I block it out. Selfishly, I don't want him to give her the Mate's Kiss.

She jumps and turns to say something to me, but I quickly cover her mouth and motion to the door. Sliding my fingers through hers, I pull her down the hallway and out of earshot.

"I'm sorry I'm late, gorgeous. When I'm working on a project, I tend to lose all sense of time."

She doesn't say anything in return, and I glance over, expecting to see anger, but she's biting her lip and staring down at the floor.

Pulling her to the side of the hallway, I murmur, "Don't think about what you heard until you can ask Daire directly."

Her eyes search mine for reassurance, and after a minute, she must find what she seeks because she gives me a decisive nod. "You're right. I'm not even sure how I feel about what he said," she states with a shrug. "Now, what's this about a project?"

I hold my finger up to my lips. "It's a secret." Telling her I'm working on a secret project is going to drive her crazy, but at least it will get her mind off Daire's comment for a while.

"Let's discuss something more important." I pause dramatically. "We have all afternoon to spend together. Just the two of us. No witches. No cadre. No quest. What would you like to do?" I trap her body against the wall with mine and lean down until my lips are an inch away from hers. "I know what I'd like to do."

Her tongue darts out and swipes her lips. "Very tempting, but there's somewhere I've always wanted to go, and Vargas would never take me."

I groan. "You want to go to the market, don't you?"

"Yep."

Running a hand over my face to hide my thoughts for a second, I quickly decide to go. Anything that puts a smile on her face is worth it, even if it means coming face-to-face with my past.

Underworld Market uses magic and illusion to lure customers to its doors. Its six-story entrance can be seen from anywhere in the city. Black beams rise high in the air framing the entrance and fire cascades down like a river on each side. Beyond its visual appeal, the entrance is a magical beacon calling seductively to all who visit the city. With barely a thought, visitors suddenly find themselves standing at the impressive entrance, eager to enter and spend their gold.

Arden flashes me an excited smile, which I try to return. I subtly wipe a bead of sweat off my forehead when she tugs me through the opening. Once inside, we're met with an explosion of sound, smells, and color. Arden tries to capture everything, her head swiveling rapidly from one side of the market to the other, but there's so much, it's impossible.

Vendors loudly hawk their colorful wares to the massive crowd shuffling past the stalls. Street urchins weave in and out, slyly patting pockets while tiny fingers quickly lift anything of value. Delicious smells from nearby food carts fill the air, mingling with the flowery and musky smells emanating from the stalls selling perfume, spices, and aphrodisiacs. Every bit of the market is designed to stimulate each and every sense until you can't help but reach in your pocket to buy something.

"I don't understand why Vargas wouldn't let me visit," she says, looking up at me for the answer. "The worst crime I've seen is pick-pocketing." A nearby vendor starts calling out ice cream flavors, and she pivots quickly toward him.

After paying for her ice cream, I wait until we're walking away to answer. "The unseen is where the danger lies. Behind the friendly stall owners and mundane goods of the main market lies the black market. It's a highly profitable and dangerous arena ruled by one man and his army of criminals, where anyone can purchase or barter for goods, services, and sex." I keep my voice neutral and stick to the facts.

I quietly explain the various areas of the black market to her. "Like the main market, the black market is also lined with stalls, but instead of the usual products, forbidden and extinct goods wait for the right buyer. Unicorn tears to heal the deadliest of poisons or a shield crafted of dragon's scales? Step up, but be prepared to pay through the nose for these rare items.

"Beyond the physical items, the black market offers buyers an array of criminal services. Need someone assassinated or tortured? Something priceless stolen? Almost anything is available, for the right price or deal. The shadows house those willing to negotiate terms.

"But the biggest moneymaker in the black market is sex. There are brothels offering the most exotic flesh and services. Surprisingly, the talent is paid, not indentured or enslaved, and the astronomical salaries ensure the application pool is always full. Everyone can apply, but only those offering something truly unique are hired."

I stop, not wanting to divulge how well I know the black market. As a young incubus, I spent a lot of time in those dens of iniquities, draining others of their sexual essence. Hedonistic and selfish, it was a dark time in my life, long before I became a member of the cadre.

Memories surround me, seeping into my skin, causing more sweat to break out on my forehead, and I can't help but look longingly at the exit. My eyes dart from side to side, searching for anyone who might recognize me, and my panic rises. Needing distance from the past and all its pitfalls, I try to steer us out of the market, hoping Arden has seen enough today. She's accepted so much of my darkness, but there's no need for her to know the depths of depravity I sank to in the past.

"Did you see the dress Daire picked out for me?"

I glance down to answer, but when I see her tongue dart out to lick her ice cream cone, memories of her licking my hard cock trip through my mind, and all I want to do is yank her out of the market to the first dark corner I can find. My body shifts, preparing to move, but I mentally slap myself. *Patience. You fucked up, remember? She needs time. Now, what was her question?* I stare down at her, hoping the answer will come to me, but I've got nothing.

"Sorry," I tell her. "What did you say?"

"I asked if you saw the dress Daire picked out for me?"

A picture of the dress flashes in my mind, and I can't help my wicked grin. "I've seen it, and you're going to look gorgeous in it," I assure her. Especially since I made a few changes to the original.

"You know, I've never been to a ball, so I'm a bit nervous," she admits softly. "Excited, too. I've always wanted to go to one but couldn't. Too many people meant safety issues. Anyway, I know it's probably a standard event for you, but it's my first ball and I want it to be perfect. Is there anything I should know or do? Anything I shouldn't do? I want to make a good impression for you. All of you—Daire, my family, and of course, Lucifer."

Frowning, I pull her into my arms and throw up a quick barrier spell to force the crowd to flow around us. "If you think about it, I'm the only member of the cadre who isn't noble or royal, and I've been to one ball prior to this one. Honestly, I was dreading the event until you agreed to be our date. Pretentious assholes aren't really my scene." I watch the relief cross her face before being replaced with laughter at my utter disregard for Underworld society.

"Making a good impression on anyone, for me, should never be your priority. It shouldn't even enter your mind. In this world, I care about you and the cadre. That's it. Everyone else can go fuck themselves. This ball is special because of you. You're going to look insane, and I'm going to be the lucky bastard standing next to you, claiming you as mine. A thousand years from now, my memories of this ball will center around you dancing and laughing. The rest will be background noise. If you forget anything, I'll help you remember." To illustrate my point, I use our shared spell to push some of my favorite memories of us into her mind.

Her lips crash into mine, and I'm knocked over by the wave of feeling surrounding me. The kiss is fierce and consuming, smashing through the barriers she put between us to keep her heart safe. Her mind and thoughts are open, and I dive into them, needing to know if I have a chance, and my knees almost buckle in relief. Everything I've been hoping for is there for me to see.

She's my reason for existing. The redemption I so desperately need, but don't deserve. The only chance for light to live in my darkness. I clutch her to me, praying to whatever goddess is out there and willing to listen to help me hold onto her.

I'm lost in the kiss, following her down to the depths of her soul, when a burst of cold wrenches me back to the harsh light of day. I shiver and break away. A drop of ice-cold liquid runs down the side of my neck, and I can't help but laugh. She must have forgotten she was holding her ice cream when she threw her arms around me. I pull her wrist away, then bring the cone forward to take a sweet bite. I'd rather be biting something else, but this will do for now.

Her face lights up, and laughter fills the air. "Oops, sorry," she says. Pulling her sleeve over her hand, she wipes the side of my neck. "You might be a little sticky, but..."

A sultry voice interjects, "Astor darling, I almost didn't recognize you. It's been ages, and I certainly didn't expect to see you in the market." She pauses. "So happy and carefree, it's like you're an entirely different person. Where's the dark, depraved incubus who spent hours in the brothels with me, inflicting sexual torture on the begging masses?"

I briefly close my eyes. Of all the memories to crawl out of sewer, this might be the worst. I wipe every iota of expression from my face and glare at the succubus standing beside me. Incredibly beautiful, with her jet-black hair and blue eyes, she exudes sexuality and charm, but don't let her close enough to strike, you'll regret it.

"Letti, I'd be lying if I said I'm happy to see you," I say in a bored tone. "Let's skip the reunion chat, shall we?"

I turn and offer my arm to Arden to escort her away from this cesspool.

Letti steps in front of Arden, and I contemplate the best way to kill her before she can open her mouth. Time ticks slowly while I breathe in and out, thinking of the options. When the answer arrives, it's both unwelcome and terrifying. I can't change the past, and I can't keep hiding from it. Arden's kiss sparked hope in me, so I scrape up the courage to let the cards fall and decide to let Letti spew her poison.

"You probably don't know this, but he's a true deviant, my dear. A master at his craft. He can wield pleasure and pain with equal dexterity, making his toys scream one minute and beg for release the next. It's truly beautiful." She looks Arden up and down. "Based on the dewy innocence you're wearing, I'm guessing you haven't met that side of him yet?" She chuckles and looks at me. "Oh, darling, you should come play with me and find your true calling again."

She reaches up, but before she can touch me, Arden's hand clamps tightly around her wrist. Letti's succubus power fills the air, but Arden shuts it down quickly.

Shock fills my face. I'm astonished to see how easily she neutralized a succubus' power. In all my years, I've never seen anyone able to neutralize a succubus. Resist, maybe, but it's as if her seductive magic has no power.

Letti steps back in fear.

"You're not allowed to touch him. In fact, if you try to touch or talk to him again, I'll permanently take away your power and put up a billboard to inform the entire Underworld. I'm sure your past victims would love to hear you're defenseless," Arden states, her voice hard with anger. Old power fills the air, and my incubus rises to the surface to peer at Arden in all her magnificence. "For the record, I don't care about his past, only his future, which belongs to me. He's mine." She glances at me, then turns back to Letti. "They're both mine. I claim them. Now, get the hell out of our way."

The crowd laughs when Letti stumbles to the side.

My incubus quietly chants in the background. *Hers. Mine. Ours.*

Screw the exit. Against market rules, I open a portal directly back to my room, leaving Letti and the past behind.

CHAPTER
SIX

<u>ASTOR</u>

When we get to the palace, I break away from Arden and pace to the other side of the room to gather my thoughts. How do I explain my fucked-up past? I glance over and see Arden sitting on the bench at the end of the bed, her face inscrutable, waiting for me to speak.

"She's right," I blurt.

Memories bombard me, and my mind slips easily into the distant past. I keep hoping I'll see some other degenerate, but it's only me. I cringe. My shadows instantly surround me. "When an incubus is young, all we think about is sex—using our power to get sex and using sex to refill our power. It's a vicious cycle, but if you try to go without, it drives you mad. I was going through a particularly rough patch when a friend took me to the brothels in the black market. The first night, I didn't even have sex. The air was so full of sexual energy, I scooped it up until I overflowed with power, then went home. For weeks, it was the same, until one night, the energy wasn't enough. I felt hollow. Hunger beat at me. I realized my incubus needed the sex, not just the power. So sex became part of my routine. For a while, we were sated." I roll my shoulders to ease my tension.

"The hollow feeling eventually returned and it was stronger than before, but I didn't know how to meet this new level of need. I started experimenting with my partners to pull more sexual energy from them, trying to fill my power enough to stay sated. The combination of pain and pleasure can produce unbelievable highs, and I learned to wield them with precision to draw the most power. When one experiment failed, I'd try another.

"One night, Letti was visiting a client down the hall. When she felt the energy, she filled her entire reservoir with the power I generated from my experiment. She hunted down the source and found me." I take a deep breath to ease the shame burning my throat so I can finish my story.

"From that night on, we were inseparable, feeding off the actions of the other. Our relationship wasn't sexual, but we were corrupt partners, addicts in our quest for more. I can't tell you how many days and nights we spent in those brothels. The sexual power I wielded grew with each depraved game we played. Time blurred, a decade slipped past, then another. I reveled in the power, the buzz I felt every night. I tried to stop so many times, but the buzz would wear off too quickly and I'd find myself back in those alleys, looking for my fix.

"Her succubus thrived on the cloud of sexual energy, and her power grew exponentially. One night, when we were extremely high and drunk on power, she failed to recognize her own boundaries and drained someone's life force. Stunned by our carelessness, I swore I'd never go back. I lasted a measly three days. Like all addicts, I couldn't stay away."

Holding my breath, I finally meet her gaze head-on. Tears fall freely down her cheeks. For the woman or me, I'm not sure, maybe both.

Clearing my tight throat, I finish the rest of the story quickly. "One morning, I lay there high but full of despair, and in a blinding flash of clarity, I knew I had one chance to stop, but I couldn't rely on my own willpower. I needed help. Before the buzz could fade, I crawled out of bed and went to the king of the underground to make a deal. If he locked me up and helped me get over my addiction, I'd give him the same amount of time in service. It remains the worst decade of my life.

"The first year, I lay in bed, detoxing. It took three or four more years for me to function, and the rest of the time to learn how to have sex without engaging in the extremes of pain and pleasure. I slowly gained control but realized it would be something I'd fight for the rest of my life.

"After I got out, he offered me a new deal. If I tattooed a truth rune on my body and served as his truthsayer for five years, he'd release me from my debt. So I did. Some days, I regret the rune, but honestly, it helped save me. The constant pain from the lies kept me focused and away from the brothels. Once I'd fulfilled my debt, I left and stumbled through the world, avoiding life, until I met Valerian. He offered me a way to redeem myself by helping the cadre save others."

Taking a couple of deep breaths, I stop. In the quiet room, my breaths sound harsh, like a gun firing rapidly, while I wait for her to speak. Her silence is devastating. With my stomach clenching, I walk over and crouch down in front of her.

"Say something," I say hoarsely.

Finally, she does. "You've traveled one hell of a road, and I'm so proud of you for making it to the other side." She holds up her hand when I try to speak. "I meant what I said earlier to Letti. Your past is your own. For me, it molded the darkness inside of you to create this version of yourself, and honestly, it sings to me and fulfills a part of me I didn't even know existed until I met you. I don't expect you to change.

"You make me feel beautiful, sexy, and powerful. You challenge the boundaries I place on myself by pushing me to reach for more. You recognize the important things and disregard the rest like inconsequential trash, and I need that. I need you. I'm interested in our future, where we make new memories, not the past." She leans forward and taps my chest. "In return, I expect you to own your feelings and be upfront with me in all matters. And whether it's Witchwood or the Underworld Market, stop letting me drag you to places full of triggers." She leans over and cups my head in her hands. "You're mine. Both of you. And. I. Am. Yours."

Darkness explodes out of me. I drag her off the bench and into my arms, raining kisses all over her.

Thank you, goddess, I repeat over and over to the one who answered my prayers.

My hand cups the back of her head, and I marvel at the fierce woman who sees something redeemable in me. Staring down into her bright green eyes, I tell her, "I've never needed anyone, but I need you. With you, I see a future, one I can be proud of living. You make my family complete. The lies falling from your luscious lips are the lightest of whips lashing against the darkness threatening to consume me. I'll work on being open, but let me worry about my triggers. Most importantly, I belong to you, and you to me."

Pain slices through me, and I wince. "To us."

My incubus nods in satisfaction.

CHAPTER

SEVEN

<u>ARDEN</u>

Bringing my legs up, I wrap them tightly around his lean waist, fusing our bodies together, trying to make us one. His hands automatically drop to hold me more securely, but I don't pause. With a simple spell, I remove our clothes, needing to feel every inch of his warm skin next to mine. I press my nose to his neck and inhale, smelling his unique scent of burnt cedar with a hint of sex. My tongue flicks out to taste him, while my hands explore the sinewy muscles beneath my fingertips. It's not enough.

Grasping his hair, I tilt his head back and find chocolate brown eyes staring at me with a delicious dark heat, while the incubus' black flashes intermittently. I smile and issue my challenge. "Show me."

He inhales sharply, then roars with laughter. "Challenge

42

accepted, gorgeous." He walks over to the wall and places my back to its cool surface.

I lean forward into the heat of his body and draw his lips into a kiss. Our tongues dance wildly, like flames in the wind, in an age-old battle, but neither of us is willing to concede to the other. Demanding but not rough, he uses every trick in his arsenal to make me surrender. He quickly finds I've got a few of my own.

With a groan, he shifts forward, and my back slams against the wall. I don't even feel the coolness of the surface this time. Balancing me on his lap, his hard cock lines up perfectly, and my hips rock back and forth a few times, sliding from root to tip. I can't help but think of how good he's going to feel once he's inside of me.

His hands grip my wrists, pulling them up on each side, and I shiver with anticipation. When I hear a clicking noise, I glance up and see my wrists restrained with magical cuffs.

Sending a small stream of magic up, I lightly test the restraints and realize they only hold me to the wall. Giving him a wicked smile, I send a small stream of magic to encircle and stroke his cock.

"Wait your turn," he growls, blocking my magic from teasing him further.

I pout and try to bring him closer with my legs.

His hands slide down to my thighs. Wrapping a hand around each one, he lifts me up and spreads me wider. Using his cock, he slides up and down my slit, coating himself in the wetness dripping from my center.

I lick my lips in anticipation, and he drops his head down to take my mouth in an unusually sweet kiss. "Savor this moment," he tells me, tracing lightly over my lips, nibbling and sucking my tongue. "Because I'm going to fucking devour you."

He steps back, and my body stays in position against the

wall, my hands shackled above me, and my legs spread wide in an open invitation.

His gaze is carnal, full of ideas for my ruin, and my body clenches in reaction.

"Tell me you belong to us," he rasps, dark emotion clouding his expression.

Shaking my head back and forth, I return a sultry laugh but no words.

Shadows descend on me, seeking those spots guaranteed to make me gasp and writhe, elevating my desire up a notch or twelve. My laughter dies in a cloud of pleasure. Tilting my head back, I moan repeatedly, loving the feel of a thousand hands touching my body, while he stands in front of me, watching. His wrists flick right and left like a conductor in front of a symphony, directing the sensual notes into a new composition.

Laughter is beyond me, but I dredge up a smile. "More," I tell him, perilously close to begging, but I manage to turn it into a demand at the last second. Sweat beads on my body and several muscles silently quiver, but my eyes continue to throw down my challenge.

Astor strides forward and drops to his knees, and I thrust my hips at him. It's the one place the shadows haven't touched, and I ache for his mouth on me. His lips kiss softly on each of my inner thighs, and I squirm, widening my legs to entice him to the center. Seductive brown eyes flick up to meet mine before his tongue glides from bottom to top, licking me straight up the center.

Nerves explode and I buck into his mouth for more, but he's too busy contemplating his next move. I bite the inside of my cheek to gain a bit of focus.

"I hope there's more. I'm getting bored hanging here," I say, taunting him with the truth, then the lie, watching him wince.

The words strike hard, and with a wicked laugh, he consumes me. His tongue and lips pay homage to me like I'm his personal goddess. Firm lips pull and suck on my nub, making it ache, then his tongue flicks rapidly up and down, pushing me to the edge over and over but stopping before I fall.

Panting, I stare at him in disbelief. Sweat darkens his auburn hair, and I use phantom fingers to push it back from his face, then grip it tightly. Trying to pull his head closer to me, I growl in frustration when he doesn't move. My body burns with the need to come.

Obsidian eyes blink up at me, and a seductive chuckle fills the air. "Naughty, naughty. I don't think you realize who you've claimed, but you will before the night ends."

Standing, he lines up and slides his hard cock into me, and I give a low moan. That's much better, but I've yet to surrender. My body clenches tightly around him. Pleasure spirals around my core, but I quickly realize the languorous pace he's set isn't enough to make me come.

"Harder, please," I implore him, moving my hips in a circle, but the pace doesn't change. I grit my teeth at his controlled movements.

"I love the feel of my cock sliding in and out of your sweet warmth, claiming you, owning you, feeling your body on the edge of surrender. Yet one glance into your beautiful eyes, and I realize I'm only waiting for you to join me. I surrendered to you long ago." His voice is gruff with emotion.

Seeing the truth in his eyes, I let my final wall crumble, and show him the naked vulnerability he deserves to see.

His hands grip my hips, and he thrusts hard and deep, my surrender causing him to lose tempo for a second. His forehead touches mine, and he stops and stares at me with new intensity.

After a deep breath, he thrusts a couple more times and slides out of me.

His cock is coated with my juices, and I look longingly at it. "Why are you stopping?"

"I need to taste you," he replies, as if the answer is obvious. On his knees, he uses his tongue to drive me crazy.

When I try to use my powers to touch myself, he blocks them. Soon, I'm promising him the moon and stars if he will only give me what I so desperately need.

Two fingers spear inside me and start sliding in and out, while his thumb moves in circles on my nub. "That's it, gorgeous. Beautiful. I'm going to give you everything you need. Are you ready?"

My hips piston rapidly, meeting every thrust of his fingers, and I nod.

"Look at me," he commands. "Fuck, I want to be inside you so badly, but seeing you like this enthralls me. The flush across your body, the low moans falling uninhibited from your sweet lips, and the small quivers I feel with each stroke keeps me on my knees, desperate to give you everything you need. Right... there. Come on, gorgeous. You're on the edge. Now let go." His lips clamp down on my nub and suck, and I scream as my orgasm hits me.

It rolls over me like a wave, powerful and overwhelming, and I let it pull me under, knowing he'll be there to catch me. The world around me darkens like I'm going to pass out, and only the light kisses on my lips keep me in the present. It finally starts to recede, and I slump forward.

Astor uncuffs me from the wall and pulls me into his arms. He strokes my back in a soothing manner and carefully carries me over to the bed.

Boneless, I fall to the mattress and stare up at him. Dark

brown and black eyes glitter with desire, and his hard cock stands at attention, almost purple in its need.

He climbs up and slides into me, setting another slow pace. Moaning, I debate whether I can go through another round of teasing. My body is overly sensitive from the first orgasm, making the pleasure sharp and intense.

He gives me a deep kiss, stroking my tongue in time with his cock. Chuckling, he informs me, "This time, you hold the power. Hard, fast, deep, whatever you need. You tell me. When you want me to come, you give the order."

When I hear him cede control to me, my mouth curves. Flipping him over, I sit up with him still inside me.

He sinks in deeper and, with a moan, starts to thrust faster.

"I didn't tell you to go faster, now did I?" I laugh and still his hips. "Let's stop for a second and catch our breath, shall we?"

Breathing heavily, he reaches up to play with my breasts, but I block his touch. He drops his hands to my hips and groans. "My sweet, gorgeous witch." He laughs loudly. "This is going to be one hell of a night."

EIGHT

ARDEN

Lucifer's throne room is filled with the beautiful and grotesque lords and ladies of Underworld's court. Demons, sirens, hellhounds, a couple of medusas, a centaur, and a lot of unknown creatures, all of them powerful and dangerous.

I walk through the crowd carefully, unwilling to touch anyone or let them touch me, looking for a familiar face or potential threat. Speculative gazes and whispers follow my path through the room, but I ignore them. Turquoise eyes meet mine, and with a sigh of relief, I head toward Solandis.

She scrutinizes every inch of my appearance, then beams and claps her hands. Gliding over, she takes one of my hands in hers and twirls me around.

"Beautiful, my darling girl," she praises. When the slit parts to reveal my leg, she frowns. "Seriously, Arden? I don't think you needed to bring a dagger to the ball." Rolling her eyes, she beckons Vargas over to us.

"This is all your fault," she informs him. "How's it going to look when she arrives at Lucifer's ball with a dagger strapped to her leg?"

"Like she's smart and capable of defending herself," he responds, then frowns. "Are you telling me you aren't wearing any weapons?" Unstrapping the small dagger on his belt, he tries to hand it to her, but she pushes it away.

"As if I'm completely defenseless, Vargas. I'm a Princess of the Fae and have more powers than most. Besides, I don't want to ruin the lines of my dress." She runs her hands down the silver beaded dress, drawing his eyes to her curves. Not only is the dress molded to her body, but the semi-sheer material displays more than it hides.

His eyes glance from her daring cleavage to the high slit in the skirt, and he slides the dagger back through its loophole. A muscle ticks in his jaw. "It doesn't matter. I'm not letting you out of my sight for even a second," he retorts, his voice hard. He turns to me and blanches when he sees my dress. Thunderclouds gather in his eyes.

I spin in a circle, distracting him with a glimpse of the Killian dagger, before exclaiming, "Isn't the dress gorgeous? Daire picked it out for me."

I hear the grind of his teeth and almost laugh. He can't debate the appropriateness of a dress given to me by the Prince of the Underworld.

Daire glides up beside him and blinks when Vargas glares at him. "Good evening, Daire. I hear you're responsible for this dress?"

I watch Solandis pinch Vargas discreetly on the side. He sighs and runs a hand down his face, muttering about the dangers of tempting monsters and expecting them to abide by the rules of chivalry.

Daire says nothing, and my amusement dies. Does he not like the dress?

A tiny frown sits between the icy blue eyes staring at my dress. "Astor," he calls out, his voice tight. "Can you come here for a second?"

Solandis raises an eyebrow at me, and I shrug. "Darling, if you'll excuse me, I need to go to the ladies' room." Turning, she sashays to the door with eyes following her every move. Vargas hurries to catch up to her, snarling warnings left and right.

I laugh at Vargas' possessiveness. It wouldn't matter if Solandis wore a sack cloth, he'd annihilate any who even glanced in her direction. I turn back to face Daire, only to find him less than an inch away.

"What's up?" Astor's voice floats over the tall vampire standing in front of me. He slides up beside Daire, and his eyes widen when he sees me. "Stunning. Sexy." His finger caresses the tops of my breasts, which are showcased in the tight, corseted semi-sheer bodysuit. He twirls his finger in a circle, and I turn to show him the full effect. "The dagger is the perfect accessory."

His blatant desire sends shivers down my spine, and when he deliberately pushes images from last night into my mind, my nipples pebble. Daire growls. Astor smirks, but I'm in too good of a mood to be irritated at him.

Daire pinches the bridge of his nose and takes in a deep breath. "This isn't the *exact* dress I picked out. What the hell were you thinking?"

Frowning, I raise an eyebrow toward Astor. Obviously, he modified the dress. "It's the same one I tried on yesterday. Solandis thought it was beautiful and perfect for the ball."

Astor scowls at Daire. Taking my arm, he escorts me over to Solandis and Vargas, who are now standing nearby. "Wait here, gorgeous. Daire and I need to have a chat. Don't worry. The dress is perfect." He strides over to Daire and yanks him out of the room.

Taking a glass of champagne from a nearby waiter, I swallow the contents in one drink, then pick up another. Half listening to Solandis' chatter, I glance around the room and find several pairs of eyes on me. Some simply wonder who I am, but others leer openly in my direction until they glimpse the red flames in Vargas' eyes. They quickly divert their attention to someone else.

Discreetly checking out the other women in the room, I almost gasp when I see their dresses. Most of them are completely sheer, with only the briefest cuts of fabric strategically covering their mounds. When they turn and flitter like butterflies, the room is suddenly a sea of colorful breasts, tails, and butts. There might even be a fin or two.

Most of the females congregate in small groups gossiping to each other, but every so often, one breaks away to glide around the room. On a seemingly random stroll, they laugh and chat with a few people, then drift away, subtly circling closer and closer to their target.

My eyes shift to the tall figure dressed entirely in black and radiating power like the sun. Divinely attractive, his golden blond aura shines brightly, eclipsing most of the males here. Deep blue eyes survey the room and its occupants like a general assessing the field of battle. While he stands with a group of demons, I don't think he's paying them much attention.

Females stroll past every minute or two, their bodies lit from behind, signaling their interest with an utter disregard for propriety. Lucifer graces them with a smile but little else. His eyes constantly scan the room, picking up minute details here and there. When his eyes land on me, he raises an eyebrow at the amusement on my face, then winks. I smile back.

Another striking blond catches the corner of my eye, and I swivel to watch him prowl toward me. Throwing back my shoulders, I watch his eyes involuntarily drop to stare at my breasts, and I smile with satisfaction to see the slightly dazed look on his face. This is the expression he should have worn when he approached me the first time.

"My dress is pretty modest compared to what I see around here," I state before he reaches me, waving my hand to indicate the nearly naked women around me. My words die when he places his finger on my lips.

"I know," Daire replies stiffly. "You're beautiful. Truly. The dress fits you like a dream. Astor did the right thing by making the alterations." He sighs. Leaning his head down, he places his lips by my ear. "Bear with me. The thought of others staring at what's—at you, pushes the limits of my control."

With him so close, I find myself distracted by the smell of the luxurious cologne he wears, and I take a deep breath, filling my lungs with his scent.

Mmm...he smells delicious.

"Honestly, I find it incredibly flattering and sexy," I admit softly.

His head pops up in surprise.

"You're always controlling your expressions," I begin with a shrug. "Until you drank from me, I didn't know how you felt. I mean...I knew you wanted me and kind of liked me, but it wasn't clear until we were connected. Even now, your face is inscrutable. We could be speaking about the weather."

He gives a slight motion with his hand to point to the crowd around us. "What I feel for you is not for public consumption. They're barely civilized at the best of times," he explains. "I refuse to voluntarily give them leverage."

Frustration beats at me. "I'm not asking you to declare your love for me in front of the court, just..." My voice trails off as I spot Solandis and Vargas. He's holding her tightly to his side, while his glare threatens anyone who glances at his mate. I wave a hand toward them. "I don't see Solandis as Vargas' weakness. He's practically feral when she's getting attention from other males, and she encourages it. See how she preens every time he snarls at another male. It's entirely silent but speaks volumes to anyone observing them."

His gaze is speculative, but he shakes his head. "It's not necessary. I've asked my father to make a statement tonight which I believe will be the best way to ensure your protection and declare your status in my life. Astor's too. Why don't we finish this discussion later?"

Let down, but intrigued, I decide to wait.

"Mmm... Love the tux. I'm a lucky woman to have two incredibly sexy men by my side tonight," I say, my change in subject giving him my answer. The black tux highlights his broad shoulders and height, but without his signature blue, he's almost identical to his father.

He smiles with relief.

"Where did Astor go?"

Lips descend on my shoulder, answering my question, while hands grip my hips from behind. Irritation crosses Daire's face, but Astor just chuckles. "Did he apologize for being an ass?"

I lift a shoulder. "He explained his reasoning," I answer vaguely.

Astor presses up behind me and peers down into my cleavage. "Hmmm... We may have to kill anyone who gets too close to you." With a chuckle, he wraps his arms around me and squeezes tightly.

I lean back against Astor and give Daire a wink.

He narrows his eyes at us both.

I stiffen, but Astor shakes his head. "No," he insists firmly. "I refuse to let anyone dictate our behavior. You're mine. I want the world to know it."

He glares at Daire. "Remember a declaration without action lacks substance." Turning back to me, he takes my hand and drags me away. "Let's find Solandis and Vargas. It's time for us to enter the ballroom."

I refuse to check whether Daire's following.

WE STAND at the threshold waiting for the Master of Ceremonies to announce us. Unlike the rest of the black and white palace, the ballroom drips with gold. From the massive chandeliers hanging from the gilded ceiling to the luxurious velvet curtains swagged to the sides of the high, arched windows, gold is the predominant theme.

The monochromatic, but opulent, setting is the perfect backdrop to the sea of color displayed by the denizens and creatures standing below. Vibrant and pale, the various hues reflect both the luxurious fabrics draped across their bodies and the bodies themselves. It's quite striking and beautiful.

The Master of Ceremonies steps forward and announces Lucifer, Supreme Ruler of the Underworld, and the ballroom falls silent. Walking alone, he strides down the stairs and across the ballroom toward the dais, where his throne sits. With a flourish, he turns but continues to stand and simply nods at the man in front of us.

The MC introduces Commander Vargas Karth, High Demon, and leader of Lucifer's armies, along with his mate, the beautiful Princess of the Light Fae, Solandis. A ridiculous number of names accompanies Solandis' introduction, and I blink. Most of the time, I forget she has all those aristocratic titles, but nobody ever forgets she's a Fae princess. Wearing a beautiful smile that contrasts heavily with Vargas' scowl, they make their way to the dais and step up beside Lucifer on his right.

Tightening my hands in the crooks of Daire and Astor's elbows, we step up to the threshold.

The once silent ballroom now buzzes with the low hum of conversation, but interestingly enough, not everyone is focused on me. Astor and Daire receive their fair share of attention. A myriad of expressions drift across the sea of faces, but speculation and lust seem to be the most common ones.

The MC announces Daire, son of Lucifer and Prince of the Underworld, First Vampire, and member of the Imperium Cadre, then Astor, warlock and incubus, member of the Imperium Cadre and Lucifer's royal court.

Since most of my background is a secret, I can't wait to hear my introduction. "Arden Karth, witch and dark elf, daughter of Vargas and Solandis, sister to Callyx, mate to Valerian, King of Dragons, heart of the Imperium Cadre, and member of Lucifer's royal court," the MC says, his voice ringing out loudly over the audience.

Member of Lucifer's royal court? I glance at the two beside me. I guess this is the statement Daire was referencing earlier. Feels rather formal and impersonal.

A muscle ticks in Astor's jaw, but his face is impassive.

Daire flashes me a smile, but I'm not sure why the title pleases him so much. It would have been nice if Daire had consulted with me before the announcement, but it's too late now. With my own smile pasted on, I let them lead me across the room.

CHAPTER
NINE

<u>ARDEN</u>

Lucifer bows to me and extends his hand. "Would you honor me with the first waltz?"

With a smile, I grasp his hand and answer clearly, "The honor is all mine."

We walk to the middle of the ballroom and assume the dance position. His power wraps around us like a living entity, and it's staggering. Daire's mother must have been an incredible witch to thrive in his presence.

A single violinist starts playing, and Lucifer waltzes me in a circle around the room. All eyes are upon us, but with the music so soft, I don't dare strike up a conversation.

On our second lap, a flash of silver catches my eye, and I watch Solandis and Vargas join us. I'm relieved to share the spotlight.

Suddenly, the music increases in volume. More violins, then the rest of the string quartet joins, and the nondescript music changes into an orchestral cover of "Royals" by Lorde. Laughter bubbles up, and I don't even try to contain it. Lucifer's dark chuckle follows mine.

I'd forgotten his dry sense of humor. "Cheeky. I like it," I quip, acknowledging the subtle positioning. "Although, I'm not sure your court agrees." My eyes catch a few frowns and scowls in the audience.

"I'm sure my ministers will convey their disagreement with my choice of music in our next meeting," he admits with a long-suffering sigh.

"I didn't realize the Underworld was so democratic," I remark. "After seeing your court tonight, I shouldn't be surprised."

"Free will and democracy go hand in hand," he intones. His eyebrows draw together. "What did you see in my court?" He stares down at me, his dark blue gaze hooded so I can't tell what he's thinking.

I think back to the civilized cocktails we enjoyed before the event. "They're much more...tame than I expected them to be, given they make up the Underworld's court. Honestly, I expected barely suppressed violence, blatant cruelty, and power plays, but I didn't see any of it. They seem bored."

His eyebrows draw down in a deep V, and I tense. "You're upset because they're civilized?"

"Sort of." I wince and try to explain my reasoning. "The light Fae court is vicious, full of power plays, sexual conquests, and ambitious aristocracy, all clamoring for the queen's attention. I expected your court to be worse."

He thinks about it for a second. "They're bored and probably a little fearful. I went on a rampage after Alain. What would you suggest I do?" His eyes sparkle with humor.

"Give them responsibilities and make them vested in your success," I answer quietly, not wanting to be overheard. "Challenge them to come up with new revenue streams and make it a competition. Start a criminal empire or steal one. Boredom is only an open invitation to anarchy."

"Maybe it's time to bring back a bit of the old ways," he concedes, studying the people around us. Several ladies pout when his gaze passes over them.

"Maybe it's also time to find a new queen," I point out, only half joking. With Daire splitting his time between the cadre and Underworld, I imagine Lucifer is bored and lonely.

"Queen, huh," he says with a snort, then frowns. He stares at my mouth. "Say queen again."

"I believe this is my dance," Vargas cuts in, handing Solandis off to Lucifer.

I raise an eyebrow toward Lucifer and mouth, "Queen."

He's thunderstruck, and I can't help but wonder why the thought of a queen leaves him speechless. Unfortunately, the orchestra plays the first few notes of the new song and I'm spun away from him.

Vargas and I dance, laughing and joking our way around the dance floor. He's the first male I ever danced with, and I can't help but smile when I remember our lessons—me standing on his feet, while he danced us around the living room.

"Have you seen Callyx?" I inquire softly. I'm surprised he's not here tonight.

"He's searching for your friend," he replies. "Meri?"

"Damn," I say with a sigh. "I guess she really is in trouble. Cormal was right."

He curses. "Arden, how the hell do you know Cormal?"

I quickly explain how we met. "He's both an ally and a threat. I think only time will tell which side of the line he falls."

Vargas' hand tightens on mine. "The power he's obtained is unnatural. Be careful around him. He first ruled the black market, and now he rules criminals everywhere. Sometimes, I think he wants to rule the world."

The black market? *Hmm, I wonder if he's the one Astor bargained with to overcome his addiction.* Regardless, I agree. Cormal's eyes burn with too much ambition and power.

"I will."

The music ends, and Vargas glances behind me. I twirl around and watch Daire's eyes flare with heat when the slit in my dress opens, giving him a brief display of my body.

DAIRE'S STANCE is formal and goes well with his polite mask. If it weren't for the simmering emotion in his ice-blue eyes, I'd think him indifferent to me. The music starts, and we move effortlessly together, our bodies in perfect sync, but silence stands like a wall between us. It's driving me crazy.

I arch a brow at him, then flick my eyes down to my breasts and back up. Almost involuntarily, his gaze follows the same path, and I arch my back, allowing him to see the globes in their entirety sitting in the cradle of the corset. Other than a small lift of one eyebrow, I get nothing. *Hmm... Stubborn.* It's been a while since I faced such a challenge, but I believe I'm up for it.

Every couple of steps, I inch myself closer to him, until my body brushes ever so slightly against his. Unfortunately, it does little. The formality and rigid dance position of the waltz isn't going to give me my best shot.

An idea pops into my head, and I barely refrain from grinning, although I must have given him some clue because he falters a half step. Seconds later, the sedate music stops, "Sway with Me" by GALXARA starts up, and Astor appears behind me. Daire looks from him to me with apprehension.

"Let's shake things up, shall we?" I quip, twirling around to face Astor. My dress flares out, and in a flash, changes from black to red. Throwing my head back, I laugh and circle Astor, then fold myself into his arms. We sway for a minute, but when the music picks up, we start dancing in a circle around Daire.

"Do you like my final surprise?" Astor asks, a wicked smile gracing his lips. He motions to the dress. "I love you in red."

"Very sexy," I assure him breathlessly. Not only has our speed picked up, but with our bodies wound tightly together, the dance is more dramatic and sensual.

His hands and shadows move across my body, the lightest of caresses finding sweet spots and lighting a flame inside me. With a sigh, I yield control, and a dark gleam of satisfaction crosses his face.

Pausing, he leans down and gives me a kiss. "I'll see you soon, gorgeous." With a flick of his wrist, he sends me spinning back into Daire's arms. Glancing down, I see my dress change back to black and shake my head at Astor's theatrics.

Daire inhales deeply, then stills. "Your desire is driving me to the edge," he whispers into my ear, his hands gripping mine. "Why do you feel the need to push my limits?" He yanks me closer with a snarl, and we stand there, staring into each other's eyes.

Suddenly whirling us around the floor, he syncs with the fast music, and we become a blur. Exhilarated, I deliberately think the naughtiest thoughts, ramping up my desire until it fills the air.

He responds wildly. Blue flames ignite when our bodies brush up against each other, and I arch into him, fascinated by this visual display of emotion and wavering control.

Sliding my leg between his, I rub and tease him, pushing at the public rules and boundaries he's placed on us.

"Will you stay with me tonight?" I murmur huskily, needing to be with him without propriety and his princely title between us.

He pauses and glances at the crowd, then back at me as his internal conflict rages. He's spent his entire life hiding his emotions from this court, refusing to give them any leverage, only demanding the respect due to him as prince and First Vampire.

I'm not sure if he realizes he doesn't need to fight for it anymore. He probably hasn't needed to in a long time, but the last battle ensured their lifelong respect. I see it in their faces—the combination of worship, pride, and fear when he walks by or enters a room.

I wait. This moment is pivotal for him and us. I don't expect him to put me first all the time, but he asked his father to make Astor and me members of his royal court. He didn't declare his love. A public gesture, the kind only a lover would make, would cement my status in his life and his in mine.

Firm lips descend, giving me a restrained, passionate kiss, enough to make a public statement but less than satisfying. Seconds later, he lifts his head and eyes the whispering crowd before swinging his gaze to Astor, who nods.

"I claim both Arden and Astor. Let this be a warning to anyone who thinks to touch or take what is mine." His voice rises to a roar, and with a snap of his fingers, the heads from the two guards earlier appear on the floor.

The savageness of the two heads dropping into the ballroom is perfect. It speaks to his willingness to protect and kill for me. I glance at Solandis and Vargas and watch them both nod in satisfaction. A small smile graces Lucifer's lips.

The crowd's whispers are quickly silenced, and all movement stops. Nobody wants to provoke the beast.

Gripping the lapels of his jacket, I bring his attention back to me. "This goes both ways, you know. You're mine too."

Like a dam breaking, his rigid control shatters and his lips capture mine, all restraint gone. They claim and worship, his tongue dancing with mine, stirring the flames simmering in the background. I can't help but revel in it all.

A column of blue flame erupts around us, creating a temporary bubble and obscuring the crowd. Drowning in heat, his kiss fills me with the very fire surrounding us, and the tiny pricks on my breast burn in remembrance of his bite. I hold nothing back, giving everything to him in return. My hands move to his strong shoulders, pulling him tightly against me.

The sound of a frog croaking jolts me out of the kiss, and with a frown, I open my eyes. Daire stares down at me, his gaze possessive and yet apprehensive. I glance up and find the night sky, beautiful and sparkling with hundreds of stars. Puzzled, I stare at them in confusion, trying to figure out if they're real. Another loud croak pierces the air behind me, and I spin around and discover a dream.

A silver lake shimmers in the moonlight and laps gently onto the shore directly in front of a large two-story white stone cottage. Flowers and plants frolic in abundance in the front yard, framing the entry with a riot of color. The fragrance of their blooms—lavender, rose, honeysuckle and more—fills the night air. The golden light spilling from the cottage windows casts a warm welcome and is the perfect finishing touch to the fairy-tale setting in front of me.

The painting we bought for Daire's room flashes in my mind as strong arms wrap around me.

"Welcome to my home," he murmurs.

CHAPTER
TEN

<u>ARDEN</u>

I stop breathing. Finding his hands, I lace my fingers through his and hold on tightly. If it were anyone else, I'd assume this visit was spontaneous, but Daire is like a general planning a battle with precision and leaving nothing to chance.

The trees sway in the distance, but everything around us is still. And I'm perfectly warm standing in the night air, wearing little more than a bodysuit and a swath of fabric.

"We're in a pocket, aren't we?" I deduce.

"Lucifer created this slice of paradise for my mother. As a witch, she thrived here. The surrounding nature rejuvenated her magic, and the nearby plants provided her with the seeds and leaves she required for her potions. It was the perfect solution for them because it allowed her to safely remain in her world, but protected from his," he explains. "I grew up here. I didn't visit the Underworld until I became a vampire capable of defending myself."

The latter statement is illuminating, and I squeeze his hands. My eyes are drawn to the abundance of greenery surrounding the cottage.

"It's beautiful and peaceful," I murmur and lay my head back against his shoulder to study the scene in front of me.

Besides the fragrant smell of the flowers, the air is heavy, saturated with love not contained by time and space, and it seeps into my bones.

He sighs, and the tension in his body eases. Cool lips skim my temple, and he pulls me in tighter. "A piece of me will never leave this place. It's embedded into my soul." Fingers slide into my hair and gently pull my head back until he can stare into my eyes. "I've never brought anyone else here, but I needed to share it with you. The world defines us by birthright and titles, but when you look at me, I feel naked, stripped bare of those superficial boundaries. I'm reminded of who I was before I became those things."

Vulnerability shines in his eyes, as if the confession is too revealing.

"Daire," I breathe, my voice barely a whisper in the night. Reaching up, I pull his head down for a kiss, wanting to show him what his words mean to me.

After a second, he pulls away. "Watching you tonight, seeing how free you are with Astor, I'm not sure I can be who you want me to be," he says stiffly.

Turning fully to face him, I loop my arms around his neck and try to find the words to explain how I feel about him. I decide to start at the beginning. "When I was growing up, your father would entertain me with stories from your childhood, but I didn't know you were already grown. In my imagination, we were friends. In my teens, I even had a crush on you." I smile at my younger dreams, with Daire playing the starring role of knight in shining armor. "It was a shock to meet you in person. You were devastatingly handsome but an arrogant jerk and nothing like I'd imagined. Every inch the First Vampire and Prince of the Underworld, you were a stranger instead of the boy from Lucifer's stories."

He tenses, and I lightly stroke the back of his neck.

"When you healed me the first time and shared Danica's story, I realized the traits I admired in my 'friend' were still there. Reassured to find something redeemable, I decided to get to know you. Physically, I was extremely aware of you, but...you were kind of a dick." I shrug.

"So I watched and learned. It helped to see you with the cadre because you're yourself around them, and your worst traits were walls you put up to hold the world at a distance. My attraction to you started changing from purely physical to something more, but the battle is where I started to fall for you. You were magnificent. It allowed me to see everything you'd been hiding."

His blue eyes blaze with emotion.

"The tremendous love and loyalty you have for the cadre, your father, and his people is inspiring. The strategy and leadership you displayed on the battlefield, your willingness to fight at the side of your men, and saving me, of course," I admit with a chuckle. "And the...breathtaking way you fight." I lick my lips in memory. "I knew I wanted more of you. I wasn't sure if you wanted me, though."

A shudder rips through his body. "I resented you at first," he admits with a wry smile. "You tugged at a side of me I thought banished long ago and I didn't want to feel again, especially for a witch. It was so *human*. I tried to stay away from you, but I was drawn to you, and the more I watched you,

the more I wanted. When you joined the battle, I was furious...
and terrified. I knew I'd been fighting a lost cause."

"So what worries you?"

"I *am* Prince of the Underworld and First Vampire, and I'm
not always free to do what I want," he remarks solemnly. "I
can't always disregard the public like Astor or challenge the
court like Valerian. Nor do I wish for that freedom. I like having
some distance between myself and my people. Is that going to
be enough?"

"Why don't you want to give me the Mate's Kiss?" I question, needing to hear his answer, even if I'm not sure I want it.

He inhales sharply. "Did Astor tell you?"

"I overheard you telling your father," I admit, pulling back
in his arms to get some distance between us.

He yanks me closer. "I dream of it. An irrevocable bond
tying us tightly together until we share one heart and a single
life force? Absolutely. I'm a jealous, possessive bastard. I don't
want to share you, not even with the cadre. I'd give anything to
steal you away, give you the Mate's Kiss, and tie you to me and
only me." He growls and runs a hand down my body, emphasizing his possessive claim, then sighs. "I won't, though. If
something were to happen to me, you'd die too. I couldn't do
that to you or them." His eyes search mine for understanding.

Something settles within me. It's the exact reason why I
don't want it. "It's enough. I only need you," I state firmly, in
answer to his earlier question.

An arrogant nod is his only response, but some of the
tension leaves his shoulders.

Wanting to lighten the mood, I slide my finger down the
side of his neck to his mouth. "I must admit, I find the vampire
part of you very sexy, especially the biting part, but the prince
thing...I couldn't care less. After all, I'm mate to the *King* of
Dragons."

His eyes widen, and he roars with laughter. "True, I'm a lowly prince and one of several royals in your life." He cocks his head. "You find the vampire sexy?"

"Mmm… It's a toss-up between the wings and fangs, but getting to see and feel your emotions? Game changer," I tease him.

He steps back from our embrace and slowly peels off his clothes until he's standing there naked. I hear a sharp snap, and black wings appear, extending high into the air to frame his magnificent body. With delicious intent in his icy blue eyes, he stalks toward me.

"Take off your clothes," he demands.

The flame from earlier roars to life inside me. Unhooking my skirt, I remove the delicate fabric, letting it fall gently to the ground. Standing in the semi-sheer bodysuit, I dip my finger into the top of the corset and stroke the pinpricks he left on me from his first bite.

Impatient, he strips the bodysuit off me and drops his lips directly to the pinpricks. Scraping his teeth over the top of them, I feel an echo from the first bite and moan, yearning for another.

"Hold on," he whispers.

A shift in space, and we're flying high above the ground. A breathless laugh escapes me. Wrapping my legs tightly around him frees my hands to roam over the hard lines of his body. His muscles thrum with unleashed power, and I arch into him, wanting to feel it coursing through my body.

Touching and flying, we're lost in the night sky and each other. All restraint is gone. His kisses demand the very breath in my lungs. Edged with possession, they refuse to let me give less than everything.

The whoosh of his wings against the night air syncs with the pulse in the center of my body. Beyond the stars, the world remains hidden in the dark. It's as if I'm floating in a sea of black ink tethered only to him. His fingers dip down and stroke my hidden folds, and I almost growl with need.

He pulls my head back, which causes me to arch up. Leaning forward, firm lips suck my hard nipples into his mouth.

Clasping his head to my breasts, I thrust against his hand, trying to assuage the ache in the center of my body. "Daire, I need you."

He gives me a hard nod and withdraws his fingers.

I can't help but sigh at the loss.

Seconds later, he's laying me across a bed. The night air, with all its sounds and smells, surrounds us, and I realize we're still outside. I smile at this unexpectedly romantic gesture.

Spreading me wide, his eyes gleam as he stares down at me. "You're so beautiful," he rasps, gliding his hands over my body. "I want to taste you." He pauses, waiting for me to answer.

"Goddess, yes," I moan. "I've been craving your touch all night."

Ice-blue eyes close briefly, and he folds to his knees. His tongue flicks against my bundle of nerves, and I move restlessly. Clamping his hands on my thighs, he does it again and again.

Crying out for relief, my hands grip the sheets, while words spill incoherently from my lips. "Please. Daire. So close," I cry out.

He bites the inside of my thigh, and my vision blackens for a brief second.

My orgasm hits hard, and I arch up. Heat spirals from my core to the rest of my body, and I explode. "Daire!"

His heavy-lidded eyes watch with satisfaction when I fall to pieces, loudly calling his name. He retracts his teeth and licks the pinpricks marking me his. Large hands stroke my thighs, and warm lips place kisses along my stomach until my body starts to calm. Standing, he shifts me on the bed, then prowls up to join me.

When his body covers mine, I wrap my legs around him, pulling him in closer. My hand reaches down to stroke his cock, and he shifts until I can grasp it tightly.

"I feel like it's been ages since your hands were on me," he confides. His finger swipes over my mouth. "And your mouth. Before the night is over, I want you in every way imaginable." He grips my shoulders, pinning me in place. "Right now, I'm already on the edge and want to finish inside you."

I caress the velvety smooth shaft in my hand, then guide the tip to my entrance. Teasing him with the wetness dripping from my body, I watch his eyes darken with anticipation. "I need you."

Surging into my body, he thrusts deep, then stops and groans. "Incredible," he remarks, taking a couple of deep breaths. Lips claim mine in a possessive kiss, delving deep, giving nothing and only taking, while he searches for control. He slides out and thrusts back in as his lips release mine.

Pleasure rolls through me with each thrust, and satisfaction gleams in his blue eyes. Cupping the back of my knee, he pushes it forward so he can go deeper, and I lift my hips to meet him. He sinks all the way in, but I feel like I can't get enough, so I grind against his fullness. A throaty noise escapes me, and I squeeze him tightly.

He grunts and thrusts deep. Hard and fast, he continues to thrust, and when his incisors drop, my heart races and my body clenches in anticipation of his bite.

He moans and moves faster toward his own release.

I'm gripping my orgasm by my fingertips, waiting for his bite to let go.

His head drops, and in the same spot as the very first bite he ever gave to me, he strikes, shredding my control and setting off his own release.

My orgasm peaks first and I cry out, then I'm swept up in the pleasure of his release, and the intensity of the two together triggers a series of smaller orgasms. I grit my teeth and ride the continuous waves, my body pulsing on his until they finally subside and my body relaxes.

Running my fingers through his silky blond hair while he drinks, I examine the thoughts and emotions slipping from him to me. Arrogant and forceful, they reflect the depths of his nature, all of which he hides so carefully from the world.

With a flick of his tongue, he soothes the pinpricks and retracts his bite. Hands push back my hair so he can peer into my eyes. "Everything I feel completely laid bare for you. Now you know the depths of my obsession," he says ruefully, but his eyes watch mine carefully.

When he sees my smile, he relaxes. "Your fierce feelings for them floor me, even if they don't all know it." He slides out of me, and we both groan at the loss. With a slight shift to my side, he pulls me into his arms and holds me. "I fervently send thanks to my mother's goddess you also feel that way about me." Kissing my temple, he continues to give me sweet words until I fall asleep.

CHAPTER
ELEVEN

<u>THERON</u>

Fury and fear wage an internal war until even my formidable composure threatens to crack. When I see ice coating the walls, I shut my eyes and start listing everything we need to do. *Wolves, stone, journal, Fallon, queen...* My mind stutters to a stop on the last item. *Fuck! I wish Fallon were here.* A thud to my left makes my eyes fly open, only to see Valerian shaking his fist in front of the new and very large hole in the wall.

"You know the walls are reinforced with magic," I chide him, my voice cool, as if my emotions are not threatening mutiny. "Once Daire and Arden arrive, we'll make a plan and figure out our strategy." My phone pings with a message. "They're on their way."

Astor, Valerian, and I get to the lobby and watch them step through the portal. I barely get a glimpse of Arden before

Valerian sweeps her into his arms and immediately heads to the elevator.

"Valerian," I snap, my anger barely contained. "The lounge." When he nods, I face Daire and bring him up to speed. "We're on high alert around here. Your father sent word via Astor. He's positive Alain mouthed the word 'queen' when he was dragged into the hole. If the Primary is a queen, Arden's enemy, our enemy, is formidable."

"A few hours after you left, he started preparing for war," Astor explains the chaos that erupted after Daire and Arden disappeared. "He got the council up in the early morning hours to get their approval, then he met with Vargas and his generals. The army is mobilizing and will be ready to go within the week. Thankfully, he can't move against anyone until he knows which queen. After all, even Lucifer isn't exempt from the rules governing royalty, and he's not about to challenge the Supernatural Council or the Wild Hunt. The lack of proof works in our favor for now."

Daire immediately focuses on the threat, sifting through the facts until he comes to the same conclusion I reached earlier. "There are three queens—the dark Fae queen, light Fae queen, and dark Elven queen. The dark Elven queen has the most to gain if Arden's out of the picture, but she's trivial compared to the other two. Also, she wasn't in power four thousand years ago. Meri's sorceress found information stating the last Primary was chosen four thousand years ago." His eyes cut to mine. "We're dealing with the Fae. I'm not sure either would be an advantage over the other. Do we have any clue which one yet?"

A sense of relief eases the tension in my shoulders. Daire slides into the place I usually reserve for Fallon, and I can't help but be grateful for the strategic backup. "No," I state firmly.

"Arden's met the light Fae queen, though. Several times. I can't imagine she would let her live."

"Unless she doesn't know her enemy," Astor notes absentmindedly, his mind analyzing the possibilities. "The assassination attempts are sporadic, leading me to believe the Primary's ability to locate her adversary fluctuates. If she knew it was Arden, she would continuously attack her. Something either triggers the attack and pinpoints the location, or she only gets sporadic opportunities. I haven't been able to find a pattern yet."

"If anyone can figure it out, it's you," I assure him, knowing he'll examine every detail until he finds the answer. Glancing at Daire, I motion to the elevator. "We need to sit down and develop a plan, but I wanted to bring you up to speed first. It will take every favor owed to us and all our resources to go up against a queen. One shot is all we'll get."

STRIDING INTO THE LOUNGE, I'm tempted to lean down and pluck Arden from Valerian's arms, but I refrain. "We need to pull together a list of everything and begin preparations. Once we start planning the battle, it will be our singular focus."

"Let me go," Arden orders, her lips swollen, likely from Valerian's greeting. Her fingers grab Valerian's chin and tug until he's facing her. "Valerian, I love you. I'm not leaving the room, but I need to get up."

His arms withdraw, and she stands before pacing around the room.

"With his last breath, Alain might have helped us out," I begin, pausing to organize my thoughts. It's one thing to know you have an unknown enemy, but it's entirely different to know a queen is after you.

Clearing my throat, I continue, "Daire, I need you to have a discussion with Vargas and Solandis about the situation. We need them to be extra careful around her sister Nyssa, the light Fae queen, until we figure out which one it is."

"There's so much to think about, but I can't wrap my head around the possibility Nyssa could be the Primary," Arden confesses, shaking her head in disbelief. "She's powerful, but she doesn't feel much different than Solandis. They had the same parents, and while she inherited a queen's power, it's similar in scale to other royals I've met, like the dark Elven queen or Fallon's father." Her voice trembles when she says Fallon's name. "I've never met the dark Fae queen, but with the only other option being Nyssa, a stranger would be better."

We're all silent while we consider the ramifications of Nyssa being the Primary.

"We have a lot to investigate," I note. "Let's tackle things one at a time, okay?"

She rolls her shoulders back and lifts her chin.

"I'll speak to my father. He's been around longer than either of them, and he might be able to give us more information on their weaknesses and strengths," Daire offers.

"Good idea," I remark, adding another task to the long mental list in my head. "Moving on. We need to figure out what you're going to do with the witches."

Arden frowns.

"I might have an another option," Astor interjects. "I've been reading the MacAllister grimoire, and I think there's a spell to create a new stone. A new coven." He glances hesitantly at Arden. "If the witches helped the Primary massacre the MacAllisters, we need to separate you from them. Creating a new stone will give you an alternative. I know you're hoping they will agree to abolish their exclusivity, and maybe at the eleventh hour, it will happen, but I'm not sure you can afford to wait."

Arden thinks about this new option. "I didn't think about creating a new stone," she admits. "According to the journals, it would take a tremendous amount of power to fuel the current stone because of the number of witches the magic supports. When it was created, it only had to support the MacAllister witch and her daughters. We may not have enough power to do it, but you're right—we should try. I highly doubt they're going to change, and this solution solves several issues at once. I could give them the old stone and explain the repercussions to them. If they don't change, I don't want to be a part of their coven anyway."

He gives her a wry smile. While he isn't going to be upset if she leaves the coven, he knows being a part of one is essential to her.

"I'll add the task to our list. It will require all three of you—Arden, Astor, and Valerian, I assume?" When Astor dips his head, I move on.

"The dark Fae library had two books on pucks," I inform Arden. "They're both in your room. I skimmed through them. Essentially, pucks have a myriad of powers mostly involving the mind—manipulating thoughts, foresight, telekinesis, the ability to influence emotions, and read minds."

Arden gasps.

Valerian and Astor swear.

I lift my shoulder. "Based on the way it's worded, it doesn't seem like they can read your thoughts, but through images and emotions, they can figure out what you're thinking."

"That's fucking scary," Valerian remarks, his voice hard with worry. "Who is this puck and which side is he on?"

Arden explains about the journal and the Killian blades.

"He seems to be on our side," she replies. "I don't think my grandfather could have created the Killian blades and made them permanently sentient without him."

Valerian grunts. "How do we find him?"

Arden shrugs and looks at me.

"When I asked, the dark Fae king told me he hadn't seen one in over a thousand years," I inform them. "The last one he saw was hanging around the light Fae queen's court." I internally wince, knowing this puts strike one on the board against Nyssa.

Her lips caress my cheek. "It's okay. Thank you for getting the info. I'll dig into them," Arden assures me. "Speaking of books, we need to find the last journal. Perhaps my mother knew something about the Primary."

"We need your father to help us find it. How do you propose we get him out of hiding?" I ask her.

She thinks about it for a few minutes. "The wooden box is a family heirloom," she replies, pursing her lips. "There might be a way to send it back to its owners with a note." Her eyes slide to Astor, who looks excited about the possibility of this complex spell.

"Blood magic," he blurts out excitedly. "Both you and the box are linked to your father and grandmother by blood. We could write a spell to send it back to them. The tricky part will be the reply. We don't want to put them in any danger, so we'll need to figure out if we can get the box to return to us without requiring the use of witch magic." His eyes gleam with excitement at this new challenge.

Another item to add to Astor's plate. I hope he's done with the spell for our secret project so I can execute the final step. I make a mental note to ask him about the status.

"We'll need to discuss the situation with allies, call in favors, and source information. It's too much activity to mask in our current state. I propose we reopen The Abbey. Any visitors will be invisible in the overall crowd."

Everyone nods in agreement.

"For now, the wolves are the least of our worries, so I think we should table any movement on that front for now." I pause and glance at the rest of the cadre. When they silently answer me in return, I turn and face Arden. "We have one more thing to discuss. It's about your room."

Surprise flits across her face. "My room?" she questions. "What about it?"

"Grab her bag," I direct toward the rest of them and pull Arden out of the lounge. "We moved you closer to our rooms. It's less private, but we're uneasy with you being on a different floor from us."

She shrugs. "Okay."

Taking the elevator up to our floor, I show her which room is hers now. "You're between Valerian and me." I point out the two rooms at each end of a long hallway. Glancing at the cadre, we all smile in anticipation.

She opens the door and steps into her new room. When her mouth drops open, we hold our breath, waiting to see what she thinks. She spins in a circle, taking in all the changes. A huge smile spreads across her face, and we exhale in relief.

"It's beautiful," she exclaims. Walking around the room, she picks up several objects and runs her hands over the luxurious fabrics. "It's similar to my room in the Underworld, all light and airy. I love it. Why, though? The other room was fine."

"Solandis was right," Daire states firmly. "This is your home now. We want you to be comfortable. This has the added benefit of being safer too. Since you liked it so much, I sent Theron pictures of your room. He and Valerian pulled this together while we were gone."

After giving Valerian a hug and thanking him, she walks over to me. "Thank you for the beautiful room," she says. "I'm going to enjoy sleeping between you and Valerian." She winks and strides over to Astor and Daire to thank them.

My cock hardens at the images her words conjure, and I mentally groan.

TWELVE

ARDEN

Valerian yanks me out of bed before dawn to work out, but I don't protest. Caged within his arms all night, I could feel the worry and tension radiating off him. Any time I shifted or got up to use the bathroom, he'd wake, muscles coiled and ready. Falling into each other throughout the night, we'd escape for brief moments, but reality returns with the new day.

For him, my safety was an illusion stripped away by Lucifer's revelation. War now sits on the horizon, and he's going to do everything possible to get us ready for it.

When we enter the training room, I realize we're not the only ones up early. Astor is my official magic trainer, so I expected him to be here, but I'm surprised to see Daire and

Theron. While they've watched my training previously, they've rarely participated.

Daire's wearing black combat fatigues similar to the ones he wore in the Underworld battle. Standing akimbo in the center of the mat, his eyes flick to mine, but he's in deep discussion with Theron and doesn't approach.

In loose black pants and matching tight-fitting T-shirt, Theron's also dressed for training. Violet eyes sweep over me with clinical detachment, and I realize he's assessing me. He motions to Valerian and Astor to join him and Daire in their discussion.

Pretending to ignore them, I begin my warmup, but my eyes are drawn repeatedly to the center of the room. Always on the move or focused on the next challenge, it's rare to see them standing still and in one place. Abandoning my warmup, I lie back on my elbows and study them.

They're all dressed in workout clothing, with acres of cut lines and muscles on display, and my hands involuntarily twitch with the need to glide over every single inch. Valerian is at one end of the muscle spectrum, with his overabundance of muscles, and Astor's lean body is at the other end, but all of them are drool worthy. And mine. How the hell did I get so lucky? All those years in isolation, I dreamt of having someone to call mine, but with an unknown destiny looming over my head, I didn't know if I'd even have a chance to find them.

Tilting my head to the side, I envision them all battling each other, and desire floods my body. I'd love to see Daire's speed against Theron's swords. Or Valerian's fighting skills versus Astor's magic. My nipples peak in excitement, and I pant a little. Silently groaning, I order myself to think of something else, or this will be the most uncomfortable training session ever.

With their battle-ready stance and lethal air, I realize why so many supernaturals fear the Imperium Cadre. It's not because of title or power, although those items certainly provide them with the necessary credentials to back up their reputations. If they were born with nothing, they would still end up at the top of the food chain. I mentally add Fallon to the picture in front of me, and I easily understand how the battle in the Underworld turned in our favor so quickly.

Fallon. My heart aches when I think of him. He hasn't messaged me, but I send him texts to keep him up to date on the important items. I'm sure Theron does too, but I try to add my own point of view, so he knows how I feel about what's happening around me. Several times, I've seen dots appear as if someone is typing, but after a minute, they disappear. Maybe one day, he'll reply.

A loud clap startles me, and I push aside my thoughts. I focus on the room and notice they're all staring at me.

"What?" I ask nervously. Astor glances at my chest and smirks, but I simply raise an eyebrow in return. It's chilly in here.

Daire steps forward and holds out his hand to help me up. "We've decided on a new training regimen for you. For the next week or two, we want you to train with us, together and indi-vidually, but without magic. You're an excellent fighter, but you sometimes rely on magic to swing the battle in your favor. The most recent skirmish in the Underworld is a prime exam-ple. We want you to have the ability to win without it." He pauses for a second. "Theron will train you in sword fighting. Astor will teach you how to keep fighting, even after you're hit with a spell. Valerian and I will focus on hand-to-hand combat with an emphasis on opponents who are stronger and faster than you."

Biting my lip, I consider the possibility of fighting without the use of my magic, and a nervous breath escapes me. I don't know why I'm concerned. Vargas started training me to fight the minute I could walk. "Is there a reason for this change?"

"Fallon recommended a few tweaks to your stance which should take your skills to the next level," Theron informs me. "I noticed several adjustments we could make to your grip to increase your sword fighting ability." He watches me carefully. "We've all been around for a very long time and learned a few things. Practicing without magic will help you focus and achieve muscle memory faster. When you add the magic, you'll be even more lethal."

Swallowing hard, I tamp down on the anger threatening to spill out of me, but the slight tremor in the floor gives me away. "Sorry, I'm a bit...peeved. Fallon can't text me back, but he can send you improvements for my training?" I wave a hand when Theron opens his mouth. "Please, don't. Who's up first?"

The first session is torture. When my back hits the mat hard for the hundredth time, I want to scream in frustration. My magic sparks in reply. Not only am I fighting each of them, but I'm also fighting to keep my magic from spilling out and joining the battle. Drained, I lie limply on the ground.

Amber eyes stare down at me. "Let's stop for now." Valerian suggests quietly. "We've been training for a few hours, and you need a break. Go get coffee and breakfast. Relax. We'll start again this afternoon."

"You have a council meeting this afternoon," Theron reminds me. "Valerian, why don't you work on a training schedule for us? We'll pick back up in the morning."

Valerian agrees and holds his hand out to help me up.

I narrow my eyes and bat his hand away, irritated with how many times he's put me down today. My eyes glide over Daire, who has one arrogant eyebrow raised, and land on Astor. When he winks back at me, I hold up my hand, and he helps me stand. Thanking him and ignoring the other two, I feel his hand glide down my ass.

"I can't help it," he says laughingly. "Those damn shorts have been torturing me all morning." Grins on the other three faces tells me they agree.

I roll my eyes, even though I want to laugh. Damn incubus. Raising my chin, I stride out the doors to the elevator. Once in my room, I strip, walk straight to my shower, turn on the water to the hottest setting, and slide down to the bench. Leaning my head back against the wall, I let the heat work its magic on my sore muscles. A sharp pain pierces my ribs, reminding me I need to take a few minutes and heal the worst of my injuries. Without the use of my magic, I've taken a beating.

This might be harder than I thought.

My bare feet stroll across the grass, and with each step, the tension drains and any lingering soreness disappears from my body. Tendrils of magic reach through my soles into the dirt, and I realize the Elven side of me is reconnecting with mother nature. I'm rejuvenated by a simple walk in the grass, and I didn't even know.

Fallon's supposed to be my teacher for all things Elven. Instead, my Elven powers remain practically useless and my knowledge nil. My patience and understanding are rapidly dwindling, with anger only too happy to take their place. Blowing a piece of hair out of my eyes, I make my way over to the chair by the railing.

Steady breathing and a good cup of coffee have me feeling better until the elevator doors swoosh open. I glance back excitedly, but when Theron strides into view, I turn my gaze to the railing so he can't see my disappointment.

My throat tightens and tears fill my eyes, but I refuse to let them fall. Instead, I distract myself with the sounds of Theron pouring himself a cup of coffee from the carafe on the table beside me. *Stupid.* I knew it wouldn't be him, and yet I couldn't stop the flare of hope.

Cool lips kiss my temple, and he tugs my chin toward him. His eyebrow twitches when he sees the turmoil and hurt in my eyes. "Mind if I join you?"

"Feel free. Nobody else is going to," I reply sarcastically.

My eyes swing to the horizon, but the fragile peace I had a second ago is nowhere to be found. Theron says nothing, and I sigh. I don't want to take my anger out on him. "I'm sorry. Fallon is everywhere this morning." I reach over and lace my fingers through his free hand while he drinks his coffee.

His eyes flick to our hands, and a tiny smile graces his lips. "How was your trip?" he asks, lightly probing. "How was the ball?"

"So much happened! Hmm...where should I start?" Deciding to omit the altercation with the guards and the private moments with Astor and Daire, I tell him about my visit to the market. "I begged Astor to take me to Underworld Market."

Violet eyes narrow sharply. "I sincerely hope he said no," he says coolly.

"You're as bad as Vargas," I tell him with a roll of my eyes. "It was fabulous and chaotic. A riot of sounds, colors, and smells designed to sweep you away to an exotic world. Astor even told me about the hidden black market, but we didn't go," I add, rushing to reassure him. "The ice cream was particularly exceptional." I'll never forget the ice cream or the moment.

His fingers tighten on mine involuntarily.

He's fighting the urge to tap, I muse.

"Solandis and I spent quality girl time together. Vargas and I danced at the ball, but he was busy with a guard situation, so we didn't see each other much," I continue rapidly, redirecting his thoughts. "I wore a beautiful dress. Want to see it?"

Without waiting for a reply, I pull up my photos and lean over so he can view my phone. Solandis, Vargas, and I forced a random demon to take a few pictures of us. Scrolling through, I laugh at the scowl on Vargas' face while Solandis and I pose outrageously beside him.

Theron inhales sharply and stops me from scrolling forward. "This is what you wore to a ball in the Underworld?"

I ignore his comment. After all, the Fae courts are worse, and I'm positive modesty isn't even a word in their language.

"Would you like me to send you a copy?" I offer. "You know what...I'll send a copy to everyone." *Including Fallon.* Opening the group chat, I text the photo to everyone.

Astor: Gorgeous.

Valerian: Beautiful. The blade is a nice touch.

Daire: Absolutely stunning.

Theron: I thought it risqué.

Astor: Positively conservative.

Daire: He's right. Practically nothing is the current trend.

Fallon: ...

The chat continues for several minutes, with them discussing the appropriateness of the dress, but a message from Callyx pops up and I tap on it.

> Callyx: Got a strong lead on Meri. Will contact Cormal.

> Arden: Keep me in the loop and let us know if you need help. XO

I attach the pic of our family, and he sends a heart back.

Tapping the phone on my chin, I think about the effort he's putting in to find Meri. Callyx is loyal to few, but the depths he'll go to for his small circle is never-ending. I fill Theron in on the Meri situation, in case Callyx needs assistance.

He scrutinizes me for a second, but I'm numb and my face is blank. I'm not even sure how I feel about her right now. Strong arms wrap around me in a tight hug. "Daire's right—you looked absolutely stunning." He drops a kiss by my ear. "When you're ready to leave for the council meeting, let me know. I'll be in the bar or kitchen ordering supplies for the re-opening."

I've been putting off this text for a while, but Callyx's message gives me an opening.

> Arden: Callyx has a lead on Meri. Didn't give his location.

> Vargas: I've got eyes on him. Did Astor tell you?

> Arden: Yes. Fae. Light or dark. Coin toss.

> Vargas: We need it to be dark. She needs it to be dark. It will destroy her.

> Arden: I know. Tell her I'll call later. Love you.

> Vargas: Love you, and be careful.

If it's Nyssa, it will kill Solandis. Their parents died a few thousand years ago, leaving them with only each other. As the oldest, Nyssa became the light Fae queen, but it took both standing united to battle the vicious and deceitful Fae court who sought to put another on the throne. As sisters, friends, and allies, describing their relationship as 'close' is an understatement. These days, their connection is a bit strained because of Solandis and Vargas' mating, but it's a tiny rift in the grand scheme of a few thousand years.

I don't know the dark Fae queen, but I squeeze my eyes shut and pray to the goddess she's my enemy.

CHAPTER
THIRTEEN

<u>ARDEN</u>

We step out of the portal at the gates of Witchwood, and I shoot off a quick text to Henry to inform him of our arrival. There's no need for him to greet us. We're quite capable of escorting ourselves. Theron stands at my side with his arm out, and I slide my hand through the crook of his elbow and grip his bicep. When he takes a step forward, though, I pull back, my knees lock, and my feet plant themselves into the ground. I feel his gaze and concern, but I need a moment.

Tilting my head, I assess the large manor in front of me, its cream walls mellowed with age and gleaming golden in the afternoon sunlight. A beacon for witches? For the right witch, maybe. For others, like Astor, it's a place of cruelty and nightmares. Acceptance or rejection. Two words. One lifts you up, and the other destroys you.

If we're able to create a new stone, a new coven, will it mean anything without the heritage? Even with the corruption, why would anyone want to leave family and friends to join a potentially weaker coven? How could I ask this of them? Even for me, with little history and few relationships, the choice isn't easy.

"Do you wish to leave?" Theron asks quietly.

"Not yet," I respond. "Soon."

He hesitates, but I tighten my grip on his arm and step forward. "Let's go."

Even with our leisurely pace, we reach the manor too quickly. The door opens, and Henry stands there with a smile on his face and a twinkle in his brown eyes.

My lips quirk, and I lean forward to give him a kiss on the cheek. "Hello, Henry. We haven't seen you in forever, but you didn't need to step away from your duties to greet us," I say in admonishment, but the grin on my face tells a different story. He's one of the few good things at Witchwood. "How is everything?"

He cocks an ear to listen for anyone close by. "Too quiet," he replies in a whisper. "I haven't heard anything since your last visit. Trouble is brewing."

I squeeze his shoulder, conveying my thanks for his warning, and continue down the hall into the council room. Leaving Theron in the audience, I find my seat at the table and return Santiago and An's greeting.

The other council members barely acknowledge my presence, except for Katarina, who gives me a cool smile. I puzzle over it but smile back. Ally or foe? I wonder where she stands on the exclusivity issue.

Caro kicks off the meeting, her voice high and bright, which makes me wonder if she's heard good news from Cassandra. The floor opens for witches to air their grievances. I try my best to pay attention, but I can't drum up any interest. The gavel bangs, another verdict passes, and my attention drifts away.

The tapestry fascinates me. Some of the branches end abruptly, which matches the history noted in Agnes' journal. They removed quite a few hybrid witches in the early days, but later in time, it dwindles to an occasional branch. The missed potential is massive. What could we have been if they hadn't taken the path of exclusivity?

I study the MacAllister line, and thankfully, find none of the severed branches, but I do notice something unusual. Several branches are slightly darker than others, and the leaves attached to those branches more defined. This includes the branch with my leaf and the two next to mine, who I now know to be my father and grandmother, even though their names have been burned out.

My gaze darts up to the other bloodlines and the places where they cut off the hybrid witches. It's hard to tell from here, but they seem darker. I'll need to get closer to confirm. Could the simple shading indicate mixed races? If so, is it because the magic is stronger?

"Arden, please give us your vote." Caro's voice rings out, her lip curled in anger at my inattentiveness.

"Should we allow the witch to sell love potions to humans?" Santiago murmurs to my left.

"No," I vote firmly.

"The vote is tied," Nico states gruffly, frustration apparent in his voice.

"No," Santiago states clearly beside me, breaking the tie. He glances at me speculatively, then at the tree. I feel him stiffen, but when I glance at him, he's staring at Reyna, who's sitting in the audience.

"This concludes the monthly council meeting," Caro declares loudly and bangs her gavel.

Tilting my head toward the tapestry, I silently indicate my intention to Theron.

"I thought you would demand a vote on the exclusivity issue today," Santiago confides. "I'm ready to back the motion, and I'm not the only one, but we do need to consider our options if the vote isn't in our favor."

Detecting a note of worry in his voice, I can't help but speculate why he's so interested in the timing of the vote and its repercussions. I glance at Reyna, then Santiago, and he nods in confirmation.

I agree. "In the next council meeting, let's nail down a date for the entire coven to vote. They may surprise us. If not, we'll discuss other options." Since he's not aware of the stone, I can't tell him I'm already working on an alternative.

Relieved, Santiago leans forward to kiss my cheek, but a smooth voice interjects, "I wouldn't."

Chuckling, Santiago inclines his head to Theron and walks over to Reyna. Taking her by the elbow, he drags her out of the manor quickly. I'm guessing they have a lot to discuss.

Sliding my hand into Theron's, I tug him over to the tree. Scanning the Martinez branch, I locate Santiago's branch. It's darker by several shades. His leaf is the same, but the veins in Reyna's leaf are more defined.

Satisfaction fills me, and I take a deep breath. My theory must be true. Darker branches indicate stronger magic in the line, and a defined leaf tells which witch is mixed. Santiago's branch changed because of Reyna. She wasn't born mixed, though. Santiago himself seemed surprised earlier, which tells me this is recent. What could change a witch? Vampire?

Shifter? Demon? At one time, she was involved with an incubus, but they don't change the chemistry of their mates. Unless she's pregnant.

Flitting from family to family, I note which branches have suddenly changed, and send a text to Santiago. If we can convince them to vote in favor of inclusivity, we might have a shot. I'm not the best person to reach out to them, though. Trust is earned, and I haven't done anything but upset the status quo. It's a monumental task for Santiago...and Katarina, whose own leaf marks her change. Now I know why she smiled at me earlier.

Theron's standing quietly at my side, watching me. Keenly observant, I can tell he's caught on to the current situation, but in this crowd, too much can be overheard. Violet eyes flick to a branch over my shoulder, and I raise an eyebrow in return. Yes, Caro's branch is darker...because of Cassandra, I confirm silently.

Something pinches the back of my arm, and I pivot to place my back to Theron.

"Oh, so sorry," Caro exclaims. With a shrug, she raises up her hand to show me her long, sharp fingernails. "I was trying to grab your attention, and I think I caught you with my nail."

Running my hand over the back of my arm, I eye her suspiciously. Theron lifts my elbow to examine it closely and rubs a thumb over the red welt. Ice forms under Caro's feet, and her eyes widen. It's one thing to toy with me, but Theron's an entirely different beast.

"We're leaving," he announces abruptly. Placing me in front of him, he deliberately puts his back to Caro and escorts me to the front door.

Spotting Henry near the entrance, I lean over and quickly kiss him on the cheek. Theron mutters something obscene behind me. Shocked, I level a look at him. "It's Henry. I sincerely doubt he's going to try and steal me away."

"You'd be surprised," Henry retorts, making Theron stiffen.

"Thanks, Henry," I respond sarcastically. "Theron, let's go home." Rolling my eyes at the two of them, I stride out the door.

CHAPTER

FOURTEEN

<u>ASTOR</u>

Training this morning was brutal. For Arden and me. She quickly adopted the tweaks Fallon suggested to make her stance more balanced and her hits harder. We practiced the moves over and over until they became second nature.

Valerian focused his training on making her use her body to attack and immobilize larger enemies, like himself, without the use of sword or magic. He reminded her of the immortal strength available to her by birthright. By concentrating on vulnerable areas like the throat, groin, and eyes, she could gain valuable seconds without depleting her magic.

Their battles were fierce, and I winced every time he slammed her onto the mat. At the same time, I couldn't help but cup myself when she successfully nailed him in the balls. Valerian would only grunt and force her to do it again.

96

Daire felt she wasn't using her instincts and other senses to their maximum potential. When she protested, he challenged her to anticipate his moves without using her sight. At vampire speed, he shifted to various spots to test her. It was mesmerizing, like a blind man trying to pinpoint his attacker. It required her to rely on the sounds echoing around her and the feel of the air shifting when he moved. Her eyes kept popping open in a fight response, so we had to blindfold her. It helped, but it will take some time to master.

Mine was the worst. Hitting her with spells and watching her combat the effects while fending off attacks from Valerian and Daire drove me crazy. Even though they were minor spells, her magic would spark in defense every time. She would snuff it out and continue fighting, but I could barely stand to watch.

Thankfully, she's a quick learner, and we should be able to get back to our regular training in a few days. I can't wait. I love the way her mind works when she's using magic against me.

Shifting my focus back to the present and my task, I use my left hand to turn the grimoire, while I use my right to cross-check the spell I'd written down. My eyes follow the words winding through the vines on the edges of the page, reading every one, then I compare it with those I'd written on my piece of paper.

When I get done, I study each line. It feels too simple, like something's missing, but I don't see any additional words in the vines. Puzzled, I lean over to study the page. There are two or three spells written on the page, and they cross over each other. Maybe I need to write out all of them.

Arms wrap around me from behind, and the air fills with the decadent scent of champagne and strawberries. My cock hardens. I grin. I don't think I'll ever be able to smell the two again without getting hard.

Pulling her around to my front, I keep her back to me and

cage her against the counter. My cock brushes up against her, and she deliberately arches her back and rubs back and forth against it. I plant a hand on her stomach to hold her tightly to me.

"One day, I'm going to fuck you against this counter, and you will stand there taking every stroke of my cock, crying out for more," I grit out while thrusting against her. My tongue whips out and strokes along her neck to lightly mark her as mine. "Until then, be still while I finish comparing these two."

She lays her head back on my shoulder and her hand on the back of my neck. Her fingers play with my hair while she watches me compare the two.

For a second, I close my eyes, savoring the feel of her in my arms. If I didn't have so much to do, I'd be content to stand here with her the rest of the day.

"Do you want me to come back later?" Valerian questions gruffly from behind us.

I drop a quick kiss on her head and reluctantly step back from Arden. "No, this shouldn't take long. I think something's missing from the spell," I say, revealing my concern. "But I want to try it." I direct them to the island.

Setting the silver MacAllister bowl on the counter, I pick up the knife and hand it to Valerian. He takes it with a light grip and stands next to Arden.

I point to Valerian. "While I say the incantation, I want you to spill Arden's blood into the bowl, then blow dragon fire on it," I state, relaying the instructions I captured.

With a slight growl, Valerian slices Arden's hand and lets it drip into the bowl until the bottom is covered. He puffs, and a small flame appears in the center.

We all three lean over and watch the blood flow to the middle, where the flame engulfs it. It burns for a minute, then slowly dies out, leaving a small dark grey stone in the bottom of the bowl.

Arden pulls the original stone out of her pocket, and we compare it to the new one. It's similar in color, but the old stone is shiny and hard compared to the one we just created.

Grabbing my tongs, I grasp the new stone to bring it closer. As soon as the tongs grip the stone, it crumbles. Arden is crushed, but I shake my head.

"I think a key element is missing, but I need to study the page some more. Maybe if I write out all the spells, I'll find the missing piece. Don't worry, I'll keep at it," I assure her. Picking up the book, I give her a kiss and walk over to the counter where I left my notepad. Determined to find the answer, I dive into the text. I refuse to let her down.

CHAPTER
FIFTEEN

<u>VALERIAN</u>

Ever since she returned from the Underworld, I haven't been able to relax without her nearby. In the building isn't close enough. I need her beside me so I can see or touch her.

"Come have a drink with me while I pack," I plead. When she agrees, I grab her hand and don't let go until we're standing in my room.

Soothing the beast, she slides her arms around my body until she's pressed tightly against me.

I shudder and wrap my arms around her. "Thank you," I mumble, slightly embarrassed by this recent compulsion. It's marginally better than the other half of me...which only wants to pulverize and destroy the world to keep her safe.

"I love you, Valerian," she says softly. "Don't thank me. I need this too. In your arms, I'm safe, and sometimes it's the

100

one thing helping me get through the day." She rests her chin on my chest and looks up at me. "Why are you packing?"

"I need to go home to get a few things done," I reply, my voice tight with worry. "Glynnis is holding a council meeting so we can discuss the possible war. I need to modify our training to include attack formations from the ground and sky. Plus, a million and one little things need to be handled."

I silently give myself five more minutes. Dropping my head into the crook of her neck, I inhale deeply to keep the scent of her in my lungs while I'm gone. My lips nuzzle her ear and drift toward her lips. Capturing her mouth, I dive into her sweetness, stroking her tongue with mine, coaxing it into a dance.

She pulls my bottom lip into her mouth and sucks, then tastes, before returning her attentions back to my tongue.

Loosening my arms first, I ease back from the kiss until only our mouths are touching. My lips cling to hers, refusing to part, until I finally find the strength to raise my head.

Her tongue slips out and licks her lips, and I track every swipe. "How long will you be gone?" she asks huskily.

My mind screams to stay, but I ignore it. "I'll be gone tonight and all of tomorrow. Promise me you'll sleep with one of the others while I'm gone. I need to know you're protected at all times."

She's lost in thought for a second but easily agrees. Patting my shoulders, she walks over to the closet and opens the doors. "What do you usually wear to a council meeting?"

Focusing on the task at hand, I answer, "A suit. Would you mind grabbing the black one?"

I sling the duffel onto the bed and throw in some necessities, including an extra pair of jeans and a shirt. I keep clothes at both places but tend to wear a select few favorites regularly. Taking the suit from her, I try on the jacket to make sure it still fits. I've been lifting a lot of weights lately to ease the roaring in my head, and my arms have bulked up a couple of inches. The jacket slides on, but it's tight around my biceps. Thankfully, the council meeting is only a couple of hours long, so this will work, but I'll need to order a couple more from the tailor.

Arden's lying on the bed watching me, her green eyes dark with desire. I groan. "Stop," I grumble, irritated I can't stay and take what she's offering.

"Sorry, I haven't seen you in a suit," she says breathlessly. "You look like a king in it—commanding and powerful. I just want you to sit on your throne and demand naughty, naughty things from me."

Images of all the things I could demand flash through my mind, and I swallow. Theron and Daire wear suits all the time. Is this the reaction they get? Hell, I might have to parade around in a suit every damn day.

"A suit, huh?" I waggle my eyebrows.

"Hmm...you in a suit. Or grey sweatpants. Although, I see a lot of those in training, so the suit might win out," she muses.

Fascinated, I listen while she lists the benefits of each one. The sweatpants outline every inch of my cock. The sweatpants are easy to slide off, and they make her want to climb me like a tree. The suit is the opposite. It makes her want to submit to me. Please me.

I almost whimper, my arousal so complete, I can barely speak.

"I see. Excuse me."

I step into the bathroom and turn on the shower. When I'm sure it's freezing cold, I walk in and let it drench me. Leaning my hands on the wall, I stay until I'm shivering and the hardness eases.

Undressing, I wash up, turn off the shower, and wrap a towel around me. When I open the door, she's gone.

Confounded, I pick up my phone and text her. She explains she'll meet me downstairs in ten minutes at the portal.

I grin and get dressed. Maybe she needed a cold shower too.

Minutes later, I'm standing by the portal talking to Daire when she walks up to us and drops a bag at my feet. Tilting my head, I consider the implications and snap, "Absolutely not." No wonder she agreed to my condition so easily. She didn't intend on staying here. "This isn't a social visit. I'm going to be extremely busy while I'm there, and I won't have time to spend with you."

"I'm going to visit Glynnis, with or without you," she retorts, her arms crossed in front of her. "I'm as safe there as I am here."

Daire smoothly interjects, "Well, technically, there isn't any place safer than The Abbey. The primal source protects the building and its inhabitants so we can deliver on the promise of sanctuary."

"Wait, what?" she exclaims loudly. "Forget it. We can talk about it when I get back. I'm going." With a mulish expression on her face, she picks up her bag and steps through the portal without another word.

Scrambling, I pick up mine and pivot toward the portal.

Daire grips my arm in his. "Don't let her out of your sight," he warns me. His blue eyes are fierce with anger and worry. "I can't... Just don't." He releases me and drags a hand through his hair.

"I love her," I state firmly, knowing he will get my meaning.

Throwing myself through the opening, I find Arden standing on the other side, surrounded by my guards. They're all laughing and joking with her. I guess her last visit cemented her warrior status. When I enter, they circle and put her in the middle. I smile in satisfaction at the protective ring around her.

My second-in-command, Drystan, walks over, and I clasp his arm in greeting. "Valerian," he greets me with a sliver of amusement in his tone, his alert eyes watching the guards to make sure they're on their best behavior with my mate.

"Drystan," I return.

We stand shoulder to shoulder, watching the scene in front of us. Arden is questioning each guard about their training. She listens to their answers and gives them some pointers for the next time.

"Drystan, what if we change the training tomorrow? Give the men something real and powerful to fight against?" I suggest. Technically, I'm king, but he's in charge of our soldiers and their training.

Hard eyes swing to mine, and he dips his chin. "It's a damn fine idea. It would allow me to assess their ability to fight against a witch in battle, then I can modify the training accordingly."

"Arden," I call out. The guards step back to let her through, and I barely contain my laugh. They won't be so chivalrous when she's standing over them with a sword at their throat or tossing a fireball at their hearts. "How would you like to train with them using magic and sword?"

Her eyes light up, and she saunters over to give me a kiss. "You know the way to my heart."

I introduce her to Drystan. "He'll set something up for the morning. I'll give you his number, and you can text him anything you might need."

She shakes his hand and beams at him. "This will be fun!"

When he roars with laughter, the guards look over at him in shock. He sees their expression and gives them an evil grin. "I've got a surprise for tomorrow's training." He bows his head in my direction, then walks over to give them the good news.

"Let's go grab supper," I drawl. "You're going to need food and a good night's sleep."

THE NEXT MORNING, the training field is packed with spectators.

"I thought we were training," she says, puzzled by the large turnout. "Why are there so many people here?"

"My mate, slayer of dragons?" I scoff, laughing at the consternation on her face. "I've got a few meetings today, but I'll be back by lunch. Don't go anywhere without Drystan. I mean it. And don't kill my men—we're going to need them for the battle—but give them hell. I want them prepared, okay?" I peck her on the lips and watch her walk across the field to Drystan. Giving him a hard look, I make sure he understands her life is in his hands. He places a fist to his chest and bows, so I leave the arena.

My morning meetings drag on, but I finally break free and head back to the training field. As I get closer, the crowd releases a loud groan of disappointment, and I hear an enraged dragon's roar in the background. Picking up the pace, I slide quietly around the corner to stand behind Drystan.

Sensing a presence, he draws his sword, pivots, and barely stops it an inch from my neck. "Damnit, Valerian," he barks, sheathing his sword. Turning his back to me, he quickly swivels to watch the action on the field.

"How's it going?" I murmur, not wanting anyone to over-hear our conversation. Glancing toward the field, I watch Arden put the red dragon in front of her to sleep. To sleep. He's snoring. The crowd jeers at him and throws their hands up to show their frustration.

"We've got a lot of work to do," he mutters. Snatching up the notepad by his side, I see line after line of changes to the training. "We've been at peace for too damn long. I need you to supply me with supernaturals for us to train against." When I nod, he jots down another note.

He points a hand to Arden. "She's younger but better than most of them. Our seasoned warriors won against her, but even a few of them settled for a tie. She doesn't act or fight like a witch. Her magic is a mixture of Fae, demon, and witch tactics. Unpredictable and lethal, when one spell or maneuver doesn't work, she pulls another from her bag of tricks. Faced with so many unknowns, they fail. Strangely, I think it pisses her off more than them. When they get up, roaring in rage, she gets in their face, explains what they did wrong, and gives them ideas to counteract those tactics in the future. Then she slaps them on the back and calls up the next one."

The sleeping dragon rises and roars. Shifting back, he immediately stalks forward and starts shouting at her. She stops him with her sword, then with a hard face and loud voice, she explains what he did wrong. The defeated dragon, as well as the soldiers on the side, listen intently. She pats the dragon on the back to console him, then points to the next in line.

"She's trained her entire life with the best. Hundreds of trainers teaching a variety of methods, but she probably learned the most from Vargas and Callyx Karth," I reveal to Drystan, watching his eyes widen when I mention their names. "Make sure you sit down and talk to her prior to our departure. There's a battle brewing, and we need to be ready." Not willing to give him more information until after the council meeting, I turn my attention back to the field.

Arden smiles and blows me a kiss. The soldier entering the field sees me and swallows nervously. They face off, and for the first time since I heard our enemy was a queen, I relax. Watching her fight and annihilate opponents fills me with confidence.

THE COUNCIL MEETING GOES WELL. Everyone's aligned on the possibility of war and willing to make the proper preparations. Once the meeting is adjourned, Arden's swarmed by people who want to meet her and talk about the training today. Beautiful in her amber silk dress, she gracefully accepts their compliments and turns the questions back on them. If it were anyone else, I'd think it a smart political maneuver, but I know she's genuinely interested in their lives, and they feel it too. Years of isolation makes her seek out others.

We adjourn to the dinner, and Arden sits quietly beside me, picking at her food. Her eyes dart from person to person, and I watch the wheels turning in her head.

"How's the food?" I ask quietly.

"It's delicious," she responds, a blush staining her cheeks. "I was so hungry after training, I stuffed myself and I'm still full."

Finishing my last bite, I put down my napkin and lean over to speak in her ear. "Put down your fork and stand up. Go to our room and wait for me. Remove your clothes but leave your heels on."

Glancing at me, her eyes drift down to the suit I'm wearing, and she abruptly stands. "Please excuse me. I'm exhausted from the day." The table nods, and she leaves.

I walk over to Glynnis and a few of the other council

members to give our excuses. Glynnis chuckles softly, but I ignore it and quickly follow my mate out the door.

When I enter the room, Arden's standing by the fire, every curve of her delectable body illuminated for my eyes to feast on. I sit in a nearby chair. It's not a throne, but it will do.

"Slowly turn in a circle. I want to see every inch of your body," I order. My hands drop to the arms of the chair, my knuckles gleaming white in anticipation.

She licks her lips and follows my instruction. As she turns, her breasts bounce lightly, and my fingers curl with need. She stops and faces me, waiting for the next command.

"Turn to the side and caress your breasts," I tell her. "Twist and roll your nipples until they're hard. Play with them. Pretend it's my hands and mouth on you."

At first, her hands are tentative, lightly brushing her breasts and nipples, which peak softly. Her chest flushes red, but I can't tell if she's embarrassed or her desire is growing. Probably both.

Without saying a word, I stand and turn toward the closet.

"Wait," she croaks. "Please."

My face impassive, I sit back down.

This time, her hands run over the smooth globes, plumping them up before cupping one in each hand. Using her fingers, she plays with her nipples, rolling and tugging until they're hard enough to cut glass. Moaning, her head drops back, but she doesn't stop. Restlessly shifting from side to side, she changes her stance, trying to ease the ache between her legs.

My eyes move between her breasts and legs, and all I can think about is spreading her wide open and plunging into her. Or releasing my cock and stroking it while I watch her pleasure herself. I do neither. Adjusting myself, I spread my legs farther apart to accommodate the beast growing in my pants.

"Sit on the edge of the chair behind you, spread your legs

wide, and touch yourself. I want to see your fingers dripping with your desire, but do not come without my permission." My voice is hard and rough with my own desire.

Gripping the armrests, I watch her follow my commands, barely stifling the groan rising in my throat when I see her pouty lips flush and wet with desire. It takes every iota of willpower in my body to sit still. It's the most exquisite torture. I'm so fascinated, I don't want it to end, and yet I need to be inside her.

She moans, and I see her chest heaving. Her finger dips down to gather moisture and up to circle her nub over and over. Red streaks her cheeks and chest. Little white teeth bite down on her bottom lip.

"Open your eyes," I demand, wanting to see the glazed look in her eyes. "How close are you?"

Green eyes, dark with desire, silently plead with me, but I shake my head. With her other hand, she inserts a finger. Sliding it in and out, her hips rock back and forth to meet it, and her finger glistens with her need.

"Stop. Come here," I order her.

She arches a brow and slides off the chair onto her hands and knees. Crawling over to me, she inches along, and I'm mesmerized by the sensual sway of her breasts.

"Who's in charge here?" I grunt, knowing it's not me.

Her husky laugh spills out into the air, and I take a deep breath, preparing to meet the challenge I see in her eyes.

She reaches my knees, spreads my legs wider, and targets the bulge straining my pants. Sliding her nails up the inside of my thighs, I meet her gaze with my own challenge, and she smirks.

When she leans forward, her breasts hang close to my hands, and I immediately fixate on all the things I want to do to them—squeezing, playing, kissing, and sucking to name a few. The images continuously bombard me, until I want to yank her in my lap and devour them, but I don't. A sliver of control remains mine, but barely. I've never been this hard in my life.

Leaning forward, she drops a kiss on the peak of my pants, leaving a perfect lipstick imprint like a brand of ownership.

I quite like it. Maybe I should have her lips tattooed on my body permanently.

"Are you done?" I question.

"That depends," she says, lifting one shoulder nonchalantly. "Are you ready?"

With a growl, I lean forward, lift her up, and spin her around until she's on her hands and knees. When she's in position, I run my hands over her body, touching her like I made her touch herself. "Beautiful. Your skin was glowing against the backdrop of the fire, and I could barely think of anything except touching and licking you." My hands find every single curve and valley, stroking and flicking, until she's walking the same tightrope of desire with me.

Unbuckling my belt, I caress her lightly with it, and she whimpers. The sound goes straight south, and I can't drop my pants fast enough. Sliding into her, I stop, giving her a second to adjust, but a second is all I can spare.

"All day, I've thought of nothing but sliding into you. It made for some damn uncomfortable meetings."

Chest heaving, my breaths are harsh and loud in the quiet room. The control I'm searching for is gone, swept away by our game, and I grip her hips and thrust in deep.

Sweet sounds fall from her lips, and I'm suddenly thrusting into her like a madman, the need for my mate overriding coherent thought until I want to roar from the rafters.

Her hips are equally forceful as they meet every thrust of mine, and I curse, knowing I can't last much longer.

"Touch yourself," I growl, barely able to form the words.

When her fingers reach down to rub, I feel them brush repeatedly against my cock, and I grit my teeth at the sensation. Everything pools down, then starts surging up, but I don't stop moving. I come hard, roaring with my release, and thankfully, I feel the answering pulse in her body at the same time. Pulling her up into my arms, I wrap them tightly around her until the last tremor ceases.

Realizing I still have my suit on, I give a low laugh. "Life will never be boring with you, lass. I feel completely wrecked by our little game."

Placing a kiss at the juncture of her neck and shoulder, I murmur my love to her and shiver when I hear those words in return. I'll never get tired of hearing them.

CHAPTER
SIXTEEN

ARDEN

"War is coming," Theron warns Maya. "Our opponent is formidable, with an army of their own. There will be no tie or truce. All or nothing. Are you willing to risk yourself and your mate?" He's not willing to sugarcoat our situation, knowing she needs all the facts to decide whether the risk is worth the potential sacrifice.

Her golden, slanted eyes shine bright, and the fierce predator inside moves behind the thin veneer of her human exterior. She shifts into an aggressive stance angled toward me, and I narrow my eyes at the threat. I'm not the same naïve witch I was when I first arrived. Too much has happened, and it's not even the tip of what's to come. Anyone at my back stands with me, or they can leave. I raise my eyebrow, questioning the sanity of her pose.

Maya blinks and shifts into a more relaxed stance. As an alpha lion, it's probably killing her to concede an inch to me, but I merely incline my head. I want her for an ally.

"We owe the cadre everything," she states bluntly. "If not for you, we would have died long ago, eliminated by our lion brethren. I'm the last royal, the purest lion shifter in existence, and I've been hunted all my life. As my mate, Syn shares my fate. The sanctuary we have here is more than we can hope to find anywhere else. If it means giving up our lives, I'd rather sacrifice them for the cadre instead of the prejudiced assholes who think they need to purge my kind in order to rule." With a lift of her chin, she waits for Theron or me to respond.

"We'd like for you to accept our invitation to come back and manage The Abbey," Theron states formally, knowing she needs to keep her pride intact.

She regally dips her chin to accept our offer, but I note the relief in her eyes.

"One more thing," Theron says, his voice cool and hard. "I trust you remember our last conversation?"

She flicks a glance at me. "I remember. I'll not allow any of the past behavior to be repeated," she assures him.

"If it happens, I'll hold you accountable," Theron reminds her. "Do not disappoint me." Ice coats the walls, and a shiver racks her body. He takes his phone out and starts tapping. "I'll send you a list of the orders I've completed, and you can pick it up from there."

Satisfied with the discussion, I place a kiss on his cheek and whisper something delicious in his ear, knowing he won't react in front of her. His eyes slide to mine with promises of retribution, and I laugh.

Maya's face flashes with surprise for a second, then settles into her usual stoic countenance. *That's right—a lot has changed since you were here last. Take his warning seriously.*

HAVING SPENT LESS time slamming into the mats today, I'm feeling victorious. I didn't win anything, but I landed a few solid hits on Valerian, managed to locate Daire twice without my eyesight, and kept my magic contained during the entire session. I didn't put a mark on Theron, but since it was our first session, I don't feel too bad. If it feels and tastes like victory, I'm counting it.

Callyx: Incoming. Front.

Running back to the training center, I find Valerian and Daire and yell for them to follow me. On the way to the lobby, I show them Callyx's text. When the doors of the elevator open, I step forward, but Valerian holds me back while Daire checks out the situation first. Tapping my foot, I wait for him to give us a signal.

"All clear," Daire calls out. "Valerian, I need some assistance."

We both run to the door, and I gasp. Brutally beaten with cuts and burns all over them, Callyx and Cormal stand shoulder to shoulder barely holding onto life, with a bloody rag doll held tightly in their arms.

I step closer to see what it is and get a whiff of something atrocious. It's a combination of burnt flesh, blood, bodily fluids, and various unidentifiable odors. Gagging, I lean back and breathe out of my mouth. Whatever it is, it's tiny. A pale hand slips from the pile, and I jump back.

Goddess, I hope it's not a child.

Cormal immediately grabs the hand and carefully tucks it

close. A sinking feeling fills my stomach. There's only one person they both care about...

When Cormal sways, Valerian jumps forward to prop him up but immediately steps back when he snarls and raises a fireball.

"Whoa," Valerian drawls softly. "It's Valerian, King of Dragons. Remember me? I've got Daire, son of Lucifer, with me. We're here to help. Let's get you inside The Abbey to safety. Isn't that why you came here?" He continues to speak in soothing tones until his words register, and Cormal lowers his hand.

"Callyx," I yell. Valerian motions for me to take it easy, but he doesn't know our history. "You look like hell. I guess you expect me to take care of you and not tell Solandis? You always do this. Take on the biggest, baddest asshole around, then whine like a baby for me to help you." I wave a hand toward the door. "Well, are you coming? If you don't want her to see you in this state, you'd better hurry. The potions are ready." It's the same thing I've said to him a thousand times before, and I know it will penetrate the fight instinct he's riding hard.

Callyx blinks, and his eyes drop to the body in his arms. "Help her first. Help Meri."

Horrified to hear my suspicions are true, I suck in a deep breath and search the bloody heap for a single resemblance to my friend, but I find none. Her features are completely smashed and unrecognizable. Tears slide down my face, and I hold out my shaking hands. Warm golden light encompasses her body, and I begin healing her.

Cormal snarls at me, but Callyx claps him on the shoulder. "Easy," he says. "It's Arden. Let her heal Meri."

Piercing dark blue eyes hold mine in a death stare, making silent promises to end me if I do anything to hurt Meri. With a solemn nod, I agree to his conditions.

Astor and Theron join us, and between the four of them, they finally get Callyx and Cormal into The Abbey. Relieved, I watch both Daire and Astor get to work on healing those two while I continue to help Meri.

Based on the number of curses spewing from their mouths, Astor's concoction must be positively vile. Color returns to their pale faces, so I know the potion is working.

Valerian brings a couch over for them to sit, and they ease down to keep from jostling their cargo.

Daire glides over to Callyx. "Astor's potion will help speed up your natural healing properties, so I'll ignore the surface wounds and concentrate on the internal bleeding." He looks over at me, and a slow smile builds on his face. A glow appears on his hands, and he places them over Callyx.

Breath rattling, Callyx lets out a string of soft curses while Daire works on him. Tears spring to my eyes, but I can't let him see them. This might be the worst shape he's ever been in, and I can't help but wonder how many they were up against. Daire pulls his hands back, and with a loud exhale, Callyx slumps down into the cushions behind him.

"Thanks," Callyx grunts, and I make a mental note to slap him on the head when he's better.

Pausing, I hover my glowing hands over Meri's body, trying to pinpoint the worst of her injuries, but they all seem to be equally bad. Taking a cue from Daire, I concentrate on her torso. Memories of all our times together flash by until I'm choking on them. I keep them on replay, pushing every one of them through my hands and into her body.

Daire moves to Cormal, but when he holds out his hands, nothing happens. Frowning, he glances at me, and I realize his dilemma.

"He guided us through the dark Elven forest. When asked, he helped Fallon search for the source of my assassination attempts. He cares deeply for Meri. He gives criminals a leader to follow, otherwise there would be mass chaos..." My voice trails off, unable to think of anything else.

Daire's hands begin glowing, and we both sigh with relief. Good thoughts are required to heal, but deep wounds require an extra push of emotion.

Cormal looks at me wryly, and I see a glint of humor in his eyes. I shrug. I can't pretend I think he's a good guy. Although, I suspect he does more than he lets on.

My body crashes to the floor, and I blink in surprise. Theron picks me up and cradles me in his arms. Looking inside, I realize my witch magic is dull and dark instead of the golden glow I'm used to seeing. Burnout. A migraine hits, and pain stabs me in the eye.

"Get up!" Cormal roars and tries to push Daire away. Using only the tip of his finger and his vampire strength, Daire holds him in place.

A tiny hand reaches up and pats Cormal's cheek. Frozen, he stops breathing for a second, but when it falls, he moves quickly to catch and cage it in his larger one. He stares down at her, hope blazing in his eyes, and waits for another sign, but she doesn't move. He's mumbling something to her, but I can't tell what he's saying.

Straining, I block out the background noise, but instead of picking up Cormal's words, I hear the faint beat of Meri's heart. It's slow but steady. My eyes meet his, and I jerk my chin toward her.

He cocks an ear and listens. After a minute, he hears it and closes his eyes, blocking me from seeing the emotion over-whelming him. A dark smile appears, and he opens his eyes. All traces of worry, anger, and whatever else he was feeling is wiped from his expression.

Theron stares down at me and quirks the corner of his brow, and to his alarm, I start crying.

"She's going to make it," I repeat over and over.

Even for an immortal, this was a close call. Theron's violet eyes swirl with anger, but his hands are soft when they wipe away my tears.

"Thank you, goddess."

Black spots dot my vision until I'm swarmed by darkness.

CHAPTER
SEVENTEEN

<u>ARDEN</u>

Pain. It drifts like smoke into every crevasse in my body and lingers until I can't feel anything else. *What happened?* My pounding head is blank. Frowning, I peel my eyes open and find I'm lying safely in my bed. The room is mostly dark, but a soft glow is coming from the corner. I lie completely still, waiting for the pain to subside, but it doesn't.

Another feeling washes over me, and I realize I'm going to have to get up. I groan and try to push the covers off, using as little movement as possible.

"Here, let me." Theron's voice comes out of the dark, followed by his hands. He moves the covers off me, then slides his arms under my head and knees. "Ready?"

I tighten my grip on the front of his shirt. "Yes," I croak, my voice rusty from lack of use.

When he lifts me, a whimper escapes, but I clamp my lips together, refusing to let out any other noises. A couple of tears slide down my cheeks. Thankfully, it only takes a few strides, and we're in the bathroom.

His thumbs hook on my underwear, but I seize one of his hands. Embarrassment floods my body.

Violet eyes fill with exasperation. "I've undressed you plenty of times," he reminds me.

The flush spreads from my chest to my face, and I weakly shove his shoulders.

"I can go to the bathroom by myself," I assert, albeit shakier than I intended.

Crossing my arms, I stare down at him, refusing to give in and let him help me further. There are some lines I refuse to cross, and I'm willing to die on my sword—or in this case, fall flat on my face—to uphold them.

My determination finally filters through, and he heaves a sigh, as if my need for privacy is illogical and impractical. "I'll wait outside," he says grudgingly.

The door closes, and I grab the counter to steady myself. It's a slow, slow process, but I finally get it done and shuffle over to the sink to wash my hands.

Callyx slips into my mind, and the recent events slowly filter one by one into my brain. I fling open the door.

"How are they doing?" I ask, gripping Theron's shoulders when he swings me up into his arms again.

Daire's tired voice floats over from where he's lying on the couch. "I checked on them about an hour ago. They're all healing, although Meri's progress is slow. Even with her immortality, it's going to take her a while to get back to normal."

I motion to Daire, and Theron carries me over to him. Sitting on the edge of the couch, I lean over and smooth Daire's blond hair off his forehead.

"You're pale," I observe quietly. "If they're on the mend, they need time, not additional healing. Do you need some blood?"

Both Daire and Theron snarl, and I roll my eyes. "Calm down," I say drily. "We have an entire bar stocked full of blood, remember? I'm sure Theron would love to go down and grab you a couple of bottles. Vintage, right?"

"I'll help you get back into bed, then I'll go," Theron replies stiffly.

"Only if Daire will join me," I tell him, watching Daire's eyebrow quirk up in surprise.

"After I have a drink or two," he promises. "I'm a bit thin on control right now, and the delectable smell of your blood is too tempting." A wolfish smile appears, and he flicks a glance down at my thighs.

Squirming at the memory of his bite, I can't help the grimace that appears when my sore muscles protest.

He scowls.

"Rain check," I reply huskily. "Thank you for helping."

He shrugs like it's of little or no consequence, but I know healing Cormal is the last thing he would have done if it weren't for me. Callyx is also a maybe.

I trace the dark circles under his eyes. "Did you get any answers from them?"

"No. Callyx and Cormal are pretty tight-lipped, but with the hell they've likely gone through, I don't blame them. I could formally force the issue, but I thought you'd prefer it if they willingly gave us answers," he remarks, raising an eyebrow.

"Yes." I shift on the couch and wince.

"That's it," Theron interjects. He swings me up in his arms and lays me back on the bed. Spotting my phone on the night-stand, he pauses. "Do you mind if I borrow your phone? Astor and I have been working on a project, and I need to add a program to it."

"After you get back," I reply. "I want to let Vargas know Callyx is here."

"I already informed him," Theron states. "Water is beside you. Do you need anything else?"

He informed Vargas. I swear my heart stutters. This man misses nothing and takes care of everything. I shake my head and immediately regret it. "Maybe a potion? My internal healing seems to be on the fritz," I whisper, not wanting my head to pound.

Theron picks up his phone and sends a text. "Astor will be here in a second," he says, tucking the covers around me. Placing a soft kiss on my lips, he picks up my phone and pockets it, then proceeds to the door. "I'll be back soon."

Astor enters a second later with a glass in his hand. "It's disgusting," he warns me, "but it will help with the burnout." Bringing the glass to my lips, he helps me drink it.

My face scrunches in response to the disgusting taste, and I stick my tongue out to air it. "That's probably the worst one I've ever tasted." Warmth races along my veins as the potion does its job. My eyes droop, and Astor helps me scoot down into the bed. Pouty lips slide over mine, and the darkness falls like a curtain.

CORMAL STIFFENS and eyes me warily when I enter the room. Ignoring him, I head for Callyx and wrap him tightly in my arms. When he grunts, I lightly smack him on the head.

"You deserve a little punishment for scaring the hell out of me," I assert.

Leaning back, I survey the damage and let out a huge sigh of relief when I find most of his cuts and bruises healed. Raising my hand, I show him my thumb and pointer finger almost touching. "I came this close to calling Solandis and Vargas."

"It couldn't be helped," he grumbles and squeezes me back. "I spoke to Vargas before I went inside to rescue her, and he ordered me to wait. Unfortunately, our intel was only good for a short period of time, so we decided to take our shot."

Keeping my arm around him, I turn and study Meri. Looking less like a bloody rag doll, she's clean and sleeping soundly in the next bed. Her color looks good, and she's breathing steadily. I'm glad. Daire healed her a couple more times while I was incapacitated. "Where was she?"

"In the bowels of hell," Cormal snarls back at me. "Does it matter?"

"I'll ask her when she wakes," I reply calmly, not willing to get into a pissing match with him. I pat Callyx on the shoulder and walk over to Meri to run my hands over her.

In a flash, Cormal's standing next to me. Holding his hands loosely at his sides, he watches my every move.

"I'm running a light check to make sure we didn't miss anything," I explain softly. After a short exam, I find nothing but good news. "She's healing and should be up and walking by tomorrow."

He exhales heavily and runs a hand through his hair. "Thank you," he bites out. "If I'd had to find a healer, she'd have been in agony, repeatedly dying and returning. Her body was already on the verge of giving up completely. Mentally, she was already lost. When we found her, she begged me to kill her."

Meri's eyes pop open, and she scrambles out from the covers and slips to the floor on the other side of the bed. Curling into a ball, her head moves frantically while she tries to get her bearings. Her turquoise eyes, filled with terror, stare unseeingly at us. I shift my feet, and the sound of my boots causes her to whimper.

Cormal walks slowly to the other side of the bed and eases down to the floor in front of her.

"You're safe, little bird," he assures her, his voice low and soothing. "I'm here. Nobody is going to hurt you." When she stares at him in disbelief, he reaches out and places a knife in her hand. "Here. If I'm lying, stab me. In the meantime, I'm going to sit here and protect you."

With a tight grip on the knife, she stares at him for a long time. Recognition comes slowly, and her terror subsides. Breathtaking fury replaces it.

"Your protection means nothing. Zero. Zilch. I should stab you in your black heart with your own knife. I want to. Goddess knows I've dreamt about it so many times in the last couple of weeks. You promised to protect me from her," she spits out, tears falling rapidly down her cheeks.

"For hundreds of years, we've played the same song and dance with each other. Every time I saw you, I begged you for sanctuary, and without fail, you'd refuse. Too dangerous. I didn't have any powers to protect myself. Didn't want that life for me. Blah, blah." She laughs derisively.

"I was already living a dangerous life, doing everything and anything she wanted. At least with you, I'd have been paid for my time. I might have gotten a decent meal or a nice *safe* place to sleep. Nobody would have sold me to *them*. True luxury," she laments.

"Nope. I worked to please her. To further her goals. The alternative was her displeasure. Do you know how creative a dark sorceress can get with her punishments?" A shudder rips through her body, and she cries harder.

I hold a tissue out, and startled, she glances up and blanches when she sees me. Giving her a small smile of reassurance, I wait until she takes it.

She swipes angrily at the tears on her face and returns her focus to Cormal. "You were my one hope. One of a very short list of people she wouldn't dare cross," she reveals in a trembling voice. "Now look at me. I'm broken. Shattered into a million miniscule pieces. I'll never be able to put myself back together."

Cormal sits like a stone, taking every single word she spits out. At the end, he reaches a hand toward her, and she eyes it in disbelief. With a short scream of rage, she stabs the knife straight through the middle of his hand.

He yanks the knife out and blood pools in his hand. Making a fist, he glances up at me for something...a tissue, healing, or possibly support with Meri, but I shake my head. He's on his own.

Meri eases to her feet, and Cormal springs up. She holds her palm out to keep him away from her.

"Thank you for rescuing me from hell," she states calmly. "I appreciate all the assistance you've given me over the years, even if you couldn't offer what I truly needed, but it's time for us to part ways. What is it you say to your associates when you're done?" She purses her lips in thought. "Oh yes, I believe our business is concluded. You may see yourself out."

"Our fucking business is never going to be concluded," he informs her with a dark laugh. "I admit, I fucked up. I didn't know how bad it had gotten. I'll kill the bitch, and you won't have to worry about it, okay?" He steps in close and stares down at her. "I'll send you word when it's done. Then I'll find you a place to work and live."

"You aren't listening. Kill her or don't," she says with a shrug. "I. Don't. Want. To. See. You. Again. I need people I can count on, not selfish assholes who only help me when it's *convenient*."

"Do you think it was selfish or convenient to come rescue you? I've always had your back. Who else has enough power to protect you from her? Arden? I doubt it. Who?" he demands, taunting her lack of family or friends.

"I..." she whispers.

Having heard enough, both Callyx and I step forward, but I reach Meri first. I put my arm around her shoulders and pull her close. "We obviously have some things to work on, but I'm your friend, Meri. You can stay here as long as you like." I lift my chin and glance at Cormal.

He laughs. "Meri, she can barely save herself right now," he reminds her. "Friends like me from the same *neighborhood* know you. I know you and embrace every beautiful flaw. She doesn't know you. Everything you told her was a lie. What happens when she discovers the real you? The one who lives in the dark?" he scoffs.

Striding confidently to the door, he opens it and glances back at her. "When you're ready, come find me."

The door slams shut, leaving a bloody handprint on the knob.

Callyx steps forward. "You have family, Meri." He gives me a pleading look. "Solandis will be thrilled to know she has a niece. I promise you."

CHAPTER

EIGHTEEN

<u>ARDEN</u>

Sucker punched by my own brother. My arm drops from Meri's shoulders, and I turn around and stare into her turquoise eyes. The same eyes I see in the face of the light Fae queen. Her mother. Almost the same eyes I see when I look at Solandis, although hers change color based on her mood. Sometimes blue, sometimes turquoise.

What's it called when you can't see something right in front of you? Scotoma? Inattention blindness? Mental blind spot? When I first met her, I asked her if she knew the queen and she said no. Didn't she? I know she didn't tell me she was her mother. I'd have remembered such an important fact.

"Nobody knows," Meri interjects, accurately interpreting my thoughts. "Yes, Callyx knows, but he found out years ago. Fae recognize Fae, especially those from the same line. When he saved me from the demon gang, he could immediately tell I was family. He confronted me, and I admitted it. Then I ran away."

Callyx picks up the story. "When you introduced your friend, Meri, in the club, I couldn't believe my eyes. I'd searched everywhere for her and never found a trace. Suddenly, there she stood."

"He's been trying to get me to come forward for weeks, but I'm too afraid," she admits. Sitting heavily on the bed, she bites her lip and explains. "I wasn't born. My guardian created me. She stole the light Fae queen's essence, and using dark, forbidden magic, she merged it with the essence of her former lover, the dark Fae king. Neither of them are even aware they have a child."

Stunned, I consider the implications of this massive secret. The sorceress used magic to create a supernatural child.

"Why?" I ask. "For power? I doubt the two kingdoms will come together for a child, especially one created under those circumstances."

She winces. "Vengeance, I think. Long story short...she used to be the dark Fae king's mistress, until he found his mate and kicked her out. Then she went to the light Fae queen and offered her insider knowledge of the dark Fae king and his court. The queen took the knowledge, then discarded her. According to the stories I picked up over the years, she went completely bonkers, disappeared for a while, then reappeared a decade or two later...with me."

Her shoulders droop. "When I turned out to be a dud instead of the all-powerful child, she turned all her hatred toward me, and I've been living in hell ever since," she states in a matter-of-fact voice.

Callyx drops down to look her in the eyes. "What happened recently?"

Meri darts a glance at me, then shrugs. "I didn't deliver the book on the Primary and ruined her little spying game." Turning to me, she grabs my hand. "I couldn't do it anymore. It's why I said all those terrible things to you. I knew if you hated me, you would walk away, and it worked." She sighs.

"Cormal is right, but he's also wrong. I did lie to you about a lot of things, but not about how I felt. I know you probably won't believe me, and I don't blame you, but our friendship is important to me. You heard Cormal. My list of friends and family is almost non-existent. If you forgive me, I promise to make it up to you. Earn your trust. Tell you the truth. Even if you don't like me afterward, at least you'll know the real me." It all rushes out in one long breath. Stopping, she waits for me to say something.

Our friendship had felt real and solid, the kind you could have for your entire life. A soul sister. Could I forgive her? I think about her situation. Would I be able to withstand hundreds of years of neglect and abuse without compromising my integrity? Doubtful. She wasn't wrong when she sneered at my sheltered life. I went from a bubble with Vargas and Solandis to a bubble with the cadre. I had food, shelter, and love, but she didn't even have the basics.

Plus, I haven't been entirely transparent with her. What if the enemy is the light Fae queen and I kill her? Would Meri forgive me for killing her mother? Even one she doesn't know?

"There are things you don't know," I begin. "About me, my destiny, the Primary. Maybe we don't know each other as well as we thought. I miss you, though. I care about you. If you're willing to try after hearing what I have to say, then I am too."

Her thin arms wrap around me. "Thank you," she says with a sniff.

I hug her tightly.

Callyx wraps his arms around both of us.

We all laugh.

An alarm blares loudly, and we break apart. It sounds like it's coming from the whole building. Callyx raises an eyebrow, but I shake my head. I don't know what it is or what it means.

Daire walks into the room. "The Abbey is getting hit with a magical attack," he states. "It's not very strong, but it's continuous. It started shortly after you arrived, and it's increased in intensity during the last hour. We're meeting in the lobby to discuss next steps."

In a blur, he's by my side. Picking up my hand, he gives it a squeeze and silently asks if I'm okay. I guess he overheard our conversation. I nod.

When we reach the lobby, the rest of the cadre is waiting, and surprisingly, so is Vargas. I shove Callyx toward him. He glares back at me.

When he gets near, Vargas yanks him into a tight hug and pounds him on the back. He examines every inch of him, then shakes his head. "You're damn lucky to get out of there alive. We're going to have a discussion later."

"I know," Callyx says gruffly. "I want you to meet someone." He pulls Meri to his side. "This is Meri." Vargas glances at me, and I dip my head in confirmation. "Arden's friend. My cousin. Nyssa's daughter."

Vargas' head whips around to Callyx, then to Meri. "I'm sure there's a long story here, but it needs to wait. The sorceress is on the hunt. I'm assuming it's for you."

Meri starts shaking like a leaf, and her eyes dart toward the nearest door.

Vargas pulls her close and pats her shoulder. "There, there. No need to worry. We take care of our family," he assures her. "Callyx is young, but he's a pretty good fighter. Me...I'm Lucifer's second-in-command and a hell of a lot more powerful. I promise I'll keep you safe from her. Don't worry. She isn't even in the same weight class."

Meri's eyes dart to me, and she raises an eyebrow.

"This is Vargas. One half of my parents. Wait until you meet Solandis," I say, only half-joking. "You're officially a part of the clan."

My eyes meet Callyx's, and we both grin. She doesn't understand what that means, but she will.

"I don't know how you can think with all this noise," Vargas loudly complains. "Callyx, why don't you and Meri come back with me? We can introduce her to your mother." He glances at the rest of the group. "With my new position, I've gained a lot of additional security, which can't hurt, right?"

An idea pops in my head. "I'll go with you." I need to start searching for my mother's journal, and there's a few things I can search through at the house. Might as well help Meri settle in while I look.

"Why don't you all come for a visit?" Vargas counters with an invitation for everyone, knowing the cadre isn't about to let me come by myself.

Astor dips his head. "Thank you for the invite, but I've promised a friend I'd help him. In fact, I've got to leave now or I'll be late." He walks over and plants a firm kiss on my lips. "I'll text you later."

Theron quickly organizes everyone, and a half hour later, we're on our way, leaving Maya to deal with the alarm still blaring in the background.

CHAPTER
NINETEEN

<u>ARDEN</u>

I gasp when I step through the portal and find a modern house, because Solandis isn't a fan of that style of home. Our old house looked like a Fae palace, with turrets and a golden grandiose design.

When the last attack occurred, Vargas moved them to this location, but I'm still shocked to see something with linear lines and minimalist details. It screams Vargas, and I can't wait to hear this story.

Solandis greets us at the huge glass and steel front door. I raise my eyebrows, and she waves a hand. "Don't even get me started on this soulless monstrosity. I bet Vargas he couldn't find suitable accommodations large enough to house our staff and all of our things in one day." She swirls her hand in a circle. "This was his answer. We're still arguing over the word 'suitable,' but I haven't come up with a logical argument to sway him. Don't worry, I'm not giving up." She folds me into her arms. "I'm so happy to see you so soon."

I laugh and give her a hug. "You might have to concede defeat on this one. Ugly and not to your taste are not good arguments. Besides, I like it."

She shudders and looks speculatively at the silver-haired woman Callyx is escorting slowly up the walk. "Callyx, I'm not sure if your father told you, but I'm very upset with you right now for taking such a huge risk with your life," she admonishes him. "It's a good thing we have company."

Callyx hunches his shoulders and scowls at me. 'Very upset' is code for livid. I shrug. He deserves it. Vargas told him to wait for backup, and judging from their condition, they barely made it out.

Meri squares her shoulders and raises her head, looking directly at Solandis. She stops in front of her and waits.

Tears roll down Solandis' cheek, and she cries out. Vargas instantly appears by her side and wraps his arm around her waist.

"This is Merindah, or Meri, as Arden calls her. She's my cousin and Nyssa's biological child, although she doesn't know," Callyx blurts out, shattering the bubble around us.

After a hesitant look at Vargas, she pulls Meri into her arms and gives her a hug. "Hello, Meri. I'm Aunt Solandis," she says tearily. "This will be an interesting story. Welcome to my home." Standing back, she greets the cadre, then waves all of us through. Sensing she needs a moment alone with Vargas, I force Callyx to give us a mini tour.

He shows us to the living room, and I glance around in appreciation. While the house is modern, the furnishings are beautiful and luxurious, making the house livable and upscale at the same time. A plush white L-shaped couch and several leather club chairs sit in front of a sleek, contemporary fireplace. Various accents of green and gold are scattered throughout the room in the pillows, throws, and other accessories. It's chic, and it screams Solandis. I think she likes this house more than she might admit.

Meri slides up beside me with a wistful expression on her face. "It's beautiful. Did you grow up here?"

"No. I grew up in a very Fae house with outrageous décor. This is very tame and quite beautiful in comparison," I answer. "I've never been here, so we're seeing it for the first time together." I link our arms, wanting her to feel at ease here.

Solandis and Vargas walk in with hands clasped together. Meri looks surprised at their public affection.

I wrinkle my nose. "You'll get used to it. They've only been together three hundred and fifty years, as they remind Callyx and me all the time. It's barely a blip in time for them. They love the human term 'honeymoon' and refer to this as their honeymoon phase. Whenever we ask them how long this is going to last, they both say 'forever.'"

Meri might as well get used to seeing them act affectionately toward each other, although they don't usually hold hands in public. Solandis is obviously feeling emotional right now, with Callyx' close call and the arrival of Meri.

"Why don't I show everyone to their rooms? Except for Callyx, of course," Solandis suggests. "Follow me."

Walking with her usual grace, she leads us to the guest wing. "Meri, you'll be here for now, but once everyone leaves, we can move you to the family wing. It will be up to you. Right now, Arden will be two doors down." The cadre are shown to the rooms surrounding ours.

Meri enters her room and stops. Her jaw drops open. "This is for me?" The room is decorated in neutral colors of white and light grey. There isn't much furniture, but there's a large closet for her clothes. A pair of overstuffed comfy chairs sit in front of the fireplace. "This is amazing, thank you."

Solandis' forehead is marred with a tiny frown for a second before she smooths it away. "Of course. Come see Arden's room, so you know where it is," she says airily, but her eyes glance toward me, and I shake my head. Meri didn't grow up with even an ounce of wealth. I silently promise to tell her later. She dips her chin and strides out the door.

My room is identical, which is why Solandis wanted Meri to see it.

Theron, Daire, and Valerian walk in a second behind us. They've already dropped their bags in each of their rooms. Daire tests the windows, Valerian assesses the security, and Theron sets up several gadgets throughout the room.

Solandis smiles with satisfaction. She loves their protective nature, and so do I. It makes me feel all tingly inside. I glance at Meri, and she's looking down at her feet. Frowning, I glance at Theron and raise an eyebrow.

"We've already checked your room, Meri," Theron assures her. "If anyone enters without your permission, the alarm will send out an immediate alert to all of us, plus Vargas and Callyx."

Her head jerks up in surprise, and she smiles at him. "Thank you. I'm not sure I'll be able to sleep, but it makes me feel safer." Walking to the door, she lifts her hand and waves. "I'm going to rest for a while. Text me when you need me."

I sigh. I hope she's able to be comfortable here. We won't be able to stay more than a day or two. It puts Solandis and Vargas into a precarious position if I'm around for too long.

"Good idea, dear. Dinner won't be served for another few hours," Solandis informs Meri. After she leaves, she turns to me. "We need to talk. Alone."

Everyone else hurries out the door, leaving us to chat. As

soon as the room is empty, she starts grilling me about Meri. I tell her everything I know and realize it's not much at all. Solandis is shocked when I get to the part of her creation.

"Meri's been through a lot, more than I can imagine or conceive," I state sadly. "She needs a safe place, family, and hope. I think she's all out of hope."

She sits there sifting through all the information for several minutes.

"I'm going to speak to Vargas and Lucifer. If they won't agree to put a bounty on the sorceress' head, I'll put a contract out. I want her gone. Forever." Her voice is hard, cold, and demanding, reflecting her royal blood. "The way she treated Meri is atrocious and enough of a reason for me to want her life ended, but to steal *essence* from other supernaturals, to create a child without their knowledge... Dear goddess, Nyssa. When she finds out..." She heaves a sigh and looks up at the ceiling.

"The lack of powers is the one piece that doesn't make sense. The ability to mimic is a powerful use of magic, but it's not power," she says, her brain already working to find the reason. "Every supernatural is born with power. It might be different levels, but magic is in our blood. I don't understand it. I need to research this topic." She taps her finger on her chin.

Now or never. "Did Vargas tell you about the possibility of Nyssa being the Primary?" I probe delicately, worried about her reaction to this news on top of Meri's appearance.

She grabs onto my hands with hers. "Nyssa's been my sister for almost forty-six hundred years. In all that time, her powers have never felt excessive, nor have I ever felt anything unnatural. Never. Believe me, in the early days, we could have used a boost of power to help us fight the Fae court," she remarks with a derisive laugh. "I've been closer to her than anyone. I would have seen or felt something in all those years."

Her turquoise eyes are light without an ounce of worry in them, easily dismissing the idea.

Tension eases from my shoulders. "Do you know the dark Fae queen?"

"We've met," she replies. "Royal meetings and formal events. She's odd. If I didn't know any differently, I wouldn't have thought her Fae."

"Is she powerful? Could she be the Primary? Why would you think her something other than Fae?" I blurt out the questions, looking for any reason to pin her as the enemy.

"She's definitely powerful. I don't know if she could be the Primary. The time we've spent together is too limited to make such a judgement call," she answers. "The Fae part... Fae recognizes Fae, and royal Fae have a special element in their blood. Royal blood courses through her veins, but the way she acts and speaks is almost...human. I can't put my finger on it." She shrugs.

The conversation is enlightening, but I can't rule either queen out. Unfortunately, it's not a puzzle I'm going to solve tonight. Getting up, I unpack a pair of shorts and a T-shirt for bed. Solandis frowns at the clothes.

"Stop. They're comfortable," I say, laughing at her expression. "Do you still have my mother's things, or did we leave them at the old house?"

"I would never leave her things behind," she says exasperatedly. "I'll have Callyx bring the trunk to your room in the morning." She gets up and gives me a hug and kiss. "Thank you for healing him. While I'm glad to have Meri in our family, I don't like the risk he took."

"Daire healed him," I inform her as she's leaving.

She pauses, then blows me a kiss. A second later, I hear a door open in the hall and Solandis thanking Daire. Knowing her, she tacked on a hug and kiss. I wonder how he'll feel about it.

Lying in bed later, our conversation swirls round and round in my brain. Solandis and Nyssa have been sisters for a long time. I trust Solandis' judgement. Nyssa was the likely candidate in my mind, but only because she's the second most powerful supernatural I've ever met. Lucifer's power exceeds hers tenfold.

If I look at the other possibility, I realize I don't know much about the dark Fae queen. I hate to add another item to Theron's list, but he's the best person to investigate her.

The door opens, and I stiffen.

"It's me," Theron whispers. Walking over, he sets something on the table, slips into bed beside me, and pulls me into his arms. "I came to bring your phone back. Also, I've missed you and I need to hold you. I thought you'd already be asleep." His hand sweeps softly over my hair, and I melt into him.

I give him the condensed version of my conversation with Solandis. "We need more information on the dark Fae queen." Her name would probably be a good place to start. I'll ask Solandis tomorrow. "Is this something you can do, or would it be too risky?" As a dark Fae, his allegiance is to his king and queen. Investigating them would call that into question.

He's quiet for a few minutes. "It's risky. I've never met her. She doesn't attend many of the court functions." He thinks for a few minutes. "I'd normally ask Cormal for this type of info, but given the situation, I don't know if he'll do it. He might. He's a businessman first. I'll call him tomorrow. If he can't, we'll find a way."

He pulls my chin up and captures my lips in a soft kiss, then tucks my head into his chest. "Go to sleep."

I STAY for a couple of days to help Meri get acclimated, but it isn't needed. At first, I think Meri reminded Solandis of Nyssa, but once she got to know her, the more she liked Meri for herself and the two became thick as thieves. I thought I'd be jealous, but there's plenty of Solandis and Meri to go around.

I didn't find any journals in my mother's trunk, just some baby items, an album, a few pieces of jewelry, and other odds and ends. I'd seen most of this previously, but this time, I scrutinized every piece. Picking up her jewelry box, I pull out every piece to see if there are any hidden messages, but I find nothing. About to close the box, I notice the felt on the inside is loose. I tug on it and see a white corner. Gripping it with my nails, I pull, and a picture slides out. It's my mother in the arms of a man, the two gazing intently into each other's eyes, with soft smiles on their faces and his hand on her belly. My father. When I see who it is, I smile. We've met. I snap a picture of the photo and hide the picture in the felt.

CHAPTER
TWENTY

At their last visit, both Theron and Astor felt the dark Elven queen's anguish and bitterness surrounding my mother's death to be sincere. Before I usurp power from my father, I want answers, and not just the ones my father insists are the truth.

Surprisingly, Astor volunteered to use his rune to help me ferret out the lies. In the past, we've always hated to ask, since it brought back so many bad memories for him and because lies cause him physical pain. Yet, since Arden's arrival, his attitude toward the rune has changed. He embraces the lies she tells him and the pain it evokes. He says it barely stings now.

Arden. Pain hits my own chest, and I automatically bring up a hand to rub it. The rest of the cadre thinks I should tell her what I'm doing, but if my father heard even a whisper about my intentions to take his throne, he would kill her, knowing it would bring me to my knees. It's better if he thinks I've chosen him over my mate.

My time is running out on both fronts. Her texts are becoming infrequent and less personal, like she's preparing to cut me out of her life, and my father is becoming suspicious of all my visits to the light Elven aristocracy. He should be, since the sole purpose is to expose his madness and ask for their support of my reign. The wind is blowing, and change is coming. Will it be in my favor?

Astor and I meet in the entry, and the butler, along with several armed guards, escort us to the queen. When we enter the room, my eyes are immediately drawn to the large painting of my mother hanging on the wall. She's younger. Her smile is broad and full of mischief and life. I barely remember her, but the anger I feel because of her death feels eternal and dark.

I hear a sniff behind me and turn to find the queen...crying. Her face is a mixture of sadness and joy as she studies me.

"You look so much like your mother. It's as if she's finally returned to me. Can I hug you?" she asks tentatively.

The guard steps forward with his hand on his sword, but I wave him away. "I'm not going to hurt her. Stand down." Walking over, I stand in front of her, but I can't make myself reach out and hug her.

She moves closer and wraps her arms around me. "Thank you," she says weepily. "All these years, I've felt so guilty for not being a better aunt to you. Whenever I finally pass on, I'm sure your mother will have a lot to say about it." She gives a soft laugh.

"I'm not sure my father would have let you visit, and until recently, I would never have sought you out, unless it was to kill you," I respond stiffly.

The guard steps forward and gently pulls her out of our

embrace. She whips her head around and orders him to stand back.

She steps over to the sofa and waves a hand at the two chairs in front of her. "Please, sit. Obviously, this isn't the reunion I thought it to be. Why don't you tell me what this visit is about?" she suggests, her demeanor cold and formal compared to a second ago.

"I'd like to hear what happened the day my mother was murdered," I reply. "Before you tell me, I must warn you. I intend to get to the bottom of her murder and seek justice. If you murdered her, I'd prepare your estate now."

Her smile returns with my answer. "I can't explain how happy this makes me. I've wanted vengeance for her murder for a long time now. Unfortunately, your father is out of my reach," she retorts. She tilts her head. "Are you prepared to kill him? I'll answer every question you ask, but I need to know you'll do whatever is necessary to eliminate her murderer."

"I am," I promise darkly.

She examines my face for deception, but apparently, finds none. She leans forward and begins her story. "Your father sent a note requesting a visit with you. Given the contention between our two kingdoms, your mother decided to meet him in a neutral location in the dark Fae territory. She left with you and a couple of guards early that morning, but nobody returned." She grips the edge of the couch.

"When she didn't return the next day either, I sent my best tracker, along with more guards, to find everyone. They found her lying in the dirt amongst the fallen leaves, her head cut off." She closes her eyes and swallows. Her voice is low when she continues, "You were missing. They found evidence of your abduction, but the guards were never found.

"I sent a note requesting an audience with your father. When I arrived, to my relief, you were sitting on the floor, playing with your soldiers. He'd never even sent word you were safely with him. We'd been scouring the countryside for you. Obviously, he was there that day. When I demanded to know what happened to my sister, he laughed. Told me he wasn't a fool. He knew I'd killed her. I tried to explain I didn't have anything to do with it, but he insisted he had proof," she recounts.

"He told me to take one last look at you, because it would be the last time I'd see you. I went back home to give him time to calm down. The investigation continued, but my tracker couldn't find anything else. Your father refused all requests to talk. In a span of a few days, I lost two of the most important people in my life—your mother and you." A low sob escapes.

"He told me you killed her out of jealousy," I state calmly. "When he arrived at the location that day, he found her dead and me kneeling by her body, crying. There were no guards. When he searched for clues, he found something of yours in her hand, proving you were there when she died and likely killed her."

"I killed her?! For what? I loved her. I wouldn't have harmed a hair on her head," she screams, exploding to her feet. She paces back and forth while she spits out her rage. "She should never have gotten involved with your father. It was a bizarre affair from the beginning, and I could never understand it. They both attended the same event one evening, and she came home enamored with him. Thankfully, it was brief. She was finished with him before you were born, but she felt you deserved to know your father, so she continuously bent over backward, trying to make sure you spent time with him. He never deserved her, yet he couldn't keep away from her. He was obsessed. He killed her. I know he did. I just can't prove it." She stops ranting and turns to face me.

"His story is completely different. He believes you killed

her because you were jealous. She was in love with a powerful king, and you couldn't stand it. Your husband was only a distant relative of the dark Elven king at the time, and the chances of him becoming king were slim to none," I say, repeating the story he told to me. A thought occurs to me, but I decide to keep it to myself.

"I wasn't jealous of her. My husband might not have been king, but he was powerful," she retorts. "I swear on my life. I didn't kill her. I could never kill her. When you find the murderer, let me know. I've had enough conversation today." She motions to the guard to escort us out.

We stand, and I look down at the wrecked look on her face. Something doesn't add up here. I need to find the proof my father supposedly has that proves she's the killer. "Thank you for meeting with me. I promise, I'll let you know when I find out the truth," I tell her. Without another word, we walk out.

I follow Astor back to The Abbey. It's the one place we know is secure. When we enter the lobby, I swear I smell Arden, and I take a deep breath. It's been so long since I've seen her or spoken to her. With a sigh, I push it away for now.

"Well?" I ask him, needing to know the truth.

"She didn't kill her," he replies. "Everything she recounted about that day is the truth. She only told one lie. She was jealous of her sister." He scrutinizes me. "If your father is the murderer, are you truly prepared to kill him?"

My body sways. I was counting on her being the murderer. Could I kill my father? Guilt already weighs heavily on me. Can I take his throne and life? Where's the line here?

"I don't know. Let's get to the truth first and figure the rest out later. Do you mind extending your services? I can set something up soon," I ask, desperate to have the answers but now afraid of them too.

"If you'll do me one favor in return," he agrees. Pulling a

phone out of his pocket, he hands it to me. "It can't be traced. Use the app labeled with an A to text, not the designated one. When it asks you for a code, enter my name. All texts will be private and inaccessible to anyone else without the code, so don't give it to anyone."

Extending my hand, I take the lifeline he just offered—a way to text Arden without my father or anyone else's knowledge.

"Thank you," I say gruffly, my voice tight with emotion for the priceless gift.

"It's for her," he returns with a shrug. "She needs you. Stop ignoring her. None of us can stand by and watch it anymore. You need to hurry up and finish things with your father before you lose her." He claps me on the back. "Text me when you have the meeting with your father set up." Leaving me in the lobby, he strides out.

My eyes follow him, but I see someone entirely different than I used to see. The insecurity and cockiness have been replaced with an inner strength and confidence. She's changed him.

Gripping the phone, I immediately send her a text.

> Fallon: I miss you. Don't give up on me. Only reply to this text. It's safe.

> Arden: …

I wait several minutes, but she doesn't reply. Maybe it's already too late.

CHAPTER
TWENTY-ONE

I need more than "I miss you" from him. The text blurs, and I hastily wipe my tears away. He's had so many chances, but he's repeatedly made the same choice over and over. It's about time I make some decisions.

Demand to see him? Demand to know why? Tell him it's over? Ignore him? All of the above? I don't know what to do, so I do the only thing I can—I let out a short scream of frustration.

The door to my bedroom flies open, and Theron stands there with his sword drawn, his eyes darting from me to the corners of the room. Finding nothing, he tilts his head, and I give him a sheepish look.

"No intruders," I assure him. "Just me, screaming out my frustration." I don't tell him it's about Fallon. He takes on enough burdens without adding this one to it.

He eyes me warily. "I see. I'll let you get back to it. I'll be back in an hour to pick you up for the council meeting."

Gritting my teeth, I smile and nod. When he leaves, I flop down on my bed and stare at the text. My mind goes in circles, trying to figure out what to do next.

A knock penetrates the fog in my brain, and I glance at the door, then my phone. I can't believe an hour passed! Scrambling up, I check my hair in the mirror and frantically smooth it down, then turn side to side to make sure there aren't any stains on my clothes. The jeans and long-sleeved T-shirt are extremely casual, but I don't have time to change, so I just head out.

Since we took a portal last time, Theron switches it up and drives to Witchwood. I let Henry know we're arriving shortly and settle back to stare at the incredibly sexy Fae sitting next to me. He's always busy, running around taking care of everyone but himself.

"I miss you," I state huskily, knowing he will understand. My hand reaches over the console to find his. "Will you stay with me tonight?"

His violet eyes darken, and he smiles. "I'd love to."

The scenery flies by, and we talk about how the plan is going. "I sent a note to Cormal to request his assistance in investigating the dark Fae queen. He told me to fuck off," he repeats with a chuckle, unconcerned with the response. "I requested Lucifer's assistance. It will give him something to focus on while he waits for this war to begin. He agreed and will get his best spies on it."

I open my mouth, but he interrupts me before I can ask.

"Not Callyx. He's got a few others he can tap into for this mission," he assures me.

"Normally, I wouldn't care, but I'd like to separate my family from this one. I think the repercussions are going to be tremendous, and I don't want it to blow back on them," I confide in him. "Also, I don't want the findings to be tainted by the hope it's not Nyssa."

"I agree," he asserts. "Any luck on the stone?"

"The first attempt wasn't successful. Astor's working on finding the key," I tell him. "Regardless, we're asking the council to set a date for the vote. It should be an interesting meeting and the first step in figuring out whether we'll have one coven or two."

His thumb rubs my hand in comfort.

Witchwood appears, and I sigh. Nothing about this place feels good to me.

He pulls up to the entrance, and I wait for him to open my door. Taking his hand, I step out and into his body. For a second, I let him shelter me, but soon force myself to take a step back.

His eyes are assessing, and given the turbulence, I'm guessing he doesn't like what he sees. "Ready?"

"Yes," I reply, but I don't let go of his hand.

Instead of allowing him to escort me, I keep his hand in mine. Screw it. Caro can go to hell. We walk into Witchwood, but there's not a soul in the entryway.

When we enter the council room, the tension is palpable. I guess word has already reached the council. It was too much to hope Santiago and Katarina's queries would remain a secret. Judging by the number of witches here tonight, it's going to be contentious.

Theron squeezes my hand, then walks over to sit in a chair with his back to the wall. I don't blame him. Always keep your enemy in front of you.

Walking to the table, I sit beside Santiago. An is across the room, talking to Katarina.

"Looks like a tough crowd," I murmur. "We're only asking to set a date for the vote, not the actual vote."

"It's going to get worse before it gets better," he replies softly. "Some of the families I spoke to were unaware their relatives had relations with other supernaturals resulting in the addition of 'tainted' branches in their line. They immediately wanted them cut off."

"What is wrong with these people?" I exclaim. "A coven of one is looking better and better."

"Don't leave us with them," he states firmly, his face serious. "If you find a way, my line will follow you. We can always find more magic. Tolerance and equality are basic tenets, and we haven't had those in a while."

I study him, then shake my head. "I promise. My intentions will be transparent and loud." Caro bangs the gavel. "Here we go."

Not surprisingly, the first order of business is a request to cut a family member from the tree. "I'd like my granddaughter removed from our branch," states an elderly woman, her voice cool and steady. She essentially requested to cut them off from their magic like she would order lunch. They won't lose it overnight, but without access to the stone, their magic will fade. The witch sitting next to her cries out, and she tells her to hush or she'll cut her off too.

The witch glares at her and stands. "I formally request you cut my leaf off the tree too." She turns to the older witch. "My daughter and I stay or we both go."

"Until we have a vote on the acceptance of witches with mixed blood, the council will not allow any changes to the branches," I state firmly and loudly.

Caro's face turns ugly. "You don't have the power to make these decisions," she screeches. "If you would like to make a motion, please do so. The council will decide *together*."

She wants to follow the rules. How about we make this public? Let's see how far she's willing to go. I metaphorically crack my knuckles one by one.

"Before we can decide on whether to cut off one branch, we need to understand the impact to the coven's magic," I begin, and she nods with approval. "The full impact. The assessment requires us to document every witch with mixed blood so we can reliably inform the coven. For example, if a witch carried the magic for five bloodlines, the loss would impact five families." I glance at the tree. "It looks like every bloodline has at least a few cases. Can I get someone to document the names?"

Cassandra's the only witch with five bloodlines, which is why I used her as the example. Several heads swivel to the tree in puzzlement, but not Caro's. She knows. The crowd hums with conversation, and Santiago gives a low chuckle.

"Stop. Quiet!" she yells while banging her gavel. "We aren't set up to take on this task yet. We should wait until after the vote. After all, we don't know how it will impact us, if at all. The coven might vote in favor of accepting all witches." She sounds calm and logical, but her mouth twists a bit at the end, unable to hide her feelings. With a flick of her wrist, she bangs the gavel again. "I motion we set the date for the vote. How about three months from today?"

"I motion we set the date for the next council meeting in two weeks. This is impacting the entire coven, every branch, except for the MacAllisters, of course. Right now, there's only me, and I'm already a member. It's a conundrum. If the vote isn't in favor of accepting all witches, does that mean I'll no longer be a member? Something to consider." Caro's eyes glitter with glee, and I realize she's hoping for this exact scenario. "Anyone second my motion?"

Katarina, An, and Santiago vote in favor. With me, it brings us to four and the majority.

"The motion carries. The vote will be held in two weeks," Caro's voice rings out, and she bangs the gavel. "This concludes the council meeting. Have a good day."

My eyes meet the other three, and I want to flinch at the hope I see in their eyes, but instead, I throw my shoulders back and find my determination. "I'll see you in two weeks. Try to contact everyone before we meet and get their vote."

The hairs on the back of my neck tingle, and I glance behind me. Caro's standing there with a maniacal gleam in her eyes and a smile on her face. Henry is right—trouble is brewing. What is she up to?

Theron takes my hand and leads the way out of Witchwood.

Sighing in relief, I get in the car and let my shoulders drop. "I'm not sure I can save them from themselves. The MacAllisters were right to be concerned, and I understand why they hid the stone. It's time to shed the cloak of secrecy. Before we vote, I'm going to tell the MacAllister story and show them the stone."

The car flies out of the gates at an alarmingly fast speed.

"'It is not power that corrupts, but fear.'"

Theron's repeat of the quote from Aung San Suu Kyi gets to the heart of the issue—fear.

"It's just so frustrating—Watch out!" I shout when a wolf darts into the middle of the road.

Theron swerves, barely missing it.

"Fuck." He smashes his foot to the pedal. "We're going to be overrun in about five minutes. Can you open a portal back to the garage?" His hands tighten on the steering wheel, and he glances in the rearview mirror.

I glance out my window and see wolves everywhere. Scrambling, I cast the magic to open a portal to the garage about half a mile in front of us. My eyes shift to the wolves running beside us and back to the portal. "I can't prevent them from going through the portal with us, but we should come out at the entrance to the garage."

"The Abbey's barriers will prevent them from entering," he reassures me. "The stop is going to hurt. Brace yourself."

I tighten my seatbelt, straighten my body, and brace my feet on the floorboard. Several wolves accidentally hit the portal and run through, but as we near it, it suddenly disappears and pain shoots through my heart.

"What happened?" Theron yells. "Are you okay? Arden? Speak to me."

Unable to breathe for a second, I clutch my chest and frantically dive inside to search for my magic. It's not there. I hit a black wall where my witch magic should be, and I gasp, taking in a deep gulp of air. "It's gone. Or blocked. Someone took my witch magic." The only magic in me is a small green orb—my Elven magic.

A barrier appears in the road, and Theron swears. "Hang on," he shouts. Whipping the steering wheel around, the car turns sideways, and I watch the barrier coming closer and closer. He curses again, and I look over. The steering wheel is locked with magic. Someone wants my side to hit the barrier first.

Theron mutters a few words, and a thick sheet of ice appears. It curls up into a circle, then twists in the middle, and ends on the other side of the barrier. The car hits the ice, and like a roller coaster uses a rail, it follows the path Theron laid out and we land intact on the other side of the barrier.

CHAPTER

TWENTY-TWO

<u>ARDEN</u>

Theron and I both breathe a sigh of relief. Hitting the barrier would have done enough damage to incapacitate me, giving the wolves plenty of time to take my head and end my life. Theron's too.

"Are you okay?" Theron asks quietly, making no move to start the car. When he sees me nod, he motions out the windows. The wolves surround us on every side. "Is your magic back?"

"No," I reply. My brain's sifting through spells to figure it out. "Only one spell can block a witch's magic—a blood spell. The only enemy who's been close enough to touch me in the last few weeks is Caro. It must have happened at the last council meeting. I thought I felt a prick when she grabbed my arm, but neither of us saw any blood. She must have covered it

153

up. Add in the fact Henry saw her speaking with a wolf on her property, and the evidence starts piling up."

The car rocks violently, and the window next to me cracks. "We need to get out of this vehicle." Reaching back, he grabs a familiar suit of armor and tosses it at me. "It's mine, so it will be a little big, but it will protect you from their claws and teeth. Don't let them bite you. I refuse to share you with anyone else, especially a damn wolf."

Humor in the face of danger. Sexy. Maybe I'm officially losing it. I slip into the suit, grateful he thought to bring it. Without my magic, I'm more vulnerable than ever. After I get it on, I pull my sword out.

He leans over and checks every inch, tugging it into place and making sure it covers me completely, then kisses me hard.

"This is going to be rough, but help is coming." The back window shatters, and Theron throws a hand up, freezing the wolf in midair. "It's going to take a minute for them to get here, but we need to get out of this car before they trap us in it. I'll freeze the wolves nearest us. It will give us a brief barrier between us and the rest of the wolves. Your sword will do the rest. Ready?" Theron separates his sword into the two halves.

Calm settles over me, and my mind becomes laser sharp. I might not have faced such terrible odds in the past, but I know how to fight. "I'm ready."

He nods at the look in my eyes and raises his hand.

The wolves around the car freeze, and their frozen bodies block other wolves from getting closer, which gives us enough time to get out of the car. I open the car door, and it slams into the wolf on the other side, shattering it to pieces. Howls fill the night air.

Stepping out, I set my stance and swing my sword at any wolf trying to get past the barrier. A paw falls to the ground. A muzzle is next. Their blood splatters everywhere, but I don't let up.

The whistling sound of Theron's swords rotating through the air is music to my ears. A deep growl sounds to my left, and a wolf leaps over the barrier. I step forward and raise my sword, stabbing up into its chest, then dragging the tip toward the tail. He falls to the ground, split almost in two, and I chop his head off before he can recover. More howls pierce the air.

The air around us shimmers, and four portals open in front of the car. Daire, Valerian, and Astor step out. Puzzled, I watch the fourth, wondering who else is coming, and to my disbelief, I see Fallon and Garrett step out. The howling stops. Silence reigns. It's one thing to attack the two of us, but the wolves must sense they're not the only predators in this fight.

I hear a few whines, but a high-pitched howl comes from the hill above us, followed by a deeper one, and suddenly, the wolves are growling again.

Theron makes a hand signal, and Valerian changes into his dragon. Within seconds, he clears a path to Theron and me. Wolves are burned to ash or crushed beneath him. Astor holds off the wolves behind us, while Daire pulls Theron and me into the center of the road. My eyes meet Fallon's green gaze, and for a second, I can't breathe. It's been so long. I note every change in his face, then shift my sight to the enemy.

With the space we've gained, I can clearly see the number of wolves we're facing, and I lock my knees to stay upright. Maybe a hundred wolves to the seven of us. Howling again. Ready to attack. Not great odds, but it could be worse. Oh right, it is. My magic is blocked.

Daire directs Fallon and Garrett to the rear, Valerian to the left, Theron to the right, and he takes the front. Astor and I stay together in the middle, me with a sword and him with magic.

The fight begins.

Theron casts a circle of ice on the ground, then encases himself in ice. Wolves slide and scramble across the slick ground, only to realize their teeth and claws can't penetrate his armor of ice. If they make it that far. His swords flash so fast, they're a blur of silver. Limbs and fur fly.

Valerian roars. A large pack of wolves circle him, thinking their sheer numbers will take him down. Several try to clamp their teeth on his legs, but his thick scales easily protect his body. Ice, fire, and shadows rain down, hitting one wolf after another, and they fall. His feet and tail do the rest of the work, crushing them to pieces.

Daire's a blur. I've never even seen him move so fast. His sword swings and decapitates them one by one.

I glance to our rear and watch Fallon and Garrett fight back-to-back, their movements so graceful and synchronized, you know they've done this a million times. One feints left and the other right, before meeting back in the middle. Wolves lie at their feet.

Astor's shadows cover us, making it harder for the enemy to see their target. He flings spell after spell at the wolves surrounding us. When they fall, I step in and take their heads.

The ease with which the cadre fends off their attacks makes me realize the wolves have little battle experience. It could be due to their age, but their actions lack the coordination and attack formations of an established pack.

A jaw locks on my calf, but the teeth are unable to penetrate the suit. Relieved, I smile, slip the tip of my sword between its jaws, and slice backward, cutting off the top half of its head. Blood and brains gush out in a thick mess.

We're all fighting, but it's never-ending. Wave after wave attacks. Theron signals to Daire, and he glides closer to him. He points to me, and Daire nods.

"I'm not leaving unless we're all leaving," I yell defiantly.

A small golden wolf darts close, I swing my sword but miss. I track it to the side of the road, where a large dark grey wolf is waiting.

Glancing up, I assess the field and realize I'm seeing significantly fewer wolves. Instead of five deep around us, it's maybe three deep now. We keep fighting.

Astor keeps trying to open a portal to get us all out of here, but something or someone keeps shutting them down. There must be another magic user close by. My eyes search the hills above us, but I only find wolves.

Fallon shouts. Dread fills me, but I can't turn and look at him. I lean in close to the wolf I'm fighting and jab his throat hard with my elbow, trying to break the bones in his neck, but it's too protected. The wolf coughs a few times, but never lets up in its attack.

It rears back, preparing to leap at me, but movement above its head catches my eye. Another wolf is flying toward its back, and I duck and roll to get out of the way. The two collide, but it's the ball of witchfire that kills them, the one that came from behind me.

Jumping to my feet, I spin around, but I don't have to search for the witch. She's standing right in front of me. Cassandra. Sheer rage fills every atom of my body, and I stalk forward, determined to end this brat's life.

Another ball of fire flies from her hand, and I jump sideways. It catches on the armor and dissipates. Hearing a scream of outrage, I smile, raise my sword and charge. It's my turn.

A flash of light surrounds her, and Cassandra's gone. A small golden wolf stands in her place, baring its teeth until it runs off. She's a wolf. That's why the branch on the tree was darker, her leaf more defined. It's probably why Caro has enough power for a blood spell to block my magic. Cassandra's mixed blood is giving her more power.

"She will never let you back in the coven," I yell, spinning around in a circle. "You're only a tool she's using to take down her real enemy—me. When are you going to realize I'm your best chance at keeping your witch magic? In two weeks, the coven is going to vote, and right now, we're losing. I guess it doesn't matter. Without me, the coven's source of magic will die anyway. Nobody will have witch magic when that happens."

"You're lying," a voice calls out from the dark. "If I kill you, she promised to let me come back home. The coven will always take me back."

"What?" a dark voice asks gruffly. "I thought she killed your mother?"

I hear a low murmur of voices, but I can't make out what they're saying. The black wolf nearby launches itself at me, and I raise my sword to meet it. At the last minute, it twists and lands behind me. I turn around to face it.

The huge beast paces back and forth, looking for an opening, but I don't give it one. The wolf feints to my left, but I stay centered until it leaps forward, then I pivot and swing my sword. The tip catches on its neck and cuts a thin line across it. Blood seeps from the cut, and I grimace. It looks like the wolf is wearing a bloody smile around its neck.

Fallon shouts, but I ignore it. The wolf chuffs. Its yellow eyes gleam with cunning intelligence, and I realize he's setting a trap. Backing away from him, so I can assess my surroundings and the potential threat, I see Fallon barreling toward me. The wolf steps forward, and I switch my eyes back to it.

Fallon launches his body toward me, but the wolf changes course and leaps to take him down. Horrified, I realize the wolf is going to meet Fallon in mid-flight. Without thinking, I flip my sword up, catch the pommel, and, with a flick of my wrist, throw it as hard as I can toward the wolf. It works, spearing its body and stopping its momentum. It crashes to the ground.

A long howl startles me, and I look over to find a huge dark grey wolf staring at the wolf on the ground. At the same time, a human scream of rage and fear comes from behind me.

Keeping my eyes on the massive beast, I slide over to grab the sword from the wolf. Yanking it out, I turn to face the bigger threat—Cassandra.

She's not looking at me, though. Her eyes are fixed on Fallon, who's lying on the ground. Garrett's kneeling beside him, but wolves are circling them, so he can't check on him.

Stumbling over, I drop to my knees beside Fallon and roll him over. A crater the size of a fireball covers his chest. Holding my hands out, I dimly realize I don't have the power to heal him right now.

I scream, "Fallon!" He doesn't stir. Fear streams through my blood. "What the hell is wrong with you?! You don't show up or text me for weeks, but now you're going to die for me? I don't think so."

Raising my head, I frantically search for Daire and finally find him sneaking up behind Cassandra. A second Cassandra appears five feet to the left of the original, an illusion courtesy of Theron. The real Cassandra disappears behind Astor's shadows, and I hear a muffled scream.

Looks like the cadre is going to end this battle a different way.

I return my attention to Fallon. "Damn it, Fallon. Don't you dare die. Do you hear me?" A sob escapes, and my hands are shaking with fear and anger. Think. *What are the tools available to you?* I hear Vargas whisper in my head. Sword. Garrett. Elven magic.

He cups my cheek with his hand. I grab it and place it on

my heart. Asking mother nature for assistance, I coax a thread of green power toward Fallon's hand. Nothing happens.

"Fallon, listen to me. You need to pull the power from me. Do you hear me? I can't do it. Remember when we were at the pond?" He smiles and mumbles something. "Come on. You know how to recognize my power, right?"

He is drifting into unconsciousness. "If you don't wake up right now and pull on my power, I'm going to die! Garrett's going to die! The cadre's going to die! Damnit. Do it now!" I scream.

Something I say punches through the fog in his brain, because a small spiral of green starts flowing steadily from me to him. It's enough to keep him from going under, but not enough to heal him. My Elven power is the equivalent of a small child.

The air turns cold. I ignore it.

Checking to see if I can pull Garrett away from the fight, I turn my head and see every single wolf around us is frozen.

Daire suddenly roars, "Surrender or I'll cut off her head!"

A deep howl pierces the air. The dark grey wolf transforms into a startlingly handsome young man. "Don't! I surrender," he shouts, his hands up to stop Daire.

"Garrett, Fallon needs your magic to heal," I call out.

Once he's sure we're safe, he leans over Fallon and sends his Elven magic into him. The hole closes about halfway, and Garrett's face turns grey. He tries to pull back, but Fallon's magic refuses to let go.

"Fallon, stop. You're going to take all the magic and his life force. Stop!" I shout, but it's like he can't hear me.

I tug on Garrett's shoulders, but the magic has locked them together. Garrett slumps to the ground. I try to stop the flow with my hands, but it goes right through them.

"Fallon, stop. Please stop. You're killing Garrett." I shake his shoulders, crying. Grabbing his face, I turn it to me and plead with him to stop. I drop my forehead to his and watch tears roll from my face to his. Remembering the kiss at the pond, I drop my lips to his and try to pull the magic into me. The magic doesn't flow, but somehow, the kiss does what all my shouting couldn't do. Fallon's magic releases Garrett.

His lips take over, capturing mine in a deep kiss filled with longing and regret, and I can't help but kiss him back, savoring the life flowing through him. All those weeks of nothing, he'd vanished, leaving me with a huge void. For a microsecond, it doesn't matter, muted by his close call with death, and I shut out the world to accept this moment, this kiss.

I hear Daire call my name, so I place my hand on Fallon's shoulder and pull back. His cheeks are flushed with color, and even though the hole in his chest is still there, it's smaller. I help him sit up.

"Check on Garrett," I tell him.

Standing up, I take a few steps back from him, and look around the battlefield.

Daire stands behind Cassandra with his sword still at her throat. Astor's arm is around Theron, propping him up, and Valerian is standing behind the young man who cried out to save Cassandra's life.

Walking over, I draw the Killian blade and press it against her heart. My blood pounds with rage, and I stare at her while I fight the temptation to end her life. I push the tip of the dagger into her chest and watch her blood flow. Her magic sparks, and Daire pulls the sword tighter around her neck.

"Stop, please. She's my mate," the fierce young man behind me shouts, pleading for her life.

Cassandra glares at him, then me.

She doesn't know it, but he just saved her life. "I'm going to ask you a few questions, and if I don't like the answers or I don't hear the truth, I'm going to carve my initials all—" I point the knife at her cheek— "over— " I drag the knife across her nose to the other cheek— "your face. Then, I'll start again with your body. Don't worry, I might not have access to my magic, but Astor can cast a blood spell to make my artwork permanent. Shall we begin?"

She shrugs nonchalantly.

I smile. "You're so fucking predictable, Cassandra. Let's have some fun, shall we?" I point my knife to the young man behind me. "Is he your mate?"

"No," she sneers, her lip curled with disgust. "Do you think I'd mate with a wolf?" Her eyes swing to the man when he bellows with rage.

"Lie," Astor's voice rings out in the night air.

Cassandra's eyes widen.

"Oh right, I forgot to tell you. Astor has a truth rune," I drawl. Grasping the blade in my fingers, I put the tip to her cheek.

"Wait!" she shouts. "Yes, he's my mate."

Ignoring her, I cut an A into her cheek, then a K. She screams and cries the whole time. Tapping her mouth with the knife, I bring her attention back to me.

"Please answer the questions truthfully the first time I ask," I instruct her. "Next question. Did your mother, Caro, cast a spell on me to block my magic?"

"No," she states firmly.

I glance at Astor who nods.

"Did you cast a blood spell on me to block my magic?" I question her.

"Yes," she spits out, looking defiantly at me.

Surprisingly, I'm beginning to admire Cassandra's gutsy, brash attitude.

"Did you get the blood and the spell from Caro?" I ask,

sliding the knife across her throat. A thin trail of blood wells up. Oops.

She presses her mouth together and glances at the young man.

"Sorry, silence isn't an answer. Either you answer the question, or I'm going to move to your other cheek," I tell her. When she doesn't say anything, I move to her other cheek and carve my initials. "It's stupid of you not to answer the question. When we go in front of the coven, they'll simply put a truth spell on you, and they will know Caro was involved in this attack."

"The council will never allow it," she interjects, grinding her teeth against the pain of my knife.

"Wow, you have been gone a long time. It looks like your sweet mother forgot to tell you all the important news," I muse.

Her gaze flicks to me, and I see confusion.

"Let's see. I'm on the council. Your father is off the council. We replaced him with An, the true leader of bloodline four. Right now, Santiago, An, Katarina, and I have an alliance, which means...yep, that's right—we have the majority. I can guarantee you will be given a truth serum. Along with your mother. You should go to more council meetings. Big news is coming, but I really don't want to ruin the surprise."

Striding over to the young man, I study him. He looks at Cassandra with love, possessiveness, and a hint of anger.

"Let's play the same game, shall we?" I tap my knife on his cheek, and a low growl rumbles through his chest.

Valerian jerks him up, and his amber eyes narrow into slits.

"Let's introduce ourselves first, shall we? I see you've met my mate," I say, waving a hand toward Valerian. "Valerian, King of Dragons." The young man swallows. I point to Daire. "Daire, Prince of the Underworld and First Vampire." I swing to

Theron. "Theron, Fae Lord of Summer and Winter." I point to Astor. "Astor, warlock and incubus."

Finally, I wave a hand to Fallon and Garrett, whose eyes are thankfully open again. "Fallon, Prince of the Light Elves, and his commander, Garrett. Most of the world knows them as the Imperium Cadre." I smile when fear sparks in his eyes. "I'm Arden. Witch, dark elf, and very pissed off." I raise my eyebrows and wait.

"Grady, Alpha of the Blood Moon Pack," he states clearly, but says nothing else. His eyes dart from one member of the cadre to the next.

"Now we have the pleasantries out of the way, I have a question for you. Rules are the same. Truth only," I say in a cool voice. "Tell me why you're angry with Cassandra." I tap the knife in the palm of my hand. When he hesitates, I remind him of the consequences. "It would suck if your mate had to look at my initials on your face for the rest of your lives."

He reluctantly gives me his answer. "She told me you killed her mother. We attacked you to avenge her death."

"I see. Obviously, Cassandra lied. Maybe she lied about one thing, maybe she lied about everything. Here comes the good news..." I pause dramatically, then glance at Daire and raise an eyebrow. "You have access to your father's dungeons, right?"

A dark smile graces his lips.

I turn back to Grady. "We're going to give you and Cassandra some quality couple time to discuss all her lies. You'll share a cell in Lucifer's dungeons. By the way, it nullifies your magic, so you won't be able to cast any spells and the bars of made of silver." Both Cassandra and the young man blanch. "Before you go, Cassandra, I need you to unblock my magic."

"The spell will wear off in a couple of hours," she confesses. "I only had a drop of your blood to cast the spell."

"Lovely," I say dryly.

It's a good thing she'll be out of my reach for those hours, or I'd be tempted to continue our little game. Who knows what I'd learn?

"Wait. What are you going to do with my pack?" Grady's voice is gruff with worry.

"I'm not sure. You're responsible for their lives, and yet you didn't even do the due diligence to investigate Cassandra's claims. You led your entire pack into war without an ounce of knowledge about your enemy. How can you call yourself alpha? Don't they deserve better? Shouldn't there be consequences? What about the wolves who are already dead? What will you say to their families?" I want to brand these questions into his soul. "I'll come visit you in a week and see if the counseling session worked." I step back, blocking out the noise of their protests.

Daire and Valerian escort the two of them through a portal and return a couple of minutes later.

"After spending a week in those dungeons, they'll tell you anything you want to hear," Daire states coolly. He yanks me into his arms and takes a deep breath.

Valerian leans down and gives me a kiss, but surprisingly, he leaves me in Daire's arms.

Astor scrutinizes every inch of me, then winks. "Carving your initials... That was dark. I liked it." He looks around the battle. "Such a waste."

Theron sways, and I rush over to him. "I'm guessing by the sheer volume of ice surrounding us, you're in burnout?"

When he doesn't answer, I turn to Astor. "What do we do?"

"The best place to replenish his strength is Winter," Astor explains. "The land will heal him within a day or so. Without it, it could take a couple weeks. He expended a tremendous amount of power."

We don't know what will hit us within the next week or

two, and we need him to be at full strength. "Let's take him to Winter."

Astor shakes his head. "I can't create a portal to Winter. I've never been, and I don't have access."

"Do we need to contact the dark Fae king?" I ask.

Can we just call him up? I pull out my phone to call Solandis to ask for advice when Fallon speaks up.

"I have access," he informs me. Easing up to his knees, he puts one foot on the ground, then another, and slowly stands. I watch beads of sweat break out on his forehead.

"Who's going to help you and Garrett get home?" I question him. If he opens a portal, the little magic we gave him will be depleted.

Valerian pipes up. "I will. Then I'll come back here to help Daire and Astor clean this up. We'll put the wolves in the field to thaw out."

I smile. He knew I wouldn't advocate killing them. They're pawns in this fight for power.

After giving Astor, Daire, and Valerian a kiss, I help Astor transfer Theron to me. It takes Fallon a few minutes to open the portal to Winter. My eyes catch his, and I close my eyes at the fierce emotion shining in them. "Goodbye."

The portal opens, and a blast of cold air greets us. I step into the unknown with an unconscious Theron.

CHAPTER
TWENTY-THREE

<u>ARDEN</u>

Within seconds of our entry, we're surrounded by an army of hard warriors, swords and magic pointed directly at us. Shifting Theron's weight, I gently ease his head back so they can see his face. I roll my eyes when none of them move. Damn Theron for training his men so well.

"Theron needs a healer," I announce loudly. "Can one of you lovely Fae go fetch one?"

Exhausted and running on empty, I literally want to break down and scream or cry. It's a toss-up. I take a deep breath, but before I can let loose, a beautiful blonde lady with brown eyes appears. "Are you the healer?"

A derisive laugh answers my question. "Hardly," she

167

sneers. "It's Lord Theron," she confirms to the men around us. "Give him to us and be on your way."

I raise an eyebrow. "I'm not giving Theron to anyone but a healer."

She gives an exasperated sigh. "You do not rule this land nor these men. I'm his mother, Lady Winter. He'll be safe in my hands. Give him to me."

When she steps forward, I greet her with the Killian blade. "His mother? The one who sent an assassin after him? An assassin with a Killian blade guaranteed to eliminate her Fae son? Kind of like this one?" I spit out. "Don't touch him."

A low murmur spreads through the soldiers. I forget the power the Killian blade has over the Fae. It's the only weapon designed to kill them.

Her face whitens, and she presses a hand against her throat. "Lies," she states loudly. "I don't know who you are, but accusations against me will get you killed." She motions to the soldiers. "Take Lord Theron to the healer and kill her."

Ignoring his mother, I point the blade at the nearest soldier. "I want to speak to Lord Theron's commander," I demand loudly.

"I'm his commander," a smooth voice calls out. A tall Fae with dark hair steps forward.

I glance at his face. "No, you're not. Someone go get the commander who led Theron's army in the Underworld battle," I clarify. "And get the damn healer."

He confers with his men, and one takes off in a run. "How did you know?"

"Obviously I was there," I respond sarcastically. "Is the healer on their way?"

"I'm here," a voice calls from the back of the crowd. A beautiful, dark-haired woman steps forward with a massive soldier by her side. "What happened?" She maneuvers around the soldier and rushes toward Theron. The soldier quickly steps up behind her and glares at me.

Protective male. Got it. "We were in a battle. He has severe burnout."

She runs her glowing hands over him. Instead of gold like mine, a blinding white light surrounds hers. When she passes over various parts of his body, she mumbles notes to herself. "It's a good thing you brought him straight here." She motions to several Fae standing to the side. "Let's get him to the infirmary where I'll be better equipped to help him."

Sliding carefully around me, they put him on a stretcher, but when I go to follow, I'm blocked by the soldiers and his mother.

"Is the commander on his way?" I ask the soldier to my right. "Or did you lie to me?"

"Fae don't lie," he replies with a smile.

"You never said the commander was on his way, ergo no lie," I retort. "My name is Arden. My guardians are the Princess of the Light Fae and Vargas Karth. One of my mates is Valerian, King of Dragons. I'm also a member of Lucifer's court. Now, have I given you enough notable names, or does this need to get ugly?"

"Stand down," a cold voice orders the soldiers.

They immediately create a path for the tall blond Fae striding angrily toward me.

"I heard you...requested my presence? I'm Commander Daevyn." Hard blue eyes stare down at me.

"We didn't get a chance to meet during the Underworld battle. I'm Arden." I smile and wait.

He stiffens, and a tiny quirk appears in his eyebrow. If I weren't watching for it, I'd have missed it. With a short bow, he extends his arm, but I shake my head.

"I prefer to have my hands free," I say, refusing his arm.

Assessing my answer, he dips his chin and turns with almost military precision to face the same direction the healer took Theron.

Nails dig into my arm, and I whip the blade up to her throat.

"Don't ever touch me," I warn her. "By the way, Theron knows. Solandis told him." I leave her with the bomb I just dropped at her feet and follow the commander to the infirmary.

A witch walking with the commander through the halls of Theron's ancestral home makes everyone stop and stare. He ignores them, so I do too.

It's a long walk, almost to the back of the...castle? I couldn't tell when I arrived, but it's massive. The inlaid marble floors are beautiful, with intricate medallions at every intersection. In white and grey, they certainly fit the winter theme. Luxurious fabrics and finishes indicate great wealth, but everywhere I look, it feels subdued and old-fashioned. It's hard for me to reconcile the Theron I know with this home.

WHEN WE REACH THE INFIRMARY, Theron isn't there. Apparently, after stabilizing him, the healer decided his bed would be the best place to recuperate. So the commander escorts me to Theron's room, where we find him lying in a massive four-poster bed while the healer treats him.

Rushing forward, I fail to see the two soldiers standing guard at the foot of his bed. They automatically move to intercept me, and I respond quickly by putting them down.

Stepping up to the bed, I realize nobody is moving. It takes me a second to realize why, and I want to crawl under the bed in embarrassment.

"Sorry," I say to everyone in the room, including the commander. "I'm kind of on high alert right now. I…" I blow the hair out of my face. "I'm sorry. It might be best if you kept your men out of here until Theron's awake."

The commander gives me an inscrutable look and calls for the soldiers in the hall to help remove the two unconscious men. With a short bow, he agrees to keep the soldiers at the door and leaves me with Theron.

The healer finishes another treatment, and I move a chair closer to the bed so I can be near him.

I stare at him. It's the most peaceful I've seen him outside of our garden. He's always running around and taking care of everyone and everything, so it's startling to see him so still. Unnerving too. "This isn't quite what I had in mind when I asked you stay the night with me."

He's my rock and my North Star. I don't know how I lived before him. He's the one I search for when I'm looking for balance or a way forward. Needing to feel him, reassure myself he's alive, I lace my fingers through his and wait.

My phone pings, and I pull it out to see messages from everyone. Relieved to see it's working, I send them all an update on Theron, along with a personal message for each of them. Except Fallon. I only send him an update on Theron.

I still can't believe he showed up to fight. All he's done is reject me for weeks. Then he dives in front of a ball of witchfire to save my life? I'm getting whiplash from the sudden waterfall of messages and mixed signals. And that kiss. Goddess, it felt good. I wish it hadn't, though.

My relationship with each of the others is evolving, growing deeper and more permanent, but the window for Fallon and me feels like it's closing. The kiss ignited the tiniest flame of hope that we can find our way back to each other, but part of me wants to smother it to stop all the pain.

A knock on the door brings me out of my dark thoughts. "Come in," I call out.

The door opens, and a tall, striking Fae saunters into the room. With his brown eyes and blond hair, he seems familiar, but I know we haven't met. He gives me a haughty look and proceeds toward the bed. He stares down at Theron, then glances at our clasped hands.

"What is your relationship?" he asks coolly, his brown eyes fixed on me, waiting for something besides my answer.

"I'm Arden," I say, introducing myself without answering his question. It's none of his damn business.

"I don't recall asking your name," he responds with an air of boredom.

"You didn't, but the Princess of the Light Fae raised me with manners," I retort. Turning away, I move my eyes back to Theron. "Did you need something, or did you come here just to be rude?" I dart my eyes to his and arch an eyebrow.

The air around us drops twenty degrees, but not a flicker of expression crosses his face. With one last look at Theron, he turns and walks out the door.

The healer comes and goes a few more times, then bids me good night. Relieved, I grab a blanket and a pillow and make myself more comfortable. I'm so exhausted, I can't even think straight anymore. The roaring fire lulls me to sleep.

THE LOW MURMUR of voices wakes me, and I realize it's morning. Smiling at the healer and the woman with her, I excuse myself to take care of business. When I get back, I find a tray of food and dive into it.

My body buzzes with power this morning, and I'm so relieved, I could cry. My witch magic is back. Searching inside, I realize both my witch magic and my Elven magic are fully restored. I pick up my phone to text everyone the good news, but it's not working. Fae magic must be interfering with it today. I put it on the table.

My eyes dart around the room, and I give in to the temptation to snoop. Unfortunately, it doesn't take long. Everywhere I look, the immaculate order to everything assures me it's his room, but it lacks anything personal. It makes me wonder how long it's been since he visited. I finally spot a few books and bring them over to my chair.

"Well, we have three options—*Fae Inventions*, *Shifter Genus and Species*, or *Agricultural Finance*." I pause dramatically. "Ok, I'll choose. *Fae Inventions* for the win." Grabbing the blanket and pillow from the previous night, I make myself comfy.

I flip through the book, reading some parts to Theron and skipping others. "Did you know the Fae claim to have invented the windmill? And the loom?"

Some of the inventions are beyond my understanding of science, but I bet Theron and Astor consume this type of knowledge. "Ooh, here's a good one. The Fae are helping humans develop a device to create electricity from thin air. Literally."

The hairs stand up on the back of my neck, and I slide the Killian dagger from its holder on my thigh. "Don't stand behind me. It could get you killed," I caution the Fae behind me. "Back for more scintillating conversation?"

The blond from yesterday slides into view. The sneer on his face disappears when he sees the Killian blade in my hand. Interest gleams in his eyes. "Where did you get it?"

I shrug. "Hard to tell. They all look alike. This one could have come from the chest of my mother," I speculate. "Or the demon who tried to assassinate me." I give him a hard stare. "You know, it could be the same one your mother handed the assassin she paid to kill Theron."

My eyes are glued to his, waiting for a reaction, but ironically, it comes from somewhere else. The tap of a single finger against his thigh—a trait he shares with his brother. "Go ask her. Theron knows."

His eyes flick to Theron, and I tense. There's something in his eyes when he looks at Theron, but I can't read the emotion.

"Tell him...Oryn would like to speak with him when he wakes." He turns and strides out with a lot more noise than he entered.

I can't really tell if he's a good guy or not, but there's something bubbling under the surface. I sit there speculating for a while. It must go both ways. Theron never even mentioned a brother. It was a wild guess on my part.

Dinner arrives when I'm in the restroom, and shortly after I finish eating, I fall into a light sleep, wanting to be semi-alert if someone enters the room again.

CHAPTER
TWENTY-FOUR

<u>THERON</u>

My veins are bursting with power when I wake. My hand automatically reaches for my phone on the nightstand, but when I don't find it, I open my eyes. Instead of the contemporary furnishings in my room at The Abbey, I'm met with old-fashioned but familiar velvets and silks. Why am I in Winter?

A chair sits close to the bed with a pillow and blanket on it. Have I been sick? Fallon is the only one with access to Winter. Did something happen? Where's Arden? Where's my damn phone?

I throw back the covers and sit up. Dizziness hits me, and I pause on the edge of the bed to let it subside. The bathroom door across from me opens, and Arden appears, stretching and yawning.

I examine her from head to toe, cataloging every detail, and my anger surfaces with what I find. There are dark circles under her eyes, her body is stiff with tension, and her hand hovers over the Killian blade. What the hell has been going on?

"Arden," I call out softly, not wanting to startle her. "What are we doing in Winter?"

Her green eyes light up, and she hurries over to me. Sweeping my hair back, she studies me like I studied her.

"You look good," she tells me. "How are you feeling? Sore? Do you have a headache? I have my powers back, so I can heal you or I can call Alix?"

When she mentions having her powers back, I begin to recall pieces from the battle. "I don't remember anything after I cast my power the last time. I assume I went into burnout?" It's the only reason I'd come to Winter outside of the strict schedule I'd set up. Tired of looking up, I grasp her hand and try to pull her down beside me, but she shakes her head.

"Get back into bed, and I'll answer your questions," she orders me.

I point to the bathroom. "I'll be back in a second," I murmur.

"Do you need some help?" she asks anxiously.

"Are you volunteering to pull down my underwear?" I tease her.

She rolls her eyes.

I laugh. "I'm fine. Wait here."

I stand slowly, but besides the sore muscles and brief dizziness, I'm feeling excellent. Until I get a whiff of myself.

"I feel amazing," I reassure her. "Maybe I should grab a shower while I'm in there?"

She frowns. "You were completely unconscious for two days," she reveals. "I'm not sure if you should be showering alone. I'll come with you."

"I've got a better idea," I say. "Wait here, I'll be back in a minute."

A few minutes later, I grab a few essentials and head back to the bedroom. When I near the chair, I see her slip the Killian blade into her hand, but when she sees my face, she relaxes and quickly sheaths it. I pause to consider the implications of what I just witnessed and decide I don't like any of them.

Grasping her hand, I pull her out of the chair and open the door. Two guards immediately step in front of me. Shocked, I stop. "Who gave you orders to stand at my door?"

"I didn't like them in the bedroom, so I asked the commander to station them outside the door," Arden admits.

"I see." I'm beginning to get a picture of the potential difficulties she might have faced with me unconscious. "You're dismissed. Tell your commander I'll speak to him later."

Hurrying away, I tug her down the stairs to a hidden door. Once inside, we follow the tight, winding staircase down a few levels. Her hand squeezes mine, and I realize she's uneasy with the darkness. "I've traveled this path so many times, it's automatic. We're almost there."

At the end, I light the nearest sconce, and the flame leaps from one to the other until the entire cave is illuminated.

She gasps at the sight. Turning in a circle, she gazes up at the sparkling ceiling, then steps forward to gaze down at the steaming water.

"It's beautiful," she exclaims. "Perfect for your sore muscles, and mine too. The chair isn't the most comfortable bed." She smiles ruefully.

Putting the towels and robes on the table beside the water, I undress us both, then lead her into the hot spring.

We both groan when we feel the water close around us, and I stand there holding her for a second, letting the heat penetrate our muscles. I step back and grab the soap, but before I can use it, she takes it from me.

"Let me take care of you for a change," she murmurs.

When she has a good lather, she washes and massages each of my muscles, taking the time to get all the knots out. Any lingering soreness vanishes under her careful ministrations. She even washes my hair several times until all the dirt is out. A smile lingers on her face the whole time as if she's enjoying it.

"Take your time and rinse off," she suggests. "I'm going to wash too."

Instead of following her suggestion, I swiftly rinse off and sit on a submerged ledge to watch her. Unlike me, she finishes quickly, but I'm rewarded when she raises her arms to wash her hair. Her beautiful breasts thrust forward, and I watch the water bead and roll down the valley between them, over her nipples and down the sides.

"Goddess, you're beautiful."

A blush stains her cheeks, and she ducks from view for a second to rinse, but when she rises, the water streams down again.

Wading over, she motions for me to get up, then sits down on the ledge and scoots back.

"Come here," she demands huskily.

When I sit in front of her, she pulls until I'm leaning back into her, then wraps her body around mine.

"Are you comfortable?" I ask, cautiously leaning back. This is certainly new.

Her lips drop to my shoulder, and her hands rub up and down my chest. "I'm perfect now that I know you're okay. I've been worried about you."

"Tell me everything. What happened at the end?"

I listen intently while she summarizes the end of the battle.

Several times, she glosses over the details, and I can't help but wonder why. I feel the undercurrents beneath her words, but without seeing her face, it's hard for me to figure out the reason.

My fingers slide between hers, needing to connect. "Tell me what happened when we arrived in Winter," I demand softly. "I know it couldn't have been easy with me unconscious. I was angry Fallon didn't come with you, but I understand now he couldn't."

"Your soldiers are extremely well trained. They didn't budge an inch until Lady Winter confirmed it was you," she remarks lightly. "It took a few minutes for them to realize I wasn't dropping you off, nor was I leaving your side. I remembered the commander from the Underworld battle, so I demanded to see him. When I mentioned my name, he escorted me to your room. I've been there ever since."

"I see." I reflect for a second on her words. It's a good thing I told Daevyn to add Arden to his protection detail after the battle. It's also time I dealt with my mother. "What happened with the soldiers?"

"Honestly, I didn't realize two of them were guarding your bed. When I stepped forward to see you, they startled me, so I asked the commander to have them stationed outside the room," she says with laughter in her voice.

"Startled, huh?" I chuckle, having a pretty good idea of what happened. "Anything else I should know?"

"I might have blurted out to everyone about Lady Winter's attempt to have you assassinated. I also told her you knew she was behind it," she says quietly. "I threatened her with the Killian blade. Your brother, Oryn, too."

Turning around, I pick her up and sit back down with her in my lap. Staring into her green eyes, I let her see how angry I am she had to go through all of them. "I'm sorry you had to deal with her, and I couldn't care less if you threaten her. She deserved it. It's past time I took care of the problem, but it hasn't been a priority until now. Tell me about Oryn."

Some of the tension eases from her body. "I'm sorry. I said it in front of your soldiers, so they wouldn't side with her, but it should have been a private matter." She sighs. "As for Oryn, he didn't really *do* anything, yet I felt uneasy every time he entered the room." A line appears between her eyebrows, and I reach up to smooth it out.

Relieved I don't have to kill my brother, I nod in understanding. "Oryn is complicated. We used to be close, but as you know, I went off the rails for a while. He grew up. Our mother filled him with grandiose ideas of becoming Lord Winter, and when it didn't happen, he became lost." I tell her, using four short sentences to explain the centuries of friction between us. "It's time he left the nest, but I don't know what to do with him."

"Do you think he'd make a good spy?" she asks suddenly.

Tilting my head, I consider the question. "I'm not sure I'd trust him to not betray us," I reply truthfully.

"Assign him to the court. Tell him it would benefit Winter to have someone in front of the king and queen as a reminder of your allegiance and power," she recommends. "It's not a lie. He needs a purpose and a reason to leave Winter. He might even meet someone and fall in love."

I mull it over and find very few potential pitfalls. "I'll inform him tomorrow." Reaching up to cup the back of her neck, I pull her forward and capture her lips with mine, diving into her sweetness over and over to show my appreciation. I drag my lips from hers, but I don't move away. "Thank you for taking care of me. I know it wasn't easy."

"The healer did all the work. I just made sure she had room to do her job," she says lightly.

"Mmm..." I say nothing in return, since I already have a plan to make sure it doesn't happen again.

Leaning her back, I cup water in my hand and pour it over her chest. This time, my mouth follows the stream, licking the sweet valley between her breasts, then gliding up the soft curve to her nipple.

Curling my tongue around the peak until it tightens, I pull it into my mouth and suck until she cries out. I replace my mouth with my hand and move over to the other one to give it the same attention. She spears her fingers through my hair to hold me in place, while she begs me to continue.

Grabbing her hands, I kiss them and hold them out to her sides. "Float on your back."

When she does, I push her out in front of me and use a bit of power to keep her afloat. I lean over and lick a long line straight down to her slick folds. Sinking down in the water, I use my considerable focus on making sure she knows how very, very thankful I am.

She tastes like strawberries—sweet and juicy. Hearing the sounds falling from her lips, I know she's close.

"So sweet. I love hearing your cries," I rasp and double up my efforts until she falls apart in front of me.

Standing, I look down to see her spread out on top of the water, a flush covering her body, and a surge of possessiveness washes over me. It's time the cadre started eliminating the threats surrounding her. I grip her hips and thrust into her. Her velvet heat squeezes tightly around me, and I groan. With all the power and resources we've accumulated over the years, not to mention the favors... A dark laugh escapes me. We protect our own.

I thrust hard and deep, wanting her to feel every inch of me. My fingers find her slick nub and rapidly stroke. When she falls apart again, back arching and body milking mine, her cries of pleasure echoing in the cavern, I claim her.

Waiting until the last wave stops, I lean over, flick her nipple with my tongue, and slowly slide in and out.

"We're just getting started, love." Truer words have never been spoken. The world will burn before I give her up.

CHAPTER
TWENTY-FIVE

<u>ARDEN</u>

With a smile, I reach out to drag Theron closer and find nothing but cool sheets and air. I sigh in disappointment. No doubt he's been up for hours checking off his to-do list. Rolling over, I stretch and feel a twinge, and it makes me smile.

Yesterday felt like a moment out of time. After spending hours in the hot springs, Theron and I rode horses and toured his land. Filled with snow and ice, I expected it to be harsh and unwelcoming, but the wintery landscape made everything feel crisp and new, untouched by the outside world. To me, it was magical. Theron insisted it was dangerous, filled with beautifully toxic plants and shaggy beasts hungry for anything that moves.

When the cold finally permeated through the hundreds of layers of clothing I was wearing, he took me to a pub in the nearby village. After a bowl of stew and homemade bread, I watched while he spoke and laughed with the villagers. It was enlightening to see how comfortable he felt in the humble surroundings and how his people looked at him. It's different here. The staff at The Abbey respect him, but the people of Winter care deeply for him.

When we returned to his room, I made us a nest by the fire and explored every inch of him. My tongue and lips the instruments of torture and pleasure, I tasted and sucked until he surrendered, then I sank down on him and stared into his eyes, wordlessly telling him how I felt, while I drove us both over the edge.

The door opening startles me. I watch him stride quickly over to the desk in the corner and grab a black ledger from the drawer. When he turns, he notices me watching, and with a slightly raised eyebrow, he walks over and tips my chin up for a kiss.

"We have a few things to do before we leave this afternoon," he informs me. "I left clothes for you on the table. I'll be back to pick you up in a half hour."

Seconds later, the door closes behind him, and I laugh. Our vacation is over. I slide out of bed and go over to the table to see what he left for me.

Lying on the table is a wrap dress in purple, its color similar to his eyes, with a matching set of delicate silk undergarments. A pair of knee-high black leather boots and a full-length black wool coat completes the ensemble. Interesting.

When he comes by, I'm surprised to see him in a charcoal suit with a tie matching my outfit. "Are we going somewhere special?"

He pulls me over to the fire and sets a large velvet box on the table. Flipping open the lid, he extracts a small silver cuff and holds out his hand.

Laying mine lightly in his, I tilt my head, waiting for him to tell me what's going on.

"This cuff gives its wearer the power to open a portal to Winter, regardless of location or magic. Typically given by the Lord of Winter to his Lady Winter, it's recognizable to everyone and signifies equal ruling power." His eyes are dark and turbulent as he explains the purpose of the cuff. "I love you, Arden, and I know I will never love another, no matter how long I live. I don't ask you to wear it lightly, but with the full confidence it's meant for you. Everything I have is yours. Will you wear the cuff?"

I inhale sharply. More than his love, he's offering me his home and trusting me with his people, sharing his roots. Tears fill my eyes, and I let him see what this means to me.

"I love you," I tell him. "Yes, I will."

He taps the cuff and says something in Fae to open it. Placing it over my left wrist, he says another word in Fae, and it wraps around and closes. Strangely, it's lighter than a piece of lace and barely noticeable. "It was created from Fae magic, many, many years ago," he informs me when I remark on it.

Stepping into his arms, I breathe in his signature scent and raise my lips until they're a millimeter from his, sparking a memory of the first time we stood this close in the hotel room. I wait like I did before, but this time, his lips descend on mine in a kiss that will be carved into my memories until my last breath. It's possessive and forceful, and it claims a piece of my heart. I gladly give it to him, but not without taking from him as well.

Breaking apart, he lifts the wrist with the cuff and eyes it with a look of supreme male satisfaction. "We need to announce it to the people. At the same time, I need to denounce my mother and inform my brother of his departure. It will ensure you are recognized with the proper authority. Are you going to be comfortable standing by my side while I deal with the two of them? A public change will result in the least amount of resistance."

I nod, and he helps me put on my coat. Taking my hand, he leads me to a large courtyard outside, where about a hundred people are gathered. Glancing around, I see a few people I know, like the healer, the commander, and of course, Theron's family. The rest of the crowd is unknown.

"Hello, everyone, and thank you for coming. I have several announcements to make. First, please welcome my Lady Winter, Arden," he says, lifting the arm with the cuff. He waits while the crowd applauds and shouts congratulations to us both.

"Thank you. We'll schedule a large celebration at a more appropriate time," he assures them. "This next topic is serious. I know many of you heard Arden accuse my mother of putting out a contract on my life. It's true."

The mood changes, and the crowd chatters to each other while glaring their disapproval at her. Their voices rise in anger but quiet when Theron raises his hand.

"As punishment, she is no longer welcome in Winter," he announces, then faces her. "You will reside the rest of your days with your mate, our father, in Summer, whether he wants you there or not. If Oryn wants to visit you there, it's up to him, but you're not allowed to return to Winter."

His mother goes berserk. "This is my home, not yours, you ungrateful bastard," she shouts. "How dare you order me to leave! I refuse. Do you hear me? I'm staying here. I'm the Lady Winter."

"If you would like to discuss your treason with the king, I'd be happy to schedule a hearing. Of course, if you're found guilty, you could lose more than just your home. Given my witness is the Princess of the Light Fae, I know my case is solid," he offers coldly, knowing she won't take him up on the alternative.

She blanches but says nothing.

Oryn sneers at her, a blatant public display of disappointment.

His mother reaches out to grasp Oryn's hand, but he pulls it away. For the first time since I met her, she looks devastated.

Theron dips his chin. "Let this be a warning. If anyone, including you, Oryn, help her return to Winter or provide her with resources, the punishment will be banishment or death."

Oryn gives Theron a sharp nod.

"Oryn, it's time we had representation at court, and I've assigned you to be Winter's official emissary at the dark Fae court." He watches Oryn's reaction to this last announcement, but other than a tilt of his chin, there's little response. "Having you at court will remind the king and queen of our loyalty and allegiance to them. Congratulations, Oryn."

The crowd claps and surges forward around both Oryn and us to offer their congratulations. I flick my eyes over and find Oryn watching me, a smirk on the corner of his mouth. Glancing away, I focus on the crowd around us to thank them for their good wishes.

An hour later, we're preparing to leave Winter, but I stop Theron. "Wait. Did you have time to ask her why she did it?"

He shakes his head. "She refused to speak to me, and I realized it didn't matter. I can never remember a time when she was kind to me. The only emotion she ever showed toward me was resentment for being the firstborn. I'm walking away without regrets."

Back at The Abbey, we enter the lounge, and three males immediately head toward me. Holding up my hands to stop them, I laugh. "I'm not a bone," I remind them, but my smile drops when I realize they're not moving. All eyes are focused on my hands. Turning them over, I look but don't see anything.

In a blur, Daire grabs my wrist, the one with the cuff, and his icy blue eyes fill with hurt and resentment. "Please excuse me," he says stiffly, leaving the room.

Theron calls his name, but Daire doesn't stop. Theron throws his hands up and stalks out after him.

I nibble on the inside of my bottom lip, wondering what to do or what to say. I don't blame him for getting upset. The cuff is a big deal. Someone tucks a piece of hair behind my ear, and I glance up.

Unlike Daire's, Valerian's amber eyes are bright with happiness, and I exhale in relief.

"Welcome home, lass," he says gruffly. "I've missed you in my arms." Firm lips capture mine in a sweet, lingering kiss. "Thank you for taking care of Theron. It looks like he appreciated it." He laughs and taps the cuff.

I give him a rude look.

Astor steps over and picks up my wrist. He stares at it for a long time, then gives me a rueful look. "I didn't think to give you something to mark our occasion," he admits sheepishly. "I'll need to get a bit creative, since I don't have this type of heritage."

I grip his arm and pull him close for a kiss. "I don't need anything but you," I state firmly. "This cuff..." I run a finger over it. "This cuff is special, but it's special to me because it gives me the means to take Theron home to heal. If it were gone tomorrow, I would find another way because I need him. I don't need material things or status or power. I need each one of you like you need me."

"We do," Theron murmurs from the doorway. "Daire left before I could talk to him. I've sent him a text so we can talk later. Let him cool off for now."

"How did everything go after we left? Did the wolves thaw?" I ask, diverting the conversation to a safer topic.

"I moved the wolves to the field using magic," Astor replies. "Gently, I promise. None were hurt. The rest of the evidence was erased."

"My car?" Theron reminds them.

Valerian winces. "It's finished. I ordered you a new one. It will be here tomorrow," he assures him.

Theron runs a hand over his head. "How did we miss the Cassandra-wolf connection?"

"There were only a few clues, and we've been so busy trying to find the journals and my father, we didn't put them together in time," I state with a sigh. I had plenty of time to think about why we didn't notice when Theron was lying in bed healing.

"Caro knew where Cassandra was hiding ever since I helped boost her location spell. Henry informed us about her discussions with a wolf on the property. The wolves often followed us from Witchwood to The Abbey, not the other way around." I walk around the room to release some pent-up anger. "At the last council meeting, I knew Cassandra's leaf showed mixed blood, but I only gave it enough thought to use it as leverage against Caro. I didn't even see Cassandra as a threat."

"How do we eliminate this threat?" Theron asks icily, his face hard and uncompromising.

"I'm not sure yet," I answer. "I want to speak to Cassandra and Grady before I call a special council meeting. Caro is finished. She deserves whatever happens to her."

The cadre glance at each other, communicating in silence, but I ignore it. When I was pacing, my eyes fell on the wooden box Elora gave me. "Astor, I'd like to send the box to my father tonight. We keep putting too many things off. Did you create a blood spell?"

"I did, but I haven't figured out how to get the box back yet," he states with a sigh.

"Fantastic," I say excitedly. "I have an idea on how to get the box back. We're going to need the tools for the blood spell, a piece of paper, and an extra dagger."

Astor leaves to get the supplies, and I turn to Theron. "One thing that keeps puzzling me. How did the rest of the cadre, including Fallon, know where we were? They all opened a portal at the same exact time to our precise location."

Theron smirks—a full-blown smirk. "I wondered when you'd notice. Astor created a spell to capture the geolocation information from the phone and use the data to open a portal directly to the coordinates. I integrated it into an app. We all have it on our phones, even you. I added it when we visited Solandis and Vargas." He looks at me expectantly.

Astor pipes up from the doorway, "It's cutting edge. How do you like our secret project?"

"Genius. Seriously, I never thought to combine the two. It's kind of scary too. If more supernaturals thought like you two, technology would open way too many doors," I admit with a shiver. "Thank you. I love your ingenuity, and it saved our asses."

Astor puffs up with pride. "Now for act two. I give you the

'vanishing box,'" he announces with a flourish. "Here's every-thing you requested." He sets a piece of paper down beside the MacAllister silver bowl and dagger. A second plain dagger is set down with it.

I bring the box over and remove Catriona's journal. I'll give it back when I can ensure it won't end up in the wrong hands. Taking the piece of paper, I look around and realize I forgot to ask for a pen. "Theron, do you have a pen?"

He grabs one from the table and sits across from us with a look of fascination on his face. "What are you doing?"

"I'm writing my father a note," I reply, tapping the pen against my chin.

Blood calls to blood. It's imperative I have the last journal. Please retrieve it and place it in the box. Once the journal is in the box, I need you to take the dagger and place two drops of blood from yourself and EAB on its blade. It's time. The box will return once the blade is inside without any assistance.

"Are my instructions clear?" I ask. I'm tempted to tell him I know who he is and I can't wait to see him again, but what if he doesn't feel the same way? Or what if he does something rash? I decide to wait.

Theron nods, and I fold and place the note in the box, then the dagger. At the last minute, I place a spell on the box to remove the insignia. I glance at Astor.

"It will work," he says excitedly. "The spell I wrote sends it by blood, and once their blood is on the dagger, it will retrieve it. Blood calls to blood. Great idea." He takes my hand, places a kiss on the palm, then slices across it. The blood drips into the silver bowl, and he recites the spell over the blood. He carefully takes a few drops and sprinkles it onto the box.

A second later, the box disappears. Now we can only hope it reaches its intended destination and returns with the necessary items.

CHAPTER
TWENTY-SIX

The lobby is quiet when I step from the portal. Astor must be running late. I send him a text to let him know I'm waiting for him. Time ceases to exist when he's in his lab. The elevator doors open a second later, and her laughter fills the air. My body tingles with awareness.

She steps out and turns toward the kitchen, not having noticed me standing here, then stops. I hold my breath. She spins around and zeroes in on my location.

"Meri, I have to call you back later," she says into the phone. "Give Solandis and Vargas a hug from me. Callyx too, I guess." She disconnects. "What are you doing here?"

"Astor and I are going to get answers from my father," I tell her. "Something isn't adding up between his story and the story the dark Elven queen told us." I know Astor told her about our visit to the queen. I'd been hoping for some response, but she isn't returning my texts. "You look beautiful."

Her skin is glowing, and even with the Primary hanging over her head, she looks happy.

"I'm glad you're getting answers, Fallon," she says, ignoring my last comment. "I know what it's like to be in the dark, waiting for answers, needing them, and getting nothing in return."

I wince at the direct hit. Striding over to grab her hands, I stop when she steps back and holds them up.

"I know I've made a complete mess of things, but please don't make any decisions until you hear me out," I plead with her. The elevator pings, and Astor steps out. *Fuck.* "What I'm doing is dangerous, and I don't want you caught up in it. You're the one thing I'd give up my entire kingdom for, and he knows it. I know we need to talk, but we must go now or I'll miss my window. I'll text you later."

Narrowing her eyes, she walks over to Astor and lays one hell of a kiss on him. I can't do anything but watch like a starving man sitting in front of a feast. She pulls back and whispers, "See you soon." She stalks over to the elevator without saying one word to me.

Astor claps me on the shoulder. "Sucks to be you," he remarks with a laugh. "Let's go."

My father is in his office when we arrive.

"Hello, Father," I greet him, reminding him of our relationship and hoping he answers my questions as a father not as a king. "You remember Astor."

He frowns. "You know better than to bring a demon here," he reprimands me. "Come back when your…friend isn't here." His gaze drops down to the papers on his desk.

"Astor is here to help me get to the truth. He also went with me to visit the dark Elven queen," I inform him. "I need some answers about my mother's death."

His head pops up, and he shoots me a puzzled look. "Why would you go to her? I've told you a thousand times. Your mother loved me and wanted to be with me. She sent me a note asking me to meet you both at the border of the dark Fae king's land and mine. When I arrived, she was lying on the ground, the guards were gone, and you were leaning over her crying," he states impatiently. "I immediately checked and found her dead, so I took you and came home. What else do you want to know?"

Astor glances at me and shakes his head. "He lied about your mother loving him and wanting to be with him. Everything else is true." Since he also heard the queen's story, he's puzzled. How can both stories be right?

"She didn't love you?" I ask in confusion.

"She was my mate. Of course she loved me," he replies dismissively.

"Lie," Astor intones. "She wasn't his mate."

My father's face turns red, and he clenches his fists. "She was my mate."

"Lie."

"She loved me!" he roars.

"Lie."

"Father," I interject softly. "Was she or was she not your mate?"

He gives me a calculated look. "She was not."

Shocked, I take a second to rearrange my thoughts. He'd

always stated they were mates. "I'm surprised you were able to have a child together if you weren't mates. It's so rare."

He freezes, and a feeling of dread falls over me. "Why does this matter? Who cares if she was my mate? All I wanted was a son. She gave me one," he mutters, shrugging his shoulders. "I'm coming down with a headache. Do you mind if we talk about this later?"

"No, we're getting this all out in the open!" I roar, pounding my fist against the desk. "Did you know she would give you a son? I don't understand. Talk to me."

He gives a maniacal laugh, his madness taking over. "I made a deal with a she-devil," he says in a singsong voice. I look at Astor, and he nods. "When I saw your mother, I knew she would give me a fine son. Out of all the candidates at the ball, I wanted her." He smiles at the memory. "She was beautiful and came from an aristocratic Elven family, even if it was from the other side."

He's always referred to the dark elves as the "other side." So far, everything he's said is the truth. "The she-devil caught me staring at her, and she laughed. Told me it was a shame, but your mother was already taken. The fates had arranged for her to meet her mate that evening. I was disappointed, but I laughed and waved my hand at all the beautiful females in the room. Plenty more."

His smile drops. "She shook her head and told me your mother was my only shot at having a son. I'd never meet my mate. It wasn't my destiny. I would live a long life, but when I eventually passed, my kingdom would go to another."

"Why would you believe such nonsense?" I scoff. Rolling my eyes, I dart a look at Astor, but he's staring at my father.

His face turns purple. "Do you take me for a fool? She knows things. I don't know how. Her power is absolute."

"Don't you mean was? Or do you still know her? Who is she?" I throw out question after question.

"Was, is, what does it matter?" he mutters and rubs his head. "She offered to blind the fates so I could swoop in and steal your mother away before she met Garrett. She said if I did, I would get a son." He lifts a hand towards me. "Here you are. My son."

"Garrett?" I ask, interrupting his story. "Your best friend, the man in charge of our armies, the man who has stood by your side for your entire reign?" Reeling, I drop into the chair behind me and stare at my father in shock.

He hunches his shoulders. "Your mother was supposed to meet Garrett that night," he admits softly, his eyes darting to the door as if he expects Garrett to walk through the door. "I don't regret it. Why should I? I got the one thing I wanted—you. Garrett didn't need a mate or a son. It would have distracted him from his true purpose. He's one of the greatest warriors I've ever seen."

"Is that how you justify it in your head?" I ask, disgusted by his treatment of the man I admire most in this world. It's sure as hell never been my father. "If you didn't kill my mother, who did?"

"The dark Elven queen," he shouts. "Why would I lie? I have proof." He opens his desk drawer, pulls out a gold ring, and flings it at me. "I found this on your mother's body. It has your aunt's initials inscribed on the inside. It must have fallen off when she killed your mother. Now get out. I've had enough of you dredging up the past."

Astor and I head to the door.

"Fallon, I don't have to warn you what will happen to your mate if you tell Garrett one word of this conversation, do I?" he asks softly. "The past is the past. It doesn't matter anymore."

"You took away his destiny, his perfect match," I return, my voice hard with anger. "It's unforgivable, the worst thing you could do to any supernatural. The only thing you didn't do is take away his son." His eyes narrow in confusion. "He's been a better father to me than you ever were."

I stride out, anger gnawing at my insides, and head directly to the portal, the ring clenched tightly in my hand. Astor keeps pace beside me but says nothing.

When we step into the dark Elven king's castle, I demand to see the queen. A butler escort us, along with several guards. I snort. As if this pittance could stop me from slitting her throat.

When we enter the same room with my mother's portrait, we find the queen standing in the middle of the room with a smile on her face. It falls when she sees my anger.

"What lies did he tell you?"

"No lies, just the truth. I made sure of it," I spit out. Waving a hand toward Astor, I inform her of his rune. I hold my hand out. "Is this your ring?"

She picks it up, turns it over, then looks at the inscription on the inside. She looks puzzled. "It's my ring. Where did you get it?"

"My father found it on the body of my mother. If it's yours, then you killed her," I shout. My hands curling toward her. "I will ask you one more time, and remember, Astor will know if you lie. Did you kill my mother?"

"I didn't kill your mother, my beloved sister," she states firmly, looking at Astor.

He shakes his head, and I roar with frustration.

"I gave this ring to someone," she informs me. "I don't know why it was found on your mother, but I will get to the bottom of it. I promise you. If this person had anything to do with her death, I'll let you know. Promise."

"You have two days," I warn her. "That's it. I want answers in two days."

She nods, turning the ring over and over, and walks out of the room.

I gaze at the portrait of my mother. "Soon," I tell her. I will avenge her death. Pivoting, I head out the door, almost bumping into the male standing outside the door.

Astor greets him. "Hello, Torin," he says, dipping his chin.

Torin follows our progress down the hall.

"Who is that?" I ask Astor, flicking my eyes back to Torin.

Astor glances at Torin. "The archivist who helped us find the name of the blacksmith."

I nod and turn the conversation back to the queen. "What do you think?"

"They're both telling the truth, so if neither killed your mother..." His voice trails off.

"Someone else did," I finish his sentence.

CHAPTER
TWENTY-SEVEN

<u>ARDEN</u>

Today is only the fifth day, but I'm wondering if I should go down to the Underworld and have a chat with Cassandra and Grady. I know I said a week, but I need to decide what punishment I'm going to ask the council to give, and I can't do that without speaking to them first.

"Arden," a voice calls out softly.

Schooling my features into a blank mask, I face Fallon. "Twice in one day. I'm honored," I retort, unable to keep the sarcasm from my voice. "Who are you waiting for this time?" Instead of his usual handsome self, he looks...broken. Devastated.

"You, I need you," he admits hoarsely. "I've been doing everything in my power to stay away from you, to keep you safe, but I don't know how much longer I can do it." He drops to the grass at my feet, plunges one hand in the green blades, and holds the other out to me. "Please sit. Listen. If you don't like what I have to say, I'll leave." His green eyes plead with me, and I find myself agreeing to hear him out.

I dismiss his hand and sit. The grass weaves between the crevasses of my body like an old friend, providing me with comfort. I fix my gaze on the garden and wait for him to begin.

"My father has always been erratic, but the last few years, he's gotten worse. I knew something was seriously wrong with him but ignored it. He could still function relatively well, and the kingdom wasn't suffering. Most people didn't even notice," he begins. "It was fine. I could hide his instability and step in to fill the cracks. Until your visit."

His face flushes with embarrassment. "When you visited, it quickly became apparent he'd hidden the worst of his madness from me. Once he knew you were my mate, he wanted to kill you. If you'd have been a light Elven mate, it might have been fine. Once he realized you were dark Elven, it was all over."

I glance over to show I'm listening, but he hasn't really told me anything I hadn't guessed yet. His green eyes, full of passion and pain, catch mine, but I look away before they can reel me in.

"Since then, I've been setting everything up to take his throne," he confesses. "Speaking to the council, the aristocracy, and our legions took time. Garnering support. Urging them to set up meetings with him, so they could see for themselves. It had to be done in secret, so I didn't tell anyone but Theron."

He moves his face in front of mine. "The tide finally turned in my favor last week when I received their support and allegiance. Not everyone supports me, but I have enough power now to challenge my father."

"I wish you had told me," I tell him. "I'd have kept your secret."

"I know. I trust you completely," he replies, grabbing my

hand. "If he finds out what I'm doing, he'll charge me with treason and kill me. Then he'll kill everyone who supported me. As my mate, he's already looking for any excuse to kill you. I refuse to give him one."

I ease my hand out from his. "So instead of talking to me about it, you decide to cut off contact to protect me?" It takes everything I have to stay calm when I ask.

"A little overstated, don't you think? I've read every single one of your texts and kept in constant contact with Theron. I didn't text back because it would have put you in danger," he replies. "You're never out of my thoughts. Even today, when I found out just how much of a monster my father really is, I could think of nothing but you. Seeing you. Feeling you close to me."

Taking a deep breath, I glance over. "Did you find your mother's killer?" I want to punch his face, but I force myself to ask the question. As mad as I am, I don't want to add damage to a potentially life-altering day.

He tells me about his visits to his father and aunt, and at first, I'm relieved he didn't find her killer, but the news about Garrett is shocking.

"Your father *stole* Garrett's mate? How is that even possible?" I ask, horrified by his father's actions. "Are you going to tell him?"

He looks bleak. "I don't know. Right now, I just want to find my mother's killer," he admits. "I gave my aunt two days to get me the information."

"I'm so sorry. I mean it. I know you'll find her killer," I state firmly. "I feel worse for Garrett, though. What if he never finds another mate? He deserves the truth." I reach over to squeeze his hand in sympathy. He captures mine in his grip and tugs me toward him. I put a hand on his chest. "Whoa. What are you doing?"

"I've thought of nothing but kissing you. When you kissed me back the other day, I felt your emotions. I know you care about me," he replies, referring to our kiss at the battle.

My jaw tightens, and I scramble to my feet. "A kiss given in the heat of battle after you threw yourself in front of a fireball to save my life does not mean 'I forgive you' or 'happily ever after.'"

"You returned my kiss," he says stubbornly, getting to his feet. He grabs my elbows and pulls me closer. "You're my mate, Arden. I thought you understood what that means to me? Everything I'm doing is for you and us. I couldn't care less about anything else."

All the pent-up anger from the last couple of months spills out of me in one tirade. "You've got to be kidding me. You rejected me. Rejected us. Mates decide things together. You made the decision to ignore my texts again and again. You made the decision to pursue your father's throne. You made the decision to drop out of my life. I don't care if you kept in contact with Theron. I'm not Theron. If you trusted me completely like you say, you would have come to me and discussed the situation instead of deciding what's best."

"I did it to protect you!" he roars. "My father wants to kill you. Do you understand what that means?"

"Tell him to take a damn number," I yell back. "Seriously, have you seen my life lately? Weren't you there the other day when we were attacked by a huge pack of wolves? If they'd been an experienced pack, we might have lost, not just the battle, but one of our lives. Then there's the matter of the Primary. Did Theron tell you it's a queen? Why not add a king to the mix! A matched royal pair." My chest heaves while I stand there glaring at him.

"You don't understand. It's my job as your mate to protect you," he says stubbornly.

"Your job?" I scoff at his poor choice of words. "Protecting me does not mean making decisions for me," I repeat, knowing he is not listening to what I'm saying. Frustrated, I look for the exit. "Go, take your father's throne. When you're sitting there by yourself, making all the decisions for the good of your people, maybe you'll realize what you lost. I'll be here in my home with the men I love." Yanking my elbows from his grip, I storm out of there.

TWENTY-EIGHT

DAIRE

"When are you coming home? I miss you," Arden asks quietly, but I hear the underlying worry in her voice.

Fuck. I didn't mean to worry her. When I saw the cuff the other day, such a *public* statement of their relationship, I lost it. I want my mark on her or a bond, a permanent one.

"In a few hours," I promise her. Lucifer walks in the room, and I mouth 'Arden.' He smiles. "Lucifer just walked in, so I need to go. I'll find you when I return." Hanging up, I sigh, knowing we need to talk, but I don't know what to say to her. I don't want her to stop wearing Theron's cuff, but I need something more too.

"Daire." Lucifer's voice finally penetrates the fog

surrounding me. "I've been calling your name for several minutes. What's wrong?"

"It's a vampire thing," I reply, shrugging dismissively. "What else do we need to do before I leave?"

"Sounds like less of a vampire thing and more of a relationship issue. Talk to me," he orders, waving his hand, and I raise my eyebrows. "I know you're not a child, but I've lived a hell of a long time. I might be able to help. If not, you're not any worse off than you are now."

"Arden came home the other day with a cuff on her wrist signifying her agreement with Theron to be his Lady Winter," I reveal. "I'm feeling the weight of my decision not to give her the Mate's Kiss. Well, our decision, because she feels the same way, but it's killing me."

"Why did you decide against it?" he asks, tilting his head to study me.

"The Mate's Kiss ties our life forces together. If something happened to me, she would die. Neither of us are willing to risk it," I say, going on to explain her relationships with the rest of the cadre. "Without it, though, I find myself wildly possessive of her, jealous of the cadre, and constantly talking myself out of kidnapping her to a remote island. So, tell me, oh wise one, what should I do?"

The ground beneath my feet rumbles with Lucifer's displeasure, but I laugh.

"Why do you want to give her the Mate's Kiss? Does she know you love her?" he asks gently.

I spent all night at the lake showing her how I felt. "She knows."

Lucifer bursts out laughing. "Well, there's your first mistake. You need to tell her, trust me," he asserts. "Why the Mate's Kiss, though? Do you think she doesn't love you back?"

"She loves me," I retort, but I realize she's never told me either.

What a mess. I feel like a teenager with a damn crush. Maybe I should send her a note asking if she wants to be my girlfriend—check yes or no. I roll my eyes at my internal monologue.

"The Mate's Kiss is an unbreakable bond. I can't explain it, but it binds us together. Like I said, it's a vampire thing," I explain, shoving away my yearning.

Lucifer is quiet for a minute or two. "What if there was another way to establish a bond without tying your life force together?" He holds up a hand when I try to answer. "Take your time."

"I don't need to think about it," I respond adamantly. "Tell me."

"You've always been impatient," he retorts. "Your mother used to get so exasperated by it. Do you remember?" He walks over to his safe and pulls out a piece of paper. He stares at it for a minute, then makes a magical copy to hand to me, and returns the original to his safe. "Once you do this, it can never be undone. I know you said you don't need time to think about it but take some anyway. Give her plenty of time to think about it." He makes me swear to do both.

He sits down on the edge of the desk to give me instructions. "It's an old ritual created by the angels. When we were assigned a human, we became their guardian angel. We used it to bind ourselves to them. The second we completed the ritual, we could sense them and their location." Silver replaces the blue in his eyes whenever he talks of those days. He glances outside, and when he looks back, they're normal.

"To have the bond work both ways, you need to complete a blood exchange. She needs to drink a bit more than a few drops of your blood, since you're not a full angel. I've translated the words into Latin, so you can both read them. Say the words together. Once it's done, you'll feel a bond and always be able to locate the other. It doesn't give her, or you, access to each other's feelings, so make sure you tell her how you feel." He sees my puzzled look and shrugs. "It's hard to describe what it does. It adds an element to the blood, almost like a tracker. While it doesn't change you physically, you become spiritually connected."

"Did you offer this to Mom?" I ask when I see the look in his eyes.

"I did," he says sadly. "She refused it, along with the immortality I offered to her. She wanted to be with Danica when she died, and I couldn't fault her. Heaven's a beautiful experience, and she should be with our daughter." He walks over to the window to look out.

"I miss them too, so much, but they've been gone for a very, very long time. Maybe Arden is right," I murmur. "Maybe it's time you found someone to be your queen."

I STAND BY HER DOOR, ready to knock, but I don't. What is she going to think of my request? What if she says no? Will I be able to continue without a bond? I think about it. Even now, in this semi tortured state, I can't imagine living without her in my life. The tight bands across my chest disappear, and I raise my fist.

"It's about time," she murmurs quietly behind me. "Would you like to come in?"

A slow half turn brings her into view. "Yes, I do." I take a small step back, giving her only enough room to slide past me to the door. Her body lightly brushes mine, and I relax for the first time in two days.

She strolls to the chair by the fire and indicates the other one for me.

Using a bit of speed, I pick her up and settle in the chair with her on my lap. "This is not a business meeting," I say mockingly. Her hair is in a ponytail, and I stare at her neck. Elegant and refined, it begs for my lips.

"You seemed to be the one dreading my company," she says with a huff. "I'm offering you the distance you so desperately need." She crosses her arms in front of her chest and raises an eyebrow.

My eyes zero in on the cuff. "I'm sorry. I reacted badly to the cuff," I admit freely. "I'll apologize to Theron tomorrow." My hand lands on the back of her neck, and I pull her closer to me. "I underestimated how possessive I'd feel without the Mate's Kiss. Instead of a mild undercurrent, my emotions became a roaring river in a matter of seconds the other day. The lack of a permanent bond is bringing out all my worst traits."

She unfolds her arms and places her hands on my shoulders. "This is only the beginning. Do you think this is going to get better or worse with time?" She sucks her bottom lip between her teeth and nibbles on it. Her green eyes search mine for answers.

"It's going to get worse, I think," I reply truthfully. "There's something inside me that feels unsettled without a more permanent bond between us."

"We could speak to the rest of the cadre," she begins tentatively.

Her generous offer tempts me, and if this angel bond

doesn't work, we may have to go that route. "I might have another alternative." I explain the angel ritual and bond.

Questions spill out of her. "I won't be changed physically by this bond?" When I shake my head no, she continues, "Our life force won't be tied together? You won't be able to suddenly read my mind or emotions? Do I have to always drink your blood or just the one time?"

I barely answer one question before she spits out another and another. Finally, she falls silent.

"I don't want you to answer right now, but think about it," I urge her. "Lucifer said it can't be undone. There can be no regrets."

"Have you thought about it?"

I smile. "Yes, I thought about it for hours."

"You want to try it, don't you?" she asks, but she knows the answer. "Why? Tell me why you need to bond with me. What could be so important you would want an unbreakable bond with me?"

There is only one answer to this question, but the words are so rusty, they stick in my throat. It's been so long since I said them. Right before my mother passed, I said them to her, but never since. Lucifer rarely uses them, and I picked up his habit.

"I love you." My voice is hoarse, strained by the three words I haven't said out loud in over a millennium.

"I think you need practice," she informs me. "Maybe you should say those words every day. You can change it up with other words too. I adore you. I worship you. I like you. I need you. I lust you."

"Arden."

"I don't want to do the bond until after we create the stone. You know, just in case Lucifer is wrong. Okay?" She waits until I agree with her condition.

"Arden."

She brings her lips close to mine. "Kiss me," she breathes.

"Tell me," I demand in return.

"I love you, Daire."

My lips meet hers, sealing the words between us, and I savor the flavor of them over and over, knowing I'll be tasting them forever.

TWENTY-NINE

<u>ARDEN</u>

Astor is staring at the wall when I walk into the lab. Nine sheets of paper are taped to it, and each one contains a variation of the three spells he copied from the page in the grimoire. He motions me over and points to them.

"Any guesses which one?" he asks with a sigh.

I read all nine, but I can't tell. "Where's the grimoire?"

He walks over to the counter, and I follow. With his finger, he traces the spell to create the stone, but he insists it's missing a line. He follows the other two spells the same way. "They all end in the middle," he says, jabbing his finger on the page in frustration. "I tried adding the last line to each of the three, but no matter what I try, none of the spells make sense."

I turn the book in a circle. The vines wrap around the page, the words sit inside the vines, and they all lead to the middle, which is blank. The entire page is an illustration, which means they deliberately left the middle blank. I wonder if there is only one answer to all three. Pulling the Killian blade from my thigh, I prick my finger and let a few drops of blood hit the center of the grimoire.

With MacAllister blood, our will shall be done, appears in the center.

Astor picks me up and swings me around. "You did it!" he shouts. "Of course, it means you'll have to say the spell for the stone. I can't believe I missed it."

"It's hard to see something new when you stare at it for a long time," I reassure him. "Thank you for all the work you did to study it. If you hadn't, we wouldn't even know we could create a new stone. Is this why you asked me to come down?"

"No, the box is back," he announces, tugging me over to the island. "I have to leave in five minutes. Do you want to open it now or when I get back?"

I prick my finger again to open the box. "Where are you going?"

The latch clicks, and I lift the lid. The first two MacAllister journals were bound in brown leather, but the leather on this one is green and it's engraved with her name, my mother—Gia Perrone. This is her journal. I pull it out and set it on the counter.

The dagger lies beneath it. Four drops of blood stain the blade. I lift it out and ask Astor for a bag to put it in. A note sits in the bottom.

"I'm going to see the dark Elven queen with Fallon," he states quietly.

I pull the note out.

Blood calls to blood. It's time. I'll see you soon. TB

Astor's response slowly registers. "I'm going with you. I need to speak to the archivist," I tell him.

"It's not a social visit," he cautions me. "It could get ugly."

"I understand. If it does, I can at least offer backup to you and Fallon," I reply, heading off any other protests. I pick up the items from the box. "I'll meet you in the lobby in five minutes."

FALLON CROSSES his arms over his chest and shakes his head. "The situation is volatile, with too many unknown factors. It's not safe for you," he says adamantly.

"If it's not safe for me, it's not safe for you two. Maybe we should bring the entire cadre?" I reply, my phone in my hand and ready to text Theron. Or we could use the new backup. "We have the new app on the phone. If something goes wrong, we can always tap for help."

"I don't want you to go," he states firmly. "Astor?"

"She's right," Astor says with a shrug. "Either it's too dangerous for just the three of us and we need to ask the rest to go with us or it's not. The new app works."

"I don't even know you these days," Fallon scoffs. "Weren't you the same one who didn't want her to go into the Under-world to battle?"

Astor smirks. "Look how well that turned out. She went, saved your ass, and came back with Lucifer's thanks," he reminds him. "Your father's making you paranoid. Now, let's go."

Fallon glances at the time. "Fine but stay close."

"All right, I sent a text to Theron to let him know where we're going," I tell them, stepping into the portal. Fallon needs to get his head screwed on straight. I blow the hair out of my eyes while I wait for them to step out on the other side.

Fallon and Astor flank me, while the butler and several guards escort us to the queen. When we pass the room with the portrait of Fallon's mother, I raise an eyebrow. Maybe they are taking us to the dungeon. After a very long walk through opulent hallways, we finally stop in front of two ornate doors. The butler opens them and waves a hand for us to enter.

The queen sits in the middle of the massive bed propped up by a half dozen pillows. Her hair and clothes are immaculate, but one look, and it's obvious she's dying. Her hands lie on top of the sheets, black and lifeless. The veins in her face and neck are also black, resembling a spider web strung across her face.

Fallon makes an inarticulate sound in his throat and steps forward. "What happened to you?"

"The truth," she says with a self-deprecating laugh. "My husband liked to collect artifacts that belonged to the old king. It was an obsession." She smiles. "I found an old dagger with the initials CB and the old crest on it. I'd been saving it for a special occasion, but this was much better. He's kind of suspicious, so I couldn't give him the dagger in the box. He'd have had his servant pick it up first, which would've ruined my surprise. I had to be the one to hand it to him." She looks down at her hands, and we follow her gaze.

"I coated it in poison, heavier on the pommel, lighter on the blade, and I gave it to him. Let him hold it and turn it in his hands. When the poison started to affect him, I yanked the gold ring off his finger." She pauses. "Her initials were in the inscription."

Fallon gasps in surprise.

She nods. "My parents gave my sister and I identical gold rings with our initials inscribed in each of them. I gave mine to my husband on our wedding day. Your father found mine on my sister's body and kept it all these years. Yet every day, my husband wore 'my' ring. There was only one answer."

"He killed her," Fallon states, shocked by her story. "Why?"

"Apparently, he loved her. When she rejected him, he turned his attentions to me. By marrying me, he could be near her. When she took you to visit your father, he thought she was leaving to be with him permanently, so he killed her and took her ring to have her close to him for the rest of his life," she intones. "My sister's killer is dead. He died a couple of hours before you got here. I'll also be dead soon. I've named you my heir."

"I don't want your kingdom," Fallon tells her. "I wanted justice, and you delivered it. I'm only sorry it cost you everything."

"Would you stay with me while I pass?" she asks suddenly. "You're the only one left."

He nods, and Astor and I excuse ourselves.

When we get to the hall, I ask the butler for directions to the library. He looks torn. "Or if you can ask one of the staff to get the archivist for me, I'm happy to speak to him here."

Relieved, he beckons to a nearby staff member, who runs off to get the archivist. I pick up my phone and jot down my number. About fifteen minutes later, the archivist turns the corner, and I scrutinize him with new eyes. Same height, dark hair, and green eyes. He locks eyes with me, and his steps falter.

"Hello, Torin," I greet. "I forgot to give you my number the last time I was here. When you find the books I requested, please call me. Here's my number." I wait until he's ready and hold up my phone. My number is scrawled across the photo I found in my mother's jewelry box—the one where he's holding my mother with his hand on her belly.

Frozen, his eyes flick from the photo to me, and he smiles. "Thank you. The books should be in soon. Why don't I give you my number too?" He recites the digits quickly, and I enter them into my contacts.

"Oh, and I'm sorry to hear about the king's death," I state with mock sympathy, pretending not to see the butler throwing a fit in the corner. I guess nobody is supposed to know the king's dead. Too bad. "The queen will soon join him. It's so sad."

"I didn't know." He glances at the butler. "Thank you for telling me."

The archivist walks away, with the butler following him.

Astor comes up behind me. "Liar, liar. What's going on?"

Fallon comes out. "The queen is dead."

"I'm sorry," I tell him, glancing at Astor and praying he won't give away my lie. "What's going to happen now?"

"I guess I'll have to figure it out," Fallon replies. He runs a hand through his dark hair. "Let's get out of here."

Ten minutes later, we're stepping into the lobby of The Abbey. Theron, Valerian, and Daire are waiting for our return.

"The Balinor family, my family, are the rightful heirs. The kingdom was stolen from them," I say quietly.

"It doesn't work that way. When supernatural royalty dies, it's complicated. Sometimes the heir automatically inherits, but on occasion, the magic chooses a new heir," Fallon explains.

"A couple of weeks ago, I found a photo hidden in my mother's jewelry box. It was a picture of my parents. I took a snapshot of it on my phone." Astor stills, knowing what is next. "I recognized the man, my father. He's the archivist." I pass along my phone to Theron. "I gave him my number today. He knows the king and queen are dead."

Theron studies the picture. "You knew for almost two weeks, and you didn't say anything?"

"I wanted to savor the knowledge to myself for a while," I say, admitting my need without shame. "Part of me wanted to test him first. Would he send me my mother's journal if I provided him with a safe way to get it to me? He did. I also asked him for two blood samples. One from him and my grandmother. He sent those too."

"He could have sent anyone's blood," Astor replies.

"I confirmed it's MacAllister blood," I inform him. "There are only three of us, so it's not like we have a lot of people willing to donate."

Fallon's phone rings. It's his father. He answers, and by the shouting, it's apparent his father is already aware the dark Elven king and queen are dead and he's been named their heir.

"I've got to go," Fallon says reluctantly. "It's almost time to end this thing with my father," he informs the cadre, and they assure him they're ready to assist. Stepping close to me, he places his hands on my shoulders. "I will do everything in my power to help your family, but I can't guarantee the magic will choose them. Tell your father I'm an ally, and I'll be in touch." With a squeeze, he turns to enter the portal.

My stomach clenches in fear. "Fallon," I call out. When he turns, I pull him into a hug and breathe in his clean scent. "Be careful. We're not finished."

He flashes me a huge smile and leaves.

THIRTY

ARDEN

Astor doesn't even stir when I slide out of bed the next morning. He'd been up late last night checking off all the last details so we can create the stone today. On the hunt for coffee, I leave him sleeping and head down to the lobby. When the doors open, I'm caught off guard by the variety of smells in the air. I completely forgot Maya opened the club last night.

Syn's in the kitchen prepping food with the staff. Unlike the first time we met, I don't feel intimidated by his demeanor. Not that I'm going to challenge the massive lion shifter in his kitchen domain, but I'm comfortable coming in here for a cup of the black nectar I desperately need to start my day.

He blinks but says nothing while I get my coffee and banana. With a wave, I leave and head to our private lounge. Theron's in there working when I arrive.

"Good morning," I say tentatively. I could tell he wasn't happy with my announcement yesterday. "I've been looking for you."

"I see," he says coolly, his face impassive. "What can I do for you?"

"I'm sorry I didn't share the information about my father sooner." After seeing the hurt on Theron's face yesterday, I realized he felt like I was hiding things from him again. I sit down across from him.

"It was like I'd discovered the answer to my universe, and if I'd told anyone, it could disappear. Irrational, I know, but every day, I'd find a new reason to justify why I shouldn't share it. I'm truly sorry, Theron." I set the coffee and banana down.

"The cadre is employing all of our resources to shut down threats, find allies, and get things lined up so when we're ready, we can attack the Primary. Finding things out later, whether it's a day or ten days, could impact those plans," he explains, his frustration evident in the tone of his voice. "Full transparency, Arden. Do you understand? If we can't rely on it, we might as well admit defeat now."

"I get it," I tell him. "I promise, no more surprises. Did Daire apologize for the other day?"

"He did," he assures me. "We also discussed this bond issue. I'm not sure I would agree to the Mate's Kiss, so I hope this alternative works." He returns to the computer in front of him, and I can tell he needs some distance from me right now.

I fervently agree. "Me too." I lean back and pick up my mother's journal.

The dedication on the first page makes me sit up straight.
Only with seven will these words be yours.
All the other pages are blank.
The only seven I possess are the bloodlines. I guess when

you need to protect something, it's best to choose a unique key. A prick to my finger, and the pages fill.

She wrote out all her visions, the rules she made Solandis follow, the things she did to ensure I stayed on the best path forward. It's all here. Unlike mine, her visions were snippets of time she viewed like a movie. They were detailed and vibrant in their telling of the future. I wonder if mine will ever reach this advanced level. I doubt it.

At the end, she writes a long personal letter to me.

My darling Arden,

As you can see from this journal, my visions guided me to create the best path for your success. I've done all I can to help you, but the rest is in your hands.

You'll not have any visions until the end. I left instructions to have your father place a small spell on Catriona's journal before it was given to you. It's for the best. With your visions intact, I couldn't find a path that allowed you to defeat your enemy. Perhaps I've meddled too much, and this is the result.

Every two thousand years, the primal source chooses one supernatural, called the Prime, to be their champion, in the fight to keep the universe balanced between the greater good and free will. Essentially, with the greater good, the Prime makes choices for the collective, and with free will, they allow the individual to make their own choices. To help them in this endeavor, the source bestows powers on them greater than any other supernatural.

Your enemy was appointed roughly four thousand years ago during a time when free will ruled the world. It was a dark time, but out of the darkness rose a young Fae filled with fire and light. They chose her to be their champion for the greater good and bring balance to world again. She succeeded, but in her zealous pursuit of her quest, she tipped the balance too far in her favor.

The next chosen was supposed to restore free will and balance the two again, but the thought of free will having equal power was so abhorrent to her, she killed the next chosen. For the next two thousand years, she did whatever it took to ensure her reign continued.

The seers she employed led to the destruction of the MacAllisters because they predicted you, a witch with the power to stop her, would come from their line. If it weren't for Gemma and Agnes, she would have succeeded. For a long time, she thought she'd achieved victory, until you were born. She's been on the hunt for you ever since. Throughout your life, you'll experience assassination attacks, but none will succeed.

Surprisingly, your protection from her does not come from me, but from another who needs you to come to power. In fact, there are several who will gamble their very lives on you winning against her. The puck who helped create the blades is one of them. Keep your heart open, for even enemies can become allies.

This letter reveals your enemy, as only one comes from the light. You've been given all the tools to defeat her, but it won't be easy. Always listen to your heart.

My last vision showed me my end, and I've chosen this place as my final destination. It holds my most cherished memories, time spent with you and your father. Stay true to who you are, and you'll succeed.

All my love to you both.
Your mother, Sia

Blood splatters the page almost obscuring the note below.

SAVE THE QUEEN - RESTORE BALANCE.

"Theron," I croak, barely able to force his name past my lips.

With shaking hands, I hand him the journal and drop my head in my hands. Nyssa is the Primary. How do I even begin to tell Solandis? It will quite literally break her heart. The woman raised me as her own child. Is this how I repay her for giving me a home and loving me unconditionally? Telling her I must stop, or possibly even kill, her sister?

Save the queen, restore balance. Was this my mother's last vision? Is there a way to save Nyssa? My head begins to pound, but the only thing I can do is call the one person I've turned to my whole life—Vargas. I need his gruff voice telling me it's all going to work out.

It goes to voicemail. Text it is, but no details.

Arden: Call me. Urgent.

I send the same message to Callyx.

Theron jerks to his feet and begins pacing, his fingers moving fast and furious on his phone. Seconds later, the rest of the cadre, minus Fallon, enters the room. He brings them up to speed with the contents of the letter.

"This is not to leave this room," Theron orders. "Daire, you cannot go to your father until we're ready. I want to have everything in place before we inform him. He's too much of a wild card, and he has the power to back it up." He waits until Daire nods in agreement. "The first thing we need to finalize is our allies. We can't plan an attack without knowing every single resource and their capabilities. For now, we focus entirely on figuring that out, then we plan the battle."

"I'll get an accurate count of dragon flights from Drystan," Valerian states. "In addition, I'll liaison with our other shifter allies, although they are few. They tend to stick more with their packs."

Daire puts his phone down. "Theron, I've sent you a text with the numbers and capabilities from our Underworld army. It's considerable, with an equal amount of physical and magical fighters." He turns to Valerian. "We should start assigning leads to coordinate the various groups. I'll draw something up and send it to you."

Needing to do something, I jump in with my immediate plans. "Astor, Valerian, and I need to complete the stone today. We figured out all the pieces, so we just need to put it together. Once I'm free from the coven, I can figure out if we have any witches willing to join us."

Theron's fingers fly as he enters everything into his phone. "I added the numbers for my legions of dark Fae. I'll need to inform the king of my intentions, but it can wait until we're ready. I've also sent a text to Fallon. I'll pull all this together, and we'll regroup each morning to update the status."

My hands are shaking, but I collect the dagger with my family's blood on it, along with the journal, and head to the door. Strong arms wrap around me from behind, and I gratefully sag against him.

"I've got you," Theron croons softly. "You're not doing this alone. Every single one of us, including Fallon, will be right by your side."

I turn around to see his face. "Promise?"

A chorus of yeses answers my question.

Straightening my shoulders, I nod several times until I gain my equilibrium. As a mental blow, it was massive, but no damage was done to me or mine. We know our enemy, and remarkably, we have a tremendous advantage over her—she doesn't know her enemy is me, yet.

"I'm good," I assure him, shaky but standing on firm ground.

He searches for any sign to the contrary, but when he doesn't find one, he gives me a hug and a lingering kiss, then passes me to Daire, who does the same.

Valerian and Astor are waiting at the door for me.

"Let's go create a new stone," I say with false cheerfulness.

It's a huge risk to leave the coven and base of power, but

it's necessary. I can't be held accountable for breaking the coven's rules if I'm no longer a part of it.

ONCE WE'RE in the lab, Astor quickly sets out all the tools—the MacAllister blood bowl, dagger, and the grimoire, and the instructions for the spell. He motions for Valerian and me to face each other.

"Only the soul bonded can create the stone," Astor reminds us. "We neglected to give that statement our full attention last time. The bond you two have as mates is a significant ingredient in the creation of the stone. We must feed the bond first, then the stone."

Valerian eyes dart to mine in question, and I smile. Astor and I worked a long time on finalizing the ritual. We added verses to it, and fingers crossed, it still works.

Astor motions to me. "Straddle Valerian," he instructs with a grin.

I walk over and stand in front of Valerian, waiting until he closes his legs.

His amber eyes twinkle. "Come here, lass." He pats his thick, muscular thighs.

Rolling my eyes at them both, I straddle Valerian's lap and slowly move up until we're joined tightly together or as close as we can be with our clothes still on. His warm breath caresses my cheek, while his hands hold my hips. I look at Astor and arch a brow.

"Sorry, just enjoying the sight," Astor murmurs. "I need you to concentrate on feeding your powers into the soul bond. Feel the threads tying you together, strengthen them with your power, and when your souls are glowing and you can see inside the other, tell me."

Adjusting myself to get more comfortable, I ignore Valerian's soft growl. Amber eyes catch mine, and I let myself fall into them. My lips find his automatically, and as we kiss, our souls light up. My mouth caresses his, lingering on the pouty lips I find so irresistible.

The scent of a bonfire on a crisp night washes over me, and I breathe in deep. Every atom of my body knows this man, and without hesitation, I let go. Diving deep, we ignite the fire between us, making our souls burn brighter. We feed the kiss, which in turn feeds our bond. The threads pull tight, allowing us to slip into each other's souls.

"Now," I gasp.

Astor pulls my hand up, slices across it, then a second later, he places my palm against Valerian's. Our blood mingles together and drips into the bowl beneath our hands. Astor quickly grabs the other bowls, placing them in a circle around the first one.

Valerian's other hand grasps the back of my neck, and he pulls me in for another kiss. This time, he's the aggressor, devouring every inch of my mouth. Our bond flares with white hot heat, and the power triples.

"All of them," I command Astor.

Our souls are so close now, they're almost touching. A whisper of spell and clothes disappear. We shift and slide together, joining our bodies. Valerian's arm bands tightly around me, holding me against him while we rock. Like the moon eclipsing the sun, our souls merge, becoming one, and we explode together. Our blood sings with the power of the bond and the pleasure racing through us.

"Valerian, fire!" Heat surrounds us.

"Arden, recite the spell!"

"Of dragon's flame and witches' blood,
The stone shall be formed.
Bonded souls burn white hot,
Power wielded and cast,
One is created from the two,
Magic true and vast.
The one binds the seven,
The seven lead the coven.
With MacAllister blood, my will shall be
    done."

Breathing rapidly, I stare into Valerian's beautiful amber eyes with wonder. When we first mated, our souls were lightly threaded together, reflecting our relationship in its fragile, new state. Not anymore. Our souls are intertwined, the threads made of steel, unbreakable.

Valerian's eyes gleam with emotion. His hands stroke my shoulders and down my back, and I arch into his comforting touch.

Astor snaps his fingers in front of our faces. "Attention, please," he demands. "If we don't get through this, I'm going to spontaneously combust."

I turn my attention to Astor and note that he's almost sizzling with power. The hairs on my neck stand up, reacting to the power he's projecting. The sexual energy Valerian and I generated must of have overloaded him.

He points to the bowl, and I look down to find a near perfect replica of the original stone, but instead of dark and grey, this stone is dark red with a brilliant white light in its center. This is what it must have looked like when it was full of power.

I hold my breath while he picks up the tongs and uses them to grasp the stone. This time, it doesn't crumble.

Excitedly, we peer into each bowl to find smaller glowing replicas. He tests each one, and they're solid too.

"We did it." I pull Astor over and lay a big kiss on him, then do the same to Valerian. "Now what do we do?"

"If there are any witches you want to add to the coven, they add their blood to one of the stones. Instead of the largest stone only being powered by the MacAllisters, you ask the leaders of each bloodline to feed the main stone. They will be tied to you and you to them," he explains.

"The dagger my father sent back has blood from him and my grandmother. We need to add them to the main stone—my stone," I instruct him. "I'm cutting our leaves and my name off the tapestry at the next council meeting."

"I'll do it next," he replies.

Valerian points to the other bowls. "Why are there six additional stones?"

"My blood is ingrained into the structure of each stone, which will be given to any lead who joins the new coven. The plan is to offer them the same option as the current coven, but with a twist," I explain.

"Collectively, we'll govern, but they'll individually be able to rule their covens. The blood of their coven will determine their strength. It gives them autonomy to make decisions that are best for their people instead of what's best for the greater good of the coven." I turn to Astor and ask, "Can you keep these in the lab?"

Astor nods and sets them aside. "Yes, definitely."

"You and Daire are welcome to join my coven," I offer tentatively, not wanting to stir up any unpleasant memories.

"For the first time in my life, I'm comfortable with who I am, and I don't want to change," he explains. "You can ask Daire, but he's probably going to have a similar answer."

I smile. "I understand completely."

Valerian stands with me in his arms. I wrap my legs around him. His voice is strained when he asks, "Are we done?"

"Yes, you lucky bastard," Astor answers with a groan. "Go savor the delicious minx in your arms. I'll be here slaving over my work."

Valerian's patience is gone before Astor utters the last word. Good thing we're not too far from his room.

THIRTY-ONE

ARDEN

I'm up early the next morning. It's been over a week since we banished Cassandra and Grady to the dungeons in the Underworld, and our conversation is long overdue. I'd thought to call a special council meeting to put Cassandra on trial along with Caro, but we're less than a week away from the council meeting and the vote. I've decided to wait and get it all over with at once. If I'm lucky, it will be the last council meeting I'll have to attend. Regardless of the outcome, I'm done.

Daire's room is dark when I enter, and I tiptoe over to the bed. Icy blue eyes filled with mirth stare back at me. I pout. "Well, I was hoping to wake you up with a kiss, but since you're already awake, I'll wait for you in the lobby."

A second later, I find myself in the middle of Daire's warm bed with a very naked, very hard body pressed up against me.

He brushes the hair out of my face, then trails his finger back and forth across my lips. "Did I hear something about a kiss?"

"A wake-up kiss to be exact, but look," I wave my hand at his face and continue, "you're already awake. Such a shame. The moment is lost." Keeping my face blank, I watch his jaw tighten.

He huffs, rolls over on to his back, and closes his eyes, pretending to be asleep.

I follow, laying my head on his shoulder, and his arm squeezes me tight against his side.

"Of course, being awake has its advantages too. Especially in the morning," I say huskily, gliding my hand down to grasp his shaft. "Awake...and ready to go." I stroke firmly up and down, and he shifts his body accordingly.

His breath quickens, and I slide a leg over his body until I'm straddling him. My hand continues to stroke while I move slowly down his body, my mouth skimming across the peaks and valleys of his abs. When my mouth is an inch away from the tip, I swirl my tongue around the head and watch his eyes darken and flare with lust. "Mmm..."

His hand drops lightly on my head, and I turn my attention back to his body. Licking and sucking, I worship him from tip to root while my hand grips and slides to bring him closer to the edge. When his fingers tighten in my hair, I take him deep into my mouth and back out, my tongue wrapping to heighten his pleasure.

"Arden, your mouth feels too good," he says with a groan. "If you don't stop, I'm going to come."

"You taste too good to stop," I reply huskily.

His harsh breaths fill the room, and his body tightens. Over and over, I take him in my mouth until he thrusts up and stills, his body pulsing as he comes. Fingers soften and he strokes my hair.

"Arden," he drawls huskily. Reaching down, he pulls me up and over his body. His arms hold me tightly to him. "I lust you so much."

Laughing, I pinch him in the side. "Now that I've tamed the beast, I need you to get up and take me to your dungeons." Wriggling out of his embrace, I stand by the bed and use my hands to smooth down my clothes and hair. I probably look a bit wild now.

Hands reach for me, but I slap them and jump back. Using a spell, I sprint through the door and into the hall, barely closing the door before hands hit it.

I hear him chuckle, then walk away, muttering something under his breath. Grinning, I make my way to the kitchen in search of some coffee.

WHILE I'M WAITING for Daire, I get a text from Fallon.

Fallon: I've worked with your father to officially remove my name as heir to the Dark Elven Kingdom. Both he and your grandmother are willing to risk the magic choosing another. If it doesn't choose them, I've invited them to stay at The Abbey with us. Permanently.

Tears fill my eyes when I read his text. He listened to what I said and did everything he could to help my family. It's a huge step in the right direction.

Arden: How long does it take?

Fallon: It varies. It can be days. I'll let you know as soon as we hear something.

Arden: With us at The Abbey?

Fallon: I've told my father I'm renouncing my claim to the throne. After all the revelations, I can't even look him in the eye, and after the discussion with you, I realized the throne isn't important to me. I'd rather be with you and the cadre, saving others and riding my motorcycle to the coast.

Arden: I feel like you're going to regret this decision and me.

Fallon: Never. I couldn't take his throne, nor could I continue to be his heir. We will decide together on what comes next. I promise.

Daire walks into the lobby, and I catch the time. Twenty-five minutes. I scrutinize his appearance and find him immaculate in a dark grey suit and green tie. He flashes me a smile and points to his tie. I shake my head.

Arden: I'm going with Daire to the dungeons to speak to Cassandra and Grady. Talk more later. I promise.

Talk about huge decisions. It's tough to believe, given he was just fighting to usurp his father. Could he really walk away? What will his father do to him? To me? I sigh.

Before he can ask, I hand the phone to Daire.

He reads the exchange and whistles. "He never says anything he doesn't mean."

Agreeing with his statement, I just nod.

He hands the phone back. "Do you realize this tie matches your eyes?" With a teasing grin, he lifts it up for my inspection.

"Do you realize it took you twenty-five minutes to get ready?" I give him a pointed look. "We're running late."

"I believe we're running late because you decided to give me…" The rest of his words are muffled by my hand.

I narrow my eyes, but he just grins.

Taking my hand, he pulls up the portal and walks through with me following. Instead of stepping into a dark, dank place, I'm surprised to find us in a cheerful, brightly lit room filled with sofas and chairs.

I tilt my head, trying to figure out our location.

"It's the waiting room for families," he explains. "I thought it would be better to bring you through here first. The atmosphere in the dungeons is designed to incite fear and chaos. It's a circular cavern about a hundred stories deep, sort of like an inverted cone, filled with cells from top to bottom, and it can be daunting when you first see it. The most dangerous creatures are held in the pit, at the bottom, with the lightest offenders at the top." He brings my hand up and places a kiss on it.

"I put Cassandra and Grady in a cell on the tenth floor, which is far enough down for them to hear the roars from below, but close enough for the guards to hear their screams of help, if needed. Also, I'm not completely heartless, I provided them with some provisions and comforts. Are you ready?" He pauses before opening the door to look at me, and I nod.

When I walk into the dungeons, I'm incredibly glad he took the time to warn me. The noise alone is deafening and filled with everything from human screams to animal roars to terrifying sounds I've never even heard before. We approach the center of the cavern, and I look down. Only the top five or six floors are visible. The rest of the floors are swallowed up by the darkness.

He sweeps me into his arms, and seconds later, we're standing in front of a cell. It's quiet for a second, then a deep growl emerges from the dark.

"Sounds like you've held up better than I anticipated," I drawl, leaning against the bars.

A wolf flies toward me and slams into them. When he bounces off, I shake my head.

"Cassandra is clearly the brains in this relationship. Cassandra, are you there?" I wait for her to answer. "If you aren't ready to talk to me, I can leave, but I won't be back for a month or two. Believe me, my calendar is booked solid."

I hear a click and a small lamp shines light into the cell. "You have no right to keep us here," she grits out. "When my mother and the council hear how you've treated me, there will be hell to pay. Grady's father is also important. He's one of their leaders, and when he hears how you killed those wolves, he'll hunt you down." She grips the bars, hate pouring out of her.

Looking past the bravado, I notice the exhaustion and fear chipping away at her. Yet she still fights. I glance over my shoulder at the cavern, at some of the other cells on this floor, and see glowing eyes in a multitude of colors watching me in return. With a shiver, I flash Cassandra a look of admiration.

"Don't worry, you'll get your chance to explain to the court why you attacked me and the Imperium Cadre, the cowardly tactics you used to block my powers, how you and Caro conspired to take me down, and how you tricked a pack of wolves into championing your personal war," I inform her. "The next council meeting is being held in a few days. We'll bring you both directly to the meeting.

"Grady, we've informed your father. He will be at the meeting, along with one of the other pack leaders," I say coolly.

Valerian had a long discussion with Grady's father. To say he's displeased is an understatement. Risking the lives of wolves for petty vengeance shows him to be a reckless and thoughtless alpha. I watch Grady's shoulders droop. He knows.

"The council meeting is not just for your hearing, Cassandra. In fact, they don't even know about the attack," I point out and smile when I see the anger in her face. "Your mother hasn't said a word about her missing daughter or the attack. I wonder why?"

I shrug. "On to more important things. We've asked for the coven to vote for the acceptance of all witches into the coven. If they vote against it, they will cut your leaf from the tree, and you from the coven. Your witch magic will slowly die until you have none."

"They will do the same to you," she sneers, although her hands tremble in fear.

I look her directly in the eyes. "I'm prepared for it. Are you? You're a smart young woman, but you have a long road ahead of you. What you do in a few days will shape your life forever. Do you want to be bitter and broken? Or do you want to be a strong witch and wolf? The choice is in your hands."

Her blue eyes hold mine steadily without an ounce of emotion, but I can see the wheels turning in her head.

I squeeze Daire's hand, and we're in the family waiting room in seconds. Grateful for the light and lack of sound, I drop my head back and take a deep breath. Guilt for leaving them in the dungeon surfaces, but I shove it away. It's going to get a lot worse for them before it gets better.

Daire strokes the back of his hand down my cheek, and I straighten up.

"I'm okay," I promise him.

Pulling me into his body, he takes a couple of steps back into the portal. When we come out the other side, we're at his childhood home.

Raising my face to the sun, I bask in its warmth for a second, letting it fill me with light and hope. He tugs me forward. Walking in the direction of the lake, I stop when I see the picnic laid out by the shore.

"You didn't really think it took me twenty-five minutes to get ready, did you?" He raises an arrogant eyebrow. "It took time to set this up."

"I did, actually," I admit, laughing. "Romantic. I'm impressed."

Sitting down on the blanket, I lean back and watch him unload the basket. He pulls out croissants with chicken salad, fruit, several slices of chocolate cake, a bottle of wine, and one of blood.

"I'm very impressed," I tell him.

He pours wine for me and blood for him, then places a portion of each on a plate and hands it to me.

"Are you not eating?"

"No, I'm not craving food." His voice husky and filled with hunger when he answers. He takes a long drink from his glass.

Neither Vargas nor Callyx texted or called me back last night. "While you're sitting there, would you text Lucifer and ask if he's seen or spoken to Vargas or Callyx?"

Sometimes they go undercover and it's hard to get a hold of them, so I'm not worried, but it doesn't hurt to check.

He sends a text and gets a reply a second later. "They're on assignment right now. Do you need him to reach out to them?"

When I shake my head no, he sends a text back to Lucifer with my answer.

I dig into the delicious food, recognizing Syn's touch in the seasoning and the fruit, which has been skillfully carved into flowers. While I eat, I study Daire. He removed his jacket and rolled up the sleeves of his white shirt, but he's left the tie on. His eyes are intense, watching every bite and expression of delight that crosses my face. A smile plays at the corner of his sinful mouth, and I wonder if he's thinking of this morning or something else. He really is too beautiful.

"Thank you for the picnic," I say, nibbling on a strawberry. When the juice drips down, I catch it with my tongue. "It's delicious. Almost as delicious as the taste of you this morning."

He chokes with laughter. "It made my top ten morning list," he informs me. "The only thing better would have been if you'd stayed the night and woke me up with your mouth."

Teasingly, I lick my lips. "I'll remember that in the future. What's in your top five mornings?" I'm curious to hear what he's found important in his long life.

He gives me a side glance. "The morning Danica was born. The morning my wings appeared. My first morning as a vampire. The last morning I spent with my mother. The first morning we woke up together."

I'm almost speechless. Having our first morning on the list is quite possibly the most incredible thing anyone has ever said to me. "That means a lot to me."

He moves over and gathers me in his arms. We soak up the peace around us while we listen to the mini waves lap the shore.

"Arden, I want to complete the bond with you," he murmurs. He pulls a piece of paper out of his pocket and hands it to me.

I read the verses written in Latin and shift so I can see his face. "Are you absolutely sure this is what you want to do?"

"I love you, Arden," he says firmly. "Those feelings will never change, but the vampire in me needs a bond to feel complete. Do you not want a bond with me?"

I shift until I'm on my knees completely facing him. "Having been reminded of my bond with Valerian the other day, I can understand why you want it. I'm bound to you regardless, but I'm willing to create something more between us."

He unbuttons his shirt until it's hanging on each side. Muscular abs wink at me from underneath, and I stretch a finger out and run it down the middle. He grips the hem of my shirt and waits. When I raise my arms, he pulls it over my head, leaving me in a racy blue bra I may have worn just for him. Blue eyes twinkle in appreciation.

"Once we've exchanged blood, we recite the verses," he tells me. "If anything feels weird or off, tell me immediately, and I'll get you to Lucifer. Okay?"

Swallowing, I signal my readiness.

He sweeps me up, then eases me down to the blanket. My head rests on his arm, and his body angles over mine. The delicious weight settles some of my nerves. His eyes search mine one last time but finds no resistance. I'm all in.

Firm lips capture mine, coaxing me to meet his, and thoughts of the ritual almost disappear. Hands roam my body, pinpointing sensitive spots, while his tongue plunders my mouth. A cloud of desire settles over us.

Pulling his shirt off, I caress the lines and grooves of his body with my fingers and nails. My hands glide to his back and find it warm from the sun. Kneading his muscles, I pull him closer to me.

Sharp teeth sink into the side of my breast, but unlike the other times, this vampire kiss is brief.

"Arden, look at me," he commands, and I raise heavy lids to find him staring down at me. "Are you ready?" The tip of a knife is held to his chest in the same place he bit me.

My eyes flick to his, and I raise up. "Yes."

He draws a thin line across and presses my mouth to it. I drink. I thought I'd be grossed out, but I guess I've tasted blood too many times when training. It doesn't even bother me. After a minute, I pull back and raise my hand to heal him.

Together, we say the verses, and I instantly feel him, like a piece of him has taken up residence inside me. It's exactly as Lucifer described.

I compare it to Valerian and our mate bond. My relationship with Valerian is warm and easy, but our mate bond is intense. With Daire, it's the exact opposite. Our relationship is intense, but the bond is light and easy.

My eyes meet his anxiously. Is this bond going to be enough? I hadn't realized I'd said it out loud until he answers.

His smile is almost carefree. "As soon as I felt the bond slip in place, all the violent, edgy feelings I've been experiencing disappeared, and for the first time in weeks, I feel like I can breathe. The possessiveness will likely never go away, but it might mellow with age." He lightly traces my features, then scoffs. "Probably not. I love you, Arden."

THIRTY-TWO

ARDEN

Theron has brought in a huge whiteboard to record all the information on our allies—numbers, magical capabilities, battle readiness, and experience. He also added the assigned leaders for each group, which Daire and Valerian put together. It's an impressive list, but our numbers are still a little light for war.

"Fallon renounced his throne," Theron divulges to the rest of the cadre. "We can't count on his elite legion of warriors, since they are independent of the king but led by Garrett. Unfortunately, Garrett is under a vow of allegiance to Fallon's father, which means Fallon needs to handle this delicately. We'll make plans without their force. We can always add them later."

Daire nods and Astor looks shocked.

Valerian gives a half shrug. "Fallon's always done everything his father asked of him. He never questioned his allegiance or duty. There were times I knew he chafed at the rigid rules his father enforced or an assignment he was given, but he never complained. If he felt the need to help someone, he used the cadre and did it in secret. There's only so many times you can bend before you either break or decide it's not worth it." He gives me a sly look. "He must have finally found something more important."

I blush and pretend to find something on my phone fascinating.

Valerian chuckles.

"Getting back to business," Theron inserts smoothly. "I've left a place blank for any witches who join us. I'm waiting to hear back from Oryn on the dark Fae king's approval, but I've added my legions to the board. Valerian, what have you heard from the shifters?"

"The wolves are grateful for our leniency in the battle the other night, and Grady's father and another leader have committed their packs to us. I'll send you the information, but it's the equivalent of five hundred wolves," he informs Theron.

Theron writes the information down on the board.

"We obviously can't ask any light Fae to join us," Theron remarks and taps the board under each of our allies. "My dark Fae, Valerian's dragons, Daire's vampires, and Lucifer's massive army make up our force for now, with tentative placeholders for Fallon's elites and any witches." They all eye the board. "It's not enough to take on the light Fae and their allies directly without the possibility of mass casualties on both sides."

"Maybe we should prepare for a two-prong attack," Daire suggests. "It's doubtful the light Fae queen will personally join the battle, and if she's our main target, we need to hunt her down separately. We could use the battle as a diversionary tactic."

The other three look at him with varying degrees of interest.

"My dragons are made for the battlefield, not stealth," Valerian interjects. "It means we'd have to split up."

"How do we guarantee she'll be in a specific place so we can plan accordingly?" Astor comments. "I think you're on the right track, Daire, but it's going to require two battle plans—one for the field and one for the queen. I agree with Valerian—we'd have to split up. Arden will have to be in the group attacking the queen, which means she'd be less protected and in more danger."

They all look at me, and I can tell how much they want me to veto this suggestion. They hate the idea of splitting up and sending me to attack the queen directly. It's the right strategy, but it leaves me vulnerable. "I agree. It's the best idea. The journal included one additional vision from my mother. Save the queen and restore balance. I don't know how I'm supposed to save someone who wants to kill me, but save or kill, I need to be near her. We should start working on a plan for a small attack group."

> Fallon: I've got great news. Meet me at the pond?

I show it to Theron who tosses my phone to Valerian.

Valerian reads it and gets up. "I'll escort you. Are you ready now, or do you need a few minutes?" He glances at the others, and they have one of their short, silent conversations.

I glance down at my leggings and T-shirt. "I'm ready." There isn't any reason to change to visit the pond.

VALERIAN AND I walk the path toward the pond. I chew my lip, wondering what Fallon's good news might be. My family on the dark Elven throne?

The clearing near the pond is empty. Turning, I close my eyes and find nothing. "Fallon's not here."

Valerian's brows come together. "This doesn't feel right."

"Let's give it a minute, and if he doesn't show, we'll leave," I tell him, also feeling uneasy with Fallon's absence.

I walk over to the edge of the pond and watch the waterfall for a few seconds. I wonder if I can still feel the water? Closing my eyes, I think about how the water felt, its consistency, the metaphorical taste of it, and a slow awareness falls over me. I feel it. I didn't forget anything Fallon taught me. My Elven power tingles, but it's not the water. Something else teases my senses, and I dig harder, trying to figure out what it is.

Opening my eyes, I look across the pond, but I don't see anything. "We should get going," I tell Valerian, turning to face him.

His eyes are scanning the area, but he nods.

I hear a roar behind me as water shoots up and surrounds me, then strong arms reach through the water and circle me. I lock on Valerian's look of rage and fear for a second, then I'm pulled under the water and into a hidden portal.

When I'm pulled out on the other side, I can't stop coughing. Water went down my airways, and I bend over, trying to get them clear. Someone slaps my back several times to help me clear my lungs. When I can finally breathe without choking or coughing, I stand up straight. Silver cuffs click closed on my wrists and shut off my magic.

Raising my head, I find Garrett standing in front of me. "Garrett? What the hell is going on?" I raise my cuffed hands to reach for my sword, but it's gone. So is the Killian blade I usually wear strapped to my thigh.

He gives me a sad look and admits to taking my weapons. "I took a vow of allegiance to my best friend and king a long time ago. If he gives me an order, I must follow it."

I read between the lines, and my heart stutters. "Your king ordered you to kidnap me? Does Fallon know?"

He purses his lips. "If the order requires me to keep the details quiet, I can't say anything. I haven't seen Fallon today," he admits.

I'm guessing he can only answer unrelated questions. Essentially, Fallon doesn't know I'm here. "Do you think Valerian saw your face?"

He tilts his head. "I'm sure of it, but the king's locked down the portals."

Despair tries to crawl up my spine, but I push it down. "You know I'm Fallon's mate?" When he nods, I continue, "Did you know he renounced his throne?" His eyes widen in disbelief. "He found out his mother was destined to be someone else's mate and his father stole her from him." He shrugs. "She was supposed to be your mate. You were supposed to meet her the same night the king met her."

"You're lying," he says gruffly. "I would too, in your shoes. Cast doubt, so you can divide and conquer. The king is mentally unstable now, but he wasn't always this way. He wouldn't have done that to me. I'm more than just his loyal commander; I've been his best friend my entire life. Let's go."

"Ask Fallon when he gets here. It's the reason he decided to renounce his throne. He's completely disgusted with his father's actions," I reply, hoping Fallon gets here sooner rather than later.

Garrett says nothing more, but simply pulls me toward the castle where the king awaits.

THE LIGHT ELVEN king circles me, then taps my cuffs. "Remarkable invention. It prevents someone from using their magic. Nobody knows who created them, but Fallon found them a long time ago and brought them home. For safekeeping," he adds, sneering at Fallon's idealism. "They've come in handy today."

My eyes dart around the room, trying to find anything I can use as a weapon, but there's nothing. The throne room is clear of everything except his throne, Garrett, and me. The only weapons are the ones Garrett is wearing, including my sword and blade, and my body. Granted, the latter is restricted by handcuffs, but at least my hands are cuffed in the front. I wonder if Garrett did that deliberately?

"Are you listening to me?" His voice is calm and mild, but his hand whips out and backhands me.

I slam to the floor. Shaking my head, I stay bent over on the floor, my hand on my cheek for a second. When he walks closer, I slam my heel into his knee and scramble to my feet. My hand jabs forward to hit his throat, but he moves at the last second and it glances off him.

A hand grabs the back of my head and digs into my hair, and he brings his other hand up to curl around my throat. Squeezing, he cuts off every bit of air, and the world starts to darken. He laughs, then throws a hard punch across my jaw, and I find myself on the floor again.

Thankfully, my face is numb, but I need to get air into my

lungs before I pass out. Taking sips into my lungs little by little is like breathing through a straw, but I eventually manage to fight back the darkness and inhale bigger breaths.

I refuse to cower before him and rise to my knees. "Bastard. No wonder your own son doesn't want your kingdom. He'd have to continue to put up with you." I spit in his direction.

He roars with rage. "It's your fault," he screams. Drawing his foot back, he kicks me hard in the stomach, and I fall forward, pain radiating from my waist. "Everything...was...perfectly...fine...until...you...came...along." He punctuates every word with a kick in my side, and I lock my jaw, refusing to give him the satisfaction of hearing me cry out. My entire body throbs, especially my ribs, but without my powers, I can't heal the broken bones.

"Sire," Garrett interjects, his voice is firm. "She's upsetting you, and you know that's not good for you. Why don't I put her in the dungeon? I can fetch her later when you're calmer."

The king laughs like Garrett just told a hysterical joke. "I didn't bring her here to put her in the dungeon." He walks over and slaps Garrett on the back. "You're going to kill her. If I do it, Fallon will never forgive me. I'll order you to do it, then I'll order you to keep silent. Simple." He flicks his fingers to me. "Kill her."

I can see the internal war in Garrett's eyes, but he slides his sword out.

"I told Garrett you stole his mate," I inform the king. "He didn't believe me." The king chuckles, making me see red. "The only reason I'm telling you is because Fallon believed you. It doesn't matter if I'm alive or not. He's disgusted with you and your actions. He will *never* come back here."

For the first time, I understand Fallon's motivations and his driving need to distance me from his father. I don't agree with the decisions he made without me, but I understand his deep-seated fear. His father can only be stopped by someone taking his power.

Anger mottles the king's face, and he grabs Garrett by the collar and shoves him toward me. "Kill her now."

Jerking forward, Garrett whispers an apology to me and raises his sword.

"Garrett, stop!" Fallon shouts, and if I weren't already on the floor, sheer gratitude would have driven me to my knees.

I slide a foot under me, then rise until I'm almost in a lunge.

"Don't touch her," the king shouts.

Hands grip me under my shoulders and haul me to a standing position. My eyes meet Fallon's, and a muscle ticks in his jaw when he sees my face.

"I told you not to touch her," the king says angrily.

Fallon gives a sad laugh. His fingers skim my cheek, and I wince. His eyes are bright green with power and rage. "If you'd ever had a mate, you would understand. Not touching her or being with her is the worst kind of torture. Seeing her like this makes me want to paint this room red with your blood. Father or not. King or not."

"Did he steal my mate?" The question slips out of Garrett.

"He did," Fallon confirms sadly. "My mother was your mate."

The sword in Garrett's hands drops to the floor, and he swivels toward the king. "How could you? I've served you all my life, been your champion and best friend, and you go behind my back to steal the only thing guaranteed to be mine? Why?"

"For a son," the king says nonchalantly. "It was my only shot. I'm a king with a kingdom, and I needed an heir. I made up for it, though. All these years, I've shared Fallon with you, fostered your close relationship. Don't think I'm not aware of how he looks up to you."

Fallon slides in front of me.

"Garrett, I gave you an order to kill her. Are you disobeying me?" The king crosses his arms while he waits for Garrett to answer his question.

Garrett reaches down and picks up his sword, then looks at Fallon for help.

"Father, let me introduce you to Torin, Arden's father, and the new King of the Dark Elves," he announces, diverting everyone's attention by pointing behind me.

Spinning, I see Torin standing there with his sword drawn. He's a stranger, and apparently a king now, yet he didn't hesitate to put his life on the line to follow Fallon into his enemy's palace. He'll be a great father someday.

His green eyes are dark with fury when he looks at me.

I give him a crooked smile in return, my face swollen from the punch I received earlier.

Stepping forward, he lifts his chin and introduces himself. "My name is Torin Balinor. I have to warn you, I'm not like the conniving, weak king who recently ruled the dark Elves. I protect what is mine, and I'm not afraid to fight for it. Kidnapping my daughter is reason for war. If you look out the window, you'll find my army ready for my slightest command."

A flash of recognition crosses the light Elven king's face when he hears my father's last name. I guess he remembers when the old king was in power.

"Take the cuffs off my daughter and let her go. Now!" My father steps forward and reaches for me.

The king calls out, "Guards!"

Several of the king's personal guards surround my father.

He backs up a step and tightens his hands on his sword, preparing to fight his way through them.

"Garrett," the king says softly.

Garrett flinches and steps forward.

Fallon steps forward until Garrett's sword tip is pressed into his chest. "Kill me first. I order you to kill me before you kill her."

"No!" both the king and I scream simultaneously.

"Fallon, what are you doing?" I question, trying to understand his reasoning.

"Garrett swore to uphold my life over his," he states simply.

I glance over at Garrett, who wears a small smile on his face. My eyes jerk back to Fallon's. "No, don't do this. I beg you. Fallon, you'll never forgive yourself."

Garrett takes a dagger out of his belt.

"He's your oldest friend. Are you really going to stand there while he kills himself?" I scream at the light Elven king.

He looks puzzled. "He should be following my order. Why isn't he following it?"

Fallon gives a mirthless laugh. "I'll tell you why. I've been collecting power from everyone for the last few weeks, along with their vows of allegiance. My plan was to take your throne."

The king stumbles back and looks at Fallon as if he's a stranger. "I don't believe you." His fist comes up, and he pulls a green ball of power from his chest.

Fallon repeats the gesture.

I look from one ball to the other. They're about the same size.

"Huh," Fallon says with a grunt. "I guess we're equal in power, which explains why Garrett is preparing to kill himself."

The king looks from me to Fallon to Garrett, indecision in his expression.

"Let's up the ante, shall we?" Fallon asks his father. "If Garrett kills himself, I will kill you and open the gates of this kingdom to anyone and everyone, then I'll walk away." He glances impassively at Garrett.

"If Garrett gives me some of his power, I will consider leaving you here to rule. Although, with considerably less power, I'm not sure how long you'll be able to hold on to your crown." Fallon nods in satisfaction when he finishes giving his father his options. "What's it going to be? Death, or live to rule another day?"

"Death," his father spits out.

Garrett smiles and shakes his head. Taking a small amount of power from his chest, he hands it to Fallon, who adds it to the ball in his hand.

"What are you doing?!" the light Elven king screams at Garrett.

"He gave us two options. I simply chose life. What do I care about a little loss of power? After all, I have no kingdom to consider, right?" Garrett hands my weapons to Fallon. He braces himself and gives Fallon a sharp nod, as if he's preparing for Fallon to strike him down.

"You will never serve this king again," Fallon orders him. "Your vow of allegiance is to yourself, not to me, or any other."

Garrett looks at him in disbelief, then straightens his shoulders. "My vow of allegiance will always be to you, whether you are king or not."

Fallon jerks his chin toward my cuffs. Garrett steps over with the key and unlocks them. My power buzzes like a nest of angry bees when the cuffs are removed.

A sweep of my finger, and the guards surrounding my

father are pinned to the wall. His eyes flick from them to me, and he raises an eyebrow.

I quickly heal the worst of my injuries, knowing the rest can wait until we're out of here. Where my hands go, Fallon's eyes follow, noting each place I heal.

"We're leaving," Fallon informs his father. "If you do anything to stop us, I'll take the rest of your power. I'd give you a warning for the future, but for some reason, I don't think you'll be around much longer. Your personal guards are the only ones left. The rest of the army is scattered, and I'm taking my elites with me. Goodbye."

The king stalks to the window, but whatever he sees drains the color from his face. "Fallon, come back here! They'll kill me. I need you. Fallon! Guards! Garrett!" he screams, frantic to save himself.

Fallon turns at the door. "You deserve whatever the Fates have in store for you."

When we get outside, I find the reason for the king's concern. Fallon's elite legions march with the massive army moving toward the castle.

"You really did bring an army," I say in disbelief.

"Of course, I did. You're my daughter, Arden," Torin—err, my father—informs me. "Thank you. Informing me of the king's death allowed me to put my plans into motion, but getting Fallon to understand our right to inherit and throw his support behind us was more than I expected." He pauses. "Can I hug you?"

"I've been waiting for a hug from you all my life," I say hoarsely. His arms wrap tightly around me, and I can't help the tears that fall. "I don't expect anything from you, but I have to say the army is a nice touch. Kind of seals the father deal."

He laughs. "I'll take anything I can get." He looks wistful. "Apart from the green eyes and height, you look so much like your mother." He fingers a lock of my hair. "Part of me is so angry with your mother for keeping us apart for so long, but if her visions can save your life, we'll have plenty of time to get to know each other."

Fallon clears his throat. "We need to leave here before the mob descends."

Torin pulls me into another hug. "We'll be in touch soon. Your grandmother is looking forward to meeting you."

"I know," I say, grinning when he gives me a puzzled look. "Elora sent a letter with Catriona's journal. I'm looking forward to meeting her too."

Torin whistles loudly across the valley and holds up a finger. The army stops, and with one last look toward me and Fallon, he steps into a portal by us and out by his army. With a flick of his hand, he opens a huge portal and marches the army into it, returning to his kingdom.

Fallon orders Garrett to lead the elites to another portal.

"Where are they going?" I ask.

"Winter. Theron offered them a home for now. Once we get past this battle, we'll decide where they should permanently live," Fallon says, watching until the last man is gone.

A portal opens to our right, and Fallon pulls me into it. When we enter the lobby at The Abbey, we're greeted by four very angry males.

Valerian immediately yanks me into his arms and holds me. "I'm sorry, lass. I failed you."

I caress our bond lightly, knowing it's the only thing that will settle him. It must have been exceptionally tough to watch me disappear right in front of his eyes. Garrett should probably avoid being in the same room with him for the next hundred years. "You didn't fail me. All of you must have moved fast to get to me so quickly."

Spinning me around, Daire looks me over from head to toe.

His eyes linger on the few small bruises remaining, and twin blue flames spear Fallon with a furious look that makes me shiver. "If the bond hadn't been in place, it would have taken us longer to find you. I located you within seconds, but Fallon's father blocked the portals. We had to track down Fallon because he was the only one who could bypass them. Are you hurt anywhere?"

"I healed the worst of it," I assure him.

Hearing I'd had to heal myself makes the tension in the room rise considerably. Ice already coats the walls and shadows swirl in the corners.

Theron is tapping his fingers on his thigh, and I walk over and lace my fingers through his. Violet eyes full of turbulence study me closely. I place a lingering kiss on his lips.

"I'm good. My father came with Fallon to save me, brought an army with him. I think he's going to be a good addition to our family," I explain, attempting to divert some of his anger, but the tic in his jaw tells me I'm not successful.

Astor twirls me into his arms and holds me tight, no quip or attempt at humor. He's silent, but when his shadows move from the corners toward Fallon, I realize that's my cue.

I spin around and pull Fallon's mouth down to mine. For thirty glorious seconds, I thank him for saving my life, for bringing my father to me, and for giving up everything to be here with me and the cadre. Knowing we have a future gives me the strength to pull away. We'll talk...later.

He protests, but I toss a look over my shoulder. "I think they want to speak with you. I'm going to leave you to your discussion and go have a hot bath." I wink and head towards the elevator. Not a second later, I hear the first punch.

CHAPTER

THIRTY-THREE

<u>ARDEN</u>

Vargas finally sent me a text early this morning to tell me he was on his way home. Apparently, the last mission had been tough, and he needed to decompress and see Solandis, but if I needed him now, he had a few minutes to chat. Relieved to hear from him, I decide it won't hurt to wait a few hours more. Goddess knows I'm not looking forward to telling him Nyssa is the enemy.

Daire and Valerian leave to get Cassandra and Grady. When they return, we put the pair in The Abbey's dungeon. I laugh when I think about my conversation with Meri. I guess I'll have to tell her she was right—The Abbey does have a dungeon, a pretty good one. The cells block magic and include reinforced bars made of silver.

We put them in the largest one, which Theron had modi-

256

fied to include a bathroom. Maya brought them some food, and for the first time, Cassandra didn't sneer at her. Maybe there's hope for her.

"You have about five hours before the meeting. I suggest you get some rest, eat, and clean up," I tell her.

Without saying a word to her, I silently cast a spell to remove the initials carved into her face. Probably not my finest moment, but given how close I'd been to killing her, it was a mild alternative.

Cassandra narrows her eyes but says nothing in return.

I accidentally brush the corner when I leave, and magic leaps inside me. It speeds through, seeking secrets, and leaves a second later. The magic almost felt sentient, like the Killian blades. Most magic needs a wielder and their intent to cast the magic. This magic wielded itself. I've never felt it upstairs, so this was new, and I make a mental note to ask Theron.

I head straight to the conference room, which we've renamed the war room.

When I walk in, all five are in there, joking and planning together, and it feels so good. Fallon is the backbone of the cadre, and he's been missed.

I glance at the whiteboard and see both my father's army —yep, that sounds weird—and Fallon's elites have been added. The only unknown are the witches, but I should have an idea over the next few days.

VALERIAN, Daire, Theron, and Fallon accompany me to Witchwood. I asked Astor to stay home, since he didn't need to be reminded of his past anymore. We portal directly to the gates and join the large crowd of witches. What's interesting is the sheer number of other supernaturals here.

We wait by the gate for Grady's father and another pack leader. Valerian spots them a few minutes later and brings them over.

A tall, very handsome older man approaches me with his hand outstretched. "I'm Duncan, Grady's father, and this is Connor, his uncle. We're two of the four pack leaders over all wolves." His voice is smooth and filled with charm. He flashes a smile full of white teeth.

"I'm Arden. Glad you could make it," I say and shake his hand. Instead of letting go, he moves a step closer, and I hear him sniff me.

Connor coughs and tilts his head towards the cadre, who've turned their full attention on Duncan.

I grab hold of Duncan's shirt and jerk him toward me. "Behave yourself, or I'll leave you outside with the other dogs." I flick my eyes to Connor. "That goes for you too."

Duncan smiles gets bigger, and he holds up his hands. "You can tell a lot with a handshake and a sniff, and I needed to know if you're worth the five hundred wolves we're sending to defend you."

I lift my chin. "Your verdict?"

"First, you're ripe with power—yours and the other five scents you wear. One step from me, and you were immediately on full alert. You aren't afraid to take on your own battles. Your firm handshake reflects your integrity, and the deep calluses on your hand tell me your sword isn't for show. Unlike most witches, you don't resort to magic as the first line of defense. Lastly, and this might be the most important thing...you aren't even remotely interested in me," he explains, finishing his assessment with a roar of laughter. His keen golden eyes watch the cadre ease back half a step.

Connor just shakes his head. "I won't shake your hand, but it's nice to meet you. Thank you for saving my son."

"I assume he was at the battle? There were a lot of wolves there," I remind him.

"Big black wolf. He said you threw a sword like a spear right through his middle." Connor's description jolts my memory. "I appreciate you not taking his head too."

"Ah, yes, the one who was trying to take down Prince Fallon. Lucky for him, I was distracted, or I might have taken his head," I drawl, watching Connor's face drain of color. "You might be happy to know he was one of the best fighters there." I glance at the cadre. "Are we ready to go? The meeting will start soon."

Theron steps up to my right and holds out his arm. I loop mine through it and take a deep breath. The battle with the wolves was easy compared to what's coming.

IT'S STANDING ROOM ONLY, but that suits both the cadre and wolves just fine. They arrange themselves against the wall to protect their backs. Tall, muscular, and handsome, they draw every eye in the place. Witches crane their necks to look at the six of them.

Everyone is seated at the council table, and I make my way over. Santiago motions to the wall and asks how I managed to add two more men to my harem. I hiss and tell him they're not mine, that they're here for the trial of one of their alphas. His eyebrows peak with surprise.

Caro bangs the gavel several times until everyone settles down. "Good afternoon. It's nice to see the entire coven turn out for this vote. We want to make sure everyone is represented, but first, we want to be sure and follow proper protocol. After all, we have a lot of guests here today." Her voice is sharp and filled with irritation when she mentions the guests. She spears me with a hard look, and I assume she's particularly upset about my guests.

"This meeting is open for new business," she states with a bang of the gavel.

I stand. "Hello, everyone, I'm Arden Karth Balinor. I have two very serious matters to discuss with you today."

I watch Caro's head swivel on a stick when I mention my new last name, which happens to coincide with the new King of the Dark Elves. Is it wrong to smirk? *Focus.* I dart a glance to Daire, who leaves and comes back seconds later with Cassandra and Grady in tow.

The entire crowd goes silent, heads and eyes swiveling back and forth from Cassandra to Caro while they try to guess what's going on.

Caro stands and bangs her gavel.

I tilt my head in her direction and wait.

"What is the meaning of this? I haven't been informed of any business beyond the vote," she sneers. "Please submit a proper proposal to the council, and we'll vote whether to include this business in the next council meeting."

I wave a hand toward the crowd. "Did you or did you not open the floor?" She nods and reluctantly sits down. Her eyes narrow on Cassandra in warning. "After the last council meeting, Cassandra, a hybrid witch and wolf, cast a blood spell on me to block my magic. Then she and her mate, Grady, Alpha of the Blood Moon Pack, plus a hundred wolves, attacked the Imperium Cadre and me." Grady slides a glance at Duncan, who returns it with a glare. "We have also learned Caro, Cassandra's mother, procured my blood for Cassandra to cast the spell. I would like to put both Cassandra and Caro on trial for this attack."

The crowd flies into an uproar, and I sit down.

Santiago whistles softly next to me. "You're never dull, are you? Is this what it's going to be like when I join your coven?"

"Who said I had a coven?" I murmur.

"Maybe we should come back to that question at the end of the evening," he concedes.

He's too damn smart for his own good, but I'm relieved to hear he'll join my coven. If I had one, of course.

Nico is banging the gavel. "Given the potential conflict of interest, I'll chair this meeting tonight. Everyone, please quiet down."

Once order is restored, he motions to the side, and Henry walks up with two vials and a broad smile. Nico flashes him a hard look, but Henry doesn't even blink.

"This is truth serum," Nico explains to the crowd. "We only use it when witches have been charged with serious crimes. It makes it easier to get to the information we need to make an informed decision."

"I hardly think that's necessary, Nico," Caro scoffs. "I'm a council member. If you can't trust my word, who can you trust?"

"Are you saying you're exempt from the same rules other witches must follow?" I ask.

"No, not at all," she says with a tinkling laugh. "I believe in order and rules. Let's proceed." Her eyes shoot daggers at me, but I ignore her.

The most interesting person here is Cassandra—the one with the most to lose, the one who is going to help my cause.

They both take the vial and swallow the contents.

"Caro, did you prick my arm at the council meeting last

week?" I pause. When she confirms, I continue, "Did you give your daughter the blood spell she used to block my magic?"

"Yes." The crowd really goes wild when she answers. Not only has Caro been against inclusivity, but she's also known for her policy against the use of blood magic. I guess all the rules went out the window when I came along.

Cassandra admits to using the blood to block my magic and the attack.

"Cassandra, are you also the mate of Grady, Alpha of the Blood Moon Pack, and a hybrid witch?" Nico asks in a booming voice.

"Objection," Santiago and I say simultaneously. I motion for him to continue.

"We have not voted on including the hybrid witches, and therefore, the question is irrelevant," Santiago reminds him.

"I think it's extremely relevant when one hybrid witch attacks another," Nico responds with mock sincerity. Quite a few witches in the crowd murmur their agreement.

I grip Santiago's wrist and shake my head. He sits and motions for Nico to proceed.

"Cassandra? Is this true?" he asks, prodding her for an answer.

"It's true," Cassandra says defiantly. I watch her eyes narrow at her mother when she says nothing to defend her. She walks up and faces her directly. "Did you ever have any intention of letting me back into the coven?"

"Of course not," Caro admits, still under the truth serum. "You made your...bed." She sneers at Grady. "Now you have to lie in it."

Pure devastation crosses Cassandra's face.

"Finally, the truth," she says snidely. With a scream of pure rage, she walks over and cuts her leaf off the tree. "I'd rather lose my magic than be a part of this coven, Mother. All my life, you've manipulated the witches to your advantage. Threatening some, bribing others. Spouting purist bullshit while secretly searching for a way to increase our bloodline's power. Yet when you have the answer in front of your face, you run.

"Why? Because you're afraid. Witches with more power than you means you'll lose your coveted role as council leader. Only the strongest rule, right? I'm stronger than you are now. Technically, I should take your place on the council." She laughs at the look on her mother's face. "Don't worry, I don't want it, but you'll not benefit from having access to my power either. Feel a little weaker?"

Caro stares at Cassandra like she's a cobra getting ready to strike. "When you make poor choices, you lose the right to be within a coven. A coven is stronger together. The decisions we make are for the benefit of all. The greater good is more important than any one person's pursuit of power."

Ouch. She's still under the truth serum, which tells me she believes everything she's saying. Pretty disturbing.

"I admit I committed a crime against another witch, but I did it for all of us—to ensure our coven had a future with strong bloodlines and the same traditions we've upheld for thousands of years." Caro walks through the crowd, placing a hand on one shoulder, then another, pleading for their understanding. Their heads bob in agreement and sympathy.

"It's time for sentencing," Nico says, interrupting Caro's performance to get on with business. "Cassandra, please face the council for your sentencing."

Cassandra steps forward, and Grady follows. He grabs her hand, and I watch her move the tiniest bit closer to him. Maybe the time spent in the dungeon helped them.

I stand. "Excuse me, Nico." I wait until he looks over at me. "Cassandra is no longer subject to our laws because she's no longer a member of this coven. The only one to sentence is Caro."

Cassandra's eyes dart from one council member to another before landing on me. She laughs. "That's absolutely right." Tugging Grady with her, she heads toward the wall, where Duncan and Connor are standing, but stops short when she sees the stern looks on their faces.

Nico bangs the gavel. "Let us confer with the rest of the council members. Arden, you're not allowed to participate due to personal conflict."

Personal conflict. I snort and watch them argue amongst themselves before Santiago throws up his hands and storms back to his chair. I guess it went in Caro's favor. Big surprise.

"Caro Pennington, we believe your intentions were good, but you did not act in the best interest of the coven. As punishment, we remove you from your seat on the council for six months. At the end of the six months, we will hold a vote for your return," Nico announces and bangs the gavel.

Caro huffs but looks satisfied with her punishment. Her dark brown eyes flash with victory, and she smirks at me.

Nico clears his throat and faces me. Sweat beads on his forehead. "Arden, we feel you should have discussed this situation with the council first. You effectively ambushed this meeting, and your actions do not reflect the best interest of this coven. We're removing you from the council, and we reserve the right to remove you from the coven, based on the outcome of the vote."

I study each member of the council to see which ones voted in favor of my removal. Nico, Amelie, and surprisingly, An. I smile. It's always good to know your enemies.

Nico straightens and raises a piece of paper. "We're passing along ballots for the vote—"

I stand, deliberately halting his speech. "Excuse me, Nico,

I'm still a part of this coven, and I have the floor. If you remember, I explained in the beginning I had two items of business. We've dealt with the unpleasantness of the first, a tedious but necessary exercise, and I'd like to discuss the second."

Nico waves a hand in frustration.

I see Cassandra heading toward the door. "Cassandra, you may want to stay for this next piece of business."

THIRTY-FOUR

ARDEN

Cassandra halts on the threshold and turns to give me a speculative look. She must like what she sees because she lifts her chin and strides back to the wall. Leaning against it, she crosses her arms and props her foot up.

After watching Cassandra tell the entire coven the truth about her mother and seeing them bury their heads in the sand, I knew they would never change. Most of them are sheep, happily following Caro to their destruction. It only cemented my decision, but I'm glad I got to watch it.

I hold up the original stone. "This is the stone that feeds all witches' powers. A long time ago, a MacAllister witch met a dragon and fell in love. In her quest for immortality, she accidentally created this stone and discovered it exponentially increased her powers. Instead of simple spells to conjure fire or heal small wounds, it gave her the power to cast real magic. When her children were born, she fed their blood to the stone, and their powers grew as well." I step down from the table and walk over to the tapestry.

"From this stone, grew the Rowan tree. It connected the MacAllisters to each other, but the main source of their magic remained with the stone. A sacred tree, the Rowan sought other humans with the potential for magic, and when they mated with other supernaturals, they became new branches on the tree, and the seven bloodlines were born." I pause and look toward the cadre for a second and smile.

"The witch never did gain immortality, but she did grow older than the average mortal. In her later years, she pulled a thorn from the tree." I walk over to the table beside the tapestry and pick up the bowl with the thorn in the middle. "Promising the witches they would collectively have greater power, she told them to place their hands upon the thorn and swear an oath. They did. Their powers increased because they collectively shared in each other's power and because they were now tied to the stone."

The crowd's voices rise as they discuss this newest piece of information.

"Feeling their most powerful, they decided to cut off—" I point to the many severed branches near the oldest parts of the tree "—every single witch of mixed blood. The strength of the bloodline weakened, but their vision of the future only included strong, pure witches, so they were willing to take a short-term loss for a long-term gain. The MacAllisters were the only branch who refused to follow this new doctrine."

I hold the stone up. "Unfortunately, human witches are the most prolific supernaturals in the world. When more and more witches were born, they, too, pulled from the source. The stone and their magic grew weaker. The MacAllisters realized the stone needed to be refueled by the same power that originally created it—dragon's flame and witches' blood. So they did, repeatedly, until they were massacred. This stone used to glow with white hot power. Now it's dark, the magic almost gone."

They break out into loud discussions, fighting over the details. Nico bangs the gavel incessantly, but they continue to ignore him.

I walk over to the tree and cut off my leaf and the Rowan name. I cut off my father's and grandmother's leaves. The coven instantly feels the loss of power, and it silences the room.

Cassandra stands up straight, her eyes dark with glee.

I hand the dark stone to Nico. "Please consider this my resignation from the coven."

He grips it tightly in his hand and shares a look of victory with Caro.

I pull out the new stone, brilliant in its intensity, and watch while it mesmerizes the crowd. "I've started a new coven. I know many of you are comfortable here with the established rules and puritanical beliefs. I wish you the best. My coven will be open to all witches."

Santiago immediately stands up with a huge smile on his face. "I resign from this council and the coven. Those of my bloodline will be given the choice of staying under your rule or following me to the new one." He strides up and cuts off his and Reyna's leaves.

The crowd gasps.

Katarina saunters over to the tree and cuts off her leaf, then joins Santiago and me in the middle of the room. "What he said," she drawls, waving a hand at Santiago.

Caro laughs heartily. "Why would anyone follow Arden? Go ahead. A coven of four isn't going to be very strong. When you're ready to come back, let me know. We'll consider it.

Except for you, Arden." She sits on the chair behind her and leans back with a smug smile on her face.

"You want to know why?" I start to recount the reasons, ticking them off with my fingers. "I'm the strongest witch in the coven, with all seven bloodlines, and I'm immortal. Our coven will include hybrid and pure witches, which means we'll collectively be stronger and will easily exceed the power of the hundreds of witches in your coven. Unlike you, I won't manipulate them." I pause. "Most of all, it's because they know they deserve to have a coven who puts them first."

Caro scoffs, but I watch her assess the witches around her to see if any of my remarks resonated with them.

Henry steps forward and bows toward Caro. "I am tendering my resignation," he informs her.

"You are bound to serve this coven for the rest of your life," Caro states firmly. "Do not test me, Henry."

Henry laughs. "If you read the contract, you'll see I'm bound to serve *a* coven of witches for the rest of my life. A small, very fine detail I made sure was included. I will still be serving a coven, just not yours." He snaps his fingers, and a contract appears in his hand. He walks over to me. "May I serve your coven?"

I slide my eyes over to Theron, who gives me an almost imperceptible nod. "Yes, we'd love to have you with us, Henry. We don't need a butler, but we can find something you want to do."

He reaches over and places the contract in my hand. "It's official. You're stuck with me."

I'm a little nervous about this last exchange. I didn't even know Henry had magic, but the appearance of the contract from thin air proved he does. Theron better have good instincts on this one.

My eyes look over the crowd to see if anyone else would

like to join, but they avert their eyes. All except one. She stands up and walks over to me.

"I, Bianca Perrone, announce my resignation from this coven," she states firmly. Walking over to the tapestry, she cuts off her leaf. Nico roars in the background.

I give her a huge hug to welcome her, then I make eye contact with every witch who has a supernatural sitting with them. Those are the ones that will join our coven. "I hate long goodbyes. If you want to join my coven, the offer is open. You can contact me, Santiago, or Katarina. Make sure you cut your leaf off the tree," I instruct them, knowing that will be the true test of their commitment to join. "Caro, Nico, An, and Amelie, I'm sorry you won't be joining us."

The cadre, Duncan, Connor, and the rest follow me out of the room. I stop at the doorway and glance at Cassandra. "Anybody who has the strength to cut off their own leaf without a parachute is welcome to join. Be very sure it's what you want, because I'm only going to give you this one warning. If you aren't loyal to the coven, or you attack me or mine again, I'll kill you."

<u>ARDEN</u>

Vargas didn't call last night. I called and nobody answered, so I'm calling again this morning. When it goes straight to voicemail, I get a tiny bit worried. When I was a child, he'd be gone for days, unreachable because of the stealth required to do his job, so it's not entirely out of the ordinary, but he knows this is urgent.

I don't want to call Solandis, because I want Vargas nearby when I tell her about Nyssa's involvement. He's the only who can prevent her from confronting her sister. As a last resort, I send another urgent text to Callyx, asking him to call me or find Vargas.

Valerian begged off training this morning to meet with Glynnis on official dragon business, so I'm luxuriating in my extremely comfortable bed. Not even coffee is enough of a temptation to make me leave its downy softness. When someone knocks on the door, I don't get up.

"Come in," I call out.

Theron strides in and stops when he sees me in bed. He raises his phone to view the time and lifts his eyebrow. "Are you feeling okay? Do you need to talk about yesterday?"

"I'm good," I assure him. "Valerian canceled training and for the first time in a long time, I don't have somewhere to be. This bed is supremely comfortable."

He walks over and sits beside me. "All the leads have been invited here tonight to discuss the logistics of the main battle —timing, location, strengths, and weaknesses of each group, etc. We'll start the meeting before the club opens. Once it's finished, the club will be in full swing, and we'll be able to hide their departures. The agenda only includes the main battle. Once we have more details on the second group, we'll inform them."

"Thank you for organizing everything," I tell him. "I know you love the planning, but it's a huge effort and I appreciate everything you're doing."

"We have one shot at her. Failing is not an option," he murmurs while he absentmindedly traces my features with his finger.

When it sweeps across my mouth, I use my lips to grab it and swirl my tongue around the tip. I release it with a laugh. Gracing him with one of my cheeky grins, I stretch, letting the sheet drop to my waist.

Instead of his signature icy look, his violet eyes are smoldering when they trace the curves now displayed in front of him.

His phone pings, and he picks it up to look at the message.

I pluck it out of his hand, slide it under the covers, and put it between my thighs. "Pay me a toll, and I'll give it back. It had better be a good one, though. Worth missing out on a delightful morning."

I raise one eyebrow in challenge, and the light of battle enters his eyes.

With a deep chuckle, he stands. "I'll pay the toll. You should know by now, good isn't a level I strive to achieve. Only your complete and utter satisfaction will do."

Yes, please. Arrogance can be so deliciously sexy, particularly when it's delivered with a promise.

He takes off his jacket and lays it at the foot of the bed. With excruciating slowness, he unbuttons his shirt, and it joins the jacket. He pulls off the tie and lays it to the side.

I'm almost panting with excitement and anticipation.

He plants two hands beside my head and leans over me. Seconds later, cool lips find mine in a hard, dominating kiss. There's nothing soft about this kiss. It's full of need and possession. The smell of dark chocolate and peppermint drifts in the air. Flattening, his lips ravish mine, demanding my passion rise to meet his.

Ice circles my nipples, and I can't help the sound that escapes. Tearing my mouth away, I glance down. Ice encases the tips of his fingers, turning them into icy tormentors. They circle my nipples, making them harden into peaks. Focusing on one, he rolls and tweaks it.

His other hand grips my chin, guiding my mouth back to his.

He switches his icy attention to the other nipple, and I give a muffled cry of pleasure.

The juxtaposition of his icy fingers against my heated skin makes every nerve stand at attention. My mind can barely focus because it's consumed with the cool touch of his hands on my body.

When both nipples are hard and aching with pleasure, he

trails a single cold finger down the center of my body until it reaches its destination between my legs. Finding his phone, he plucks it out and lays it to the side, then returns.

My legs fall open, and his icy finger travels from the bottom of my slit back up to the top. When the tip lands on my nub, it's no different than a wet ice cube, and my mind zeroes in on that one frigid point. Ice cold drops slide from the top to the bottom, and I can't help but seek more.

My green eyes meet his violet ones, and I'm ensnared by the emotion I find. He likes seeing what his touch does to me. They burn fiercely with desire, sparking each time a tremor pulses through my body or a sound escapes me.

My breath catches when his clever fingers increase their speed, and I surrender, letting his icy magic shatter me into pieces. Not once do his eyes leave mine, not until my body calms.

Wearing an incredibly satisfied, very male smile, he leans down and murmurs, "Was the toll worth it?"

"I feel like I owe you some change," I say huskily. "Ice, huh? I won't be able to think of anything else for a while."

His violet eyes flash in agreement.

Both our phones ping, and we grab them. The world is intruding.

Within a minute, he's gone, and I'm rushing into the shower.

THE REST of my morning is filled with visits from witches wanting to join the coven. Bianca, Santiago, and Katarina stop by first. They add their blood to my stone, and I give them each one of the smaller replicas.

When they look at me in surprise, I explain how I want to structure the coven. "As leaders of the larger coven, we'll work together on policies and laws, but you'll govern your individual covens. Recruit whomever you want instead of relying only on the original bloodlines. The more mixed the heritage, the stronger your coven will be overall, and the more you'll thrive. There are only six smaller stones. I'm selecting the leads carefully. Any questions?"

Katarina and Santiago have a ton of questions. Some I can answer, but others we'll have to figure out over time. Bianca hasn't said a word the entire time.

I lay my hand on hers. "Is everything okay?" I'm worried she's regretting her decision to leave.

"I don't want to lead my own coven. I was hoping I could become part of yours," she explains softly. She twists her hands together.

"You're family. I'd love for you to become part of my coven," I reassure her.

With a relieved smile, she hands me back the stone.

"If witches don't choose to join one of our individual covens, we can decide together where to place them," I tell Santiago and Katarina. "I'm going to need you both to take point on the influx of new witches, though. I'm going to be busy preparing for war."

If this coven is going to work, we need transparency. They need to understand what's happening right now. I explain all about the Primary, my life, and our intention to attack.

Santiago and Katarina share a look.

"If you have witches who wish to join the fight, send them my way, but nobody is obligated to follow me to battle," I emphasize the last part.

They give a relieved nod.

Surprisingly, Bianca looks intrigued. "I'd like to go to war." She laughs at the expression on my face. "I'm the best portal creator on this planet. I've been everywhere and nobody has ever known. Best of all, I've been to the light Fae queen's palace."

"Somebody's been hiding their talents," I joke. "This is huge. When we start planning the second piece, I'll bring you in to help."

She beams.

I sit in on the first part of the planning meeting, but battle strategy requires a lot of knowledge and expertise, none of which I have, so I decide to check on the club.

Sitting in the VIP section, I order a drink and watch the crowd below. Eyes and heads turn in my direction, and I know they're speculating on my identity and relationship with the cadre.

"You know you're supposed to have one of us with you at all times," Astor reminds me. He signals for the server and slides into the booth across from me.

I eye the five feet between us and give him an icy glare.

"Don't give me that look," Astor admonishes me. "Someone else called dibs on you this evening, gorgeous. I'm just honoring the deal."

"You're calling dibs now?" I question him.

"It's not like it sounds," he says, exasperated. "Don't worry."

A beautiful man with thick, wavy, caramel colored hair

catches my eye. I've seen him walking around all evening. Even before the meeting, I glimpsed him at the bar. I thought he may be a new server, but he's not waiting tables. My senses are tingling, and I continue to follow him. He's not with any group, and he never sits at a table. Alert, his eyes constantly scour the room for someone or something.

"Who has you so intrigued?" Astor asks in a hard voice. "Is it a threat? Do we need to alert the others?"

"Yes."

He immediately picks up his phone and calls Theron. "Get down here. We might have a potential threat in the club. I don't know. Arden's instincts are screaming."

Not even a second later, Daire's standing beside me. Bending down, he follows my line of sight and murmurs, "Brown-haired guy? Blue suit?"

I nod.

He disappears.

Theron, Valerian, and Fallon arrive.

Astor explains what's going on while I frantically search for the guy.

Theron's phone pings. "Daire went to grab him, but he disappeared."

"What do you mean disappeared?" I challenge him. "Like he lost him in the crowd?"

"No, he literally disappeared in front of me," Daire replies, walking up the steps.

I'm about to question him further when the dance floor lights up, and Maya steps into the center. Heaving a sigh, I shelf my frustration for now.

"We have a special treat for everyone tonight. Please clear the floor."

The lights go down, and huge males line the edge of the dance floor. The low beat of "Born For This" by The Score starts. Beating their fists to their chests, they walk forward into the light, and Valerian pulls me to the rail. When they see us, they bow low and begin the first words of the song.

When the chorus hits, they stomp their feet in a choreographed beat to the song, then the song's lyrics kick in and they sing. The crowd goes wild. Every time they sing about having the same name, the crowd shouts, "Dragons!"

Watching these normally stoic men raise their voice and declare themselves dragons is compelling and magnificent. As the last bars of the music play, they stomp into a circle and face the center. A column of flame appears for a brief second. When it's gone, a necklace floats in the air. They look up at Valerian and me.

Valerian grabs my hand and pulls me down to the dance floor.

Glynnis appears and walks over to stand in front of us. "Before you go to battle, the council wants the world to know you are protected and claimed by dragons. Until you came along, we floundered. Our time had no purpose, our king had few followers, and we were stuck in the old ways with no path forward. We're a proud race, but we'd forgotten what it meant. You reminded us. Honor is non-negotiable. It would be our honor if you would accept and wear the Eye of the Dragon on behalf of all dragons."

Floored, I stare up at Valerian and see the pride and tears shining in his eyes. "The honor would be mine. I accept," I state clearly.

Glynnis takes the necklace in her two hands and hands it to Valerian.

I turn my back to him, and he places it around my neck and closes the clasp.

She gives a sharp look to the dragons standing around, and they all drop to one knee with their fists on their chests.

Unable to help myself, I pull Glynnis in for a hug. "Thank you," I whisper.

When I step back, I walk over and shake every one of the dragon's hands. Most of them I met during the training session, so we laugh and joke with the familiarity of old friends.

When I'm done, Valerian swings me around in his arms. "I'm so proud of you." His pouty lips capture mine, and the crowd cheers.

CHAPTER
THIRTY-SIX

<u>ARDEN</u>

Pounding on the door pulls me out of my sleep the next morning. Valerian gets up to answer, and I hear the low murmur of voices.

He closes the door and eats up the distance between us. "Arden, we need to go. Get dressed, put on your armor, and gather your weapons. We're meeting in the lobby in ten minutes." Walking to his closet, he pulls on his own clothes and yanks out a large duffel from the bottom of his closet.

Alarmed, I sit up. "What's going on? Are we under attack?"

"Lucifer's here. He says Vargas is in trouble," he throws over his shoulder, moving to the bathroom to finish getting ready.

Scrambling up, I race out the door and down the hall to my room.

Hard, battle ready faces greet me in the lobby. Lucifer, the

280

cadre, Daevyn, Garrett, and Drystan are waiting for my arrival. The sight of the commanders makes me wonder what we're walking into, but I don't get a chance to ask.

Theron opens the portal, but Lucifer leads the charge. When we step out on the other side, I open my mouth in a silent scream. Instead of the beautiful modern showcase we left a couple weeks ago, Solandis and Vargas' house looks like a bomb hit it. Rubble is everywhere. The metal and glass door is torn halfway off its hinges, and half the panes are missing. Windows are shattered. Smoke billows from inside.

I'm hot on Lucifer's heels, racing toward the house. When we pass the front door, I see a high-heeled shoe lying beside it. It belongs to Solandis. Fear clogs my throat. I clench my jaw to keep from crying out their names. I don't know if their attackers are still here, but if they are, I'm not warning them of our arrival.

Lucifer pauses and closes his eyes.

Watching intently, I realize he's trying to sense Vargas' location. Interesting. I didn't know they had a connection or a bond.

While we wait for Lucifer to lock onto Vargas, I look at Valerian. "We should split up and search for Solandis and Vargas separately."

He nods, uses a few hand signals to inform the others, taps Drystan and Daevyn on the shoulders, and leads them to the right.

Fallon and Garrett head to the left.

Theron and Daire remain with Lucifer and me.

"This way," he directs. We hit the hallway and silently make our way to their bedroom. "Wait here." Lucifer slips inside, hardly more than a shadow, to look for Vargas.

A minute later, he comes out with Vargas' body in his arms, and I clamp my hands around my mouth so I won't cry out. In all my life, I've never seen Vargas go down. He's grey and bleeding from several areas. Lucifer hands him to Daire and orders him to get him back to The Abbey.

"Wait," I whisper. I bend over and place my mouth near his ear. "Hold on, Vargas. Do you hear me? I love you. Solandis and Callyx love you. Hold on." Tears slide down my cheeks, but I ignore them. Kissing Vargas' cheek, I silently beg Daire to do whatever he needs to save him.

He dips his chin and leaves with Vargas held tightly in his arms.

"Where are the guards?" I murmur to Lucifer. "He's supposed to have additional security here." I dart into a few rooms. "The staff is also missing."

"I don't know." Lucifer thrusts his hand through his hair in frustration. He stiffens when a low whistle reaches us.

We run to the living room and find Fallon with Solandis in his arms. She's missing her shoes, blood drips from a gash on her head, turning her golden hair a mottled brown, her arm's bent at an odd angle, and her clothes are torn. She fought hard.

I sway and reach out to the wall to steady myself. "Go, get her help."

Fallon and Garrett rush to the portal to get Solandis back to Daire and The Abbey.

The rest start to follow, but I shake my head. "Callyx?"

Lucifer places a hand on my shoulder. "He's on a mission. I haven't been able to get a hold of him for the last two days," he admits softly. "My men are searching for him."

Sagging against the wall, I try to stop the world from spinning, but it's like trying to hold onto the wind. Turquoise eyes flash in my mind. "Meri!"

I take off in the direction of Meri's room. When we get there, it's empty. The bathroom too. Maybe the kitchen? I start to race out of the room, but Theron grabs my arm.

"Wait," Theron demands. "The security feed will tell us if she left on her own or..." He lifts his phone and taps on it.

Or if someone took her.

He brings up the video of the room. We see her entering about three hours ago, lying on the bed for a nap, then nothing happens for the next hour. Suddenly, her door flies open and Solandis enters. Golden aura surrounds Solandis on the screen, which tells me she's using magic. A bubble appears in the room. She pulls Meri over to it, but they argue. She glances frantically over her shoulder, then Solandis shoves Meri into the bubble. It disappears with Meri in it, while Solandis rushes out of the room.

Nothing else appears on the video for the next forty-five minutes, then the door slowly opens. Nyssa, Queen of the Light Fae, strides confidently into the room. She stops, and the white aura surrounding her tells us she's using her magic, but nothing happens. With a frown, she walks around the room, looking into the closet, under the bed, and in the bathroom. It hits me—her magic didn't find Meri, but she refuses to believe she's not here. Ten minutes later, she walks out.

Rage. Pure, unadulterated rage pours through me. Other than mild irritation, Nyssa showed little emotion the entire time she was in this room. Not once did she look remorseful or guilty or upset, yet she'd already fought both Solandis and Vargas. I can understand Vargas, since Nyssa hates him, but how could she not be upset about attacking her own sister? She hurt Solandis, then left her here to die instead of taking her to a healer. Why? A message for Meri? It's not adding up for me. I close my eyes and reign in the anger. We need to locate Meri.

If Nyssa didn't find Meri, it means Solandis didn't use Fae magic. The only other magic in the house...Vargas.

"Lucifer, she used Vargas' magic. Can you sense anything in the room? A void or an abundance of demon magic?"

He walks slowly around the room but finds nothing until he gets near the closet. "Here." An incantation spills from his lips, and a translucent bubble appears.

Meri is still inside, banging her fists against the bubble's walls, but we hear nothing. She sees us and stops. I see her mouth the words, 'Get me out.'

Lucifer's hands hover over the bubble, then he punches directly through it. With a pop, it disappears.

Meri rushes into my arms. "Solandis? Vargas?"

I hug her back and lift a shoulder. "The guards or staff?"

Meri shakes her head and walks toward the door. "I don't know what happened to the guards. Solandis gave the staff the day off."

Her words have my head whipping around in a second. "She gave the staff the day off?" Not once in all my years of living with Solandis did she ever give the staff the day off. "Damnit. She invited Nyssa over to tell her about you."

Guilt hammers me. Why didn't I try harder to get a hold of Vargas? If Solandis had known Nyssa was the Primary, she wouldn't have invited her here.

Meri's face also fills with guilt.

"Fallon sent a text. He forgot to mention that they checked the rest of the house and didn't find anyone except Solandis. Lucifer, what do you want to do about the guards?" Theron asks him. "Daevyn and I can help you look?"

Lucifer nods. "Thank you, I'd appreciate it. I want to make sure they're not here before we leave. I don't think anyone should come back here."

I walk over to Meri's closet, grab a bag, and start filling it with the few clothes hanging in there. She grabs things from her dresser and the bathroom and tosses them on the top. I zip it up and hand it to her.

"Can you help me grab some of Solandis' and Vargas' clothes?" Anything to keep us busy while they quickly search for the guards.

Everything's replaceable, but they'll need some clothes and toiletries for the next few days. I also grab a few of the photographs sitting on Solandis' nightstand. She'd framed one of the silly ones we took at the Underworld ball a few weeks ago. My knees give out, and I drop heavily to the bed to stare at the happiness on our faces. It feels like so long ago. What if we never find our way back to silly pictures?

"Let's go," Theron says hoarsely from the door. His face is white, drained completely of color, and his violet eyes are filled with shock.

"What happened to them?"

He refuses to tell me, just sweeps his hand toward the front door.

Lucifer is standing outside with his face turned up to the sky. Rage is pouring off him in dark waves, and the ground is trembling. When he turns to watch us walk out of the house, flames burn brightly in his red eyes.

I walk over and stand by Lucifer. Instead of facing the house, my eyes scan the hills and forest surrounding the house. "I didn't figure it out until I came outside and saw you perfectly silhouetted against the backdrop of the house. She left Solandis here, by herself, badly hurt and bleeding. It floored me."

Lucifer stiffens when he catches my train of thought.

There's not a whisper of sound nor any movement anywhere. "She's here somewhere. Originally, I think she was waiting for Meri to show herself. Now she's watching us. If it had been you with some of your men, she wouldn't have thought twice. Or me, by myself or with a friend. Nothing. You and I showing up with the Imperium Cadre and their commanders? Her instincts are screaming. We'll have to move the timetable up." I turn to face the destruction before us.

He squats and picks up a handful of dirt. With a few whispered words, he blows the sand out of his hand. Moments later, the house and all its contents disappear. "Don't worry, I sent it to a safe place." Behind the house, the remains of his men lie scattered in pieces everywhere. With a sweep of his arm, fire burns in a large circle around them. More words from Lucifer's low voice, and the flames are replaced by a unit of fire soldiers, comprised of remnants from their original bodies and the hellfire Lucifer created.

They line up in front of Lucifer. "Go, hunt your killer," he commands them. They march off toward the forest. "It will keep her busy for a while, but you're right—we need to finalize our planning and mobilize in the next few days. Let's go."

CHAPTER
THIRTY-SEVEN

<u>ARDEN</u>

We rush back to The Abbey. Maya shows us to the room where Daire and Alix are working on Solandis and Vargas. They both look like they're running on empty, drained of their healing power, but they're still working on their patients.

When we enter the room, Daire looks relieved. "Vargas needs one more healing to fix the worst injuries. Our main concern is Solandis. She isn't responding to any of the treatments."

I head straight to Solandis. Her beautiful features are still covered in dirt and blood, but it looks like Alix healed the cut on her head. I check her arm and find it fixed and resting at her side. Hovering my hands over her, I expect to find internal injuries, but there's nothing. Nothing torn, bleeding, or broken. I give Alix a puzzled glance.

"I healed every physical injury on her body. I've never seen anything like it," she replies with a sigh. "I don't know why she isn't waking up. I'm going to go back to Winter to do some research. For now, we should make her comfortable."

"Thank you for helping her," I say, switching my gaze back to Solandis. "If you can find anything, I would greatly appreciate it."

With a little magic, she's clean and dressed in her favorite loungewear. I tuck her into bed, pull the sheet up around her, and lean over to kiss her cheek. I'm not sure what's worse—thinking she's dying or seeing her in this state and not knowing how to fix her. Either way, I am utterly powerless, and my rage comes roaring back. I hate this feeling. My hands clench into fists, and I barely hold in the scream threatening to burst out of my throat.

"Arden." Daire's smooth voice injects a sliver of calm into me. "Vargas needs you."

I take a few deep breaths and flash Daire a grateful smile. Straightening my hands, I walk over to Vargas and give him one more treatment. When it's done, his body falls into a deep but restless sleep. I clean him up and place him beside Solandis, hoping the proximity will help, but it doesn't. He continues to mutter incoherently, and his sleep is far from peaceful.

Daire wraps his hands around my shoulders and eases me back against him. "The cadre will take shifts guarding them."

"We can't," I say regretfully. "Nyssa knows we were there tonight. She doesn't know what we're planning, but any element of surprise will be lost if we don't move in the next few days."

"I'll stay with them," Meri offers from the doorway.

"We can also help," Maya interjects. She stands beside Meri with Syn at her side.

Leaving Solandis and Vargas in anyone else's care goes against every instinct in my body, but I can't give Nyssa too much time to figure things out either. "Thank you. I appreciate it."

Maya and Syn tell Meri they'll be back later to relieve her.

Daire places a kiss on my forehead and leaves to refuel and get a shower.

Meri comes into the room and stands beside me. Tears roll down her face. "I've known more...everything in the last few weeks than in the entirety of my life, all because of her," she says, reaching down to grab Solandis' hand. "She's so incredible. I didn't even know laughter could make your face hurt until I met her." She gives a broken laugh. "I can't stand to see her so still."

"I know. I'm sorry," I cry out. "This is my fault. I should have done more to get in touch with Vargas to let him know Nyssa was the Primary. He would have kept Solandis from contacting her."

Meri shakes her head sadly. "No, he wouldn't have been able to stop her. Solandis' view of Nyssa is completely warped. I've been trying to convince her I didn't want to meet Nyssa, but she refused to believe it. I couldn't tell her the truth. Nyssa is screwed up. She's not even remotely close to Solandis' rosy picture of her." Her lips curl in disgust.

"You've met her?"

Meri shakes her head no. "My guardian sent me to Rivan to get a tattoo." She taps behind her ear, and I remember her telling me about it when we first me. "Just as he was finishing it, we heard screaming in the hallway. Rivan shoved me into a closet and told me not to come out, no matter what I heard, or she would kill me. Having my own psychotic guardian at home, I quickly understood what he was trying to tell me." She shudders, and I squeeze her tightly.

"The punishment she laid on Rivan with her own two hands... It was so bad." Meri's voice drops to a whisper. "At the end, she laughed, thanked him for being so unbreakable, then left. I waited for two hours before I came out of the closet. When I saw Rivan, I puked. His beautiful skin had been completely shredded by her nails. The only part she left intact was his face. I raided the infirmary, made up my special blend of healing potions, and stayed with him for three days. When I was sure he was going to make it, I left."

Appalled, I shake my head in disbelief. "I haven't spent much time around her, but she always seemed kind of cold to me. I've never even seen her in a rage, but I know she went into one when she found out Solandis and Vargas were mates. Solandis glosses over the incident, but it took a while for her and Nyssa to get back on speaking terms, so I know it must have been bad."

Shouting fills the hallway. I quickly hand Meri one of the Killian blades and shut her in the room with Vargas and Solandis. When I reach the corner nearest to me, I slide a look around the corner and see Cormal shouting at Lucifer. My eyes widen. I'd previously thought Cormal to be pretty damn intelligent, but now I'm not so sure.

Another man comes into view and leans heavily against the wall. "Cormal, this isn't helping."

I start running and slide to a stop in front of him.

"Callyx," I say, tears clogging my throat.

I wrap my arms tightly around him and squeeze as hard as I can. He's alive. *Thank you, goddess.* Sobs well up, and I can't hold them back. Burying my face in his shoulder, I don't even try. I need my big brother right now.

He pats me awkwardly on the back. "I'm a little banged up, but not too bad. A little healing from you, and I'll be good."

I grip him tighter and move my head back and forth.

Lucifer's voice is low when he fills him in on the attack.

Callyx stills, then wraps his arms tightly around me. "They'll be okay. Dad's too tough to kill, and Mom..." His voice breaks. "She can't stand to miss out on anything. You know she'll wake up in a few days and chide everyone for making a 'fuss.' Then she'll milk it for every last drop, and we'll be waiting on her for weeks."

As intended, I laugh, hiccup, then laugh again. She loves to be the center of attention. I get myself under control and wipe my face. When I lean back, I see Callyx's eyes are red and shiny, but my tough brother won't shed his tears in front of Lucifer.

"Do you mind using some of your wonderful powers to heal my broken bones?" He waves a hand down his body.

Most of the wounds, cuts, and broken bones are easily healed. The deep cut in his abdomen takes a bit more time.

"Every time I see you with Cormal, you're hurt. What did he get you into this time?" I raise an eyebrow, waiting for Callyx to explain this one.

Cormal loudly protests, "This fuck-up isn't on me. Talk to the supreme ruler here." He motions to Lucifer.

Callyx looks at Lucifer for permission, and when he gives it, he turns back to me. "I've been following the sorceress for the last week. My orders were to kill her, but when I saw her meeting with the dark Fae queen, I decided to wait and see if I could gather any intel to indicate she's the Primary. They went into the sorceress' house, then an hour later, an urchin came running to the door. The queen left out the back, and I decided to follow her. When I rounded the corner, I looked back and saw Nyssa confronting the sorceress in the street. I figured it was time those two had a conversation, so I chose to keep following the queen."

He closed his eyes. "It's a good thing I did. About a mile from town, a huge boom filled the air, and I turned back to see this force race across the ground, flattening everything in its radius. The edge of it reached me and knocked me flying about a thousand yards. It's the last thing I remember until I looked up to see Cormal's face."

Puzzled, I glance up at Cormal.

"The Queen of the Light Fae, Nyssa, leveled the town and everything in it." The rage on Cormal's face is identical to ours. "And everyone. Quite a few of my men lived there with their families." He looks at the wall for a second. "Wives and children, all of them gone."

I freeze. "She killed everyone in the town?" I blink in shock.

What kind of monster kills an entire town of innocent people? I can't even comprehend the mindset it would take to do something so horrifying, not to mention the power it would take to commit such an act.

"Dear Goddess." How the hell am I going to save or defeat her?

THIRTY-EIGHT

<u>ARDEN</u>

Cormal left to take care of a few things but promised to be back in a day. Vengeance makes for strong allies, and we're going to need every ally we can get. Meri wasn't too happy to see Cormal, but when she heard about the town, she fell apart. Apparently, it had been her home, her neighborhood, for about a hundred years, and she knew every single person who had lived in it, especially the children. She silently called out their names one by one. I couldn't hear her words, but I saw her lips moving.

She went back to guarding Vargas and Solandis, but the news broke something fundamental in her, so I made a note to check on her in a couple of hours.

Thankfully, the club is closed on Sundays. Exhausted but hungry, I go down to the kitchen to grab something for dinner. When the elevator doors open to the lobby, I see the cadre standing in a circle, staring down at something. I walk up to stand next to Theron, who eases to the side so I can see what they're looking at, but it's not a what, it's a whom.

The same beautiful guy who disappeared into thin air the other night sits on a chair, while the cadre towers over him. "Arden, I've been waiting for you," he says in a smooth voice. When I raise my eyebrows in return, he points to the blade on my thigh. "I can't tell you how delighted I am to see you got my gifts."

The cadre gives me an incredulous look, but I shake my head in denial. I have no idea what he means.

"Your gifts?" I question.

He puffs up with pride. "The Killian blades. I'm Bran, and with the help of your great-grandfather Conall, I created them. They're my finest work."

"You're the puck?"

"The puck...and Henry," he says, and in a flash, Henry is sitting in the chair.

We all pull our swords and level them at the—him.

He raises his hands, then looks at Theron. "Did you read my contract of service?"

Theron studies him for a good minute, then sighs and puts his sword away. "Your service forbids you from hurting anyone without the express permission of the coven leader who owns your contract, which is now Arden."

"Henry or Bran or whatever your name is...I need food and maybe some coffee. It's been a long and very fucked-up day. You're welcome to join me." I leave him sitting there and head towards the kitchen.

Nobody is in the kitchen when we enter. I pull out the ingredients to make sandwiches, and Fallon moves beside me to help. I glance up at him, and he winks. With a smile, I continue setting out the food.

Theron and Daire grab drinks for everyone, while Astor and Valerian keep Henry company, much to his amusement. A few minutes later, we all grab a seat at the rustic kitchen table and dive into the food.

Henry's eyes dart around the table, and he flashes a wry smile before taking a bite of his sandwich.

"Do you find something amusing?" Daire asks him, his brow arched high.

"Don't mind me," he replies, laughing. "I'm only eating sandwiches with some of the most powerful supernaturals in our world. The casual approach is a bit of a shock."

"I'm sure Daire or Theron could show you how they treat lesser mortals, but most of us are pretty relaxed," I joke. Neither Daire nor Theron find this amusing, but the rest have a good laugh. I finish half my sandwich. "I'm starting to feel less cranky. Let's talk. Do you prefer Henry or Bran?" I wave a hand at his body.

"Bran, but I've gotten so used to being forced to show Henry, I can continue to hold this form indefinitely," he replies cautiously. "Which would you prefer?"

"I'm going to miss sweet Henry," I lament with a sigh. "He had a wicked sense of humor and a complete disregard for Caro's authority."

A second later, Bran sits at the table.

The cadre unconsciously sits up straighter and puffs out their chests, and I laugh silently to myself. I'd react the same way if a gorgeous woman suddenly sat at our table.

"Why don't you tell us how you got here?" Fallon suggests quietly, his bright green eyes fixed intently on Bran.

"The story doesn't paint me in the best light, but I hope you'll let me tell it in its entirety." Bran looks directly at me when he speaks. "Almost two thousand years ago, I met the light Fae queen at a ball. Expecting a benevolent but boring queen filled with goodness and light, I found a conflicted queen filled with insecurity, greed, power, anger, and a whole host of personal demons. For a puck, she was a feast for the mind, and I quickly became enamored with her."

His smile twists. "A puck is a rare thing, and she loved to collect rare items. She invited me to stay in her court indefinitely. While I studied and learned about her, she did the same. Unfortunately, the man became less important than the puck."

Daire nods in understanding, having experience with those who were more interested in the vampire than the man. I reach out and slide my hand into his.

"Foolish and arrogant, I failed to figure out her games until it was too late. Quite a few of my powers focus on the manipulation of the mind, and I thought nothing of showing them off. I even shared a couple of them with her. At first, she used them against her court, and I found it amusing. I failed to understand they were merely test runs." His jaw tightens. "By this time, Rivan and I had become close friends, and he warned me, but I didn't listen.

"The sole purpose of her personal seers was to find potential links to her replacement. Not as the queen, but her other role." Bran waves a hand.

"We call her other role the Primary," I offer to him.

He nods. "The seers sent her information on Catriona's parents. She found them on their way home one night and manipulated their minds into thinking they were each the enemy. They turned their powers on each other. Shocked at the deaths of two innocent people, I confronted her. She locked me in the dungeons. It took me a while to get out of there, but I eventually found myself back in her good graces, or so I thought."

He grimaces. "Long story short...she needed to know how to make the world forget the MacAllisters ever existed. The original spell could only make one person forget, but with her powers, she found a way to amplify it. When I gave her the spell, I didn't know what she intended, but it doesn't matter. I knew I was responsible." His eyes plead with me to forgive him.

"I knew she was involved in their massacre, but I couldn't prove it," I say stiffly.

Bran runs his hand through his wavy hair. "I didn't know how to stop her, but I knew I could look. A puck can call on the power of foresight. It requires a sacrifice or a toll, so I hesitated to use it." His expressions changes to one of sadness. "Rivan changed my mind. He'd left to run an errand for the queen, met Sima MacAllister, and fell in love. The queen killed her and bound him to her court permanently. Devastated, he couldn't even kill himself. I knew something had to change. If she continued to accumulate power, she would eventually rule us all."

"The power of foresight led me to Conall and the creation of the Killian blades. I didn't know they would become sentient. I only knew we needed to create them, because they would serve a purpose in the future," Bran explains. "In my vision, I saw you, a witch and the Rowan, and I knew I had to find a way to bide my time until you arrived. I drew up a contract and sold myself in service to the coven. It allowed me to escape the queen, pay my toll, and stay near the witches. I've been waiting so long for you. I'll do everything in my power to help you defeat her." His brown eyes burn with vengeance and guilt.

The cadre looks at me with doubt and hesitation in their eyes.

"My mother left me a message in her journal," I say slowly. "Do you know who might have been able to hide me from the

Primary and how they might have done it?" I don't tell him she also told me the puck would be a good ally.

"I've kept in touch with Rivan. When he saw a witch about to win the Guardian of the Light, he knew you were the one. The queen originally planned for the winner to get a priceless Fae artifact, but she didn't want it to go to a witch. Rivan offered one of his tattoos as the alternative prize, and she accepted," he says, laughing. "He included a couple of extra runes to help hide you from her and the seers. It wasn't fool-proof, but it was the best he could do in the short time he was given."

Astor pounds his fist on the table. "I knew it. Her ability to find you is completely random. She must have them searching all the time."

"My mother told me you would be a great ally," I inform Bran. "I guess we can add Rivan to our team, as well. I appreciate you telling me your story. Welcome." I stand. "If you'll excuse me, I need to check on my family and get some sleep. We're regrouping tomorrow to plan the final battles. I hope you'll join us. We could use someone who knows the layout of the palace. I've only been to a few areas."

Leaving them all in the kitchen, I head out. My mind sifts through the new information, trying to find anything I can use against Nyssa, but I find nothing.

MAYA IS STANDING guard over Solandis and Vargas when I check on them.

"Any change?" I ask her.

"No, I'm sorry," she replies quietly.

I didn't expect there to be, but it's disheartening to hear. "How's Meri?"

Maya shrugs. "She's fine. Told me she would be back to relieve me in the morning."

I'm guessing Meri didn't tell her about the town. "I'm going to grab some sleep. If anything changes, please let me know immediately."

I give them each a kiss and tell them I love them. I'm on the other side near Solandis when I see Vargas' eyes flash open. Startled, I rush over, but when I get there, they're closed. Maybe it was a trick of the light, or maybe he's starting to wake. Regardless, nothing happens for several minutes. Giving him an extra kiss, I say goodnight to Maya and step out of the room.

"How are they?" Fallon asks softly. He's leaning against the wall across from their room.

"No change," I tell him, closing the door behind me. My eyes latch onto his. "Would you stay with me tonight? I don't want to be by myself." All day, I've felt like I've been walking a tightrope, with a long fall below me and no safety net. "If you don't, I can ask one of the others."

He steps forward and cups the back of my neck. "Don't you dare," he rasps. "I need to hold you in my arms, hear your heart beat next to mine, and know you're not a ghost come to torment me in my dreams." He scoops me into his arms and heads toward the elevator.

THIRTY-NINE

FALLON

A tiny frown appears between her eyes, but I gently smooth it away. I pull her in tighter, and she gives a small sigh. Her head turns until it's pressed into my chest, and she places the lightest of kisses near my heart. I close my eyes to savor this small moment. When you don't think you'll get another one, it becomes more valuable than an entire kingdom.

Or former kingdom. It's going to take time getting used to this new life of mine. I don't regret the choice for a second, but I'll miss my people. The responsibility for their care never weighed on me. I enjoyed finding ways to make their lives easier and more prosperous. The cadre's purpose assuages some of the need, but not all. Maybe there's a way I can help them in an unofficial capacity.

Arden cries out, and I wrap my arms tighter around her.

After a few minutes, her body relaxes, and her breathing tells me sleep has claimed her again. Not willing to risk her waking, I continue to hold her tightly. She's only been asleep for a couple of hours, but I doubt she'll sleep long tonight. With Solandis and Vargas incapacitated and the horrific stories of Nyssa's abuses of power, there's too much on her mind.

I've met Queen Nyssa at several royal functions, but she'd always come across as a sharply cold person. My father always seemed too happy to attend to her himself. Knowing the depth of her power now, I can't help but wonder if she was the one who intervened with fate's plans for Garrett and my mother.

My father sent a note yesterday, asking me to meet with him to broker a deal. He proposed we split the kingdom in two, but it's not the best course for the people. It would also require me to accept a royal role in ruling the other half, but I'm not going back to a life of pomp and restriction.

I've got another deal in mind, but it will take all my negotiation skills to get him to agree. With the battle coming, I don't have the time to meet with him anyway, so I refused his invitation. I didn't give any reason. Let him wonder whether I'm even interested in making a deal. It will give me leverage when we do meet.

Arden cries out again and leaps from the bed, frantically searching for something only she can see. I ease out of bed and stand behind her. I don't want to startle her awake. My hand accidentally brushes the plant behind me, and I reach back and pluck a few of the leaves. With my power, I guide a leaf into each of her hands, then use the third to stroke along her bare shoulders and neck.

Her Elven side picks up on the comfort provided by the leaves, and she slowly wakes. "What in the world?" She curls her hand protectively around the leaf and stares down at it.

"You were having a nightmare, and I didn't want to chance waking you. The leaves helped," I murmur behind her.

She spins around and finds me close. Launching herself at me, she wraps her arms and legs around my body. "Thank you for being here. For everything. I haven't had a chance to talk to you about your decision to leave it all behind, though. I'm worried you'll regret it."

"Would you rather I go back to being a prince?" I question her intently.

She shakes her head. "No, but…"

Relieved, I smile. "Good. I don't want to be a prince, not anymore. I do want to find a way to help my people, but not in the same role."

She licks her lips and leans closer. Soft lips touch mine in a kiss, then pull back. Another kiss, and again, she pulls back, but this time, she takes my bottom lip with her. Her green eyes flick to mine, and she angles her head. This time, she kisses me like I've been gone for ages and she can't get enough of my taste. Her mouth moves purposely on mine, and I fall into the kiss with her.

Shifting her in my arms, I stride over to the bed and ease us down. Settling into the kiss, I tell her how much I've missed her, how much she means to me, and how I can't live without her. I lower my body down to hers.

She slides her mouth to the right to get some air, and I switch my attention to her neck and jaw. Inhaling the sweet scent of strawberries, I pepper her with little kisses and give her time to decide if she wants to stop here or continue.

Rising on my elbows, I stare down into her beautifully bright green eyes—Elven eyes. "Is everything okay? We can take it easy. I just want to kiss you and feel you in my arms."

"That's too bad," she says huskily. "I want complicated, not easy. I want you inside me. I want to feel your commitment to me with every stroke. I want your actions to tell me you missed me."

Inhaling sharply, I tell her, "You slay me. I knew the minute I laid eyes on you that you would change me. I'm so damn lucky you did."

My mouth captures her in a slow, drugging kiss. I don't want to rush through this night. I kiss her until she's panting and restless for more. Sliding my mouth to her shoulders, I lick along her collarbone and nibble up the side of her neck to her ear, where I whisper all the things I want to do to her. Her body arches up and into mine.

I ease her into a sitting position and stretch her arms up over her head to take off her tank top. My mouth follows her back down, and I worship every inch of skin I can find.

"You're so beautiful. Here." I kiss the juncture between her neck and shoulder, and she gasps. Moving down, I trail my mouth and tongue to her beautiful breasts. When she arches up, I place my hands under her back to hold her up.

"Here." I trail my tongue around her hard pink nipple and watch it harden for me. My lips capture the hard peak, and I suck on it until sounds spill from her lips. Then I switch my attention to the other. "Definitely here."

Her hands move from the back of my head to my back, and her nails dig in when I latch on to her breast.

I love the feel of her marking me.

She rakes her nails down my back and across my sides until she reaches the soft sensitive skin below my abs. When her fingers glide across, I can't help but push my body into hers.

"Sensitive?" she asks with a husky laugh.

"Your hands feel too good," I grumble. "I'm not nearly done worshipping your body yet."

Pulling her hands up above her head, I hold on with one hand and continue using my other hand and mouth to drive her crazy. I'm so consumed with finding every peak and valley, I don't even notice when she uses her magic to strip my pants off, until I lean in and her hot, wet core wraps around me.

She wraps her legs tightly around my body and slides against me.

Gripping her hips, I drop my head to find my control.

Tempted by the wetness I feel against me, I slide my hand down to delve into her sweetness. "Goddess, you feel so good, so wet and swollen. I just want to slide right into you."

"Fallon, I don't want to wait any longer," she murmurs.

Unable to resist, I slide into her and stop for a second to capture this moment. The tingles we felt for each other before come roaring back, and we both gasp at the sensation.

I pull back and surge into her heat. "You feel so damn good," I say with a growl. The tingles move up my back, and I clench my teeth. "I don't know if this is a mate thing, but I'm not going to be able to take it slow."

"Good," she says firmly.

Letting go of her hands, I brace myself and thrust into her hard. Damn, that felt good. It's the last coherent thought I have for a while. My body sets a hard, steady pace, and I watch the desire flit across her face with every stroke. Sweet moans slip from her lips, and it makes me wild. Her cheeks flush, and I know she's close, so I slip my hand down and help her over the edge.

When her body clenches mine, it triggers my own release. I thrust hard a couple more times before settling deep within her body.

Breathing heavily, I lift my head to make sure she's okay and find a dazed expression on her face. "Everything okay?"

"Better than okay. We should have done this long ago," she says, laughing. "I love you, Fallon."

"It's better now," I tell her. "I love you, Arden."

FORTY

<u>ARDEN</u>

Fallon and I are watching the sunrise and enjoying our coffee from the roof when Theron rushes into the garden. When I see the frown on his face, my stomach drops.

"What is it?" I whisper, afraid to almost ask. "Solandis? Vargas?"

"Vargas and Meri are gone. She took the Killian blade you gave her, and Vargas helped himself to a few of our weapons. They left you a note," he says harshly, handing me a piece of paper.

I snatch it out of his hands.

> Arden,
>
> I don't know if you'll understand my actions,

but I hope you won't try to stop me. Or I should say, us.

When I woke in the middle of the night, I felt nothing but a black hole in my heart where Solandis used to reside. I could see her lying beside me, but no matter what I tried, I couldn't punch through the stasis that bitch Nyssa put her in. I can't tell if she's even alive. My heart and mate bond say she's gone. I need to know one way or another. Even if it means my life, then, so be it. It doesn't mean much without her anyway.

Meri refused to give me the Killian blade unless I took her with me. It's the only weapon that will kill a Fae, so I agreed. Yes, I know I could have taken it from her, but the need to kill burns brightly in her too. Who am I to deny her?

Meri reached out to Rivan to help us get into the palace. If I can send word to you, I will. There are so many words I want to say to you, but I know I've said them all your life. I couldn't be prouder or love you more if you were my blood daughter instead of the daughter fate gifted to me.

I left a separate letter for Callyx. Take care of each other.

I love you,
Your father, Vargas Karth

P.S. Meri says she hopes you forgive her too.
She couldn't stand on the sidelines anymore.

Reeling, I drop the paper in my lap. "How long ago did they leave?" I ask Theron.

He shakes his head. "Maya said Meri relieved her around three this morning. I'm guessing they left shortly after. I didn't even feel the portal open." He looks puzzled.

"Vargas has some secret way around portals," I say biting my lip. "We need to get our plans into place and strike tomorrow."

"I've already sent word to everyone. They'll be here by noon," Theron confirms. His eyes drop to Fallon's hand on my knee, and he quirks his eyebrow. He leans over, captures my lips, and knocks Fallon's hand off me. "Don't be late."

Fallon narrows his eyes and grunts at him.

THE ROOM IS PACKED when I arrive, but I see a flash of red hair and head immediately to the couple in the corner. Torin stands stiffly, unsure how to greet me, but I ignore the awkwardness and pull him into a hug. He immediately hugs me back.

A finger taps on my shoulder, and I ease back from my father. "I'm Elora, your grandmother, and I'd like a hug too." She sniffs and holds out her arms.

I fall into the beautiful redhead's arms. "Nice to meet you. I'm Arden. I got your letter, and it couldn't have come at a better time. I'd been feeling pretty down about getting Catriona's journal without finding my father."

"See, I told you," she says, hitting my father's arm lightly with the back of her hand. "I'm not sure why the magic picked you to rule instead of me. Clearly one of us is smarter than the other."

I laugh. "Why do you think the magic chose him?" I'm curious to hear her answer.

"He has more dark Elven blood, than I do, since I'm half witch," she explains with a shrug. "I couldn't pass up the chance to tag along today and meet you. Is it okay? I'm sorry to hear about Solandis. Would you mind if I stayed with her while you two go off to war?"

Tears come to my eyes. "I'd love it," I assure her. "It would be nice to have family watching over her while I'm gone."

I chat with them a couple more minutes until I spot Bianca in the doorway. "Excuse me," I tell them.

Bianca lights up when I approach. "Thank goodness. I was a bit nervous to come in with all these warriors. I know they're probably wondering what I'm doing here."

Looping my arm through hers, I pull her to the front to sit beside me. The cadre stands before us, facing the room. Lucifer enters quietly and leans against the wall. Cormal follows him. The rest grab chairs around the room.

Theron points to the whiteboard. "We went over the main battle the other night. Is everyone still good with the plan?" He waits until he sees their agreement. "Good. At Daire's suggestion, we are going to hit the queen with a separate force. We need your help to plan the best attack for this group. It's our only shot at her. Daire."

Daire steps forward. "The second group will consist of around a hundred people, that's it. More and she'll pull her troops back from the battle. Less exponentially increases the risk and decreases our chance of success. This group will include Fallon, Theron, Arden, Astor, Bran, Garrett, myself, and

Fallon's Elven elite. We'll start on the battlefield with the rest of the troops, then we'll portal to the palace. Before I detail out the strategy, is there anyone I'm missing?"

"Callyx—" I watch as he writes down his name, "—and Bianca," I add. "She's the best portal creator on the planet. We need a way to get a hundred people from the battlefield directly to our designated spot at the palace, and it will take a tremendous amount of skill."

"I had Bran assigned to open the portal," Daire says frowning. He glances at Bianca and Bran. "Thoughts?"

"We need someone on the other side to open a portal, then we need to bridge the two. If not, an automatic alarm will sound. Only a select few have keys to use the portals without her permission. It's either me or Rivan for that task. If Rivan's already with Meri and Vargas, he won't be available. I'll check my access after this meeting and make sure it's still good."

Daire makes a note. "Good. Make sure you coordinate with Bianca."

Cormal steps up. "I'd like to go with the smaller group. My expertise is in getting in and out of secure places. I'm not of any use on the battlefield." He pauses. "Also, if you know where we're entering, I can pull together a report on how many guards we'll encounter."

Fallon whistles and looks at Daire.

"You just earned your ticket to enter," Daire informs him with a speculative gleam.

Interesting. I'm sure every royal here is wondering if he can access their guard rotations, too. Cormal raises an eyebrow, and I smirk. It cost him quite a bit to reveal his secret to them.

"Once everyone's on the battlefield, the smaller group will take off and head straight toward her army. Fallon's elites will go first and create a tunnel for the rest to follow." He draws two parallel lines leading up to an X on the map. "Bianca, you'll have to open the portal at the very last second. If it's too early, they'll catch on to our plan. Can you do it?" He bores a hole in her.

"Absolutely," she says confidently. "Why don't I show you this afternoon?" She knows he's going to keep questioning her until he's confident in her abilities.

Relieved, he agrees.

Valerian taps the map. "They should start running toward the designated point, but when they get about halfway, the rest of the groups standing on the front—" he circles a couple flights of dragons and Lucifer's front lines "—should also start running. The battle begins at the same time we send them off to meet the queen."

Daire thinks about it for a second. "I was wondering how we were going to shield the smaller group, but this works."

Lucifer also nods. "I agree."

Daire looks at his notes. "Bran, can you ask Rivan to help pinpoint where the queen will be so we can enter the palace at the point closest to her? This is the most critical and risky part of the operation. If we miss her location, she could flee before we reach her or call in more troops."

"I'll send him a text now," Bran says, bringing up his phone. His fingers fly across the keyboard. Without looking up, he assures Astor the phone is protected from anyone trying to intercept the messages.

Astor snorts, but throws me a wink. I think Astor likes Bran.

"Once we're in with the queen, we'll do what we do best— fight," Daire states firmly. "Arden will have one Killian blade, and I'll have the other. My speed might be the only thing that gets us close enough to her."

"Plus, Meri or Vargas have a blade," I add.

He nods and jots down a note. "It's a pretty straightforward plan, but there's a lot of risk and we have a very small window of opportunity. Unfortunately, it's our only plan," he says solemnly. He looks over at Theron.

Theron motions to Valerian and Lucifer. "These two will be in charge on the battlefield. Run any side plans by them. We know things change in the middle of the battle, but we want to be sure everything is coordinated through them."

When everyone nods, the meeting adjourns.

"Bianca, once we're at the palace, I want you to stick with Garrett, okay?" I pull Garrett over to us. "Garrett, she will be your shadow once we enter the palace. Got it?" I wait until he agrees to protect her. "Good."

Entering the lounge, I find the cadre in deep discussion. "Would you like for me to come back later?"

Fallon comes over and takes my hand. "We want to talk to you about something." He sits down on the couch, and I sit beside him. "I started the cadre with the intent to help others. At first, it was because I couldn't always help people in my official capacity. Sometimes, the things I needed to do fell into grey areas. My plan worked too well. It soon became overwhelming with the number of requests I received for help. Thankfully, Valerian came along, then Theron and Astor. Last, Daire joined us."

I tentatively smile not sure where this is going. "Yes, I know."

"When there were five of us, we found this sanctuary and the magic accepted us. It bonded us with each other," he explains. When I nod, he continues, "It also bonded with us.

The magic comes from an ancient, primal source. We want you to be a part of the cadre—part of us."

Theron leans forward. "It's not because of our personal relationships with you. We're asking you to join the cadre because you hold the same beliefs and honor that's essential for someone who's helping others."

"You're an incredible fighter," Daire interjects, "but fighting doesn't rule you."

Astor grins. "Loads of power and magic at your fingertips, but you don't automatically attack or kill with it. Even when you're provoked, you hold back."

Valerian leans over and taps my chest. "You have heart and compassion."

Tears roll silently down my cheeks. "I would be honored." This is the purpose I'd been looking for all along.

WE HEAD to a large cavern below the basement. Markings and dates on the wall go back further than our earliest known dates in history. In the center of the cavern lies a circle, which is ingrained with a pattern of swirls and symbols.

Theron strolls up. "This has been a sacred place since the beginning of time, at least that's what the source told us." He positions me in the center of the circle, then moves to the outside.

The rest of the cadre flow around the circle to specific points.

Fallon takes a half step forward. "We call upon the ancient magic of The Abbey to request an addition to our cadre. We know this person exhibits the traits to be a strong warrior in our fight to provide sanctuary for others, to help those weaker than us, and to approach the world without prejudice."

The swirls on the floor transform into smoke and glide up my body until I'm surrounded by a veil of shadow. It pokes and prods, then enters through my skin. I tense and glance at Fallon who gives me a reassuring nod.

Images from pivotal points in my life flash by, and I watch while the magic observes and judges each one. When it gets to the battle with Cassandra, I wince at the image of me carving my initials in her cheeks, but it follows with me removing them. Then the images stop, and the magic stills within me. I hold my breath, waiting for its verdict. The smoke dissipates.

Disappointed, I glance at the floor, but nothing else happens. I guess I didn't pass the test. Worried about their reaction, I tentatively glance up.

Fallon strides forward and yanks me into his arms for a crushing hug, then hands me off to Valerian. They all take a turn congratulating me.

"I don't understand," I say with a frown. "Did I get in?"

Theron pulls my hand up to show me the infinity symbol glowing on the back of it. His violet eyes twinkle.

"You're officially a part of the Imperium Cadre and this sanctuary," he confirms. "The symbol will only shine in this cavern." He pulls his sleeve up, and I see it glowing on his forearm.

"The magic will protect you and this sanctuary as long as you fight for others," Daire states.

I tilt my head. "If someone attacks me, it will protect me?"

"Yes. It may lend you magic, or it may simply protect you. It's hard to tell. Why?" Astor asks.

"I might have an idea for the battle tomorrow." I quickly outline my plan and wait while they digest it.

Astor is the first to comment. "It would take tremendous power, but I can do it."

Daire nods. "The timing is tight. We'll need everyone to be ready at the same time. If we're not, we'll have to abort the plan."

Theron, of course, makes a note on his phone. "I'll send a text to Bianca."

Daire stops him. "She's going to display her portal skills for me in about a half hour. We'll add this to the agenda."

Valerian, Fallon, and I look at each other and laugh. Daire is becoming more like Theron every day.

NONE of us wants to be alone. Knowing we'll get very few hours of sleep tonight, we pile blankets and pillows in the lounge and spend the remaining hours laughing and teasing each other.

Those without armies to command, like Bianca, Elora, Callyx, Cormal, and a few others, join our relaxed festivities. We bring Solandis to the lounge as well, hoping she might hear the laughter and decide to wake up.

It's a glimpse of the future I'll fight tooth and nail to preserve.

CHAPTER

FORTY-ONE

<u>ARDEN</u>

Dawn is cresting the horizon when we line up on the border between the Land of the Light Fae and The Wilds on a large swath of land abandoned by all. With its proximity to the forest and all its dangers, it's home to no one, which makes it the perfect battlefield.

Arcs of light shine brightly as large portals open simultaneously and our armies march from their kingdoms to the field of battle. Rulers and their commanders direct soldiers in setting up necessary battle support stations, like armories, food supply tents, and infirmaries. It's a hive of coordinated activity.

Bran and Rivan text back and forth all morning, trying to pinpoint the location of the queen. When she recreates a virtual model of the battlefield in the throne room, we immediately get the information to Cormal so he can get us the location and numbers of the guards we'll be facing.

315

Two hours after we arrive, the land in front of us starts filling with our enemy. Her army alone is massive, and when her allies start to arrive, we count and shift our soldiers accordingly to match their strengths. By noon, we're all in place.

Cormal's source doesn't bring us good news. The throne room is the most protected area of the palace. Fortunately, it's a place familiar to several of us, and we're able to quickly map out the exits and create several escape plans.

Bran leaves to sneak into the palace, and I know it's almost time. I duck into a tent and pull on my armor and weapons. Finding my center, I walk through the plan in my mind, then I send prayers to the goddess to watch out for my family and friends. When I open my eyes, I'm focused and ready.

We're lined up directly in front of the enemy's left side. Fallon's elites slide into place in the front of our group. Since Bianca is human and doesn't have our speed, Garrett is carrying her to the designated spot. They stand behind the elites with Daire and Fallon beside them, while Cormal, Theron, Astor, Callyx, and I bring up the rear.

Without any signal, we start running toward the enemy. Startled to see movement, they scramble to get magic users and weapons trained on us. Magic shoots into the air, but it hits our shield and fizzles out. Five hundred yards reduces to four hundred yards.

Arrows of fire and ice shoot through the air toward our group. A couple of them spear through the shield, but none of our group is hit.

Three hundred yards, and we're almost to the second mark. The enemy pulls more soldiers to its front lines to face us— exactly what we hoped they would do.

Two hundred yards. I look directly to my left and find Valerian. He mouths 'I love you' and starts running parallel toward the enemy from the center of the field, a flight of his most senior warriors with him. To his left, Lucifer's front lines also begin running. The enemy spreads their front lines out to meet all of us.

At one hundred yards, Valerian and his men start shifting into dragons. The enemy's front lines erupt into chaos while they try to defend themselves against the bigger threat. Valerian's dragons get close enough to send streams of fire and ice down on top of them.

At fifty yards, Fallon's elites line up in two parallel lines. Garrett and Bianca hit the mark, and she opens the portal. Half of Fallon's elites head directly into portal, and half stay to provide protection for the rest of us. In mere seconds, we're through. The rest of the elites following us, then Garret and Bianca drop in last, and she closes the portal.

Once Bran started opening the portal on his side, we knew he'd be vulnerable to attacks. He assured us he'd be able to hold the portal long enough for us to get through, and he did, but it must have been a tough fight. We find him on the other side of the portal, slumped against the wall. Several guards litter the floor around him, but the only blood is on Bran. He's bleeding from several places but wearing a huge smile on his face.

I raise an eyebrow, and he laughs and taps his temple. "Never mess with a puck," he jokes. "We'll scramble your mind."

Bianca gives him a couple of potions to speed up his healing.

Astor swoops down and slings Bran's arm across his shoulders, then we head in the direction of the throne room.

It's the elites' job to get us to the queen. They form a perimeter around the rest of us, and we move as one entity toward our destination. The elites take on the brunt of the fighting against the palace guards. They're an incredible fighting machine, and few guards make it past them to us. When they do, we dispatch them quickly.

When we get to the throne room, we find Meri, Rivan, and Vargas have started the battle without us. They're fighting through the aristocratic Fae and her personal guards. The queen isn't even looking at the fight around her. She's studying the battlefield.

The Elven elite station themselves at the entrances and secure the room. Astor sets Bran behind a pillar and moves to the center of the room. Bianca stays with Bran. Cormal, Callyx, Fallon, and I immediately jump in and help fight. Theron joins Astor in the center of the room, and they turn slowly in a circle, trying to memorize every inch of the room.

Seeing all the guards surrounding Vargas, I head straight to him. When he sees me, we shift into one of our favorite fighting formations.

"Your form's gotten better," he states, praising my improved fighting stance. "Are you mad at me?" He finally cuts down the guard he's fighting and swivels to catch the next one.

"I was. I'm not now. I'm glad you're here," I admit.

"Solandis?" His eyes dart to me when he asks.

"No change," I reply. We're down to only a couple of guards when I spot Meri in the corner. "You got these two? I believe Callyx is coming to have a chat with you."

Callyx slides into my spot next to Vargas.

I duck and weave my way over to Meri.

When I reach Meri, I cut off the head of the guard closest to me and continue to attack from the rear. Another turns to face me, and Meri uses magic to set him on fire. Shocked, I stare at the burning Fae for a second, but when I see him putting the fire out, I quickly remove his head from his body.

"Where did you get the magic?" I say, moving to her side so we can face the last two together.

"Apparently, I can tap into dear old Mom's Fae powers," she sneers, but the flush in her cheeks and sparkle in her eyes tell me she's enjoying the magical perk.

"It's a good thing, or you'd have been dead in the first minute," I remark. "Still have the blade?"

"We've kept it moving between Rivan, Vargas, and me," she says, freezing the two guards in front of us. She waves a hand. "Hurry up. I'm not sure how long they'll stay this way. These powers didn't come with a manual."

I swing, cut off their heads, and start laughing.

"Shut up. I don't know why this looks so easy when you do it," she grumbles.

"Umm, three hundred and twenty-eight years of practice," I inform her with a smirk. When we're not attacked by anyone else, I yank her behind a pillar and fill her in on our plan.

She gives a relieved sigh, but it's interrupted by a scream.

"Rivan," she whispers and takes off.

Very few of the enemy remain standing, and we skirt around the fighting to get to other side of the room.

The queen has pinned Rivan against the wall, and she's using force to drain his magic.

Daire and Fallon are fighting to get closer, but there's a shield around her.

Meri looks at me helplessly. She's not used to wielding magic, so she didn't learn anything beyond the basics and some defensive elemental magic.

Instead of trying to punch through her shield, I wrap a strong shield around Rivan. It temporarily stops her. Infuriated, she snaps her fingers, and a cell appears. She flings him in it and seals it with a magical lock.

We're all spaced out around the room. I glance at Daire.

Daire's eyes dart to the markings on the floor, and he nods

his head. *Everything's in place. We only need to find our window.*

The queen turns and frowns when she notices our group has joined the fight against her. Her gaze sweeps over each member of the cadre, and she shifts until her back is to the wall. She sneers when she sees Vargas, Callyx, then me. Cormal generates a flicker of interest. Bianca is easily dismissed, but I see her shocked fury when she notices Bran. Out of all of us, though, she locks on Meri like she's her biggest threat.

"I knew you'd eventually turn up. Poor Solandis was completely convinced you were my daughter, but you're not, are you? The sorceress told me you were the next Prime. She swore she didn't know when she found you abandoned in a shack on the outskirts of that disgusting little town," the queen sneers.

Anger makes Meri stand up straight and face the queen without fear. "You mean the one you destroyed?" Meri snaps back. "That town was full of innocent people, including women and children. Why not just kill the sorceress? The people in the town were no threat to you. What kind of monster are you?"

"The town filled with Cormal's criminals?" she scoffs. "Please, I did the world a favor, and when I find your guardian, I'm going to do worse to her."

Meri's face drains of color, but she rallies quickly. "She escaped? You couldn't kill one sorceress?" Meri says tauntingly, then snorts. "A queen outsmarted by one mediocre sorceress. Age is clearly taking a toll on your powers. Maybe you should step down and let someone younger take over."

The queen's head snaps back like Meri punched her. Fury fills her face, and she raises her hand.

I glance at Daire, and he shifts into place.

"Meri, run straight for it," I order her.

The queen was so focused on Meri, she didn't notice the *human* witch move across the room to the left of Meri.

Bianca takes a deep breath and opens a portal, then Meri runs straight toward it.

Infuriated, the queen screams and rushes to intercept her before she can get away.

Theron taps his foot on the floor to open the hidden portal.

Astor focuses all his attention on the queen.

Meri dives into the portal, and it closes behind her.

The queen stalks toward Bianca.

Daire slips by and stumbles into the queen. She reaches out to grab him, and he spins her around.

I signal to Garrett. He whistles, and the elites back off from the exits. Light Fae guards and soldiers start filling the doorways.

Using magic, I slide Bianca to Garrett on the other side of the room. She stands and sways, but Garrett steadies her. Her magic must be low.

She lifts her hand to open a new portal, but it's weak and barely formed.

"Bianca," I yell. "Pull on the magic of our coven."

Theron, Astor, and the queen disappear.

Daire whistles, but I wave him on. Icy blue eyes narrow, and he shakes his head.

Fallon strides over to help Garrett and his men.

Reaching inside me, I find Bianca's thread and shove magic down the line.

The portal strengthens, and the elites, Callyx, Cormal, Fallon, and Bran get out. Garrett grabs Bianca and throws the two of them through, then it closes.

"Vargas," I shout. "We need to go."

Puzzled, he locks onto Daire, who points to the almost

translucent portal near the cell, but it's closing. Vargas starts running toward it and slides through right before it closes.

Daire and I stare at each other, then turn toward the guards who are rushing into the room.

Rivan shouts, slides the Killian blade I'd given to Meri through the bars of the cell and across the floor to me, then points behind us.

A small portal opens. I glance back at him, and he shakes his head sadly. "Leave me. Maybe I'll get lucky and they'll kill me."

I grab the blade, and Daire immediately pulls us through the portal.

We end up in the lobby of The Abbey. He picks me up and uses his vampiric speed to get us to the cavern where we've set our trap.

He sets me down but doesn't let go. "Remember, she must attack you first or The Abbey won't help you," he reminds me.

CHAPTER
FORTY-TWO

Theron, Astor, Meri, Vargas, and the queen are the only ones in the room when Daire and I enter. Bianca's portal took the rest back to the battlefield. Fallon was supposed to be here, but at least we gained Vargas.

The queen immediately pauses when she sees Daire and me walk in. She tilts her head, looks behind me, then back to the center of the room. She starts clapping.

"As a Fae, I'd have seen through an illusion, but you managed to make me see my throne room in my head like I was still there. You must tell me the secret," she trills with a laugh.

Astor releases the spell and falls back against the wall in burnout. He'd been using our shared spell to make her think we were all in her palace, and it had taken a tremendous amount of power to project the spell for that long.

While Astor held her mind, Theron created a hidden portal and covered it with an illusion of the room. Then Daire spun her around, and she unknowingly went through the portal to this cavern.

When Daire and I entered from a different location, we must have entered the "throne room" from somewhere unusual, like a wall, causing her to notice the anomaly immediately.

"It's one of the spells passed down to me from the MacAllister side of my family," I inform her. "You remember the MacAllisters, don't you? Most of the world doesn't, but you do. I can see it in your eyes."

"You're lying," she states confidently, glancing from me to Meri. "You're trying to protect your little friend."

I flash the tattoo of the Rowan on my inner wrist. "The Rowan is the only witch with all seven bloodlines. The one destined to save witches and their magic. The one destined to stop the Prime—to stop you. Any of this ring a bell?"

She looks speculatively at me, then Meri. "Then who is she?"

"She's your daughter. Solandis told you the truth, but you didn't stop to wonder if it was actually true, did you? So busy protecting your Prime status," I sneer. "The sorceress, you know, the one who managed to escape right from under your nose?" I deliberately wave her failure in her face hoping she'll get angry and attack me. "She stole your essence and created Meri. Did you not even check to see if Meri was your daughter? Go ahead. Fae recognizes Fae, right?"

Her eyes drill into Meri, and she snarls when she finds I'm right. "That bitch. I'm going to skin her alive."

"Don't you want to know who the father of your child is?" I quip, then clap my hands together as if I'm delighted to share the news. "The dark Fae king." I howl with laughter at the look on her face. "Here you are, the Prime, protector of the greater good, and your child is full of free will."

Enraged, she curls her hands, but instead of attacking me, she spins around to attack Meri. Thankfully, Daire moved Meri across the room.

Fuck.

She stalks toward her, but I create a dozen Meris to slow her down. Flinging her hand out, she mimics my move and creates a dozen illusions of her.

Theron and I look at each other, then immediately start searching for the real queen. When I find an illusion, I shine a spotlight on it to let the others know it's not her, while Theron uses his Fae power to make his disappear.

We're down to two when she reaches the real Meri. She picks her up by the throat and squeezes. Meri uses her borrowed power to try and fight back, but since it's the queen's own power, it does nothing to her.

Daire sweeps in close to grab Meri, but she uses Fae fire to keep him at bay. He dodges, then moves in again.

Vargas is inching up behind her with one of the Killian blades in his hands.

I place a shield on Daire and yell for him to get Meri out of there. He yanks Meri away and tosses her across the room, and I catch her with my magic and set her down gently.

Theron and Daire move in closer to the queen, and I follow.

It's time we set Plan B in motion.

"Nyssa, I must tell you. We're in The Abbey, which is a sanctuary. There are rules you must follow. The most important one is you cannot harm those who are bonded to uphold the laws of sanctuary," I tell her.

She backs away from Theron and Daire. It doesn't occur to her that I might also be part of the cadre.

Vargas is close enough to strike.

Her nose wrinkles, and she disappears. A second later, she reappears behind Vargas and captures him with her magic. "Did you think I wouldn't smell your demon stench?" she hisses at him.

Screw the rules. I raise my hand to attack her with my magic, but I'm not fast enough.

A sword appears in her hand, and she cuts off his head. Vargas' body falls to the ground, his head falling to the side of it. She flicks Fae fire at him, and his body turns to ash.

I scream and scream until the rage burning deep inside of me explodes like a volcano. It's unending and deep. Rage from the fear and anger I felt each time assassins attacked me. Rage for the death of my mother. Rage for a childhood spent without my parents. Rage at the years of isolation and training I had to endure to get to this point. Rage at her attack on Solandis. Rage for killing Vargas. For annihilating the MacAllisters and Meri's town. So much rage.

I throw spell after spell at her, but her shield is impenetrable and her power too great. Chest heaving, I watch her smile at my attempts.

Her smile triggers something dark in me, and I laugh. She cocks her head, then waves an elegant hand to dismiss me.

I laugh because I'm going to kill her. The knowledge settles into my bones like it's part of my DNA. When the roads lead to a single point, you have no choice other than to believe it's meant to be. My hand clenches on the sword, and I picture it sliding through skin and muscle and bone. I see her blood spilling from her body, coating the blade and my hand. When I yank it out of her black heart, I will twist the blade until her insides are entirely shredded. Then I'll thrust the point of it through the middle of her throat and slice off her head using two strokes instead of one. I want her to hurt. I need her to know her reign of power is over. I stalk toward her.

She chuckles and spots something on the ground. Bending over, she picks up the Killian blade that had been in Vargas' hand. She turns to face Meri across the room. Holding her palm out, she floats the blade above, then uses magic to send it hurtling directly toward Meri.

Both Daire and Theron try to stop it, but her magic prevents them from grasping it.

My head swivels from her to Meri and back. I can either kill her or try to save Meri, but I can't do both. My hands shake with the need to kill her now, but not at the cost of Meri's life. Changing directions, I sprint toward Meri, praying to the goddess I get there in time. The blade rushes toward its target, and I give myself a magical boost. I'm almost there.

Meri scrambles to move out of its way, but the queen's magic is locked on her, not her location, and the blade follows. She stops running and straightens her shoulders, facing death head on.

Knowing the dagger can't kill me because I'm not Fae, I slide in front of Meri and brace myself.

Male shouts echo in the chamber.

It stops an inch from my head and quivers.

It whispers to me, and this time, I decide to whisper back. "Find the true enemy, the one you were born to kill." The blade turns around to the queen, and it shoots straight into her heart. I didn't even see it move from me to her, it was so fast.

Neither did she. She stares down at her chest in shock and crumples to the ground.

I run over, raise my sword high, and cut off her head. It rolls near my foot, and I spit on it. Leaning over, I yank the Killian blade out of her chest and wipe the blood off.

I can't help but look over at the pile of ash behind her.

It's the last thing I remember. Darkness sweeps over me.

FORTY-THREE

ARDEN

I'm floating in a sea of nothing with voices all around me, but I can't tell what they're saying. "Who's there? Where am I?"

All noise stops, and I drift for a few minutes. Then a light appears, and I watch as it moves forward to encompass me. At the last second, I close my eyes against its brightness.

"Hello, Arden," a woman's voice greets me.

Opening my eyes, I look around and find myself near a stone cottage at the edge of a forest. A woman stands to my right in a long dress. Her hair and body are a rich brown color. Deep green eyes study me intently. I automatically scrutinize her in return to determine the level of threat, and surprisingly, I find it quite high.

I tense. "Hello. Where am I?"

She looks intrigued, but shrugs. "The individual usually

chooses a place where they experienced the most happiness. I find it odd you don't recognize the location."

I look more closely at the cottage, but it doesn't seem familiar. Leaving the stranger, I decide to walk around the house to view it from another angle. In the back, I see a gravestone with an abundance of flowers surrounding it. I hesitantly move closer.

Gia Perrone, Beloved Mother and Mate, Seer. The dates of her birth and death are listed.

The stranger glides up next to me. "This was your mother, correct?"

"Yes. I don't have any memories of this place, but it feels right to be here when I'm at the end of my journey," I tell her. "Who are you?"

Is she the goddess who guides our spirit to the next life?

She laughs, but it's hollow, as if there isn't any real amusement in it. "I'm not a goddess, and you're not going on to the next life. I'm an extension of the primal source. We are the source of all magic, and throughout the ages, we have done whatever we must to ensure magic's survival. One of our tasks is to choose a Prime to help us keep the supernatural world in balance."

I fold my arms across my chest and stare her down. "Can the world not balance itself? Why does it need two sides?"

"Neither side can exist without the other. If free will were to reign, the world would be chaotic and without purpose. If the greater good reigns, the world is rigid and without creativity. We need both. We tried to let the world balance itself, but it couldn't, and in each case, magic either dominated or disappeared. The Prime was our solution," she explains.

"Why did you choose Nyssa? She doesn't seem like the ideal person for the position," I question her.

Her eyes flash black, making me take a step back. "When

we chose Nyssa, free will had ruled for many, many years. Dark Fae killed her parents. When she found out they had done it for sport, she vowed to fight for the greater good, to dedicate her life and power to it. She was a good choice for the Prime."

"Until she wasn't," I say dryly. The rage tries to surface, but I push it back down. "She's gone now. I suppose you need to find a new Prime."

"Long before you were born, we chose you to be the next Prime. It took many, many years of planning," she says and waves a hand toward my mother's grave, "and sacrifices to get the right people and resources in place to give you the best chance at defeating her."

Well, damn. "My mother told me to save the queen and restore balance," I retort. "I didn't save her."

"Sometimes, the meaning of a vision is open to interpretation," she says solemnly. "If we are to give you the power of the Prime, which side will you favor?"

"Neither. Both." I shake my head and explain, "I'm a child of both. Why would I choose just one?"

Cocking her head, she contemplates my answer. "We've never had a Prime who has chosen both. It would be a good experiment," she replies. "What will you use your power to do first?"

"Can I bring Vargas back?" I immediately ask.

"No, we don't have power over life and death," she says. "Anything else?"

My heart breaks with her answer. "Can I heal Solandis and make her whole again?"

She looks off in the distance. "I think you'll find she's already healed. Nyssa's death broke whatever spell she was under."

Relieved, I think about it, and for the first time in my life, I have almost everything I want. "What can you tell me about the Prime's powers? Can I share them with others?" I ask, thinking of Meri and people like her who are powerless.

"They differ with each Prime. You get the powers you need to balance the world," she says vaguely, her voice fading a bit.

"What if I refuse?" The words are out of my mouth before my brain processes them, but once they are, I know they're the right ones.

"We've never had anyone refuse." Her voice is hard when she replies. "Why would you turn down an offer of this magnitude?"

Who am I to dictate to others? "It doesn't help the world to give the power to one individual. It's why the balance is temporary and why Nyssa became corrupt. It's why the light Fae flourished while other races struggled. She manipulated rulers and annihilated threats to her reign. What did she do for the individual? The supernatural who's living life day-to-day?" I watch her digest my answer.

"Do you have a solution, or are you just commenting?" she asks, her tone sharp.

"Replenish the primal power supporting the sanctuaries. Let the cadres use it to help those who need it most. Foster an environment to help all supernaturals, not just those favored by the one in power," I answer, throwing out my suggestion and knowing this is the right thing to do. "Plus, the cadres are bonded to the sanctuaries and its rules, which helps control any potential corruption or abuse of power."

She tilts her head and considers my suggestion. "Let me confer," she says, fading away.

I'm tempted to go into the cottage, but I have no desire to see where my mother died. She chose this as her resting spot, and it's enough to know it's beautiful and peaceful. I sit on a nearby bench to wait.

She returns. "We agree with your suggestion. It will be

interesting to see the impact this solution has on magic. If the balance starts to tip too heavily, though, we will return to the proven solution. We'll be watching you closely." She fades out.

The world fades along with her.

CHAPTER
FORTY-FOUR

<u>ARDEN</u>

When I wake, darkness still surrounds me, but this time, it's filled with shadows and shapes familiar to me. Valerian lies next to me in my bed. Theron and Fallon are in chairs nearby. Astor sleeps on the couch, and Daire paces at the foot of the bed.

I close my eyes and cast my senses into The Abbey. It's humming with power. Relieved to find I'm not the Prime, I can't help the smile stretching across my face.

Daire sees the small movement and rushes to my side. He sweeps the hair back from my face and pulls me into his arms. "For a while there, I couldn't feel you," he rasps. "It's as if you didn't exist. Don't ever do that to me again." Burying his nose in my neck, he takes several deep breaths. "I love you, Arden."

I squeeze him tightly. The bond must not have worked in

that other...realm or whatever it was. "For a second, I was gone. Thankfully, I'm back and still me. I feel the bond between us, so it's not gone." I glide my fingers over the place on his chest where I drank from him to remind him. "I love you too. So much."

I look over his shoulder and catch the turbulence in Theron's violet eyes. Tapping Daire on the shoulder, I ease out of his arms and crawl into Theron's lap.

His body is cold, which tells me Lord Winter locked away his emotions while I was gone. Fingers circle the cuff on my wrist, and he taps it quietly, needing some reassurance that it's me he's holding.

"I'm home," I assure him. "For good. I love you, Lord Winter."

He shudders when he hears my words. "I love you, Lady Winter." His hand cups the back of my head, and cool lips descend on mine in a brief kiss. "I can't wait to hear about your latest journey." He's anxious to hear where I've been and what's happening next so he can plan accordingly.

"I've got a lot to tell you," I tease him.

Astor comes up behind Theron and yanks me up into his arms. I wind my legs around him, knowing he needs to feel all of me squeezing him back. "Gorgeous, you fucking scared the hell out of me. None of my spells or potions worked. If you'd have stopped breathing, I would've contemplated following you to whatever comes after this life."

My breath stops at the thought. "I didn't see whatever comes next. So we'll just have to stay here and drive each other crazy for several thousand years, okay?"

He crushes his mouth to mine, and I kiss him back just as fiercely.

"You're mine, both of you, and I'm not giving you up so easily."

"Ours," he says in a gravelly voice, which tells me the incubus has joined us.

He carries me over to Fallon and sets me down in his lap.

"Arden." Fallon's voice cracks for a second, and I throw my arms around him. Tingles leap between us, and I feel his hands grip the back of my shirt.

"When I realized I was at the battlefield instead of the cavern, I immediately tried to open a portal, but The Abbey had gone into some type of lockdown. I couldn't get in. Even Lucifer tried and couldn't break through the barrier. I went out of my mind." His voice is wild and full of emotion. "I'm so sorry I wasn't there instead of Vargas. If I had been, he'd still be here."

I place a finger on his lips and shake my head, recalling what the lady told me. "Not even the most powerful have control over life and death. Vargas knew the risk, and he accepted it before he left to hunt down Nyssa. I honor his choice, and as a warrior, you should too."

He closes his eyes and takes a couple of deep breaths. "When I finally saw you again, you were absolutely still, frozen in a moment of time. I've been praying every minute you've been gone for more time with you." He cups my face and places a soulful kiss on my lips. "I love you, Arden."

"I love you too. I've got incredible news for you—well, everyone—but first, I have one more hello," I tell him and turn to face the quiet dragon watching me from the bed.

Fallon stands and places me in Valerian's arms.

For a second, I can't breathe. It's not the massive arms holding me tightly. It's our bond. He's flooded it with his emotions—worry, anguish, rage, love. It's overwhelming. I fuse my mouth to his in a kiss and pull on the strings between our two souls. When he feels the two merge, he begins to calm. His lips claim mine in a breathless kiss.

Needing air, I pull back and rest my forehead on his. "Are you okay?"

"Like Daire mentioned, we couldn't feel you. I had a void in my soul," he says hoarsely. "I almost lost it. The only thing keeping me sane was the sound of your heart beating. I can't live without you. Do you hear me?"

"I love you, Valerian," I cry out. My heart hurts to hear everything he went through while I was gone.

The rest of them pile onto the bed with Valerian and me. Our hands touch frequently, needing to reassure ourselves we're still here and together.

In a quiet voice, I tell them what I experienced during my time away from them.

"You were chosen to be the next Prime?" Theron asks, repeating my statement to make sure he has it correct. His eyes are lit with both intrigue and relief. "I bet they were shocked when you turned them down."

"Apparently, I was the first to refuse," I confide with a laugh. "Seriously, I couldn't imagine having all that power. Also, I don't think it helps everyone. It only supports the Prime's agenda."

"What are they going to do? Find another Prime?" Astor questions me.

"I gave them an alternative solution which will help a lot more people and hopefully maintain the balance," I reply, then look at Fallon. "I suggested they replenish the sanctuaries to give the cadres more power to help all supernaturals."

Stunned, he stares at me for a second, then swoops down and plants a huge kiss on me. "I'm assuming they agreed?"

"Yes, so you'll need to let the other sanctuaries know," I reply. "How long have I been out?"

"Three days," Theron replies stiffly. "We burned Nyssa's body."

"How's Meri doing?"

The cadre share a glance, and I tense.

Daire answers me. "Meri inherited Nyssa's power. She's now the Queen of the Light Fae."

Save the queen and restore balance. Maybe this is what my mother's vision meant? "Wow. How's she doing? Going from no power to queen in a day?" I ask, unable to picture her with magic, much less the ruling power of a queen.

"She's adjusting. Bran went back and helped Rivan escape. They've been holed up in the guest rooms near Solandis," Astor informs me. His eyes widen. "Oh, that's right. Solandis..."

"She's awake, right? Back to normal?" I blurt out.

He raises an eyebrow, and I explain how I know.

Daire takes my hand in his. "She's awake, but she's in denial about Vargas. No matter what we say to her, she refuses to believe he's gone. Although she admits he feels far away."

"What does Lucifer feel through his bond with Vargas?" I ask, not willing to totally discount Solandis' belief that Vargas still exists somewhere.

Daire looks shocked. "What bond?"

"Your father has a bond with Vargas. It's how he knew he was in trouble the day Nyssa attacked them," I tell him.

"He never said a word," Daire says with a growl. "We'll ask him when he gets back. Apparently, he had an urgent errand to run."

"What about the battle? My father? Bianca, Daevyn, Garrett? Did everyone make it back okay?"

Valerian chimes in with an account of the battle. "We took some hits, but once the queen was dead, they scattered like leaves in the wind. I'm sure they're scrambling to grab power right now. Meri's going to have a hell of a fight on her hands. It's a vicious court, which has been ruled by an iron fist for over four thousand years, so it's going to be a bloodbath."

I bite my lip. "Well, she has a hell of a support system. If she needs help, we'll assist her."

Valerian and Daire sigh, but I see the sparkle in their eyes. They love a good challenge.

"I feel like I've been gone a year instead of three days," I say with a sigh. "My father and everyone else are okay?"

"Everyone's been worried about you, but they're good," Theron assures me. "I'll let everyone know you're awake." He picks up his phone. "I think we should invite everyone to The Abbey to thank them for their help. What do you think?"

Astor snarls. "Let's give it a few days. The six of us need some time together."

"I agree," Fallon chimes in, while Daire and Valerian nod.

WHEN SOLANDIS COMES by a few hours later, we both cry at the sight of one another. She crawls in bed with me, and we hold each other tightly.

"I'm sorry it was Nyssa," I tell her, knowing how she felt about her sister. She knows the blade killed her, but I confess my role in it. "I didn't just want her dead. I wanted to kill her. Like Vargas, I wasn't willing to walk away."

She kisses me on the forehead. "Meri told me everything that happened, including what Nyssa did to the MacAllisters and the people in Meri's town. I feel guilty." She sighs. "I should have known something was off about her, but around me, she always acted the same. The only time she seemed angry was when she spoke about Vargas."

"She hid her powers from a lot of people," I assert, not wanting her to feel guilty for Nyssa's actions. "I'm surprised you didn't inherit her crown." It's the one thing that's been bugging me since I heard Meri became queen. Not because I don't want Meri to be queen, but it's odd.

"I abdicated my right to the throne when I mated with Vargas," she explains. "I knew I would never want it. Even if he is...gone, I don't want it. I never did. I'll help Meri, though. Rivan says the court is calling for The Wild Hunt to investigate their queen's death and Meri's right to rule. They'll put her and Rivan on trial. Bran was never a member of the court, or he'd probably be on trial too."

"The Wild Hunt, seriously?" I reply, shocked they would call for them. "When is this happening?"

"We're waiting to hear," she says, rubbing her temple. "Did those handsome men of yours tell you I'm acting crazy? I feel Vargas." She places a fist on her heart. "I swear."

"I don't know," I admit. "But I saw her cut off his head and burn the body. I don't know how he could recover from it."

"I know," she says, leaning her head back. "Maybe I'm just not ready to admit he's gone."

"Then don't," I tell her. "You're the only one that can make the call. What does Callyx think?"

She frowns. "He's avoiding me, but he believes Vargas is gone."

I'll have to smack him on the head when I see him. "He'll come around," I say convincingly. He'd better, or I'll kick his butt.

We stay in bed together for a few hours, talking and laughing. Solandis informs me she and Elora have been getting along great, and she likes Torin, but she hasn't been around him as much. We both realize our world is changing, and we're sad to let go of the old. Thankfully, we still have each other.

CHAPTER

FORTY-FIVE

ARDEN

The party is scheduled to start in the afternoon and go all night, since we wanted to give everyone time to have fun and visit. Syn has been preparing for days. He decided a barbecue buffet would be the best way to serve everyone, so Theron sent the word out, and a pair of shifters came by and dropped off a smoker and an industrial grill two days ago.

The delicious smell hits me when I enter the lobby, but my mind is on coffee, not food. I'm walking toward the kitchen when I hear my name called.

Without turning around, I warn her, "You'd better be here for good reasons, Cassandra. I haven't had my morning coffee, and I refuse to be held responsible for killing anyone before coffee."

She gives a strangled laugh, then coughs to cover it up. "I'm here to join the coven," she says defiantly.

"I'll be right back," I tell her. The kitchen is buzzing with people everywhere. I head straight to the coffee maker. After pouring a large cup and swiping my usual banana, I take a few sips and savor the second of—

Pans crash to the floor behind me, and I realize peace isn't going to be around today.

When I get back to the lobby, I notice Grady is with her, along with a very good-looking, dark-haired man whose piercing golden eyes are watching me intently. Not in a sexy kind of way, but in a 'if you hurt her, I'll kill you' way. Given how close he's standing behind Cassandra, I figure he's with her.

"Cassandra, Grady, and whoever you are, come join me." I drop into a chair at a nearby table, then take a couple sips of coffee, peel my banana, and observe the three of them. It's an interesting dynamic. Grady's deferential to the other man, but not subservient. Cassandra's frequently touching Grady but ignoring Mr. Broody, who is definitely not ignoring her. Cassandra huffs, and I narrow my eyes.

"I'm Connor's son, Liam, Alpha of the Blood Moon Pack," he says, holding his hand out for me to shake.

I guess Grady lost the right to lead the pack after our battle. Liam won't make those mistakes. He screams alpha. After shaking his hand, I look at Cassandra. "Here's the deal. Right now, we have three leads. Myself, Santiago, and Katarina. I plan on finding another four leads, but it will take time. The seven will govern big policies, but each lead will run their own coven."

Her eyes widen. "So you're establishing seven different covens?"

"Technically, but the leads pick who they want to join their covens. It's not dictated by bloodlines, but by those who are willing to give them allegiance and be a good fit for the coven," I explain further.

She deflates and stands. "I see. Let's go, Grady."

"If you can give me your vow of allegiance, you can join my coven," I offer her. "The allegiance isn't a joke, though. If you break it, the consequences will be severe and could mean your life."

She scoffs. "So you can constantly belittle me and keep me at the bottom of the coven? No, thank you." She motions for the two of them to leave, but Liam stands firm.

"I'm offering you the chance to join the most powerful coven—mine. I'm doing this for two reasons—one, I want to keep an eye on you, and two, you have potential. You're ballsy and smart. With some practice, you might be a decent fighter." Liam and Grady snort. "If you left your ego at the door, you could be a powerful witch."

She scrutinizes my face. "Who else is in the coven?"

"My biological father and grandmother, MacAllister witches and dark Elven mix, Bianca, and myself. If you don't want to be in my coven, you're welcome to interview with Santiago or Katarina," I say with a smirk, knowing she won't consider them. "I need an answer right now. Does your gut say yes or no?"

"Yes." She jerks in surprise.

I pull out the stone. "Blood donation is required, along with your vow."

She does both.

"Great, welcome to the coven. Heed my words, and we'll get along fine. You and your mates are welcome to come back for the party. It starts in a couple of hours."

"That's it? When's the next coven meeting? Also, Liam's

not my..." She gives a cry of surprise when he jerks her around and growls at her.

"We'll figure out the coven stuff later. Go and take care of things," I tell her, stifling my laugh.

Liam puts his hand on the back of her neck and marches her out the door. Grady follows with a grin on his face.

"Dominant fellow. Exactly what Cassandra needs," Bran says with a chuckle. He walks over and takes a seat across from me.

I study his face and notice he looks a little lost. "You know you're welcome to stay here as long as you want, right?"

He tosses me his trademark smile. "Where else would I go?"

I slide an envelope across the table and watch while he opens it. "Wherever you want. It's your contract. I took the liberty of tearing it up. Without you, this would have ended very differently. I can't thank you enough, but hopefully, this is a start. Friends?"

His brown eyes sparkle with emotion. "Friends. You know, pucks bet on the odds. If someone had told me the odds when all this started, I'd have never bet on us. I'm glad I didn't know." He stands up. "I'd give you a kiss, but the damn Fae is standing in the corner waiting for a chance to turn me into a block of ice." Dipping his chin to Theron, he heads to the elevator.

Cool lips bend down and kiss mine. "You've been busy this morning."

"It's almost like I have a plan," I retort.

He narrows his eyes.

"Torin and Elora invited us to spend a week with them. All of us, including Solandis and Callyx. They want to get to know everyone," I inform him. "I accepted." When he pulls up his phone, I stop him. "You need a break, and I know you want to get to know my father."

"I do, actually," he says seriously. "When do we leave?"

"At the end of the week," I reply and stand. "Now, if you'll excuse me, I need to shower. If you want to swing by in thirty minutes, I'll be sure to answer the door wearing a towel just for you."

"You know how busy I am," he says icily.

"Mmm. I do, but the offer stands." I throw over my shoulder and get in the elevator.

THE PARTY IS in full swing when I finally join a bit later than I originally intended. A delicious-looking cocktail is waved in front of my face, then handed to me.

Astor leans down to whisper in my ear, "Someone looks very satisfied. Care to share?"

I roll my eyes and take a sip of the drink.

"Daire?" he prods.

Daire bends down and smells my neck. "Theron." He stills. "Fallon too. You have been very busy today."

Blushing, I look around the crowd to find a distraction. "Excuse me, I see Bianca."

Astor whistles, while Daire chuckles. I ignore them both and head over to Bianca.

"I invited Cassandra to be a part of our coven," I inform her. "She accepted."

Bianca takes a deep breath. "She'll be a handful in the beginning, but if she can grow up and be an adult, she'll make a fine witch."

"I agree," I reply.

Garrett comes up and hands Bianca a glass of wine. He greets me, but his eyes never leave Bianca's. Pink flares across her cheeks.

"Meri's waving to me, got to go," I say, although I'm not entirely sure she heard me. Apparently, a battle is a great place to meet someone.

Meri stands close to Solandis, and I weave my way to their side.

Putting an arm around each of them, I squeeze them both. "What are you two plotting over here?"

Meri tenses and looks quickly at Solandis.

"When Meri is acquitted," she says, emphasizing the *when*, "I'm going to stay and help her learn how to be a queen. She'll need allies, and the Fae aren't known for their generosity of spirit."

"That's a wonderful idea!" I exclaim, especially since it helps both Meri and Solandis. She continues to deny Vargas' death, which means she's not ready to move on and make any permanent decisions. A temporary stay with Meri will help keep her busy. "You should see if Callyx will stay for a while too." He decided to opt out of today's party, and I have a feeling he's avoiding us.

"Really?" Meri asks, biting her lip.

"Yes, it's perfect. For all of you," I reply with a slight tilt of my head in Solandis' direction.

Relief crosses Meri's face. "Oh, by the way, I found this on my bed this morning." She pulls a Killian blade from a sheath at her thigh. "Here."

I put out a hand. "If it comes to you, it's yours. I've come to understand they know things we don't, and if it's sticking with you, you're going to need it." I pat the one on my thigh. "Trust me."

Determination flashes in her eyes, and she nods.

"You know, we make powerful allies," I tease before getting serious. "We'll be there in whatever capacity you need."

She throws her arms around me and squeezes tight. "Anyone who would jump in front of a flying knife for me definitely has my back. Thank you."

"Is that all it takes to show my loyalty? Quick, someone throw a knife at me," Cormal states snidely. His blue eyes darken when he stares at Meri.

"I'd be happy to throw a knife at you, as long as you promise to hold still," Meri spits out. "What do you want?"

"Just thought I'd say hi to the new queen," he sneers. "You've got the power you always wanted, but let's see if it makes any difference." He raises his glass in a toast and saunters off.

"Infuriating man," Meri grits out.

Solandis laughs. "You should invite him over for a chat." When Meri gives her an incredulous look, she continues, "The court is vicious. Chatting with Cormal will help you prepare for it." Solandis tugs on Meri's elbow. "Come. I need another drink. Arden?"

"I'm good," I say, shaking my head. My neck tingles, and I feel eyes on me.

Looking around, I don't see anyone, so I look up toward the VIP section. Bingo. All five of them are standing up there watching me with hard, possessive looks on their faces. Yummy. A waiter walks by, and I grab another drink off the tray and make my way to them.

"The party is quite the success," I say, walking over to the rail to stand next to them.

From here, I see several people I need to greet. Glynnis, Santiago, Alix, Rivan, and a lot more. Even Oryn came to the party. So many new friends and allies. I spot Torin and Elora. New family too. We're only missing Vargas, Callyx, and Lucifer.

Clinking my glass to get everyone's attention, I wait until they're looking up at us. "I propose a toast...to all of us. Every single one of us fought hard for a better future. Here's to... tomorrow." I take a large drink.

Everyone raises their glass and drinks. When I look down at each face, I feel blessed by the goddess. It's amazing. My life of isolation replaced with all these people.

Valerian, Theron, Fallon, Daire, and Astor move in close to me. I turn and smile at each one. "In my wildest dreams, I never envisioned the path to my destiny would bring so many wonderful changes and this incredible life. All these people. The Abbey. Most of all, the five fiercest, and sexiest, warriors to call my own. I love you."

"My life changed the minute you walked through the front doors and saw through my illusion," Theron reminds me.

"The instant I collided with a gorgeous witch," Astor says huskily.

"When you walked into the elevator and informed me you were The Executioner's daughter," Daire states with a smirk.

"The first time we sparred together," Valerian says with a laugh.

"When I saved you from the dark," Fallon murmurs.

"May our life be filled with love, family, purpose, and good battles," I say, raising my glass to them. "But most importantly, with each other."

EPILOGUE

LUCIFER

On the hill overlooking the River Acheron, I watch the demon stare into the grey waters. He makes no move toward Charon and the boat waiting at the dock, but neither does he look for a way out. This is an unexpected consequence of our bond, which I likely should have foreseen, but hindsight and all.

I nod my thanks to Charon for letting me know he found him and stride over to stand by Vargas. "I've been looking for you."

Vargas nods. "I know. It appears this bond of ours is giving me a choice."

"It's never happened in the past, but they were human, not demon. I'm not immortal, I'm eternal. You have a choice. If you want to continue your journey to whatever's next, it's an option. Or you can choose to stay in our world until the day you're ready to go on," I inform him, laying his options on the table. "I'd be happy for you to continue as my second-in-command."

"What about Solandis? Is she still the same?" He finally turns to look at me, and I see the torture in his eyes.

"I can't tell you. Fate is dictated by blind decisions and leaps of faith," I state with a shrug, knowing it sucks.

He heaves a sigh. "I figured. If I go on, who's to say we'll end up in the same place? If I go back and she's gone, I don't know if I can live without her," he says hoarsely.

"You can," I assure him. "Living without part of your soul is excruciating, but you do whatever it takes to make it through each second. Eventually, seconds become minutes, then days, and so forth. The pain never goes away, but it changes. Softens. Our lives are so long, we eventually come around to the idea of finding someone again."

He snorts. "Your pep talk sucks. You know that, right?"

I chuckle. "Daire has told me the same on several occasions."

Vargas looks at Charon and raises his hand to salute him. "I'm not ready for retirement, so I guess I'm going back with you." He pauses. "If Solandis is gone, I can't promise to stay, but I'll let you know before I leave."

"I understand." I clap him on the shoulder and turn around to guide him back to the Underworld.

He clears his throat. "I'm going to need a body."

"We'll find one along the way," I assure him.

Silence. "Good-looking demon and human form. Chaos, preferably. A strong fighter. Tall. Thick hair..."

He continues to give me a list of requirements for this new body during the entire journey back to our world.

THANK YOU!

Thank you for following along on this incredible journey with Arden and her Imperium Cadre. Ideas come from the oddest places. This one started with a song.

Arden's journey as the main character is at an end, but I'm busy plotting a few spin-offs and she will appear in those books. Some loose threads from the first three books will be resolved in future books and some will not be. Sometimes I think our imagination is better than the book so I leave a few open to your interpretation.

If you enjoy this world and these characters, keep an eye out for future books in 2023. Follow one of my social channels to get the latest news.

A special thanks to you—the fans! I write that word and I still can't believe it. You have emailed me, followed me on social media, joined our FB group, and signed up for my newsletters. And the reviews!!! Wow! Thank you. You truly rock!

*If you find an error, please feel free to email me at Stellabrie@stellabrie.com.

To get a free eBook copy of my first book, My Salvation, just subscribe to my newsletter.

Website: https://www.stellabrie.com/my-salvation

ACKNOWLEDGEMENTS

When I started this journey, I had no idea what it would take to create this world. It took more than I thought possible, but I loved almost every moment of its creation. There were days when I wanted to pull my hair out because I couldn't get the story to move forward or a character to do what I wanted, but it eventually worked itself out. I couldn't have done any of it without the support of my husband, my mom, and my girl, Bailey. (My beautiful golden retriever who passed shortly after this book was released. I miss her greatly!)

My beta team is awesome. They're incredibly supportive and they have been more than flexible with their schedules and time. Their insights are a tremendous help to me. Without them, Arden's story wouldn't have been near as good. Huge shout out to Nia, Bianca, Iliana, Melissa, Rachel, and Debbie for all your feedback! I don't know how I got so lucky, but you are the best!

Book two was the first time I had an ARC team, and I want to send a special thank you to them for making the process seamless and for promoting the book. I swear, I'm going to get better at giving you guys stuff to share before the book releases!

My gorgeous cover is by Mayflower Studio. Amala does fabulous work! Check her out.

Rockstar editing and proofreading by two lovely ladies, Meghan at Bookish Dreams Editing and Katie at Kaye Kemp Book Polishing.

Playlists for each book can be found on YouTube https://www.youtube.com/@authorstellabrie

About the Author

Stella Brie lives with her husband outside of Nashville, TN. After mentioning her desire to write a book a million times to her husband, he challenged her to sit down one day and write a paragraph. Instead, she wrote her first book, *My Salvation*.

She decided to trade in her career in digital marketing, working on big brands, for this wildly creative one. Armed with a notebook crammed full of ideas, she's constantly writing about bold heroines, sexy men, and HEAs. Whether it's a paranormal book full of creatures and magic or a contemporary romance full of heat and drama, she's always thinking about how she can bring her books to life.

Latest News and Updates:

Facebook Group: Stella's Stalkers

TikTok: @stellabrie_author

YouTube! Playlists (all books): @authorstellabrie

Instagram: @stellabrie_author

Website: Stellabrie.com - Exclusive sneak peeks, cover reveals, giveaways, and more!

BOOKS BY STELLA BRIE

PARANORMAL WHY CHOOSE

KILLIAN BLADE SERIES

The Rowan (1)

The Rowan's Stone (2)

The Rowan's Destiny (3)

<u>Spin-offs:</u>

Wicked Savior - Lucifer's story (MF Romance) - Book 3.5

The Light Falls (4) - Meri's story

The Dark Rises (5) - Meri's story

CONTEMPORARY WHY CHOOSE

THE SAVAGES SERIES

Savage Traitor (1)

Savage Ruin (2)

Spin-off:

Lethal Vengeance (Standalone)

My Salvation (Standalone)

To get a free eBook copy of my first book, My Salvation, just subscribe to my newsletter.

Website: https://www.stellabrie.com/my-salvation

ARDEN'S WORLD

- <u>ARDEN KARTH BALINOR</u> – WITCH, DARK ELF, SEVEN BLOODLINES – THE ROWAN, WITCH + ELVEN POWERS, 328 YEARS OLD, BLONDE + HAZEL (FORMER) BRIGHT GREEN EYES (CURRENT), SMELLS OF STRAWBERRIES AND HONEYSUCKLE, WARRIOR, LOYAL, HONORABLE

<u>THE IMPERIUM CADRE</u>

- <u>VALERIAN</u> – KING OF DRAGONS, ALL THREE DRAGON POWERS (FIRE, ICE, SHADOWS), BLACK HAIR + AMBER EYES, BLACK DRAGON, SMELLS OF BONFIRE ON A CRISP NIGHT, LOST, INTROVERT, BIG HEART, GRUFF
- <u>DAIRE</u> – PRINCE OF THE UNDERWORLD AND FIRST VAMPIRE, PART ANGEL, BLOND + ICE BLUE EYES, MOTHER (D.) – HEALER, SISTER DANICA (D.), SMELLS OF LUXURIOUS COLOGNE, ARROGANT, STRATEGIST, WARRIOR, HEALER
- <u>THERON</u> – FAE LORD OF SUMMER AND WINTER; PREFERS WINTER, BLOND + VIOLET EYES, SMELLS LIKE DARK

Chocolate + Peppermint, calls Arden love + Lady Winter, Arrogant, OCD, Highly Intelligent, Strategist

- Astor – warlock and incubus, Runic, Blood and Sexual Magic; Prefers the shadows; Dark Auburn Hair + Chocolate Brown Eyes. Smells like burnt cedar + sex, calls Arden "gorgeous, minx", Seductive, Charming, Fun, Scientist
- Fallon – Light Eleven Prince, Creator of Imperium Cadre, Elven Magic, Dark Hair + Bright Green Eyes, Prefers the light, Solitary, Thinker, Strategist, Idealist

Arden's Family

- Solandis – Princess of the Light Fae, Mate to Vargas, Parent to Arden + Callyx, Sister to the Queen of the Light Fae
- Vargas Karth – Underworld Executioner (Former) High Demon, Lucifer's Second-in-Command (Current), mate to Solandis, Parent to Arden + Callyx
- Callyx Karth – Demon + Light Fae, son of Solandis + Vargas, Brother to Arden, Lucifer's Spy
- Gia Perrone – witch, Arden's Mother (d.), Seer with Six Bloodlines
- Torin Balinor – MacAllister witch & dark Elven, Arden's Father, Archivist, King of Dark Elves
- Elora Agnes Balinor – MacAllister witch & dark Elven, Arden's Grandmother
- Catriona MacAllister Balinor (d.) – MacAllister witch, Arden's Great-Grandmother

- <u>Conall Balinor / Keir Balanthir</u> — Son of former dark Elven king, blacksmith, Catriona's mate, Arden's Great-Grandfather, Co-creator of the Killian blades

DEMONS / VAMPIRES

- <u>Lucifer</u> — Ruler of the Underworld, father to Daire + Danica (d.), Former Archangel
- <u>Daire</u> — (see reference above)
- <u>Alain (d.)</u> — Lucifer's Second-in-Command (Former)
- <u>Vargas Karth</u> — (see reference above)
- <u>Callyx Karth</u> — (see reference above)
- <u>Solange (d.)</u> — daughter of Alain, Daire's former girlfriend
- <u>Sorceress</u> — Guardian of Meri, former mistress of Dark Fae King
- <u>Letti</u> — Succubus from Astor's past
- Dumb Demons Guarding Vargas' Door — Meh, Who cares?

WITCHES

Bloodlines + Leaders

- <u>Bloodline One</u> — Portals + Seer Abilities
- Nico Perrone (Leader)
- Gia Perrone (d.)
- Gemma Perrone (d.) — Greatest Seer in History of Witches, Visions predicted The Rowan, MacAllister massacre, downfall of the witches
- Bianca Perrone

- ESSA PERRONE (WITCH IN CASSANDRA'S GROUP)
- ELLA PERRONE (WITCH IN REYNA'S GROUP)
- ORIGINAL HERITAGE: ELVEN & HUMAN

- <u>BLOODLINE TWO</u> – ILLUSION + GLAMOUR
- AMELIE VON DIETRICH (LEADER)
- NATASHA VON DIETRICH (WITCH IN CASSANDRA'S GROUP)
- LUKAS VON DIETRICH (WITCH IN REYNA'S GROUP)
- ORIGINAL HERITAGE: FAE + HUMAN

- <u>BLOODLINE THREE</u> – SPELL CASTING + POWERFUL SHIELDING
- CARO PENNINGTON (LEADER)
- CASSANDRA PENNINGTON (BLOODLINES 1, 2, 3, 4, 5)
- MATE TO GRADY, FORMER ALPHA OF THE BLOOD MOON PACK
- CHARLOTTE PENNINGTON (BLOODLINES 1, 2, 3, 5)
- ORIGINAL HERITAGE: DEMON + HUMAN

- <u>BLOODLINE FOUR</u> – HEALING + POTIONS
- ADAM PENNINGTON (FORMER LEADER)
- AN LEE (CURRENT LEADER)
- ORIGINAL HERITAGE: ELVEN + HUMAN

- <u>BLOODLINE FIVE</u> – ELEMENTAL (FIRE, EARTH, WATER, AIR)
- KATARINA IVANOV (LEADER)
- NIKOLAI IVANOV (WITCH IN REYNA'S GROUP)
- ORIGINAL HERITAGE: FAE + HUMAN

- <u>BLOODLINE SIX</u> – TRANSFIGURATION
- SANTIAGO MARTINEZ (LEADER)
- REYNA MARTINEZ (BLOODLINES 2, 3, 5, 6)

- Original Heritage: Shifter + Human

- <u>Bloodline Seven</u> – Blood Magic + Stone Creator
- Arden Karth Balinor (Leader)
- Catriona MacAllister Balinor (d.) – Arden's Great-Grandmother
- Elora Agnes MacAllister Balinor – Arden's Grandmother
- Torin Balinor (Arden's Father)
- Original Heritage: Dragons + Human

- <u>Council Leader</u> – Caro Pennington
- <u>Council Members</u> – Nico Perrone, Adam Pennington replaced by An Lee, Katarina Ivanov, Santiago Martinez, Amelie Von Dietrich, Arden Karth Balinor
- <u>Butler</u> – Henry / Bran, puck, Co-creator of the Killian blades

<u>MacAllister Witches</u>

- <u>Agnes MacAllister (d.)</u> – Matriarch of MacAllister witches at the time of the massacre; friend to Glynnis + Gemma
- <u>Lara MacAllister (d.)</u> – Orphan, One of five survivors, died outside of Kingdom of Dragons
- <u>Aileen MacAllister (d.)</u> – Orphan, One of five survivors, died outside of Kingdom of Dragons
- <u>Sima MacAllister (d.)</u> – Orphan, One of five survivors, went to Light Fae territory, Fell in love with Rivan
- <u>Fiona MacAllister (d.)</u> – Orphan, One of five survivors, went to Light Elven Kingdom, Friend of

ELDER LO

- CATRIONA MACALLISTER (D.) – ORPHAN, ONE OF FIVE SURVIVORS, WENT TO DARK ELVEN KINGDOM, (SEE REFERENCE ABOVE)
- MOIRA MACALLISTER (D.) – FIRST LOVE OF VALERIAN
- TORIN BALINOR – (SEE REFERENCE ABOVE)
- ELORA AGNES BALINOR – (SEE REFERENCE ABOVE)
- ARDEN KARTH BALINOR – (SEE REFERENCE ABOVE)

FAE

- SOLANDIS – (SEE REFERENCE ABOVE)
- NYSSA (D.) – QUEEN OF THE LIGHT FAE (FORMER), SISTER TO SOLANDIS, PRIME
- MERINDAH (MERI) – DAUGHTER OF THE LIGHT FAE QUEEN AND THE DARK FAE KING, QUEEN OF THE LIGHT FAE (PENDING THE WILD HUNT'S INVESTIGATION), ARDEN'S FRIEND
- THERON - (SEE REFERENCE ABOVE)
- ORYN – BROTHER TO THERON, WINTER AND SUMMER FAE
- LADY WINTER – (FORMER) LADY WINTER + MOTHER TO THERON AND ORYN
- LORD SUMMER – FATHER TO THERON AND ORYN
- ALIX – WINTER HEALER
- DAEVYN – COMMANDER OF WINTER ARMY

LIGHT ELVEN

- FALLON – (SEE REFERENCE ABOVE)
- LIGHT ELVEN KING – ELWEN, FALLON'S FATHER
- GARRETT – COMMANDER OF LIGHT ELVEN ARMY AND ELITES

- <u>Elven Elite</u> – Elite legion of soldiers; Legendary in battle

DARK ELVEN

- <u>Conall Balinor / Keir Balanthir</u> – (see reference above)
- <u>Elora Agnes Balinor</u> – (see reference above)
- <u>Torin Balinor</u> – (see reference above)
- <u>Fallon</u> – (see reference above)
- <u>Caprina (d.)</u> – Fallon's mother, sister of the Queen of Dark Elves
- <u>Queen of Dark Elves (d.)</u> – Former Queen of Dark Elven, Fallon's Aunt
- <u>King of Dark Elves (d.)</u> – Former King of Dark Elven, Fallon's Uncle

DRAGONS

- <u>Valerian</u> – (see reference above)
- <u>Glynnis</u> – Agnes' friend, Showed Arden the path to the Rowan tree in the Kingdom of Dragons, Newly appointed to Dragon Council, Has two grandsons, one of which is also appointed to the council
- <u>Drystan</u> – Commander of the Dragon army

WOLVES / SHIFTERS

- <u>Grady</u> – Alpha of the Blood Moon Pack (former), Cassandra's Mate
- <u>Cassandra</u> – Witch + Wolf Shifter (see reference above)

- <u>LIAM</u> – CURRENT ALPHA OF THE BLOOD MOON PACK, POSSIBLE MATE TO CASSANDRA?
- <u>DUNCAN</u> – ONE OF FOUR ALPHA LEADERS OF ALL WOLF SHIFTERS AND GRADY'S FATHER
- <u>CONNOR</u> – ONE OF FOUR ALPHA LEADERS OF ALL WOLF SHIFTERS AND LIAM'S FATHER

<u>MISCELLANEOUS CHARACTERS / PLACES</u>

- <u>CORMAL</u> – KING OF CRIMINALS, UNKNOWN ORIGIN, FRIENDS WITH MERI
- <u>RIVAN</u> – TATTOO ARTIST OF BOTH RUNES FOR ARDEN + MERI, SIMA MACALLISTER LOVER, UNKNOWN ORIGIN
- <u>MAYA</u> – ALPHA OF THE LION PRIDE, LAST PURE ROYAL LION SHIFTER, MATE TO SYN, MANAGER OF THE ABBEY
- <u>SYN</u> – ATE TO MAYA, CHEF AT THE ABBEY
- <u>PRIMAL SOURCE</u> – WOMAN WHO OFFERED ARDEN THE POSITION OF PRIME
- <u>THE ABBEY</u> – ONE OF SEVERAL SUPERNATURAL SANCTUARIES; NAMED FOR THE ANCIENT CHURCH WHICH STOOD IN ITS PLACE PREVIOUSLY; LEY LINES AND PRIMAL MAGIC AT ITS SOURCE, OWNED AND MANAGED BY THE IMPERIUM CADRE
- <u>WITCHWOOD</u> – WITCH HEADQUARTERS
- <u>VARIOUS CASTLES / PALACES BELONGING TO THE SUPERNATURAL RACES</u> – LIGHT + DARK ELVEN KINGDOMS, KINGDOM OF DRAGONS, LIGHT + DARK FAE KINGDOMS, THE UNDERWORLD

www.ingramcontent.com/pod-product-compliance
Lightning Source LLC
Chambersburg PA
CBHW051203190726
48288CB00006B/1780